WAR GAMES

WAR GAMES

THE INDIAN WHO SUCCEEDED ALEXANDER THE GREAT

B RACHANA APPACHOO

Anecdote
Publishing House
For the love of quality reading!

Anecdote
Publishing House
For the love of quality reading!

Anecdote Publishing House
2nd Floor 2/15 Lane no. 2 Ansari Road,
Daryaganj, New Delhi-110002
Email: info@anecdotepublishinghouse.com
Website: anecdotepublishinghouse.com

Published by Anecdote Publishing House

First Edition 2025
ISBN 978-81-982589-0-8
MRP ₹ 699

Book Promoted and Marketed by Champ Readers Pvt. Ltd.

Edited by: Papri Sen Sri Raman & Ashwin Raj
Cover design by: The Book Bakers
Layout by: Graphic Tailor
Printed by Thomson Press (India) Ltd, New Delhi

To God the Father, Mother Earth,
Dadda, Mom, Sakala and the
Indian Armed Forces.

Thank you.

Alexander: Greece-Macedonia-Asia-Egypt (356-323 BC)
Chandragupta Maurya: India-Pakistan-Afghanistan (356-295 BC)
Darius III: Iran, Northwest India and parts of Eurasia (d 330 BC)
Bessus: Uzbekistan, Tajikistan, Afghanistan, Iran (d 329 BC)
The Nandas: Patliputra (now Patna in Bihar) to north-western India (ruled 329 -321BC)

Nandawati (near Uchh on the Indus) is the western capital of the Nandas; the historical Patliputra is the eastern capital. Morvati is a village east of Sauvira in the lower Indus Valley. Varana is ancient Aornos, now in west Pakistan. India of that time was made up of independent republics and small kingdoms.

Aristotle: (384-322BC)
Chanakya/Kautilya: (375-283BC)

Mudrarakshasa is a Sanskrit-language play by Vishakhadatta that covers the ascent of Chandragupta Maurya as king. This is the most detailed account of the rise of Mauryan power and is open to interpretation. It is dated variously from the late 4th century CE – this account of Chandragupta's life is believed to be written at least 700 years after his time. Chandragupta is also mentioned by Plutarch.

Chandragupta was both a military and political leader, who waged wars to take over Alexander's conquests. A Diadochi. He replaced Seleucus and assassinated many of Alexander's satraps. Twenty years after Alexander died, he had captured and finally freed India's northwest from foreign domination, whether Achaemenid, Alexandrian, Seleucid or other Macedonian satraps. What he did for ancient India was huge.

The five main surviving accounts of Alexander's life are by Arrian, Plutarch, Diodorus Siculus, Quintus Curtius Rufus and Justin. In addition to these five main sources, there is the *Metz Epitome*, an anonymous late Latin work that narrates Alexander's campaigns from Hyrcania to India.

Alexander was a king of Macedon, a southern European kingdom, now a part of modern Greece. In 335 BC, he took control of Thrace and parts of Illyria before marching on the city of Thebes. Alexander then led the League of Corinth, in a campaign against the Achaemenid kingdom of Persia in Turkey, that lasted ten years and led him to occupy not only Persia but the west banks of the Indus, Jhelum, Chenab and Ravi.

The *Behistun Inscription* is a relief with accompanying text carved 330 feet (100 meters) up a cliff in Kermanshah province, western Iran. The work tells the story of the victory of the Persian king Darius I (522-486 BC) over his rebellious satraps when he took the throne of the Achaemenid Empire (550-330 BC) in 522 BC. The relief is accompanied by text in three languages – Old Persian, Elamite, and Akkadian.

Contents

Prologue

In 323 BC, Alexander the Great died in Babylon. With his death, the Macedonian king's vast empire split into four entities – Antigonid Macedon, Seleucid Asia, Ptolemaic Egypt and Thrace. One more division, which took place quietly, cited in Greek historian Megasthenes' *Indika* (written about twenty-five years after Alexander), mentions a king of India – who later historians called Sandracottus.

Centuries later, scholars discovered that Indian king Chandragupta (Maurya) and Sandracottus were the same person. If history is a chronicle of events and places, India's historic age begins with Megasthenes' account, *Indika*.

Architect of a pan-Asian culture, Alexander earned the title Shahenshah, 'king of kings' as well as the sobriquet, 'Accursed' from the Persians for his rampage of Persian lands, but his steamroller ride freed northwestern Indian territories from Persian satraphood.

Seemingly out of a clear blue sky, in 321 BC, the Maurya dynasty bursts into play in northwest India. Vishakadutta's composition *Mudrarakshasa* describes the intrigue and deception to win Nanda chief minister Rakshash over to serve the Maurya dynasty in the former Indian colonies of Alexander. In the West, Greek and Roman historians wrote from the Greek-Macedonian point of view. This account tries to combine both points of view to settle at an Indian perspective.

The tale of the *War Games* of Alexander, Bessus, Chandragupta and Darius unravels a chain of events that destroyed Graeco-Persian colonization in Asia. The Mauryan empire united India in a new, never-seen-before avatar, combining the Indus Valley and Ganges plains. And for the first time in 220 years, Chandragupta (who ruled from 321 to 298 BCE) stopped the practice of giving 360 + 170 talents (17,490 kilos) in gold dust as yearly tribute to empires west of India – Persian, Macedonian or Seleucid.

A silent witness of that tumultuous time is Kautilya's *Arthashastra*, a classic on wealth creation by the state. The *Arthashastra* mentions that the ideal kingdom should be buffered by sea, rivers, steep mountain terrain and desert. In the 4th century BC, all four features – Arabian Sea, the Sapta Sindhu river system, the Hindu Kush, and the Gedrosian desert (in today's Balochistan) – were found surrounding a riverine island called Patala near the mouth of the Indus river area, located in current day Pakistan and probably buried with the passage of time under the waters of a shifting, flood-prone river (see Maps at the end).

This account is of how, thanks to Alexander the Great, an Indian dynasty – the Mauryas – was raised phoenix-style in the war games of the Indo-Persian-Greek kingdoms that Alexander thrashed. In the book of history, the page on Alexander and Chandragupta is a note on vanishing empires, lasting kingdoms, war and peace. ***War Games*** covers the theatre of war where an Indian king – the founding Maurya – took over Indian territories seized by Alexander after his death. Other major players include the Indian king, Dhananananda, the Persian King Emperor, Darius Codomannus (Darius III) and Bactrian Bessus. This interpretation begins with Alexander's birth and ends twenty years after his death, in 303 BC, when Indian territories of Seleucus Nikator (formerly Alexander's conquests) became a part of the Mauryan empire. It also unveils how the unification of the Indus and Gangetic areas that lead to one of the most glorious kingdoms India has ever had, happened. As a page in India's history, this is no moral lesson on goodness and evil, just a witness to extinction and survival through war.

ASCENT OF
ALEXANDER

356 BC Macedonia

Birth of Alexander

IN 356 BC, FOUR events occurred that were connected to Macedon. A son was born to Myrtale, princess of Epirus and Philip, king of Macedon; Philip's racehorse won in the Olympics; Philip seized Potidea on the peninsula of Chalcidike; and the temple of Diana at Ephesus (one of the seven wonders of the ancient world) was burnt down.

After Myrtale gave birth to her son Alexander, she was renamed Olympias, after the Olympic win. Olympias – daughter of King Neoptolemus I of Epirus – was the fourth wife of Philip II and a member of the snake-worshipping cult of Dionysus. Olympias' father traced his descent from Achilles, the ancient hero, and her mother, from the ethereal Helen of Troy.

Like the mothers of many great people (Gautama Buddha for example), Olympias had a dream, before consummating her marriage to Philip… a dream that she was struck by a thunderbolt in the womb, which spread a flame 'far and wide' before dying away. Shortly after the wedding, Philip too had a dream – that he had secured his wife's womb with a seal that had a lion's image. Their little boy, Alexander, was a cherub at birth – blond-haired and blue-eyed, with a milky white complexion. He brought with him many gifts. The incidents around Alexander's birth were portents – his adulthood would be filled by war, victories and a deep connection with the gods of his time.

356 BC Sapta Sindhu

Birth of Sashigupta in Northwest India

AROUND THE SAME period in faraway India, courtesan Mura was pale and exhausted. After a nine-hour labor in the modest courtesan quarters of the Nanda palace, she had just given birth on the night of a *purnima,* a full moon. Though her firstborn did not know this then, he too would come in contact with Alexander.

A lowly *dasi* or maid ran to inform the king, who was in his usual posture, slouched sideways, gravity having taken a large portion of his squishy midriff off the couch. A couple of bawds oversaw a large array of alcoholic drinks strewn all over. Fellow drunkards including Dhananandaʼs siblings had fluid dribbling through slack jaws, a sign of how much they had imbibed. The king merely grunted contemptuously, 'Low caste bastard!' when he got the message, forgetting his own father had been a low caste barber. Nor did he ask Mura to visit him, filled with disdain for his low caste concubine.

Mura was too thrilled with her delicate-featured firstborn to feel upset with the cold response of his father. 'I will name my firstborn Sashigupta after the full moon,' she told the dasi, making up her mind to groom him for a better future.

344 BC Macedonia

Alexander and Bucephalus – a Love Affair Begins

BACK IN MACEDONIA, Prince Alexander was displaying signs that would predict the ruler he would become. Alexander was a feisty boy. He proved this when he tamed a wild Balkan horse called Bucephalus. *Bucephalus* means 'ox-head'; the horse so named for the ox-head mark on its thigh. A horse trader from Thessaly had offered Bucephalus for 13 talents. Everyone who tried to tame the horse narrowly escaped with their limbs intact. But twelve-year-old Alexander succeeded. The young prince observed that the horse was afraid of its own shadow, so when he worked the horse, he always made it face the sun, so that no shadow spooked the temperamental animal.

When Alexander came to his father after taming Bucephalus, a proud King Philip kissed Alexander on his head and said, '*Son, find yourself another kingdom when you grow up, Macedonia will not be big enough for you.*'

344 BC Northwest India

Sashigupta and the Acharya

MURA'S HEART GAVE a thud of joy; an urchin had run past her open door, screaming, 'Letter for you has come!' Only her firstborn Sashigupta could send her a missive, Mura knew. He was now spending the entire year in his acharya's gurukul, a school many miles south. Rushing to the village square, her two youngest sons racing in front of her with two indie hounds, she squatted down at the letter writer's feet, waiting patiently for her turn.

'Dear ma,' the letter writer read aloud, 'I will not come for the annual village festival as acharyaji is training me in hands-free martial arts and weapon making.' The letter ended with loving wishes for his younger brothers.

Mura thanked the letter writer and paid him some coins for reading her letter.

340 BC Macedonia-Thrace

Alexander Becomes a General

IN MACEDONIA, KING Philip had many reasons to trust his intuition regarding his son. Alexander displayed precocious military understanding from a young age. When the prince was sixteen, in complete faith, Philip left him in charge of Macedonia as regent while he himself warred against the people of Byzantium. Alexander proved worthy of this faith. A tribe of the Maedi rebelled in a wild outpost of Thrace and Alexander led an expedition that squashed it. Alexander celebrated his win by establishing the first city named after himself – Alexandrapolis Maedica. Thrace was one of Alexander's earliest exploits in the theatre of war. King Philip was appreciative – he made Alexander a general in the army.

Philip's Wedding Feast Again, 339 BC

A year later, King Philip, quite the debauch, married young Kleopatra Eurydice, niece of his general, Attalus.

At the wedding feast, a drunken Attalus spoke out loud. 'Macedonians, pray to the gods for a lawful successor to the throne through my niece.'

'And Alexander?' one doubting member of the drinking party asked.

'Alexander doesn't count as heir because his mother Olympias is Epirian, not Macedonian by birth.'

Alexander, who was present but not drunk, angrily threw a goblet at Attalus, growling, 'What am I then, a bastard?'

Philip, the inebriate, decided to side with Attalus and charged at Alexander, sword raised but slipped and fell.

Alexander looked down and mocked his prone father: 'This man plans to conquer from Macedonia to Asia but cannot even march from one table to another.'

Alexander then left both banquet and Macedonia for Epirus, with his mother Queen Olympias and his sister Cleopatra.

Sometime later, an old friend visited a sober King Philip, who asked him 'if the Greek states were at peace with each other?'

The visitor laughed and commented, 'How strange that you worry about Greece when your own house fragments with so many wars.'

Philip, sober, was no fool and got the point; he called Alexander home.

In the meantime, Olympias – a fine schemer – had wasted no time in exile. She had secretly poisoned the food of Philip's other son, Philip Arrhidaeus, which affected the child's brain. This, she hoped, took Arrhidaeus – bastard son of the Thessalian dancer Philinna of Larissa – out of the race for the throne.

End of the Gay Sacred Band, Thebes 338 BC

After father and son reconciled, Alexander assisted Philip at the battle of Chaeronea against the combined armies of Greek city states, Athens and Thebes.

The first thing Philip asked Alexander was a military favor: 'Son, lead the army against the Sacred Band of Thebes – the elite force of the Theban army – consisting of 150 gay male couples led by General Gorgidas. He believes gay lovers make invincible soldiers.'

Alexander, a lover of young men himself, was unimpressed. With his men, he slayed more than 250 of the 300-strong Sacred Band.

The battle of Chaeronea was an important one; it gave control of Greece to Macedon. This early lesson was well learnt, and Alexander would always thumb his nose at giant reputations for the rest of his military life.

March 336 BC Sapta Sindhu

Nandawati

A FEW YEARS had passed. The Nandas had successfully conquered Gedrosia,[1] a small republic of Kshatriyas, a warrior caste, southwest of the Sindhu River on the western boundaries of their kingdom. The victorious army trooped through the capital Nandawati, with sedate generals on horseback and a Nanda prince atop a decorated female elephant, having fun showering silver coins on jubilant subjects. To revel in the victory, within weeks, King Sarvarthasiddhi – the eldest Nanda – invited neighboring kings, heads of republics, troublesome vassals, and their children and nephews for a celebratory feast.

Egged on by his brothers, he also invited his sons from his former concubine Mura, sons whom he had never acknowledged in public before.

Mura, the low caste mother of his sons, the younger ones still studying and the older being coached in the ashram of their martial arts acharya, cautioned them on how to behave

1 In coastal Balochistan.

with their father who they had last met ten years ago.

'Your father, Raja Sarvarthasiddhi, is nicknamed Dhanananda for his wealth. He likes to show off. He might insult you in public with his putdowns. Promise me that you will be composed,' Mura said.

Mura's six sons promised her and set off with gifts for their father.

They arrived in Nandawati, the western temporary capital of the Nandas, on the morning of the feast. The Viceroy who usually ruled had been sent to one of the Persian capitals on a diplomatic mission and the Nanda cohort had taken over. Near the palace, sounds of merriment could be heard outside the court entrances. Before entering the court, they had a brief powwow and decided the youngest brother Dhruv would present gifts to their father, the king.

'Mura's sons!' the court caller shouted, and the 13-year-old walked, trembling, to his father and handed him the gifts. Behind him at the back of the hall, Dhanananda and his brothers could see a tall youth, hair tied in a ponytail – his firstborn, Sashigupta – with a few younger boys, his remaining sons from Mura.

'Is this for me? *Sivi* cloth! Specially made for a king… ah ha ha!' King Dhanananda smirked, grinning at his brothers. None of the siblings were drinking, thanks to the briefing by Rakshash, the chief minister.

Dhruv, Mura's youngest son stiffened, hurt by his father's behavior, a reaction that did not escape the king's eyes.

'O, puppy, sensitive, are we?' the king waved at the boy, winking at his brothers. 'Go to the chamber; there's a special feast for you, son of Mura.' He waved his hand and a courtier stepped forward to lead the six brothers, and their attendant, to an ornate new stone hall behind the palace.

'Our Father is Dhanananda'

An air of festivity filled the chamber, festooned with ropes of jasmine and lotus flowers on the door, and vapors of *khuskhus*, vetiver, perfuming the air. Sashigupta, Dhanananda's firstborn, waited till all his brothers had walked down the steps to the stone chamber. The rest of the guests were ushered in group by group, vassal king after vassal king, republican following republican to the huge underground chamber, the specially-made dining hall for guests. Bodyguards and attendants stayed back as their masters went in. Inside the hall, the carved stone walls of the dining hall arched high into the roof in a sharp curve that kept the chamber cool. A series of foot-sized skylights let in light and fresh air where the two walls met.

The two flights of steps that led from the ground level to the chamber below had a huge, magnificent silver inlaid door. Dhruv ran his hand over the bas-relief depicting overdressed kings and well-armed gods on the door.

'Beautiful, isn't it? Pure silver, do you think?' Dhruv asked. He had forgotten his father's misbehavior in court with the generosity of youth. 'Well, our father *is* Dhanananda – the wealthy Nanda,' Prince Sashigupta remarked.

The brothers and luminaries from different kingdoms took their places at the two massive tables and waited.

Sanctified Pots of the Underground Chamber

Percussion music wafted in from beyond the ornate door. A sandalwood haze perfumed the air from a *homa*, a fire ritual, in a corner of the hall, which had innumerable small clay pots. Sashigupta looked curiously at the pots, all filled to the brim with cooked rice. Dhruv noticed it too. 'Why are all the pots in the homa in the corner?' he asked his eldest brother.

'Probably to sanctify the place,' Prince Sashigupta answered with a twinge of unease, he himself did not believe it.

But all around him, there was an air of jubilation and celebration in the chamber. The assembled guests waited for King Sarvarthasiddhi and his retinue to walk down the steps, but no one came. As minutes dragged on to half an hour and then an hour, the gathering became restive.

'I'll go up and see what's keeping our father Raja Sarvarthasiddhi from coming here,' Dhruv announced restlessly to his brothers.

He had just gone up the first flight of stairs yelling for the attendant they had left outside when a loud noise – the metallic clank of barred steel bolts dropping – silenced the jubilant group with shock. Immediately, the crowd in the dining hall became alert with suspicion that all was not going according to plan.

'What's happening?' Prince Pushkarashakti, vassal from Gandhara yelled, drawing his sword and racing up the steps. Other princelings – Kathoians, Siboi, Kshudrakas, Agalossoi, Ossadai, Abastoi, Malloi, Xathroi and many others who were vassals of the Hindush satrapy – with swords drawn ran up two steps at a time to the thick doors and kicked them. They slashed at the silver plating with their swords, but the assault was futile.

'My bodyguards are keeping watch outside. They will open the doors,' one of the princes – a Malloi, shouted. He yelled loudly to his bodyguards outside, but no response came through. 'Why does no one answer?'

'The doors are soundproof,' Prince Sashigupta said calmly. 'And they are probably all dead,' he added grimly as more princes and kings rushed up the steps, shouting for their attendants and the silence continued.

'Pushkarashakti and I pay gold talents to the Persian King

Emperor as yearly tribute, Dhanananda won't dare kill us like this,' Prince Siddharth, an Ashvaka princeling, said.

'But that is precisely what they are doing,' Sashigupta said soberly to his brothers. He was overheard by Prince Siddharth.

'Rubbish!' Prince Siddharth snapped to mask his nervousness. 'Don't be negative.'

The rest of the kings glared at Sashigupta as though he was responsible for their predicament.

Desperate Kings

After more than an hour of utter chaos, the assembled princes and kings came down from the steps.

'Let's all search for an underground tunnel,' someone suggested.

'I bet there is none,' Prince Sashigupta said in a low voice to his brothers, shrugging his shoulders.

He was right. The entire day was spent in a frantic search of the walls and tapping the floor, but in vain.

'Let us use our daggers to try digging a tunnel through the floor,' Prince Siddharth said, hunger making him unreasonable.

But it was futile, the stones under their feet were seven to eight feet thick – tunnel proof thick – and only blunted or broke blades that were meant to be used against human flesh or chain mail.

Two days later, now desperate, the only place they thought they could have escaped was through the foot-sized holes in the arched roof, which let in streams of light when the sun was up and some fresh air.

With increasing hopelessness, the kings and princes piled up the furniture to try to reach the roof but the stones around these holes were too high. Wooden torches in sconces kept the place lit with a reddish glow throughout the day. A couple of kings tried to set fire to the silver-plated door, but as the metal grew hot and radiated blistering heat, they realized the door was not wood plated with metal, but entirely made of metal. Prince Sashigupta had guessed right. Even piling furniture next to the door and setting fire to it did not work. This disheartened the kings, already demoralized by the lack of food and now the near pitch-black chamber.

'Who will Last till the End?' April 336

Above the chamber, every day, Raja Sarvarthasiddhi and his courtiers snickered at how easily, without battle, they had captured so many troublesome vassal kings and even been given gifts.

'Like spitting out chewed up betel leaf,' Dhanananda contentedly spat a mouthful into a silver spittoon. 'Let's bet on who lasts longest… I say the king of Kosala will be the last to die... what say you?' Dhanananda asked his siblings.

'I say one or two Mallian princelings,' Prince Kaivarta wagered.

'Ashvaka!' his sibling bellowed.

'Kshudraka!' one more sibling yelled.

The other brothers roared in fraternal camaraderie, taking sides. Chief minister Rakshash was silent.

Meaning of the Rice in the Clay Pots, May 336

Below in the chamber, three weeks had passed. Weak with unaccustomed hunger, thirst and hopelessness, as their body systems failed, one by one, each of the men in the dark treacherous stone trap (the torches were now ash) asked for Prince Sashigupta who seemed unaffected by thirst or hunger. They got him to promise them that their deaths would not go unanswered.

'Sashi, you, being Dhanananda's eldest, I count on you to take revenge for this treachery,' Prince Pushkarashakti of Gandhara whispered faintly, his parched mouth smelling of impending death. The chamber reeked from the odors of feces and urine.

'Your father Sarvarthasiddhi's nickname is Dhanananda – the fabulously wealthy Nanda. Many will be bought over by his gold, including Asura king emperor Darius to whom he pays a whopping yearly tribute.'

'He pays a lot of it on behalf of many princes,' Sashigupta said gently.

'Therefore, he kills me as revenge for gold he pays on our behalf. Promise our deaths will not be in vain.' The Gandharan held out his right hand, weak and bony. 'My signet ring will be proof to the Gandharans to be loyal to you. And my waistband will give you a little money to continue to work.' The Gandharan handed his signet ring to Sashigupta, who slipped it on his right hand and the broad gold waistband fit snugly under his upper body cloth.

As prince after prince and republican after republican died, each of them beseeched Sashigupta, quiet with pain for all the deaths, to take revenge. Each of them stripped off the best of their jewels and handed them over to Sashigupta, who slid them under the cloth covering his upper body, or on to his angular hands.

The meaning of the rice filled, clay pots in the corner was now clear – it was an advance homa, for the souls of all the men destined to die in the hall. When Sashigupta's fingers counted in the darkness, the number of pots more than equaled the number of people in the chamber.

Sashigupta wanted to die too, as his younger brothers one by one perished, holding his hand. 'You will live, just make up your mind,' Sashigupta lied to each brother as they clung to him during their final moments.

The last to die was his youngest brother, Dhruv, and Sashigupta lied again and again to keep the boy's morale up. 'They will open up by evening, just hang in there,' he lied stoically, but it was of no use.

Sashigupta, the Sole Survivor

Finally, only Sashigupta remained alive but barely able to lift his head, when the doors were flung open to the stench of the dead. The general who climbed down the steps, an upper caste Kshatriya, buried his nose in his shoulder cloth to avoid the putrid smell of rotten flesh and dried feces.

'Take them away, cremate them all,' the general barked orders to the soldiers behind him.

'General, one of them is alive, Raja Nanda's eldest son,' a soldier whispered to him.

The general went back to the private court and reported to the king, who was in the process of imbibing some very fine *Vacha* alcohol:[2] 'Raja Sarvarthasiddhi, all prisoners are dead except your son Sashigupta.'

'Exchellent *newj*!' the king bellowed, smacking his lips. 'Kill, kill him too.'

'Not right now, your majesty!' chief minister Rakshash interrupted hurriedly. 'We can engineer his death when he is outside. Within the city, let your subjects (and Sashigupta) think he will be left alive'.

---

2 Acorus calamus Linn. (Acoraceae), also known as Vacha in Sanskrit, is a mid-term, perennial, fragrant herb which is used in Ayurvedic (Indian traditional) and the Chinese system of medicine. Used often as a sedative.

'And that low caste bitch will curse us less, if we let one of her sons live,' Prince Kaivarta said, displaying an understanding of public relations his drunk brother lacked.

Dhanananda waved his hand impatiently, not bothered whether his illegitimate son lived or not.

'Okay, don't go on and on, Amatya,' he said peevishly to Rakshash. 'My bastard son can live. Let him finish the last rites of his brothers.'

'And let us see him one last time, to check his reaction,' Prince Kaivarta said.

Dhanananda nodded. '*Exchellenth idea*!' he said, turning to Rakshash who bowed in agreement.

The Chandala at the Sangam

Weak and heartbroken, Sashigupta attended the early morning funerals of his brothers and friends. As the pyres died out, the acrid smell of burnt rotten corpses filled the air for miles around, making it hard to forget. All the *Chandala*, low caste workers whose job it was to cremate the dead, had their turban cloths wrapped tightly around their noses to shut out the stench. 'What happened to the bodyguards of the kings?' Sashigupta asked feebly.

The head Chandala grinned. 'Guess!' he said.

'All killed?'

Chandala nodded. 'Brutally,' he said with relish. 'Dhanananda's elite guards overwhelmed them,' the Chandala smirked at the recollection.

Dhanananda's servants were louts like their master, Sashigupta thought, hiding his feelings behind a nondescript expression. Hardly able to stand, he gathered the ashes of his late brothers and the dead kings in individual covered mud pots (eerily similar to the rice-filled ones in the cursed chamber) on bullock carts and immersed the ashes in a *Sangam*, the confluence where the River Sindhu met two other rivers. Sashigupta made a silent vow to avenge the deaths, tears streaming down his face. Behind him, a courtier from Dhanananda's court oversaw the immersion. The pots floated away or gurgled to the riverbed. Sashigupta then stepped into the river, and as a ritual poured water over his head. As he wiped his face on his filthy sweaty shoulder cloth, the courtier stepped forward.

'Collateral Damage'

'Prince Sashigupta, his majesty, King Sarvarthasiddhi has asked you to attend court before you go anywhere,' the courtier informed him. 'We have new clothes for you to wear,' he handed over a set of new white clothes reeking of antiseptic herbal medicine.

Dazed, Prince Sashigupta changed behind a tree, taking care to cover himself carefully so the jewels were not visible. He then accompanied the courtier in the same bullock cart that had carried the ashes of the dead.

At the palace, two sentries accompanied Sashigupta to the public court presided over by Dhanananda. It was late afternoon. A turbaned horn-blower used a long, curved brass horn and announced to the courtiers, 'Sashigupta enters the court.'

The highly adorned courtiers became silent as he walked towards his father, the king. Some of them visibly winced at the smell emanating from him, others waved their shoulder cloths as if to fan the foul odor away.

Prince Sashigupta walked right up to the ornate rope that kept ordinary mortals from getting too close to the mighty Dhanananda. There was a silence during which time the king and his brothers exchanged looks with raised eyebrows. Finally, someone cleared his throat and started to talk – it was chief minister Rakshash.

'We are sorry your brothers died. Our actual targets were heads of republics. Your brothers got caught in the middle… collateral damage,' Rakshash finished lamely.

'Looted the Dead Bodies'

Sashigupta looked numb. Rakshash gestured to a lowly official nearby, who walked forward with a bronze plaque sealed with an iron ring to hang it by. Rakshash picked up the bronze plaque and a small, jeweled bag, and held them out.

'Prince Sashigupta, your father, the generous Dhanananda hands over this pouch of gold and the title for the island of Patala for your own.'

Sashigupta remained still, too dazed to move. With a gesture from Rakshash, some official took the jeweled bag and thrust it towards Sashigupta, veins popping out on his forehead in an effort not to break down in front of his father.

'Is there anything we can do for you?' Rakshash asked politely.

'I need a mount, I can barely walk,' Sashigupta croaked.

The court stared at Sashigupta in silence, the ones close to him, still holding their noses with grimaces to avoid his stench.

'Go to the stables and pick a horse. Do not worry about taxes for your island. This deed is exempt from paying us any revenue,' Rakshash broke the silence in a placatory tone.

'You may go now,' Raja Sarvarthasiddhi growled and at the sound of his father's voice, Prince Sashigupta finally bent his head in acknowledgement.

'I will take leave of you, O king!' Prince Sashigupta said in his normal voice. He bowed and Raja Sarvarthasiddhi waved his goblet at him. But Rakshash noticed that even though he spoke normally, the young prince's fists were clenched so tight, the back of the hands looked white. Then Prince Sashigupta turned and walked towards the exit.

'He's taking it quite well,' Raja Sarvarthasiddhi muttered.

'No, your highness, he is acting, and he has far more gold *kada*s on his wrists than when he first came here.'

'My bastard son probably looted the dead bodies,' Raja Sarvarthasiddhi said spitefully.

The rest of the court laughed out loud.

'I think your eldest born is very deep,' Rakshash said quietly. 'Keep an eye on him,' he snapped at the Governor General, who nodded obediently.

The Gifts

'Before you leave the fort walls, choose a horse for travel,' the lowly official said condescendingly, handing over the bronze plaque to him.

Even the lowest of the low sounded like trained but inferior replicas of his arrogant father, Sashigupta thought.

'Raja Dhanananda has given Patala to you,' the copycat said pompously as though the gift was his decision.

Sashigupta remained stone-faced. He knew that, acting on chief minister Rakshash's advice, Dhanananda had gifted the small riverine island, Patala, to make up for his crass behavior. Sashigupta walked slowly from the court to the royal stables, mounted a bronze-colored horse called Vijayta, nodded stiffly to the copycat, and rode up the highway. As soon as the citadel gateway was out of sight, Prince Sashigupta took one of the small paths that meandered through green crop fields. While in Nandawati, Sashigupta had remained quiet from the pain.

And it continued while he rode silently, crossing the Sindhu river, and towards his mother's village, which lay towards the east. He avoided the highway or townships as much as possible, stopping only to rest briefly at night or eat wild fruits which he shared with his horse.

Chanakya Enters Dhanananda's Court, May 336 BC

The excitement about the dead kings had not yet died down. It was a Friday – the day Sarvarthasiddhi bestowed his patronization of the arts and sciences on deserving souls. His audience chamber was crammed to bursting.

Each scholar's sycophantic address to the king as a sponsor of fine arts was in the hope of getting royal patronage for their respective fields.

None of this made any impact on the king. With disdain for the worthy scholars present, Dhanananda was getting more inebriated by the hour, his corpulent midriff oozing sideways, his eyes glazed like a dead mackerel. His siblings looked on with mirth as almost all scholars tried to flatter the king with similar expressions.

'O savior of the world…'

'O master of the arts…'

Variations of the same theme had gone on for nearly three hours when the last scholar's name was called.

'Chanakya…!'

A wiry man with pockmarked skin and hair tied in a top knot came to the front of the king's throne. He bowed and spoke without flattery in a gravelly voice. Addressing the king, he said, 'Brought here by Shaktar, your courtier. I am Chanakya, a scholar in politics and economics.'

Shaktar, the Courtier

Raja Dhanananda was sagging sideways, a trickle of fluid dripping from the right side of his mouth. Chief minister Rakshash, worried that the king was in imminent danger of sliding off his throne, or worse, saying something unspeakable, decided to intervene. Dhanananda, however, botched this good intention. With the haste and coarseness of an uncontrolled drunk, the king pointed crudely at Chanakya and roared, 'Look at that, an ugly man who says he's a *sholar*.'

'Brother, don't you know, the uglier the scholar, the more his brains,' Prince Kaivarta joked rudely.

The Nanda siblings bellowed in shared insulting laughter, the courtiers joining them. Chanakya observed that one middle-aged man with luxurious locks, seated to the right of the king, was solemn and silent.

'Do not offend a scholar, your majesty,' chief minister Rakshash began, but his voice was drowned by a powerful shout from the wiry man.

'For this insult,' the scholar spat, 'I will not tie my hair in a top knot till I see your kingdom end.' In one swift move, he undid his hair with his left hand and vanished through the main exit.

The court was stunned to silence as the scholar disappeared, all flattery and mirth evaporating into the air. It took a couple of moments to sink in before the king and his drunken brothers realized what the wiry scholar had just said and they yelled in collective outrage.

'Stop *dat* bandicoot!' Prince Kaivarta, who having imbibed half the amount of Vacha alcohol as the king, bellowed in delayed umbrage.

'*Capshure* him!' Dhanananda shouted drunkenly, spraying everyone closeby with spit.

Shaktar, the courtier, drew his sword and blocked the exit giving Chanakya time to mount his horse, and ride to safety. After fifteen minutes of adroit fencing, Shaktar was captured and dragged in front of the king minus his sword and turban.

'Why did you protect *dat* ugly man?' Dhanananda's speech was slurred. 'Who, who *ish* he to you?'

'I did not want you to sully your hands with the blood of a Brahmin and he is a famed scholar,' Shaktar said with dignity.

'Throw *thish* lover of Brahmins into prison for stupidity,' Dhanananda snarled.

Soldiers grappled with Shaktar, stripped him of his civilian armor and marched him out of sight towards the royal prison.

'*Dat* warty old *sholar* should be in prison too,' Prince Kaivarta said furiously and demanded, 'Governor General, give me a report on that old bandicoot.'

'As the administrator of the city and countryside, I will bring him in if he has *bahirika* status,' the Governor General said. He stomped out in a swish of silk to the barracks to instruct his men.

June 336 BC Morvati

Mura's Home

MEANWHILE, STRICKEN BY bitterness and grief, Sashigupta continued to ride east towards Morvati village, his mother's birthplace and residence, which lay east of Sauvira. To avoid people, he crossed the river, took the inner roads, grazing grounds, pathways around villages, staying away from public highways. He lost count of days before he reached Morvati village. Mura, his beautiful mother, was waiting for him patiently in her tiny thatch-roofed hut. There was no need to talk, her calm lovely face had aged twenty years and her hair had turned completely grey. Choking with pain, he touched her feet forcing words out of his stiff mouth.

'I bring you bad news,' Sashigupta croaked.

'Your brothers are dead,' Mura said calmly.

'You know, mother?' he asked in pain.

'The wandering troubadour informs us every month about all the surrounding kingdoms. Three days after you cremated my other sons, the troubadour came here. What took you so long?'

'I wanted to avoid the highways.'

'Of course!' Mura said, looking curiously at the bronze plaque.

'My father has gifted me an island, Patala and Rakshash has waived off any future taxes,' Sashigupta said as he laid the bronze plaque at his mother's feet.

'Then it must be a worthless barren piece of land,' Mura was contemptuous, pushing the plaque back towards her son with her left foot. 'As if the grant of land will recompense for my five dead sons.'

Mura looked into the distance, a faraway look in her eyes. Then she turned stern, tired but stern.

'You must avenge your dead brothers,' she said.

'I agree. But how can I pull this off alone, mother?'

Mura's Advice

Mura shut the door tight.

'Your father is immune because of his wealth. He makes enemies every day. Many of his enemies would like him dead. Some of those enemies, small or large, are your strength.'

'Which enemy would dream of taking on the Nanda might as it is right now, and where do I start, mother?' Sashigupta wondered.

'The latest news by the singing troubadour is that your asinine father Dhanananda has insulted a respected teacher from the northwest, Chanakya, who is very distantly related to us. His other name is Vishnugupta,' Mura said.

Even as Sashi asked, 'You want me to…'

'Contact Chanakya who fled for his life from the Nanda court. Each of you have the same goal, to vanquish Dhanananda.'

'My father knows that you stay here. He might target you, mother, my only remaining family,' Sashigupta's voice cracked with the effort not to break down. He scratched his back vigorously, an action that did not miss his mother's eyes.

'Don't worry about me, the king abandoned me and my sons eleven years ago. (I did everything possible to win him back, went to an expert for love potions, but to no effect),' Mura shook her head at the recollection.

'Not worth the trouble, mother,' Sashigupta said.

'I agree. If your father chooses to kill me, after my sons' deaths, I do not mind dying. So do not think of me. Focus on your goal instead,' she said.

'Besides, you, unlike your father, have no craze for power– a quality that makes for a good king. I trust you will bring justice to this land, justice that will not bow to your father's gold,' Mura told her son.

Dhananandа's Wealth

Mura stretched out a brass tumbler full of aromatic buttermilk. Her son drank it in one go and wiped his mouth with the back of his hand.

'Who will support me, mother?' Sashigupta scratched his back with a small twig.

'In Dhanananda's territories, there is a tremendous disparity of wealth. Dhanananda is the richest man in the kingdom. All surplus wealth from the gold mines, taxes and trade in the kingdom belong to him. Across the kingdom are his high officials who earn upwards of 48,000 *pana*s a year. The lowest government workers earn 60 panas a year. The ratio of highest to lowest is 1000 to one. Your father is an unfair ruler,' Mura sighed softly.

'And there are lakhs more who earn even lesser than 20 panas a year,' Sashigupta said as he scratched his right shoulder.

Poisoned Clothing

'Why do you scratch so much?' Mura asked sharply.

'Ever since I wore these clothes, my body itches all over. I guess it is because I haven't had a proper bath yet. I covered myself to hide the jewels I carry,' Sashi said.

'Were the clothes given by your father?' Mura asked to which her son replied, 'A courtier gave them to me.'

'How can you trust your father, Sashi? The clothes must be steeped in poison. Change into something I have woven. And throw the rubbish you are wearing into the fireplace,' Mura said with concern.

Sashigupta went and stripped off his clothes. Now that his mother had pointed out that his clothes might be poisoned, he became aware of the stale medicinal smell emanating from his clothes, strong enough to drown his own body odor. He threw the clothes into the kitchen fire and rubbed a coarse towel dipped in boiling turmeric water over his skeletal body. When he had changed into clean clothes, Mura said, 'You have boils all over.'

Mura slid a sword from the wall behind her, towards Sashigupta.

'I should have given you this before you left to meet your father. It will help you in your goals.'

Sashigupta picked up the sword and unsheathed it. His finger moved deftly over the blade.

'*Wootz* steel, mother. The same southern steel is used for the famed swords of Damascus and Persia. I won't waste any more time.'

'Do what you must for justice for this land. Meet the *Gramika* before you leave,' his mother advised.

Mura put the jewels into a wizened goat skin pouch.

Sashigupta buckled the sword below his waistband. He covered the bulging goat skin pouch and gold stomachers with coarse home spun cloth. Sashi then straightened and stepped out of his mother's hut. Mura had rubbed dye over Vijayta when he was bathing and the horse was now as black as a crow, except for a faint white diamond patch on its throat.

'Wait for the dye to dry, and then mount the horse,' Mura advised him.

'Yes, mother!' Sashigupta gave his mother a tight hug and turned away after touching her feet, so she would not see his tears or he, hers.

The Gramika

Sashigupta walked his horse to the gramika, the village headman, who was seated under a peepal tree in the village square surrounded by elders. The headman was a distant relative of his mother Mura and he welcomed him warmly. When Sashigupta stooped to touch his feet, the headman hugged him tightly. The gramika waved his hand at the elders saying, 'These are the *gramavriddha*.'

'We have a small piece of rice-growing land that was your maternal grandfather's, which you can inherit now,' an ancient gramavriddha spoke.

Prince Sashigupta bowed humbly in acknowledgement.

'I prefer the income goes to my mother as always. What do you do as gramika?' Sashigupta asked.

'I tend the pillars that mark the boundaries of the village, control grazing rights and expel law breakers.'

Sashigupta felt a trifle puzzled, why had his mother asked him to meet the gramika?

There was a silence.

'Anything we can do for you?' the gramika asked.

'I need to bring justice to the land. Where do I start?' Sashigupta asked.

Chanakya, the Kingmaker

'There is a guru on the run from Raja Sarvarthasiddhi, called Vishnugupta or Chanakya,' the gramika said.

'Or Kautilya,' a toothless gramavriddha added.

'My mom mentioned him too,' Sashi said.

'This is his maternal grandmother's natal village. He will support you in your goals,' the headman said.

'How will he help?' Sashigupta was curious.

'The rumor goes that Chanakya was born with a full mouth of teeth. The intuitionist that his mother consulted said he would become a king. Frightened, his parents had the entire set of teeth removed from the baby's mouth. Chanakya's luck then changed to that of a Kingmaker.'

'Besides,' the gramavriddha added, 'he is an expert on the science of government and knows how to maintain civil society through *danda niti*, the art of punishment.'

'Not through heavy taxes, fines and jail time, which is Nanda *niti*,' the gramika said.

The crowd guffawed.

'He will teach you justice where all are equal before the law, the king's son, an enemy king, a high-born minister or a nobody,' a wrinkled gramavriddha added.

Sashigupta was silent for a minute.

'Please give me directions to meet this guru who was insulted by Dhanananda,' Sashigupta requested.

'I will send my son to direct you to a shortcut that bypasses the highway but leads to all important destinations. Preran!' cupping his hands, the gramika yelled towards a long-row house behind him.

A young boy in his teens came running towards them.

'Mount the horse and lead Prince Sashigupta to the nearest road. Avoid the highway, show him a route that will lead to the Jhelum. This is my lunch, please take it,' the gramika said as he handed over a banana leaf packet to Sashigupta.

'The old man is being hunted down by the Nanda soldiers. Every few weeks, he goes to a different ashram, but he still stays on the same circuit of ashrams and villages. The Nanda soldiers came here too, to harass your mother about the old man's whereabouts. But Mura told them even if they killed her, she did not know where the guru was hiding. They think, not wrongly, that Chanakya is related to your mother.'

'My mom?' Sashigupta looked aghast.

Brave Mura

The gramika shook his head at the memory, 'It was unbelievable, ten soldiers surrounded your mother, pushed her around, but she was brave, held her ground and denied knowing the old man. Didn't your mother tell you?'

'No!' Sashigupta's stomach churned with anger. He swore and slashed his sword at the branch above him, scattering wood chips.

The gramika and elders waited miserably till he got back in control.

'I need to take leave,' Sashigupta spoke quietly after a few minutes.

There was silence.

'May your quest bear fruit,' the gramika said.

'It will,' Sashigupta said grimly.

He bid the old men farewell and mounted Vijayta. The dye had dried. Preran and he rode out of the village onto a narrow path through green rice fields, water glistening silver between the sharp stalks. Next to the fields, vast *maidans* housed massive indie cattle.

'This land is very fertile, Preran,' Sashi told the young boy.

'Probably, sir. I don't like farming, that's for my father and his brothers.'

'You don't look like a farmer, Preran, you have good command over your mount. What do you like to do?' Sashi asked.

'I always wanted to be a soldier, live the gallant life of a Kshatriya. Farming is for people who live a sedate life.'

'If I want a soldier, could I recruit you?'

'I would like that. To serve you and this land.'

They rode up to the crossing and the young boy showed Sashigupta the narrow road to be taken through the fields.

'After you cross the river, avoid the highway travel lodges. State appointed Nanda poisoners, the *tikshna,* run the lodges and poison any citizen they consider a danger to the Nanda kingdom,' Preran advised.

'That's smart thinking, who taught you?'

'I studied for a couple of years under teacher Chanakya, who you want to meet. He taught us to think,' Preran explained.

'I can't wait to meet the old man. Thanks for the warning about those poisoners,' Sashi told Preran, adding, 'I must top their list. There's probably a contingent on the lookout for me on the highway in their territory. Thank you!'

Sashigupta slashed the air with his sword in farewell and swiftly rode ahead. The boy waited till Sashigupta was a speck on the dirt road, then rode back to his village.

July 336 BC
River Jhelum, Airawati

Sashigupta meets Chanakya

AT THE RIVER crossing, with renewed vigor and a sense of purpose, Sashigupta set off on Vijayta.

Riding from village to village, bathing in small streams, away from the highway, but close to the villages, Sashigupta asked for the old man's whereabouts until fate led him to a small village, Airawati, near the Jhelum river. A cowherd pointed out to him the ashram of the teacher Chanakya. The thatched roof ashram hut was so miniscule it could easily pass off for a one-cow shed.

In the small mud hut that nestled on the bank of a stream, Sashigupta saw the old man, spiritedly teaching eight to ten-year-old boys economics and politics in the verandah.

Sashigupta dismounted, tied Vijayta to a peepal tree and bowed humbly in the direction of the old man, who nodded briefly, and ended the lesson.

'Go and collect dry, fallen firewood,' he instructed the youngsters.

The boys obediently left the tiny hut to do their guru's bidding.

Sashigupta introduced himself and touched the old man's feet respectfully.

'Welcome to my *Gurukul,* my forest school. Why are you here?' the old man asked after a brief silence.

'I want justice for my brothers and my friends,' Sashigupta said. He hesitated for a moment and then told him about the deaths of his brothers and friends.

'I know, the troubadour passed by with the news. Do you realize who you are up against. Dhanananda, richest satrap of Persian King Emperor Darius,' Chanakya said.

Normal and Abnormal

Sashigupta placed the bronze plaque with a sealed ring at the old man's feet. 'Maybe, we can start here, Guruji,' he said.

The old man picked it up and silently read the bare wording gifting the island of Patala to Sashigupta.

'I don't know what it is worth,' Sashigupta said quietly as the old man continued to read. 'Rakshash said there would be no taxes. This could mean the land has no agrarian value or mines. There may be no forest or natural resources. I don't know why he bothered to give me anything.'

'Thanks to your father's popularity, he is practiced in conciliating enemies,' Guruji said drily, continuing to add, 'Topsy turvy.'

'Meaning?' Sashigupta raised his eyebrows.

'The four methods of dealing with enemies are *sama* (conciliation), *dana* (giving rewards and gifts), *bheda* (introducing dissent) and *danda* (using aggression). This order is *Anuloma* (natural). Using punishment, followed by donation of gifts, is *pratiloma* (abnormal).'

'If he has no value for the island of Patala, he may not keep tabs on the place,' Sashigupta said slowly.

'I think not, but we have a place you can call your own. The value of land is what you make of it,' the old man said as he looked at the plaque.

The old man read the deed again.

'Good start! Acquiring territory can be extensive, like half a kingdom at a time or slightly, like a single village, fort,' the old man said in a low rough voice.

'Or Patala,' Sashigupta added.

The Kosa

Feeling encouraged, Sashigupta unhooked the stomachers around his waist, opened the bulging goatskin pouch strapped around his body and emptied its contents on the floor beside the old man. Signet rings, armlets, necklaces, huge precious stones. The personal adornments of the kings and republicans who had met their deaths in the underground chamber, a fortune, clattered down. Sashigupta stripped the gold bracelets off his wrists and added them along with the small leather pouch containing gold coins to the pile on the ground.

Minus the goatskin pouch, Sashigupta's stomach looked shrunken and wrinkled, obvious signs of his period of starvation. The old man stared at the gaunt stomach without expression, then abruptly picked up the signet rings and checked them out one by one.

'Gandharan, Mallian, Sind, Sauviran, Kshudrakan, Kambhojan. The future cost to the Nandas will be huge. I wager most of his vassals will ditch him now and choose independence over Nanda protection. A treasury with gold coins, silver, precious stones and expensive jewelry is a good start. In times of war or natural catastrophes, with no income, the treasury saves the kingdom from bankruptcy,' Chanakya explained.

Sashigupta nodded in agreement.

A Kingdom Begins

The old man smiled. 'Congratulations, Sashi! Of the seven features of a kingdom, you have one already – the *kosa,* the secret treasury, the wealth of the state.'

'And the remaining six?' Sashi asked curiously.

'The king, loyal ministers, faithful subjects, armed citadels, the army and navy. And lastly, dependable allies.'

'Who will ally with us against a Dhanananda so rich, so powerful?'

'Allies can be bought or ditch you in an emergency for profit. By getting rid of troublesome vassals, Dhanananda has made many enemies,' Chanakya explained.

Sashigupta was silent.

'Will people support a prince of lower stock? My mom's lineage?' Sashigupta broke the silence.

'Lower stock? You are a prince by birth, Sashigupta,' Guruji's gravelly voice rose indignantly. 'Your father Dhanananda's own father was a lowly and traitorous barber who killed the king and his children. Dhanananda's mother was queen of the Shishunaga dynasty. Why worry your mom is low caste when Raja Sarvarthasiddhi is himself a lowborn king?'

There was a long silence as Sashigupta digested this information.

Guruji continued, 'You have other qualities that a king's subjects look for… noble mien, discipline, honesty, toughness, respect for elders and scholars, and keeping the company of good men, or so I have heard the troubadours sing.'

Prince Sashigupta frowned, looking down at the floor.

'Besides attack on an unjust king will always succeed because his subjects will be indifferent in battle, calamities or peace time. They couldn't be bothered,' Guruji said calmly.

The old man noted Sashigupta's pain and quietly drew a map on the cow dung-swabbed floor after dipping his finger into a brass pot with water. 'Let's play,' he said.

Sashigupta looked down silently at the rough map of Patala, then marked the floor after dipping his finger in the water. Then he poured more water and washed away the map.

Chanakya nodded in approval. That one gesture from the boy was enough to assure him that Sashigupta was no fool, that he understood secrecy and mutual trust would be inherent in every activity.

'It is a king's responsibility to maintain law and order in his kingdom, look after the well-being of his people, and protect the borders against external aggression. If you were the king, what would you want to do first?' he asked Sashigupta.

'Build Patala into a hub for republican rule. If Patala develops into a citadel, it can become a scourge for enemies and the base of a larger republican kingdom,' Sashi suggested.

'I prefer a monarchy, but that takes time. The signet rings will kickstart the moving of loyalties from the dead kings to you,' Guruji nodded approvingly. 'Let's build Patala into the capital of your future kingdom, with imperial authority over republics, petty kingdoms and tribes.'

Kosadanda – the Army and the Treasury

'I want to start recruitment, Guruji,' Sashigupta said as he bowed to Chanakya.

'We need the best in military science and economics,' Guruji said.

'Where do we start?'

'The Nandas usually neglect their people during natural calamities. Their only sure intervention is during invasion or a foreign military exercise on their territory. We recruit disgruntled villagers who have faced floods, droughts, famines. We can offer tech support for agriculturists and rural traders, and then recruit their young men,' Guruji said.

Sashigupta nodded as he thought it over and said, 'We will offer administration for a just taxation policy, and infrastructure for law and order.'

'Ah! The *kosadanda*!' Guruji grunted.

'What?' Prince Sashigupta asked puzzled.

'Kosadanda is a combination of treasury and army, for effective statehood. Dhanananda's rule has unfair taxes and punishments and, in the west, Taxila's Ambhi Raja's reign, too much leniency.'

Guruji and his new protégé talked till past sunset. Both men had moved beyond Dhanananda.

The Pigsty is Safest

That night Sashigupta visited the Airawati gramika.

'I request you for a place to sleep in your compound,' Sashigupta said humbly.

'Couldn't you sleep in the ashram compound?' the gramika said peevishly.

'Guruji warned of many snakes, scorpions and centipedes,' Sashigupta apologized.

'Okay, but leave early tomorrow. I don't want the Nandas to hear you stayed the night. Our village will suffer,' the gramika sounded cranky as he led the way.

Prince Sashigupta guessed that if the Nandas heard about the fugitive guru and prince meeting in the village, it would look like the headman had consented to the meeting.

'I need to recruit an army. Do you know any boys with a Kshatriya bent?' Sashigupta persisted, talking to the headman's back as he walked ahead with a lantern.

The headman looked nervously at a haystack as though a Nanda spy was closeted within and whispered, 'There are two boys who want to become soldiers. And two teenage orphans we want off our hands.'

Sashigupta grunted as he surveyed the pigsty, saying, 'Do you have a better place to sleep?'

'No, the pigsty is safest because my pigs are vicious and will alert you if there is an intruder, whether snakes or men. Let me lead you in so they trust you,' the headman said as he walked ahead.

Walking into the pigsty, in the dim light, Sashigupta searched for a place free of dung and carefully shook a pile of hay to remove ants or anything worse. He settled in for the night, his stomach churning with a familiar sensation, hunger, his nostrils twitching from a new odor, fresh pig droppings.

Military Engineering

The next day, after the headman sent word to the families of the two boys and the orphans, all four teenagers went to the ashram. Sashigupta, waking early, had gone to meet Guruji. The old man was already prepared.

'Be seated!' he said waving towards the tiny verandah to the boys. 'Why do you want to become soldiers?' he asked as they settled down.

'I would like to serve this land on a horse,' one boy said.

'I want to remove injustice,' another boy said enthusiastically.

'Very good!' The old man nodded. 'And you?'

'I would like to serve your court,' a teenager spoke, evidently under the impression that Sashigupta was already a king.

'You?' Guruji asked the second orphan.

'I would like a job with a lot of travel, and stratagem.'

The old man looked straight-faced.

'Okay. You will be trained as all Kshatriyas in military science. Tactical movements, strategy, logistics, engineering and communications are the art and science of war. Open that box,' Guruji said pointing to a flat square box.

The boy nearest opened the box. A chess set with elephants, cavalry, infantry and fortresses, kings and queens, half in dark wood and half in fawn colored stone, lay in the box.

'You will learn chess as a method to strategize on land and sea. You will also train as engineers, building bridges over ravines and water and leveling roads. Military engineering is a must for the battles we will fight,' Chanakya told the youngsters.

Confused silence met these words.

'Do all of you know chess?' the teacher asked.

The orphans looked even more confused.

'Both of you must teach the other two chess. Go to the platform under the peepal tree and learn it,' Guruji pointed at the tree. The first boy bowed to Guruji, picked up the chess set and dashed madly towards the tree followed by the other three running furiously behind him.

'Our work starts, Sashigupta,' Guruji said slowly, looking at the boys chatting animatedly to each other. 'Our orphans will train in juggling, and interpreting codes, and body marks. Plus, palmistry, numerology, astrology, face reading, intuition and reading the future, and interpreting bad and good omens…'

'That's a long list. How do we use them?' Sashi asked, perplexed.

'As secret agents to kingdoms.'

The First Treasury, August 336 BC

A few weeks later, Sashigupta suggested, 'I think we can move to Patala over the next one month.'

'Good idea, we must consult a fort builder for a blueprint for an island fort,' Guruji sounded enthusiastic.

'I will send out a message for one,' Sashigupta said.

'But first things first. You cannot walk around carrying all this jewelry with you, you might be killed. Leave it with me.'

'What must we do about the gold?' Sashigupta said as he unstrapped the goat skin pouch around his stomach.

'There is a murderer in the next village who escaped from prison, condemned to death by the Nandas. We'll use him to make a secret treasury, only the three of us should know where the treasury will be. When he is caught, he can walk to his death with the secret dying with him.'

'You are right. All kings have a secret treasury for emergencies. Dhanananda has countless treasuries in his kingdom. This will be our first,' the young prince undid the gold stomachers and laid them at the old man's feet. The old man immediately wrapped them in homespun cloth.

Sashigupta looked up again. 'Guruji, going back to the *kosa*, where is that fugitive?'

'Dhoomal, come here,' Guruji called.

A teenaged orphan with a faded turban too big for his head, came over.

'This is Prince Sashigupta. Take him to the Vasundhara village gramika,' Guruji said.

Prince Sashigupta mounted Vijayta, lifted the boy, and rode towards Vasundhara. He had an idea about where his first kosa could be buried. But he would tell the convict only on the day he was supposed to work on the kosa. In Vasundhara village, he met the convict, Revi.

'You can travel to Patala and work there incognito,' he told Revi, who looked delighted to meet Prince Sashigupta, and for a chance to escape Nanda justice.

September 336 BC
Mouth of the River

Barren Patala on the Indus

OVER THE NEXT one and a half months, in a hectic monsoon season, both guru and prince moved south towards Patala, a barren and low-lying island of the Sindhu river, which was below Nanda territory. On the way, Sashigupta and four excitable teenagers scouted villages from republics and kingdoms on the borders of Nanda territory to recruit villagers to whom the signet ring of their late chief was a war cry for justice. He also visited villages that had suffered recently from natural calamities.

In each village, the gramika promised to aid Prince Sashigupta.

'We need to avenge the death of our noble chief. How may we help you?' a gramika said.

'You can send tribute so that we can maintain an army. And your able-bodied men can become part of our army,' the young prince appealed.

Every village he visited, Prince Sashigupta exhorted the young men to enlist. Many more boys joined the group as they traveled towards Patala.

Within weeks, Prince Sashigupta and Guruji arrived in Patala, the barren island where a pitiful ramshackle hut stood with just enough roof for one man to sleep under.

'There is nothing here to tempt a thief or Nanda taxmen,' Guruji said in his rasping voice. 'Let's make our own destiny, unharmed by your father's affluence.'

'No wonder Rakshash so generously waived the taxes,' Prince Sashigupta said, shading his eyes from the sun with his shiny new gauntlet (the wootz steel armor, a gift from Guruji).

'We will build the entire citadel with seasoned wood and waterproof bricks, no matter how long it takes,' Sashigupta said. He called the teenage boys who had accompanied them.

'Maraj and Dhoomal,' he addressed the first two, 'You get wood for construction. Cross to the west bank of the river wherever there is wild forest. Bring back as much seasoned wood as you can with each boatful. Do not aggravate the villagers on the riverbank. Go only to places uninhabited by people,' the young prince advised.

'We will take care not to challenge the Chandalas, and dog the *Svapakas* who live in between villages,' one of the youths commented.

'Svapakas?' Sashi asked curiously.

'Dog breeders, Prince Sashi,' the youth replied in a mischievous tone.

'Get lost!' the amused prince said as he aimed a kick at both boys, who gleefully jumped into a coracle with instructions for the boatman.

Hauling wood from the forested west bank to the island was a task and treating it by steeping it in river water took longer than anticipated. River water during the flood tides would wash over the river beaches of Patala. A waterproof wall with fired bricks and jaggery-lime-sand cement kept river water from overflowing on to the island. Gradually over months, Patala turned into a citadel – a parallelogram. Prince Sashigupta had a modest residence near the west gateway, with a private jetty connected by a welcome arch to the rough river. Soon, their peaceful little world would admit a wind of change from far, far away.

The Shenanigans of Philip II, October 336 BC

It was sundown. The villagers from the riverside nearest to Patala were gathered around a fair-skinned young traveler with pale sand-colored tresses, plucking a three-string instrument and swaying, enjoying his own music.

'Where are you from, young man?' Sashigupta asked.

'I come from distant Macedonia. Ask and I will tell you,' he sang in a western accent.

'Who will you tell us about?' a wiry man with a ponytail asked in a voice that sounded like powdered gravel.

'A special king of Europe,' the troubadour said.

'Boys!' the wiry man rasped loudly.

A few teenagers leaping several feet in the air practicing martial art kicks came bounding up.

'Okay, begin,' Guruji Chanakya spoke, for it was he who had asked the man plucking the strings.

'Philip II was king of Macedon till this year. Born in Pella, Philip was the youngest son of King Amyntas II and wife Eurydice. In his youth, for three years, Philip was held hostage in Thebes, where he learned military science from their toughest army leaders. After Philip returned to Macedon, the deaths of his elder brothers, Alexander II and Perdiccas III, accelerated his takeover of the throne of Macedonia. In 359 BC, Philip, regent to his nephew after his brother died, became king instead,' the young traveler sang.

'Did no one try to stop him?' someone interrupted.

'They couldn't! King Philip, a master military strategist, attacked Greek towns with the successful phalanx formation, an infantry attack as opening strike, cavalry for knockout strike. Within a few years, Philip controlled most of Greece and his power extended north to the Danube river.[1]

'Did no one anticipate Philip?' another boy asked.

'One man did! In Athens, Demosthenes ranted about Philip's ambitions in his speeches, the *Phillippics.* He raised the Athenian and Theban armies against Philip, who defeated them in the battle of Chaeronae. Philip formed Greece into a political organization, the League of Corinth and became its president. All Greek city states (except Sparta) were represented by the *Synhedrion,*' the troubadour continued.

'Synhedrion?' Sashigupta asked.

'Council. But Philip had grand plans to conquer Asia this year that came to nought,' he said.

Pausanius vs Pausanius

'How so?' Sashi's curiousity was aroused even more.

'King Philip's plan to conquer Asia faced two setbacks. When Parmenion, Philip's trusted general, was defeated by Memnon, mercenary general of King Emperor Darius Codomannus in Magnesia…,' the troubadour began.

'And the second setback?' Sashi asked.

'When he was assassinated.'

'Philip the unconquerable, assassinated?'

Shocked expressions followed this pronouncement as the village square was now in a bit of an uproar. The fair-skinned

1 In modern Germany.

troubadour raised his hand to get their attention.

'Assassination of a king of Europe? But how?' Guruji's normally gravelly voice sounded like rocks hitting a stone.

'King Philip's weakness was of the flesh. Though he had wives and courtesans enough to satisfy his lust, he had a weakness for teenage boys. One of Philip's youngest lovers, Pausanius of Orestis, was a friend of his son Alexander,' the traveler said.

'Why was he special?'

'Pausanius was a *somatophylake,*' the troubadour explained.

'Somato…?' a confused onlooker asked.

'Seven elite bodyguards for the king, Somatophylakes are Select Companions of Macedonian nobility. Pausanius had been Philip's lover for a while, when the king, a compulsive debauch, took a younger, prettier boy, also named Pausanius, as his lover.'

'Pausanius versus Pausanius!' one of the students snickered.

'Yes! Pausanius of Orestis was so jealous of pretty boy Pausanius who had taken his privileged place as the king's lover that he taunted the younger Pausanius. Mocked unbearably by his older namesake, pretty Pausanius gave up his life in battle. After he died, his friend General Attalus, a relative of King Philip's latest wife Kleopatra Eurydice, took revenge against Pausanius of Orestis.'

'Revenge against the king's ex-lover?' Prince Sashi asked.

'Revenge very rare… Attalus invited Orestis Pausanius to dinner, got him drunk and with two friends, raped him. The next day, Pausanius complained to King Philip that, "Attalus got me intoxicated and raped me when I couldn't defend myself."

Philip was unsympathetic. "That's because of your allure as my former lover," Philip said crudely to Pausanius.

"At least chastise him in court, please, Sire," Pausanius begged Philip.

But King Philip was adamant. "Chastise Attalus, who will soon leave to establish a bridgehead to invade Asia? Nah!"

Pausanius argued with Philip, saying, "But Sire, he is just one of your many commanders."

"My hands are tied. Attalus' niece, Eurydice is pregnant possibly with my future heir," Philip had said firmly.

"Future?" Pausanius sounded confused.

"Well, I divorced Alexander's mother. Eurydice will be my consort after my daughter marries Alexander's mother's brother, the king of Epirus."

"But Sire, the invasion and the future of the monarchy need not be linked," Pausanius tried to reason it out.

"Do not pester me anymore. Out!" Philip had roared impatiently. And Pausanius hurriedly scurried out of the room.'

Pausanius of Orestis meets Alexander

There was pin drop silence as everyone waited for the troubadour to continue.

'And then?' an orphan asked.

'Well, a humiliated Pausanius went straight to Alexander. Alexander had no clue about his father's rotten behavior.

"What's up, mate?" Alexander asked.

Pausanius told him, "I want justice for what Attalus did to me... Your father is trying to protect Attalus, because he thinks his future heir is through Eurydice."

"Do not worry, the baby is yet to be born. I will consult my mom," Alexander consoled Pausanias.'

Revenge of Pausanius – Philip Dies

'But Pausanius was not comforted. He decided to act on his own,' the traveler continued.

'How?' the students asked breathlessly.

'Well, the wedding day arrived. The venue for Cleopatra's wedding to King Alexander of Epirus was an ornate theatre where noblemen and royalty had gathered for the celebration. King Philip was jubilant – his wife Kleopatra Eurydice had given birth to a boy, Caranus and his daughter Cleopatra was now wedded to his former brother-in-law. He ordered statues of the twelve Macedonian Gods to grace the stage.

'To show off how much he trusted his people, King Philip, in white ceremonial cloak stepped on to the stage alone without bodyguards or his usual somatophylakes and that's the last thing he ever did. Everybody heard the roar, the crashing of footsteps and saw Pausanius Orestis rush to the stage behind Philip. He thrust a sword up to the hilt into the king and stretched him out dead on the stage. Before the shocked crowd realized what they had witnessed, Pausanius leapt down and escaped with the king's two bodyguards at his heels. Outside the theatre, as he ran towards his getaway horse, Pausanius tripped over a vine root and was speared by Attalus, a bodyguard of the king. Behind Attalus, two other excited guards came rushing out and speared Attalus and Philip's other bodyguard chasing Pausanius.

'The crowd in the theatre poured out and froze, gawking at three dead bodies, four deaths within minutes. No one spoke. The stunned silence was so powerful it felt like a wall immobilizing everybody,' the fair-haired traveler said as his audience listened in rapt attention.

'Since Cleopatra was now wedded to her uncle, Alexander of Epirus, the new bride and her husband departed for his kingdom.'

Alexander begs Aristotle

'And then?' all eyes were fixed on the sandy-haired speaker.

'Late that evening, after his father's assassination, a disguised Alexander went clandestinely to Aristotle's house.

"Please help me, teacher," Alexander begged Aristotle. "You have influence more than most. I don't want to be branded as my father's killer."

"Were you in any way connected?" asked Aristotle.

"Pausanius of Orestis complained to me, but I had nothing, nothing, to do with my father's assassination," Alexander confessed.

"Very well. I will address the Counselors tomorrow," Aristotle nodded.

"What can I do in return?" Alexander asked him.

"Make my grandnephew Callisthenes of Olynthus your official historian."

"As soon as I am crowned king," Alexander replied.'

Alexander crept home in the dark, going through deserted footpaths back to the palace. Nervously, he waited for the coming day.

Aristotle to the Rescue

'A small hall was the venue of the emergency meeting the next day. Arguments of the circumstances surrounding Philip's death were bandied about until the whole crowd – public relations officers of Macedonia, Aristotle's coterie and officials from the city states – was sick of it.

'Halfway through the private meeting, Marios, the seniormost, stood up.

"What do you say about the fact that there were two horses at the kill site?"

'Aristotle chuckled, shook his head and said calmly, "Over

and over again, I state that only one disgruntled somatophylake was responsible for the assassination."

"And what do you say to the rumor that an ex-wife of Philip was responsible for his death?" asked General Attalus, who as uncle of Philip's consort Eurydice, wanted her newborn son to become crown prince.

"Well, that is one rumor with no evidence because assassin Pausanius of Orestis and Philip's two bodyguards, one of whom killed Pausanius, were killed too. The trace goes cold as there are no witnesses. One more rumor says that Persian royalty engineered Philip's murder. Who knows the full truth?" Aristotle was calm.

'Aristotle then used his formidable stature to state the official position. "This is my final statement. The assassination of King Philip was the act of a lone mad man. Instead of rumormongering and wasting time, let us pass a resolution for Prince Alexander to be crowned king."

"We agree," the majority of members said, and the resolution was passed without opposition.

"As soon as possible, let's coronate Prince Alexander as king and support his resolution to conquer Persia in revenge for Greek defeat," a senior dignitary, Claudios, said, adding, "all in favor say Aye."

'There was a chorus of "Aye" and most in the throng raised their hands in concord. The Greek city states, represented by the Synhedrion, were especially vocal in their support.'

Alexander's Coronation

'And how did they work it out?' Guruji asked.

'Well, the next convenient day was designated for the change of monarchy to witness the coronation of the young Prince Alexander,' the troubadour said.

'How old is he?' Guruji asked.

The troubadour replied, 'Twenty'.

'And he had everyone's support?' Guruji probed.

'Well, the Synhedrion was fully represented at the coronation. When the date for the coronation was announced, a messenger went to the boudoir of Queen Mother Olympias, Alexander's mother. Poor man!'

'Poor? Why?' Guruji was curious.

'When the messenger entered, Olympias was seated on a gilded chair in a dark room, stroking two silvery 11-foot king cobras on her lap.'

'Two king cobras! Wow!' a young student exclaimed.

"Good news, your might… mightiness," the messenger stuttered. "Prince Alexander will, will be… be crowned king," he stammered, his legs trembling, his bladder perilously close to emptying its contents. And with good reason. One of the cobras had stretched its silvery hood three and a half feet to his face. A couple of coir baskets lined against the wall had lids that moved, no doubt by their slithery occupants.

'Queen Olympias was gleeful. She threw her head back and laughed and screamed.

"Take this," Olympias threw a necklace towards the messenger, who caught it and hurriedly departed from the snakes and their mistress.'

Crucifixion of Pausanius of Orestis

'After the coronation, as a lesson to all, King Alexander crucified the body of Pausanius Orestis. Aware that the two had been close childhood friends, this act terrified many into submission to Alexander's authority. Alexander then executed General Attalus, uncle of Kleopatra Eurydice, Philip's widow. It was her turn next. After Attalus died, Olympias executed

Kleopatra Eurydice,' the troubadour continued his story.

'Alexander has no rivals for the throne?' one of his listeners asked.

'Olympias made sure – she had already poisoned Philip's other son Arrhidaeus, making him a blubbering idiot,' the traveler said.

'Is that all?' Guruji asked.

'No! Olympias built a *tumulus,* in honor of Pausanius, for a job well done,' the young troubadour bowed politely.

A few coins changed hands.

Alexander Destroys Thebes, 335 BC

In the cold foggy night, a sing-song male voice accompanied by drumming of a clay pot could be heard clearly through the dense river fog.

'Hear, O people, about the city state Thebes which revolted this year and allied with the city state of Athens. When the army of Alexander of Macedon reached the gates of Thebes, his soldiers destroyed every house, with one exception,' he sang.

'One exception? Bring him here,' Guruji commanded, huddled around the warmth of a bonfire, fog swirling around his head.

Two young boys raced away and came back with the singer who wore high-heeled boots and settled down near the bonfire.

'Name and designation?' Guruji asked.

'Xerxes. Pony express man,' the singer replied.

'You said the Yavana made an exception in Thebes, who was it, Xerxes?' Guruji asked the singer.

'The poet Pindar's residence,' he said.

'A culture-sensitive fiend,' Prince Sashigupta snorted, asking him, 'What else?'

'He nobly spared temples dedicated to Macedonian and Greek gods,' Xerxes said.

'And?' Sashigupta probed.

'Sold 30,000 people into slavery.'

'That's not so noble,' Sashigupta commented.

'Put it this way, Thebes is no more an independent city state,' the man told the group around the bonfire.

'And then?' someone asked.

'It is rumored that like his father Philip, Alexander has his eye on Asia,' Xerxes said.

'So, the Yavana could come knocking on the doors of the King Emperor?' Prince Sashigupta asked.

'That is a distant dream. The King Emperor has a vast navy, satraps, mercenaries, deadly war chariots and foot soldiers,' Xerxes said confidently.

'Well, dreams sometimes come true,' Prince Sashigupta laughed, adding, 'Have dinner and stay the night in the soldiers' mess.'

The pony express man pocketed the money and left after a deep head-on-the-ground bow.

The Making of an Economy, 335 BC

Many months had passed, time well spent. Catamarans, coracles, fishing boats and barges – Sashigupta's 'merchant' watercraft brought weekly provisions to the island via the western jetty.

Using the signet rings scrupulously, as Prince Sashigupta forged alliances with different chiefs and republicans, Patala became the political heart for republican rule.

Every few weeks, Prince Sashigupta traveled to various places, and forged relationships with Kushans, Bactrians, Scythians, Ashvakas, Gandharans, Koshas, Mallian princes,

Mongols and Persians. People on the borders of Dhananandaʼs kingdom, whose kings and chiefs had starved to death, now routinely came to Sashiguptaʼs court.

Prince Sashigupta would report all progress to his teacher.

'Nanda tax collectors – forced to listen to hard-luck stories about flooding, failed annual harvests and less fish catches than normal – collect less tribute than previous years,' he would tell Guruji.

'How much exactly?' his teacher asked.

'A mere one-tenth to tax collectors, another tenth to Patala, compared to the years before us,' the Prince said.

'Other details, Sashi?' Guruji would ask.

'All waters belong to the king, in this case us. Users pay a water tax for irrigation. Villagers pay for water tanks we build for them,' Sashi said.

'And?'

Sashigupta would elaborate saying, 'To get revenue from riverside villages, a fishing tax, ferry tolls, fines and service charges have been imposed. Easy-to-fish areas are leased directly to our people. Areas difficult to fish are leased to outsiders. Several fishing villages on the Nanda northwest are now sending tribute, a trickle but enough to acknowledge they have accepted a new leader. All thanks to your guidance, Guruji.'

Guruji had his own agenda to build goodwill. The old man never gave up a chance to mine a public relations catastrophe. Nanda villages suffering from floods, drought and insect invasions would beg him for help.

Guruji unfailingly obliged, 'I teach villagers superior agricultural practices, Sashi.'

'Like?' Sashigupta asked.

'Growing flood-friendly rice that shoots up six feet to survive flood waters as well as requests to grow lentils, oilseeds, sugarcane and cotton,' his teacher said.

'Soon,' Sashigupta said cheerfully to Guruji, 'another secret *kosa* would have to be buried, probably on the mainland.'

Guruji nodded.

'A few more villages have agreed to pay tribute,' the accounts officer added.

It was true. Every few months, a couple more villages paid tribute and taxes to the Prince of Patala, in return for protection and justice.

'Sashigupta, settle uninhabited lands between villages on the mainland, get revenue through direct cultivation or lease land to farmer tenants,' Guruji instructed him. 'Also, Brahmins and certain officials in office should be exempt from taxes for goodwill,' he announced to the accounts officer. While Prince Sashigupta consolidated his fledgling republic, there were rumblings of war in the northwest.

Achaemenid Emperors of Persia, 334 BC

It was a humid day.

'During monsoon, entertainers don't travel between villages so as not to disrupt crop planting,' Guruji sounded aggrieved.

Both Sashigupta and he were seated on the parapet of the verandah of Guruji's small hut observing young boys trying out martial tactics with ropes and staves.

As though in answer to Guruji's complaint, just then, a singing voice interrupted him.

'I come from a faraway land, the land of the mighty Asuras of old. Let me tell you about Ahura Mazda country,' a bard sang to a group of appreciative islanders near the north jetty.

'How old, Guruji?' Prince Sashigupta craned his neck to hear better.

'Older than me. The Persian Achaemenid Empire began 216 years ago,' Guruji chuckled ruminatively.

'That's a long time,' Sashigupta made up his mind. 'Oye, come here, O bard,' he yelled.

Taking a cue from him, some boys added enthusiastic yells to attract the attention of the distant singer. For a few moments, there was pandemonium. But it worked. Minutes later, a colorfully-attired man with long curly beard tied in fine twine and head covered in tight, damp curls hove into sight. He entered with his boots on and twanged his sparse stringed instrument to tune it.

'How much do you know about the Achaemenid Empire, O bard?' Sashigupta asked.

'From the beginning to the recent battleground.'

'Bard, we would appreciate a brief history of the Acheamenid Empire,' Guruji said politely.

'Boys, story!' Prince Sashigupta yelled.

The boys galloped in with anticipation.

'Okay, all of you, hear how empires are formed in far-off lands,' Sashigupta announced.

'Well,' the bard said as he settled in front of his eager audience. 'More than 220 years ago, the Persians were subjects of the Medes.[2] But they broke free under Persian king Cyrus II, who then ruled both peoples. Babylon surrendered without a fight when the Persian army raced across the Eastern frontiers of the Babylonian empire from the Persian Gulf to the Black

2 The Medes or Medians were a group of Indo-Iranian-speaking people from Central Asia who migrated to northern Iran around the end of the 2nd millennium BCE. By the end of the 7th century BCE, they founded the kingdom of Media, which was absorbed into the Achaemenid Empire by Cyrus II c. 550 BCE.

Sea. Cyrus II[3] annexed Central Asia.'

'So much work by one king?' someone asked.

'No, Cyrus' son Cambyses acquired Egypt and Lydia.'

'Like father, like son,' Sashigupta commented.

'Then his successor Darius I organized the Persian Empire into satrapies,' the bard continued.

'Satrapies?' a boy with a floppy turban held up his hand.

'Kingdoms that give tribute to the empire, all linked by a vast road network and pony mail express,' the man explained.

'Three generations. Wow!' Sashigupta sounded impressed.

'Darius next crossed the Hellespont into Thrace to attack the Scythians and also added areas of India, west of the Indus,' he said.

'Dhananandas vassal territories among others,' Guruji growled sotto voce.

'In the past, the Persians got lucky with India,' the bard said.

'Lucky? How?' the turbaned boy asked eagerly.

'Three Persian emperors, Cyrus, Cambyses and Darius I conquered gold-rich northwestern India[4] in tiny pieces,' he said.

'Proving the old Persian saying, Cyrus was a father, Cambyses a tyrant and Darius a tradesman,' Guruji chuckled, displaying knowledge his protégé guessed was just a drop in the ocean.

Bagaos the Eunuch Dies

'After that?' asked one of the curious boys.

'Recently, Emperor Artaxerxes III and his sons were assassinated by Bagaos, an elderly eunuch,' the bard continued.

3 Cyrus I was grandfather of Cyrus II, also known as Cyrus the Great.

4 Gold was mined in Indus river bed, called placer gold.

'Oh! Artaxerxes' male line is now extinct?' Sashigupta asked.

'Bagaos made sure. He coronated Darius Codomannus (Darius III), a cousin of Artaxerxes, as King Emperor and became vizier to the new emperor. But sometime later, Darius deduced that his vizier had become greedy for power.'

'How?' the prince asked.

'Darius was warned. When Bagaos offered him wine with a leafy odor, he forced the eunuch to swallow the poisoned drink, thus killing him,' the bard continued.

The boys clapped, thrilled with the real-life tale of blood and gore.

334 BC Patala Hears of a Predator

In Asia Minor – The Battle on the Granicus

AS EVENING FELL, the travelling bard from Persia continued with his story, pausing with the death of Bagaos, the Eunuch.

'That ended all danger?' Sashigupta asked.

'Only within. A predator outside Persia still prowled.'

'Predator?' the Prince asked again.

'King Alexander established a bridgehead in Asia, vanquished the Persians in their first battle of the Granicus river.'[1]

'How did the fiasco happen?' the turbaned youth asked.

'Alexander crossed the Hellespont Strait with a 40,000-strong army,' the bard began to explain.

'That's one-seventh the standing Nanda army,' Sashigupta commented.

'And then engaged the Persians, led by mercenary Memnon.'

---

1 A river in modern Turkey

'Who is this Memnon, the King Emperor trusted so much?' Prince Sashigupta wanted more details.

'Memnon is brother to Mentor of Rhodes and brother-in-law of Artabazus of Phrygia. The Granicus battle was fought in May. Alexander crossed into Asia Minor with artillery, cavalry and infantry in 150 triremes,' the bard continued.

'Triremes?' a thin hand under a large turban waved about for an answer.

'Boats with three banks of oars. Alexander lacked money, food and fodder. Memnon knew this and adopted the "scorched earth" policy,' the man explained.

'Scorched earth?' another curious boy asked.

'Yes. He destroyed all food, fodder and pack animals so Alexander's troops would starve.'

'All?'

'All. Fields, granaries gone. Roads, bridges, lodges razed. But here is a true winner...'

Guruji's voice rasped out, 'Lesson, boys.'

'Sources close to the Persians said that the Macedonian forces were skint for money. But that did not deter the Yavana,' the bard said.

The Granicus Battlefield

'Dear bard, could you draw a map of the battlefield?' Guruji said as he pushed a waterpot and a river shell towards him.

'I will,' the man dipped the shell into the water and drew the battle formation on the floor.

The boys craned their necks.

'Here,' he pointed, 'the Persians camped on one bank of the Granicus. Heeding his generals, Alexander waited till dawn so his troops would be fresh. Then he stormed downriver across the swift, 60-foot-wide river with 13 cavalry squadrons. His

40,000 men met the 75,000 strong Persian forces.'

He scratched the floor.

'The Macedonian battle formation,' he made more scratches, 'infantry phalanx in the middle, flanked by cavalry on both sides began with a cavalry-infantry-cavalry charge on the Macedonian right…'

He drew a triangle, 'Alexander used a triangular arrow-tip battle array to pierce the center of the Persian battle formation. Persian cavalry charging Alexander's men were viciously killed by Alexander and his elite bodyguards.'

'Bodyguards for the boss,' Prince Sashigupta whispered to Guruji.

'Alexander was attacked by the Persian nobleman, Spithridates, satrap of Lydia and Anatolia, with an axe, but Cleitus the Black cut off his arm and saved his king,' the bard drew a crude armless figure.

'And Alexander?' one of the boys asked.

'Alexander then killed the King Emperor's son-in-law, Mithridates, by piercing his lance into the face.'

'And then?'

'The Macedonian cavalry moved left and engaged the Persian formation which then unraveled like a loose thread. The Macedonian infantry phalanx crashed into the leaderless Persian, Indian and Greek infantry at the back of the Persian battle formation, routing the entire Persian army,' said the bard describing the action.

'The entire Persian army?' someone exclaimed.

'The whole lot.'

Alexander the 'Accursed'

The motley group stared at the bard in silence.

'The victory opened up Asia Minor for Alexander.'

'How many losses?' Prince Sashigupta asked.

'The regular Persian army lost 1,000 cavalry and 3,000 infantry men. Alexander lost less than 350 men.'

'Wow, 350 max!' one of the boys exclaimed loudly.

'Alexander's stars must be in the ascendant,' Prince Sashigupta said quietly. 'How is he when negotiating?' he asked.

'Merciless. The Greek mercenaries under Memnon later tried for a ceasefire but Alexander refused. His soldiers massacred several thousand mercenaries, took 2,000 prisoners, chained and sent them to Macedonia as slaves for the mines.'

'He must be really popular,' Prince Sashigupta said laconically.

'This battle earned Alexander the moniker "Accursed"', the Persian told them.

'How surprising!' Sashigupta whistled.

Dhanananda Sends Some Soldiers

'How did the Indian satrap Dhanananda react?' Guruji asked.

'Dan what?' the bard looked confused.

'King Sarvarthasiddhi,' Guruji explained.

'Oh him. When Darius III requested him, Sarvarthasiddhi sent Indian infantry and cavalry troops to the King Emperor, but they were used poorly in battle against the Yavana.'

'Ah, knowing cheapskate Dhanananda, he would have sent third-rate non-Kshatriya troops that were no match,' Guruji grunted.

'Which side will win?' Prince Sashigupta asked.

'It doesn't matter, either way, it serves our purpose,' Guruji said.

The bard was silent, listening to Guruji and the prince converse. Sashigupta realized his mistake in time.

'Thank you very much, bard sir,' he respectfully dropped a few coins into his outstretched hand and pointed him towards the fragrance of fish curry-rice wafting from the soldiers' dining hall. 'Please eat before you leave.'

The bard left. Prince Sashigupta waited till he was out of sight.

'How will the outcome of the battle affect us?' he asked.

'The balance of power between the satraps of Asia, including Dhananananda, rests on the Yavana's Asiatic offensive. If the King Emperor assumes that all battles will end in victory due to superior power, he is pursuing a foolhardy hallucination,' Guruji said.

'One that will impact all of us,' Prince Sashigupta replied.

Guruji smiled and went back to work on his manuscript, the *Arthashastra,* that described features of a strong, just nation kingdom.

A Lesson in Kingship, 333 BC

It was early afternoon, with a scorching sun overhead. Both Guruji and Prince Sashigupta were seated on the parapet of the tiny verandah that encircled the hut. A yellow dust haze hung above the ground around them.

'A strong kingdom includes a dissent-free country and intelligent foreign policy with allies and enemies. The king who balances both is a *vijigishu,* an aspiring conqueror,' Guruji said. He was instructing Sashigupta on the necessary features of his future kingdom.

'To be vijigishu, we need intelligence reports from in and around our future kingdom,' Prince Sashigupta said, practically.

'The ideal Indian kingdom for an Indian King Emperor should begin from the Hindu Kush in the north, to the

(Arabian) sea in the south and a thousand *yojanas* wide from east to west, bordered by desert and rivers,' Guruji explained.

'I am just a prince in waiting, I wonder how the Asura King Emperor is faring with his ready-made kingdom,' Prince Sashigupta said reflectively.

'There is a woman mendicant newly come from the land of former Asuras. Dhoomal,' Guruji yelled at one of the youngsters impatiently waiting his turn for combat with the martial arts acharya. 'Go, fetch the mendicant from the mess hall,' he ordered the boy.

'At once, Guruji,' the teenager galloped away, delighted to be moving.

A Mother from Halicarnassus

Minutes later, an amber-eyed woman with matted hair, glowing dark skin, adorned in multihued clay bead chains walked up to the hut. She prostrated before Guruji and settled down comfortably on the baking hot, bare ground.

'Come on, chaps,' Prince Sashigupta hollered, bowing apologetically to the acharya.

The youngsters prostrated before the acharya and rushed over.

'Update us, Mother. We know about the Yavana till the battle of Granicus. But not after,' Prince Sashigupta bowed to the mendicant.

'Let's see. After the debacle of Granicus, the Persians retreated. Alexander sent Parmenion, his trusted second-in-command, to occupy the coast around Issus,[2] while he captured Miletus last year,' the mendicant said. 'Starting this

2 Issus is in southern Anatolia, Turkey. Miletus was a Greek city in Turkey.

year, Yavana Alexander marched along the coast to Syria.'

'Does the Yavana ever tire?' Sashigupta asked.

'Never.'

The mendicant moved her feet out from under her hips.

'Next, he besieged Halicarnassus on the southwest coast of Anatolia in December last year. Halicarnassus was regional administrative center of the Persian Empire as well as the Persian naval base,' she continued.

'A strategic territory,' Guruji remarked.

'The rightful queen of Halicarnassus, Ada, had been cheated of her throne by a devious relative, who later died. Alexander went to Alinda town where Queen Ada was living in exile. She willingly gave up her army and Alexander promised he would restore her to the throne. Both bonded well. Ada discovered that Alexander had a sweet tooth, and she spoilt him with many delicacies. Alexander preferred the calmer woman to his own biological mom, so much so he began calling Ada "mother". She became his adopted mom.'

'Don't blame him, Olympias is overpowering,' Guruji grunted.

The Siege of Halicarnassus

'Mercenary Memnon of Rhodes defended the citadel of Halicarnassus. The sea route was defended by his navy, so there was no entry point from there,' she said.

'Alexander used the land route?' Sashigupta asked.

'He did. When his men demolished the outer walls of Halicarnassus, they found an inner wall. Halicarnassus would have withstood a long siege, but Memnon died in August in the siege of Mytilene. And Ada's throne returned to her,' the mendicant said as she paused, her eyes glowing like a wild cat at night.

'After Memnon's death, King Emperor Darius appointed Athenian Charidemus to head the army. Darius was of the tribe of leaders that surround themselves with sycophants, classic "yes" men. When Charidemus made unsavory comments about Persian commanders at a meeting, Darius, infuriated, foolishly had him executed, losing the only general capable enough to succeed Memnon,' she explained.

'Suicidal,' Guruji grunted, 'Then?'

'Memnon's brother-in-law Pharnabazus, a classic "yes" man, was appointed successor to the slain army chief.'

The Battle of Issus

'And Alexander?' Sashigupta asked.

'First, he summered in central Turkey near the Gordian Knot.[3] Next, he advanced south of Issus through the Pass of Jonah. In November, news of the Persian army's march into Syria reached Alexander. Darius raised a large army, prepared and fortified a riverbank near Issus, behind Alexander,' the mendicant said.

'Issus was the next battlefield?' Sashigupta was in factfinding mode.

'It was. The battle of Issus occurred in southern Anatolia, south of the village Issus, near the source of River Pinarus. After the debacle of Granicus, King Emperor Darius decided to take personal charge of the battle, a damn poor idea,' she commented.

3 The Gordian Knot is a Greek legend associated with Alexander the Great in Gordium in Phrygia, which is a place and people representing central and western Anatolia, Turkey. In 333 BC, Alexander was challenged to untie a complex knot on a rope tied to a bullock. Instead of untangling it laboriously as expected, he dramatically cut through it with his sword.

'Poor when a king emperor takes command?' Sashigupta sounded surprised.

'Not everyone is capable as you, Sashi. Most heads of state make bad military strategists,' Guruji chuckled. 'Continue.'

'The Persians captured Issus and hacked off the hands of the sick and wounded, left behind by Alexander,' the mendicant continued.

'Brutal, bad karma,' Guruji growled.

'What occurred next?' Prince Sashigupta asked.

'Darius' army cut off Alexander's supply chain… food, fodder and water. Darius sent a mercenary, also named Memnon, who concentrated his cavalry near the coast. Behind Memnon's cavalry were Darius' Greek mercenaries. Parallel to both was the Persian infantry, camped along the riverside and foothills. When Memnon, advancing north, reached River Pinarus, his scouts and double agents informed him that Alexander too was marching north,' she said.

'A major use of intelligence?' Prince Sashigupta asked keenly.

'But Alexander's spies kept him better informed about Persian army stats,' she replied.

'Which were?'

'Eleven thousand cavalry, 12,000 Greek mercenaries and 10,000 Persian Immortals, elite forces that were both standing army as well as the Imperial Guard that protected the emperor.'

'Did Alexander use his signature cavalry-infantry-cavalry battle formation?' Prince Sashigupta asked.

'He did. His infantry phalanx was flanked left by Thessalian cavalry led by Parmenion and to the right by Companion Cavalry, led by Alexander,' the mendicant noted.

'So how did the battle go, Mother?' one of the older boys asked, drawing the Persian-Yavana battlefield with a river shell.

'Parmenion faced the first charge by the Persian cavalry. Crossing Pinarus, holding the battlefield long enough to give the Companion Cavalry time to strike the Persian army. Alexander attacked Memnon, who fled the battle. Minus leaders, some divisions of Darius' army ran away chaotically.'

'Ruinous,' Prince Sashigupta whistled.

The Alexander Phalanx

'It was. The Yavana continued north and ripped the combined Persian-Greek-Indian army ranks with his special phalanx,' the mendicant was getting into more details.

'Why special?' Prince Sashigupta asked.

'Because the phalanx, feared in Europe and western Asia, is an offensive battle formation of armed infantry troops in tight ranks. Alexander's father, King Philip armed the Macedonians with *Sarissas*, long spears. Alexander extended the length of the Sarissas to 5.8 meters.[4] Their carriers were 16-deep, protected by overlapping shields. The phalanx needs cavalry support because though it has great striking power, it is not flexible.'

'The Persian high command expecting a fight downhill, set up a cramped base there, but instead Alexander's army made a feint uphill, across thorny scrub. Alexander's Companion Cavalry sliced through the Persian right flank killing Darius' bodyguards and several top generals. The battle, raging on both sides of the Pinarus river, was so brutal that bodies piled up in the river, turning the water red with blood. King Emperor Darius fled, Alexander personally chasing his chariot

---

4 Persian measures were cubit & foot. Cubit was their 52.1-52.2 cm. Greek measures of length were named after parts of the body, such as daktylos the δάκτυλος, or fingers, which was about 19mm.

for nearly 25 kilometers before giving up the pursuit.'

'Why did Alexander stop?' Sashigupta asked.

'Both his left flank, and center were in trouble with Persians and Greeks who were still fighting. These Greek mercenaries were as fierce as Alexander's own Greek troops. So, he charged the Greek mercenary positions which split into smaller factions and retreated... the Persian army also fled when the King Emperor and their commanders took flight.'

'So, the mercenaries fought even without leaders?'

'They did. Chasing the Persian army, the Macedonians killed so many escaping soldiers that they rode for miles on enemy corpses scattered on the battlefield,' the mendicant said, giving gory details.

'And Alexander set up another Alexandria?' the Prince commented.

'A military garrison near Issus. But that was not his only win,' the mendicant smiled.

Sisygambis and Alexander, November 333 BC

'What was his second win?' Guruji asked.

'Darius lost his family too. Mother Sisygambis, wife Statira, daughters Barsine and Drypetus, and son Ochus. All of them, protected by women troops, were captured by Alexander who ordered his men to treat the women with honor, setting an example himself,' the mendicant explained. 'After capture, Sisygambis went to Alexander's tent, where he and Hephaestion were deep in discussion, and begged for mercy. Her error, she addressed Hephaestion, who was taller, mistaking him for Alexander. Very nobly, Alexander forgave her mistake, even calling her "mother."'

The mendicant bowed in conclusion and left for the military mess, her hand clutching some coins.

'Okay, my brilliant ones, come after lunch for a lesson in kingship,' Sashigupta told the boys, who dashed away to the mess hall.

'What do you conclude about Alexander's treatment of the King Emperor's family, especially his mother, Sisygambis, Guruji?' Sashigupta asked.

'Alexander is moved by royalty and has a mother complex,' Guruji remarked.

Another Lesson in Kingship

The boys were back. Sashigupta's mess cook, who truly believed an army marched on its stomach, had done wonders with some goat meat, curd and rice. Today's 'army' included some hungry teenagers, who, now full, were noisily kicking a cloth-and-straw football with more gusto than skill. Guruji clapped to get their attention, and after some pushing and shoving, they settled down on ground that had cooled a bit in the shade.

'Everybody, from the beginning, what are the qualities of a just king?' Guruji asked.

'Being a king,' one of the smart alecs said.

'Very just,' another student said.

Several snickers greeted these answers. The look on Guruji's face repressed more merriment.

'A just king should be a *rajarishi*, a sage king. What is a rajarishi? Dhoomal?'

'A wise king, disciplined and humble.'

'Good. Maraj?'

'A sage king who begins his day two hours before sunrise.'

'In *Bhrama muhurta* time,' Guruji added. 'Revi?'

'A king immune to the deadly six. Lust, greed, anger, conceit, arrogance and foolishness.'

'Ravana coveted another's wife and Duryodhana refused to part with even one village for his Pandava cousins,' Sashigupta added quietly.

'Preran?' Guruji barked, quelling the leader of the fidgeters.

'A king with self-control over hearing, touch, taste, sight and smell.'

'What else does a sage king need?' Guruji probed further.

'Smartness.'

'By?'

'Keeping one's eyes and ears open through spy rings, within and outside the kingdom.'

'Guruji, Dhananda is a bad man. How come he has so many loyal followers?' one of the cadets asked.

'He has a noble chief minister like Rakshash. What should a chief minister make the bad king do?' Guruji grunted.

A brief silence filled the air.

'Become an expert in creating wealth for his citizens. Lasting prosperity from sound economics,' Sashigupta said into the silence.

'What else is necessary for the king?' Guruji asked.

'A wise king listens to his advisors, when he makes a mistake,' Dhoomal said.

'The effective leader controls all aspects of his fighting forces,' Preran added, sounding like the textbook he had memorized.

'Why is it necessary to be a sage king?' Guruji asked.

'His subjects will follow him to his death,' one of the boys said.

'Excellent. What lessons did you learn from the mendicant?' Guruji looked at one of the fidgeters.

'If the leader abandons his men, the army can't work,' the boy replied.

'And, you can chop off the hands of enemy prisoners,' someone said brightly.

Into the silence following this statement, a guttural sound that could chip rocks was heard, Guruji in full growl. 'Karma, bad karma,' Guruji smacked his forehead in shock.

'And bad kingship,' Prince Sashigupta laughed aloud in a spasm. 'Theory versus practice.'

'Punishment, boys, for not understanding the real deal about kingship,' Guruji looked irate. 'Each of you will fill up 20 pots of river water for the mess kitchen every day for a week and also give me a discourse on good kingship based on real life kings.'

The boys groaned, Guruji's punishment always included mental and physical chores.

'Now go back to train,' Guruji said grouchily.

The boys dashed back to the acharya, Prince Sashigupta's former teacher who was waiting patiently under a tree.

Both men observed their boys who had slipped back into martial arts mode.

'All action is west of the Sindhu river,' Guruji said.

'Therefore, we wait for more info,' Prince Sashigupta cheerily added.

The Troubadour in Patala, 332 BC

The wait lasted for a few months.

Back in Patala, life fell into its usual routine. It was a busy weekday in the Patala court. Cases of land, looting and other petty crimes of the villagers of the west bank of the Sindhu were being tried at the pan-village court that Prince Sashigupta and Guruji presided over once a week. Two fine brains were needed to catch the truth from all the lies.

A man with rare musical instruments, wearing heeled

boots and a twine-tied beard had entered, when administration work was at its busiest. He was asked to sit down to the right of Guruji. When one especially ornery case wound to a close, Guruji held up his hand and gestured. The trumpeter blew a long low note, signaling a break.

'Tell us some news, troubadour!' Guruji requested. 'From the West, Persian and Yavana.'

'I will try,' the troubadour replied as he twanged an elaborate stringed instrument. 'Last year, Alexander defeated Darius at Issus.'

The Hot Sands of Tyre, 332 BC

'After Issus, Alexander turned towards Phoenicia this January. He captured the port of Tyre,[5] which was actually two cities, one on the mainland and the other, an island. For the island, Alexander built a causeway and besieged it from January to July. Neighboring cities sent their naval squads to Alexander as safeguard to escape his army's looting. Tyre used a new weapon, one which the Macedonian soldiers encountered for the first time. The Tyrians filled massive metal containers with sand and gravel, and then after heating them till they were white-hot, flung them on enemy soldiers who came within range of the containers. The hot sand would get under the armor of the unfortunate soldiers and burn their flesh, forcing them to retreat,' the troubadour said.

'Why haven't we thought of that?' Guruji grunted aloud.

'Tyre resisted for seven months but lost its nerve in the face of the stubborn Macedonian siege. Alexander killed 8,000 Tyrians and sold 30,000 into slavery.'

---

5 Now in Lebanon.

'Oof!' Prince Sashigupta exclaimed.

'When news of this massacre spread, nearby towns surrendered to Alexander rather than face the fate of the Tyrians.'

'Better safe than sorry,' Guruji scowled.

The Siege of Gaza, 332 BC

'The entire region submitted to him except one Persian governor of Gaza,' the visitor continued.

'Poor man!' Prince Sashigupta said, adding, 'I can almost predict what happened.'

The troubadour nodded at the prince.

'Between September and November, during the siege of Gaza, Alexander was wounded, first he broke his leg on an artillery stone, and then was wounded again when an arrow pierced his inner garments, making him very intolerant. Outside Gaza, Alexander constructed a mud mound 250 feet high, with a base circumference of a quarter of a mile, on which he mounted special Torsion catapults to launch rocks, stones and other projectiles at Gaza.'

'Torsion catapults! A new thing to learn,' Sashigupta sounded excited.

'After three months, when Gaza fell, it was treated shoddily like Tyre. The garrison-in-charge, an enormous eunuch called Batis, was dragged around the city by his foot from a chariot until he died. Alexander gave his men permission to loot and raze Gaza, as a warning to other hostile kingdoms. Men were killed, women and children sold as slaves,' the visitor said.

'Bad karma, selling children,' Guruji growled disapprovingly.

'Then, Alexander went to Jerusalem which surrendered without a fight. News of Alexander's ruthlessness reached an already-nervous King Emperor Darius.'

'Why did Alexander make Darius nervous, when the King Emperor had a great navy, dangerous chariots and more infantry than anyone in the world?' Sashigupta sounded surprised.

'Alexander had a fiercely loyal army. In every conquest, he had absolute sway.'

'And it was opposite for the King Emperor,' Sashigupta summed up.

Entry into Egypt, 332 BC

'And next, troubadour?' Guruji asked.

'In December, Alexander invaded Lower Egypt. The Egyptians cheered him as a liberator who freed them from their oppressive Persian tormentors. They crowned him for both Upper and Lower Egypt, which made him a Pharaoh, and an incarnation of both Ra and Osiris. Olympias' prediction came true, her son was now a god, even if it was only in Egypt. Alexander constructed, on a strip of land between the Mediterranean Sea and Lake Mareotis, Alexandria by the Nile, which is predicted to become a world center of Greek culture.'

'So soon? How so?' Guruji was intrigued.

'Many Greeks have migrated to Alexandria by the Nile. It may soon become the long-term capital of Egypt, such is its accelerated cultural and political development,' the troubadour concluded.

'Thank you. Please eat before you leave,' Prince Sashigupta said as he dropped a stream of coins into the hand of the troubadour, who beamed. The aroma of rice flour-coated fried fish wafted towards them.

Siwa Oasis in Riverless Libya, 331 BC

The court was filled with people. Xerxes, the pony postman had walked confidently into the audience chamber to meet Prince Sashigupta, now his friend, and Guruji. Both men acknowledged him by asking the trumpeter to blow a long low note, to signal a break in court proceedings. Xerxes settled down at Guruji's right.

'What's up with the Yavana and the King Emperor?' Prince Sashigupta asked.

'Darius? Myopic. After he killed Charidemus, he had no reliable military strategists. And Alexander vexed the King Emperor with his trip to Libya,' Xerxes said.

'Why did the Libya trip irk Darius?' Prince Sashigupta was curious.

'Because of Olympias' proclamation that god Zeus-Ammon was his true father.'

'Alexander believed her?'

'Conveniently, yes. So, while constructing Alexandria by the Nile, he made a dangerous 300-mile trip to the temple oracle of Zeus-Ammon in the Siwa Oasis of the Libyan Desert, guided by crows. There, after animal sacrifices that placated the priests – meat being scarce – Alexander was proclaimed by its grateful oracle and the priests as son of god Zeus…'

'God of sky and earth, and king of all gods,' Guruji explained.

'And a world conqueror, words his mother had dinned into him in childhood.'

'Words Alexander desired to hear, no doubt,' Prince Sashigupta smiled.

'After that trip, Alexander referred to Zeus Ammon as his true father and minted coins of himself with ram's horns.'

'No posts?' Guruji asked.

'No, I just came to catch up with you,' Xerxes spoke casually, confident his friend would not misunderstand.

'Thank you, eat before you leave,' Prince Sashigupta put some coins into Xerxes' chest pocket. The pony express man grinned and left.

September 331 BC
Prosperous Patala on the Indus

The Lull Before the Storm

SEASONS CHANGED, YET remained the same. Entire villages by the lower riverside had chosen to side with Prince Sashigupta, finding the modest tribute he asked for water rights, better than the outright looting by the Nandas.

In Patala, Guruji quizzed his scouts who came once or twice a week from the mainland.

'How is everything?' Guruji asked them.

'Our villages are brave and secretly prosperous. They live their lives without impediment and oppose the Nandas secretly,' one of them said.

'Almost all the villages who side with us have a history of famine, drought, destroyed or flooded cropland, or assassinated leaders. Even during calamities, the Nanda administration taxes them,' Sashigupta remarked.

'Well, our subjects are happy and that's what counts,' Guruji said.

Happiness, though, is hardly ever a two-way street in politics. Guru and protégé were about to find this out.

In Nandawati: Dhanananda and the Prinsh

For several months, news of loyalties and tax monies transferring to Prince Sashigupta was steadily passed to the Nandas by pony express.

This was one more such occasion.

A pleasurable ambience flowed through the opulent gold and sandalwood public Nandawati court where a nimble-footed dancer was entertaining the court. Dhanananda, a connoisseur of dance, was slouched, multiple chins squashed against his chest, ogling the dancer. Into this cheerful environment, a pony express man walked up to chief minister Rakshash and handed a sealed cone-shaped letter carrier to him.

The Amatya read the message silently and offered it, without much hope, to Dhanananda. As a man of no great intellect, the king could only do one thing at a time, in this case focus on the dancer, whose extremities had a tinge of blue skin.

'She has fed on mercury,' one of the Nanda princes drawled to the king who was ignoring the letter.

Rakshash again offered the letter to the king. But the small chit completely escaped the king's attention.

'*Whash*?' Dhanananda growled incoherently.

'A couple of riverbank villages have refused to pay tax. No money they say, but our double agents swear they pay tribute to Prince Sashigupta,' the chief minister informed.

'*Prinsh* Sashigupta? *Prinsh*?' Raja Sarvarthasiddhi snapped drunkenly. 'Who gave him the guts to call himself that?'

Rakshash bravely ventured an answer, 'The Brahmin scholar we insulted, Chanakya.'

Mention of the name had an effect the letter had not made, the king and his brothers stared at their Amatya.

Intelligence Gathering by the Nandas

'*Shana, Shanakya?'* the king spluttered in rage, his attention now distracted from the dancer. 'Did I not tell you to destroy both my son and *dat* ugly man?'

'General, did you hear?' Rakshash snapped at the general, demanding, 'What is taking you so long?'

The General stammered: 'They went missing, no reports came in, not that I forgot, by all the gods, no.'

'Update us, how is Patala set up?' Rakshash turned to the pony express man.

'Iron ore is transported by watercraft to the island. Prince Sashigupta, an expert metallurgist, has set up an ordnance factory on the north of the island, churning out Wootz steel swords, daggers, arrow and spearheads for his soldiers. *Devadanda,* beams with nails and *Urdhvabahu,* heavy pillars torpedoed by machines, protect the citadel on its blind corners between the four gates.'

'Our next step?' asked Prince Kaivarta, more sober than his eldest brother.

'Send a warning to Sashigupta to pay tribute. If he doesn't, we go to war,' Rakshash ordered.

'*Shime* to kick his Mura arse,' Dhanananda spluttered angrily.

'Here's what we can do, your highness,' Rakshash spoke pacifically. He beckoned to the letter writer, who unrolled a tight curl of leaf parchment, and dipped his pen into an inkpot. 'Take this message for Prince Sashigupta.'

'Leave out the '*prinsh*', Raja Sarvarthasiddhi snapped.

Rakshash signaled to the letter writer who nodded.

Pigeon Posts, September 331 BC

Early next day, a lone pigeon post, followed two days later by a delegation of messengers on horseback, was sent to Sashigupta to ask for tribute. Sashigupta greeted the team of messengers who had come by a commercial water vehicle over the choppy, wild Sindhu river, hospitably and directed them to the soldiers' canteen for lunch of river fish and rice gruel. He sent them back without an answer. Guruji stayed out of sight. However, all women and children were sent to the riverside villages on the west bank just in case.

Rakshash was persistent. He sent another pigeon post. No answering post came back as reply. He thought it prudent to not tell the king this, giving Sashigupta one more chance.

The third pigeon post contained a warning, but Sashigupta contemptuously ignored it, only making a mention of it to Guruji. Rakshash was forced to tell Raja Sarvarthasiddhi about his son's reaction.

'I told you and the Governor General to kill the ugly old man, and my bastard son,' Dhanananda snarled, spraying alcohol laced spit on everyone near him. 'And you overlook it for so long?'

'I wanted to safeguard your highness from negative curses, Mura would have cursed us malevolently and killing a renowned Brahmin scholar would gain us bad publicity. We will send one more message to fool them into thinking we expect a diplomatic solution,' the chief minister explained.

'But prepare for war,' Dhanananda growled. His brothers nodded.

Intelligence Gathering by Sashigupta

The same night, two of Sashigupta's spies, an ironmonger and a widowed cook, came by a fisherman's catamaran to tell him that drunken Raja Sarvarthasiddhi had ordered a full-fledged assault on Patala. And that he wanted both Sashigupta and his teacher Chanakya killed, and the diplomatic message was an eyewash.

'Prince Sashi, most villages on the northwest bank near Patala are being occupied by Nanda forces to deter you from fleeing there, the villagers evicted,' one of them informed.

'Most?' Prince Sashigupta asked quietly.

'The Siboi are best avoided – murderous, half naked – they bludgeon strangers with wooden clubs. Complete anarchy there,' a fisherman who cast his nets near both banks of the Sindhu river, informed them.

Guruji was silent.

'What's on your mind, Guruji?' Prince Sashigupta asked.

'Well, Preran, on a sortie, had the same info, which means the news is true. I need one more confirmation,' Guruji said.

'Let's prepare to fight the Nandas' all out annihilation attempts, even though we are outnumbered,' Prince Sashigupta said.

Going to the jetty outside the prince's modest apartment, both had a serious discussion under moonlight with two of their commanders. By midnight, they had more visitors. A hunch-backed jester from the court of Raja Sarvarthasiddhi and two nuns.

'The Nandas' military preparedness?' Prince Sashigupta asked squinting at multiple silvery moon reflections on the river.

'The Nanda assault forces have equal number of infantry and cavalry, double that number of mercenaries, most strangers to water travel. And massed on the west bank, to choke you into staying in Patala,' one nun said. 'No horses.'

'No cavalry for a river fight,' Sashigupta said ironically, 'Great!'

The nun had confirmed what the ironmonger had told them.

'Well, as Patala is a riverine island, our men are adept at fighting over water. But we don't have a proper navy,' Prince Sashigupta's eyes became steely.

'The Nanda navy will not come upriver or downriver, Sire,' a nun added.

Prince Sashigupta asked, 'Why not?'

'They are doing naval exercises in the sea south, more than two days' travel.'

'That's a relief,' Sashigupta said. 'The jester and the nuns must leave early in the morning,' he instructed.

Patala's Battle Preparedness

One hour later.

Guruji was staring coldly in the direction of the Sindhu river's west bank, as if he could see the Nanda army trooped there.

'Summon my commanders,' Prince Sashigupta ordered a young scout.

Within minutes, the commanders came to the impromptu meeting on the jetty, vaulting over the ornate rope, which kept the public away.

'Commanders, this is war,' Prince Sashigupta stated.

His secretary held up a lantern to a rough map of Patala, the river and the mainland on the west bank. Both Guruji and Prince Sashigupta made markings of the coming battle formation aided by the commanders. All knew that the future of Patala, their liberty and lives, depended on their defense of the island citadel.

'After the meeting, Commanders, leave to instruct your men. We have less than 12 hours to prepare a "hot" welcome for our uninvited guests. Right now, our men cannot go to most of the west bank as the Nandas have infiltrated the coastal villages. The east bank has hostile tribes and the Indian desert. We fight from here or die,' the prince briefed his officers.

Scouts from the mainland kept arriving at the north jetty and were taken to the meeting.

'Double agents,' Prince Sashigupta said, 'Anything to help us in the coming battle?'

'The Nandas have a huge contingent of infantry, cavalry and mercenaries, and far too many commanders. From villages, abroad, upper caste Brahmins, Kshatriyas, tribals and so on,' Sashigupta was informed.

'No unity,' Prince Sashigupta said shrewdly.

'Also, Sire, during bad natural calamity, the army is stretched a lot,' one of them said.

'How does that help us?' Sashigupta asked.

'There is a dire famine near the western desert frontier in Gedrosia, so bad that the Nandas and their vassals are engaged on a war-footing to help the *nagariks*,' he said.

'With less soldiers to attack us,' Prince Sashigupta said, 'What will this war be like, Guruji? Open, secret, undeclared?'

'Open war,' was his response.

A young fisherman landed at the west jetty.

'What news do you have of the west bank?' Guruji asked him.

'On the northwest bank of the Sindhu, villagers loyal to Prince Sashigupta are doing "nothing,"' the fisherman replied.

'Nothing?' Guruji said sharply.

'Villages loyal to Patala have hidden coracles and food, and sent away their able-bodied sons to escape recruitment. Villagers, who want to fight, are sailing to Patala as I speak,' he said.

'Good news. Now the next step,' said Guruji.

The Nanda Army Base, End September 331 BC

Across the river, back in the chaotic Nanda army base camp, a lone pigeon post had arrived for Rakshash, who summoned the commander-in-chief and senior commanders.

'General, Patalites have been busy. Crocodiles in the Patala moat, booby-trap gates and jetties, poisonous thorn shrubs to deter climbers. Sashigupta is working non-stop to give our army a fitting reception,' Rakshash read out the post.

'Sire, we outnumber the Patalites five to one. No escape when they are so outnumbered. If we land between gates, there may be no booby traps,' the General smirked.

His commanders smirked back in agreement, confident that strength in numbers would win the battle for them. Rakshash had a small niggle of doubt, but stayed silent in case it demoralized the commanders.

Inside and Outside Patala, October 331 BC

Sashigupta had been busy the entire night, inspecting the preparedness of his citadel.

He checked the archers, each manning six-way lookout posts, their choice of six-foot bows of palmyra, bamboo, wood, bone or horn. Arrowheads designed to tear into bone and sinew were collected from the underground armory. Fire arrowheads, dipped in highly flammable python oil, were also stocked at the lookout sniper posts.

He barked orders as he walked past the armory.

'Commander, next to the moats, *Panchalika*s, wooden planks studded with nails. At the four corners of the fort, Devadanda, beams with nails, to take care of the blind sides. Urdhvabahu, heavy pillars released by machines, will target Nanda men if they come up the walls between gateways,' the prince barked out commands.

'Good work, men,' Sashigupta said, as he walked towards the peepal tree that was his power center.

But he had other worries.

'For waterfront vehicles that will transport Nanda soldiers, what are the preparations?' Sashigupta asked Ramagupta, his senior-most commander.

'On the west, our moat walls between gateways are below the water line. If any oared watercraft comes too near our citadel walls, they will stall on the mud bars, their oars will stick or break,' the commander said.

'Good. I need to address the men now,' Prince Sashigupta buckled his tri-blade and leapt on the peepal tree platform.

As the horn blower gave a long summoning note, all the men hurried to the platform.

'All right, my fighting machines! Protect this island as best as you can. Each of you tie a white cloth on your left arm. Anyone not wearing the white arm band must be killed. Eat, and man your posts immediately. Our scouts have warned us of an early morning assault.'

'Yes, Commander. We are battle ready,' Commander Ramagupta said.

'Excellent,' Prince Sashigupta slashed the air with his triblade and in turn, his men roared an ululating war cry, slashing the air with their own swords.

The Nanda Offensive

Before the sky turned orange, and the sun rose, the Nanda army bullied docked merchant boats on the Indus west bank, plus their own watercraft into a rough bridge. They crossed over the rough waters to Patala, confident they could annihilate the islanders through sheer weight of numbers. Though warned by double agents, the vicious defense that Patala Island put up took them by surprise.

The first line of Nanda soldiers, wounded by the hailstorm of arrows, beat a hasty retreat across the water to the west bank of the river. Several soldiers drowned when their pilotless boats capsized in the rough waters after their navigators were struck by poisoned arrows.

A few boats stalled on the underwater moat walls and were also pummeled by a blitz of arrows. These injured men too retreated across the river to the Nanda base camp. Some boats survived the treacherous moat walls, the dangerous Panchalika, but fell prey to flaming arrows that set them on fire. Some Nanda soldiers, escaping the fires, fell into the raging river that swept them away.

The Nanda Commander-in-Chief

When report after report of the brutal hammerings by the Patalites reached the Nanda high command, the commander-in-chief decided to personally lead his troops, to boost their morale, in a big merchant vessel accompanied by smaller vessels. As the C-in-C's boat neared Patala, the loud intimidating sound of many horns announced to the islanders that an important person was approaching.

The storm of arrows faded to a scatter and the biggest vessels managed to land at the abandoned west gateway cum jetty.

'Scared them silent,' the commander-in-chief commented.

His commanders guffawed.

'Maybe, they want a deal with us,' one of them remarked.

Together, Nanda commanders, along with their commander-in-chief buffered by a massive barricade of bodyguards with arrow-proof shields, climbed on to the quiet jetty. There was silence. Just a few footsteps forward, the wooden welcome arch gave an ominous creak.

'Devadanda!' a loud roar put dread into their hearts. The commander-in-chief and his men had barely time to look up when heavy beams with thousands of sharp rusty nails, the Devadanda, rained on them. Under the weight of the human brigade and the metal beams raining down, the wood floor of the jetty caved in, plummeting them all into the swirling river water below.

Confused shouts filled the air.

'The commander-in-chief is drowning.'

'We are being drowned alive.'

'Where are the damn boats?' the commanders were heard shouting amidst the mayhem.

Nanda soldiers struggled to pull away their unconscious C-in-C from under the now defunct jetty, battling against the swift tidal flow of the river and unable to reach their watercraft.

The South Wall

Meanwhile, an ominous sound filled the air. A few Nanda watercraft had landed at the southern, more sheltered, moat... and about 500 men uttering war cries had clambered swiftly over the fort wall, braving thorny poison shrubs. These boatloads of infantry men had one and only one instruction – to capture or kill Prince Sashigupta. Sashigupta himself, clad in common soldier's attire, was the first to spot the line of red-clad Nanda soldiers scaling the wall like an uncontrolled hemorrhage.

'Devadanda! South wall!' the Prince ordered.

At Sashigupta's roar, many soldiers rushed to man loading posts, vacated by soldiers who were defending the jetty.

Manned again, heavy beams with nails crashed down on Nanda soldiers who were climbing freely over the scantily-manned south wall.

As Prince Sashigupta roared 'Urdhvabahu,' more soldiers rushed to aid men manning machines unloading heavy pillars on Nanda soldiers, clawing their way up the walls. The yells outside the walls were proof that the Devadanda and Urdhvabahu were doing their job.

'Nandas!' Prince Sashigupta shouted as he charged Nanda soldiers who scattered and were brutally felled by Sashigupta's bodyguards and his troops.

By the time Nanda soldiers guessed who the white-booted, black-faced defender was, it was too late. Prince Sashigupta remained to secure the south wall, and when the near endless line of Nanda soldiers stopped, he turned to the west gateway, where a few enemy soldiers were fighting fiercely like cornered rats to protect themselves and their injured commanders. No one knew how long the battle lasted, but only when it was over, the Nanda soldiers abandoned Patala, their weapons, and their dead, and sailed swiftly away with their maimed brethren.

After the Battle

It was early evening. A huge orange sun glowed at its reflection on the river. Crows and naked-necked vultures circled each other under a cloudless sky, and landed one by one on a battlefield littered by corpses inside the fort wall, and near the west jetty. A short distance away, waves crashed on the shore or on brick-lined walls, dulling the sounds of pink flamingoes screeching to eachother.

A tall rangy pony-tailed youth in a lowly soldier's attire, his face and hands smeared oil black, walked briskly through the battlefield, his gait at odds with his face, which was lined with exhaustion. The young man slowed next to a pile of loot, examined a rusty blade and threw it back on the pile.

'Greetings, Prince Sashi,' the head Chandala bowed between loadings of corpses, identifying his leader under the lamp black through his height and white, high-heeled boots. Sashigupta noticed Nanda corpses being unceremoniously offloaded into the river.

'How many of theirs and how many of ours, Brighu?' the prince asked.

'Roughly five to one, Prince Sashi,' the head Chandala answered, adding, 'Their weapons are not as sharp as ours, they are already rusting.' He picked out a *Nishtrimsa,* curved sword, which had flecks of rust on the blade, and held it up.

'Any unusual weapons? *Kutara* - axe, *Chakra* - discuses?'

'If there were any, they wouldn't have retreated,' Brighu stretched out a double-edged sword with his right hand gesturing 'ours' and a rusty single-bladed sword with the other as 'theirs'.

'Point! That's what helped our boys, superior weapons and assault skills,' Sashigupta said.

'And they had you as their leader. Patala took its worst beating since I can remember, Prince Sashi. One more thrashing like this and Patala will be an abandoned island on the Indus. Would surrender to your father save Patala?'

'Surrender is genocide. Thanks to my father's hospitality, I have no brothers,' Prince Sashi said grimly.

'And the Northwest and East fewer kings,' Brighu finished. He turned back to loading corpses on rough cloth to be thrown into the river.

Prince Sashi walked up to a lone, tiny, mud cottage on the north of the island and entered.

'You are late', said the tonsured old man inside with a ponytail, his face blackened too, sounding exhausted as the young man touched his feet.

'Guruji, I just walked through the killing field,' Prince Sashi sagged against the wall.

'Dhanananda's intent is clear – total annihilation. Our next battle, if we have one, will be our last,' Guruji's voice was devoid of feeling.

'With their elephantine forces and endless mercenaries for combat....'

'Genocide is your father's aim and the loyal Rakshash backs him.'

'Such loyalty we can use,' Prince Sashi said bleakly, staring as the old man carefully put a dry leaf in a manuscript.

'Covert activities in the *Arthashastra*,' he said to the unspoken query.

The door opened to reveal two infantry men.

'Come in,' the old man said.

Mura

Both men sat down beside Prince Sashigupta, who said quietly, 'First, Patala news.'

The tanned foot soldier was the first to speak.

'The Patala west gateway collapsing on the Nanda commander-in-chief made the Nandas withdraw to rethink their next maneuver,' said Ramagupta's familiar voice.

'But an attack is expected?' Prince Sashi asked.

'From the south, north and east water gates,' he answered.

'Good, Ramagupta, congratulate the gatemen,' Prince Sashigupta turned to the other soldier, whose pale gold skin, epicanthic eyelids and glinting star earrings proclaimed him to be Digvijay, the Kushan.

'Digvijay?' Prince Sashigupta prompted loudly when the Kushan refused to speak.

Digvijay stammered.

'Your, your mother Mura was found with her throat slit in her hut,' Digvijay croaked out with difficulty. He held out a curl of parchment.

Prince Sashigupta read it, in painful silence. Guruji growled in condemnation.

Abandon Patala

'Ramagupta, Digvijay when do you expect the next attack?' Prince Sashigupta asked, his voice cracking, but face expressionless. He had regained control.

'Tonight,' Ramagupta answered. 'More Nanda troops are amassing on the west bank of the river. The fatally wounded commander-in-chief has angered the Nandas. That much anger can translate into multiple attacks.'

'One more battle could annihilate all my men,' Sashigupta said. 'We need to rejig our future course.'

'Do we abandon Patala?' Ramagupta asked.

'Immediately,' Sashigupta said.

'His father is a master at genocide,' Guruji explained. 'So relocating is survival.'

'How about Kashmir or the Gandhara satrapy in the northwest? We need allies,' Guruji said. 'Like Parvataka Raja, greedy, independent, mountain king of the North *parvat*s, mountains?' he suggested.

'Great idea,' Prince Sashi said.

'Ramagupta, meet Parvataka Raja and promise him half of any combined conquest. We will send a pigeon post to Parvataka Raja and back it with a sealed letter from me,' Prince Sashi said. 'Right now, we are so outnumbered we could be completely decimated.'

'Boss, we abandon now this island,' Ramagupta paused.

The old man looked searchingly at the commander, 'Why,

Ramagupta?'

'The Nandas will cut off all exit points by nightfall. That was their plan when the welcome arch crashed on their C-in-C,' Ramagupta said.

'I heard different,' Digvijay said apologetically. 'Thanks to the C-in-C, the Nandas are rethinking their strategy.'

'Ramagupta?' Guruji asked.

'A tonight battle.'

'No, a tomorrow battle,' Digvijay protested.

'And?' Sashigupta prompted.

'Dhanananda's brothers are with him at the base camp, baying for our blood. Their next assault will be more efficient. Except, the Sindhu river is in a late stormy flood state. The moment the water calms a bit...' Ramagupta trailed off.

'I am convinced, call our men. Change into a commander's uniform,' Sashigupta said. 'You too, Digvijay.'

'Okay, Commander Sashi,' Digvijay touched Guruji's feet and left.

'What instruction will you give?' Guruji asked.

'Abandon Patala, relocate beyond my father's reach. My father, richest satrap of the Persian Empire, buys his way with gold,' Prince Sashi spat.

'Don't lose heart. A king should be just, not greedy,' Guruji remarked. 'The need of the hour is to play games...'

'To?'

'Increase our wealth.'

'Well, our goldsmiths can use every trick to increase our gold and make quick money,' Sashi said.

'Ask the head goldsmith to come here at once,' Guruji shouted to a little boy, who was aimlessly walking about, unaccompanied by an adult.

The Goldsmith

A man in green guildsman's clothing entered within minutes.

'How can we increase our gold?' Guruji directly asked.

'With spurious matter. We mix salt and sand when making gold leaf. We use inferior stones like cheap jadeite instead of high-quality emeralds,' the goldsmith said.

'We might need to adulterate some gold for relocation,' Prince Sashigupta said.

'Where do we relocate?'

'Maybe Kashmir, Bessus of Bactria,' Prince Sashigupta said. 'Or Parvataka Raja and Gandhara'.

'Summon our man from Bactria. I want a clear picture,' Guruji instructed a commander.

'I prefer satrap Bessus, equal to my father in status.'

'"Satrap" means "protector of the land", hopefully Bessus is better than Dhanananda,' Guruji said.

'For a parched man, any drop of water is welcome' the prince said.

Sashigupta thrust his neck out and yelled, 'Oye hoi! Send the pony express man. Our pigeon post faces dangers of eagle and kite attacks on the way, unlike pony express,' he added in an apologetic tone to Guruji.

Greek States

Within moments, the pony express man entered the hut.

'Educate us Xerxes, on the land west of the Nanda satrapy,' Guruji said.

'Sure. In the west, there are rumbles of battles between Persians and the Yavanas, who are moving in on all satraps.'

'How tough are the Yavanas?' Guruji asked.

'Young, use Macedonian military phalanxes. Commander-in-chief Alexander wins every battle.'

'Battle readiness?' Guruji asked.

'Awesome. One example is four years ago, a rumor that Prince Alexander was dead encouraged Thebes and Athens to rebel against Macedonian rule. When informed, Alexander, away north subduing barbarian tribes, marched into Thebes. His soldiers destroyed every house, with one exception,' Xerxes explained.

'Let me guess, the poet Pindar's residence?' Guruji said.

'Good guess. Thirty thousand people were sold into slavery, crushing all rebellion,' Xerxes said.

'Sounds like the man to beat Dhanananda,' Sashigupta commented.

'Yes, Alexander inspires his men,' Xerxes said.

'The Yavana are tough enough to stop Dhanananda from taking over Persian satrap territory. Right?' Prince Sashi asked.

'Right!'

'Let us divide our troops between Kashmir, Bactria, Parvataka Raja and Gandhara. That way, they will be safe when away from us. And I will send two pigeon posts each to all the kings. Thank you, mate!' the Prince said.

Xerxes left.

The Treasury

'We need a digger,' Guruji said.

Sashigupta thrust his neck out again and yelled to the little boy.

Within minutes, a muscular and coarse-looking man entered, a plough in hand.

'Dig the corner beneath the water pot,' Guruji said, pointing where two walls met.

The man dug the tightly packed earthen floor for a couple of feet, till he hit a rectangular stone.

'Call Commanders Digvijay and Ramagupta,' Guruji said to the little boy, who was peering in.

In minutes, Digvijay and Ramagupta entered in uniform.

'We need the *kosa* to fund our future travels in the lands of Emperor Darius' satraps,' Guruji said as he waved towards the corner.

The men got busy.

'What does a satrap do?' Digvijay grunted, sweat pouring, his slippery hands grappling with a rod beneath the cornerstone, his forehead veins bulging.

'They protect the land.'

'Not kill kings?' Prince Sashigupta panted, wrestling with another rod beneath the stone.

Finally, the four men reached their prize, a large bronze pot, lid sealed in parchment. The sound of rattling metal filled the hut as Sashigupta tipped it over.

'Commanders, before the Nandas blockade our north side, let's give our men wages and dry rations. Take the salaries for your men, with two months extra.'

'Okay, Prince,' Ramagupta replied.

Both men counted out silver and gold coins, and stuffed them into leather pouches.

'Send our treasurer,' Guruji said quietly to the digger, who stepped out and hollered.

'I also need to address our men,' Prince Sashigupta told the commanders, who barked an order to their men outside. After Sashigupta had stuffed the remaining gold and other valuables into two pouches tied around his stomach, he, Guruji and the two commanders walked to the North Gate platform.

'Update me,' Prince Sashigupta said to Digvijay as they strode together.

'There is a tent for our wounded. Patala dead are buried in

mass graves. Nanda dead, dumped in the river,' Digvijay said.

As Sashigupta neared, a man with a six-foot curved brass horn blew a long, low note. The Prince leapt on to the platform around the peepal tree, his power center, to address his men. His pet mongoose, who protected the Prince from poisonous snakes while he slept, was draped round his neck. The old man slowed to discuss something with the treasurer and his protégé bent nearly double, to hear the old man's instructions. Then Sashigupta straightened.

Preparing to Become Invisible

'Greetings, men!' Sashigupta began.

The assembled troops raised their swords in acknowledgement.

'For your information, the west gateway crashed on the Nanda commander-in-chief, wounding him fatally,' the prince said.

A roar of elation drowned the rest of the sentence.

'This has given us a small advantage but the Nandas intend to launch an attack now. Before that happens, abandon Patala. Infantry, divide yourselves between Digvijay and Ramagupta. My troops will only comprise cavalry,' he instructed.

Both Digvijay and Ramagupta raised their swords on either side of Sashigupta. Their respective troops split up.

'One group goes to Kashmir, another to Bactria and a third with me. You will take two months' advance pay, ten days provisions from the canteen office, and all your weapons. Chandalas and women agents, you too. Physicians, prepare the wounded for travel and give enough medicine for a fortnight at least. My troops and those for Bactria, will cross the river on the northwest, the ones for Parvataka Raja will travel north-northeast,' Sashigupta told his men.

'When Commander?'

'Within an hour. Better scatter and live than be killed by Raja Sarvarthasiddhi. Each place you go, present yourselves as superior infantry men for mercenary positions. Be tough, this journey will only last for a year or two', he explained.

'How do we keep in touch, Prince Sashi?' an infantry man asked.

'Pigeon posts in Kashmir, pony express for Bactria or Parvataka desh and Gandhara.'

Sashigupta gestured to the trumpeter again. 'Call my group to me now.'

The men who were going with Sashigupta, gathered around their commander. 'Get your weapons and mounts ready at the north gate jetty. I will join you shortly,' he said. 'Prepare a few rafts into a pontoon bridge for the horses to cross over to a calm place on the opposite shore,' he added.

'We need time, Sire,' one of the soldiers spoke out.

'This is an emergency, man. You have less than an hour to depart. Digvijay, cross into Paurava territory before you go to Parvataka desh, I will send a pigeon post on our next move. Send Xerxes to the pigeon cote. Come for last minute instructions,' Sashigupta said sotto voce to Ramagupta and Digvijay.

'Farewell, men!' Sashigupta slashed the air with his sword, the soldiers ululated and did the same.

Patala's Pigeon Post Office

Impatient to send the pigeon posts, Sashigupta sped to the pigeon cote. The smell of pigeon excreta and the sounds of dozens of feeding pigeons made it hard to think. A lesser man would have flinched at the odor.

The pigeon man, filthy with pigeon droppings, asked,

'How many, Sire?'

'Seven. Two for the king of Kashmir, one each for Bessus, Parvataka Raja, the man in the fortress, Gandhara and Raja Paurava,' the prince said.

'Messages, Sire?' the pigeon handler asked.

'Ready to send,' the prince indicated.

The pigeons were prepared for flight. Small brass cylinders carrying the messages were tied to their legs.

'What about eagles on the way, Sire?' the handler was worried.

'Good question. One more pigeon each as backup,' Sashigupta said.

'What messages, Sashi?' Guruji asked.

'Simple. Ask the king of Kashmir to recruit my men as mercenaries. Ditto for Bessus, Raja Paurava, Gandhara and the fortress at Varana. Ask Parvataka Raja for an alliance for more territory,' Sashigupta said.

The man at the pigeon post prepared more carrier pigeons.

'Xerxes,' Prince Sashigupta addressed the pony post man, who was patiently waiting, 'Messages for the King Emperor's northwestern Indian satraps.' He dictated a couple of messages to Xerxes.

'Will teacher leave today?' Xerxes asked respectfully.

'Everyone, including you. My father has a simple agenda, he only wants to kill all my men,' Sashi said.

'Send your pigeons now and pack up the rest,' Guruji instructed before he walked out with Sashigupta.

Patala Abandoned

At the north jetty, three large merchant ships were docked. Soldiers with tents folded into small parcels, weapons and ready-to-eat food packed, readied for the boat ride. The cavalry men were preparing their horses at the point where the jetty was crowded three deep with barges, canoes, merchant vessels and a few large catamarans. To keep safe on the waves, each catamaran had a *plava,* an extended bamboo float stretching out on one side. The special anti-wave technology ensured the catamaran did not capsize, no matter how violent the waves.

In less than two hours, men left for their various destinations, the team leaders briefed by Sashigupta. First, troops with horses left, then foot soldiers, spies in varied disguises, the Chandala and common citizens. The wounded, the pigeon post man and Xerxes were in one of the boats headed east upriver.

Guruji, Prince Sashigupta, their bodyguards and horses were the last to leave on a merchant ship. Guruji looked on amused as the Chandala barge sailed away, laden with weapons looted from the battlefield. Low caste dog-breeding Svapakas shared space with the Chandalas, keeping a tight grip on their hunting indie hounds. As sparrows, crows, vultures and pelicans returned to their roosts, quiet took over Patala. Only a raging Indus crashed against the outer walls.

'Do they have any safe landing spots on the northeast shore?' the old man had asked Ramagupta and Digvijay repeatedly.

'Yes teacher, a private beach north-northeast is ready for us,' Ramagupta replied before boarding his boat, not revealing any more. Guruji's hands were clenched tightly, as were his lips. It dawned on Sashigupta that his invincible guru had a tiny flaw, a paralyzing dread for water travel. The boats navigated carefully upstream against the heaving waters.

331-330 BC Sapta Sindhu
The Riverside Camps

In Nandawati

LIKE MANY RULING families, the Nanda cohort were control freaks. Nowhere was this more evident than their military lineup. 'Yes-men' of all descriptions filled top positions. The new Commander-in-Chief, General Bhadrasala, was no exception.

Downriver on the west bank, but upstream from where the Indus met the sea, in their palace, the Nandas made fresh plans to capture Patala, Prince Sashigupta and his guru.

But the new C-in-C, a cautious man, wanted many precautions in place before launching another Patala attack. 'Let's check and double check so that my troops have the minimal exposure to any trap in Patala. I want archers with fire arrows to be on the forefront of the troops,' General Bhadrasala said.

Raja Sarvarthasiddhi seethed at the delay.

'Tell the old dotard to start work,' he hissed at Rakshash, spraying a foam of spit on his own chest hair.

He was not the only one angry, his five younger brothers were furious, each one muttering under his breath, impatient with the loss of time. Only a calm Rakshash kept them from inflicting physical harm on the C-in-C.

'Making sure there is no booby trap, Sire, just making sure our men don't die in vain. Let them fight fair and square, one on one,' General Bhadrasala said, when gently prodded by Rakshash.

'But we lose time, while you are making sure,' Rakshash said patiently.

As voices rose in argument in the private court where the Nanda siblings, Rakshash and the Commander-in-Chief were meeting, a man in clothes filthy and smelling of bird droppings distracted them with a shout at the entrance. In his hands, he held a grey and white pigeon. Rakshash waved his hand so the king's bodyguards would let him through.

'Mighty Sire, news,' the pigeon man gasped.

Rakshash opened the missive. 'Ah, too late!' he slapped his forehead. 'Patala is being abandoned. General, immediately instruct your men to leave for the northwest and northeast gates of Patala and stop their escape,'

General Bhadrasala stood up.

'Go now,' Rakshash said firmly. 'Wreck Patala,' he ordered.

General Bhadrasala left, looking important. The Nandas muttered till their C-in-C was out of sight.

'*Wash* the hell is happening?' Raja Sarvarthasiddhi snapped, his drink forgotten.

'We are going to annihilate Patala,' Rakshash spoke in a low voice.

'What took you so long, Amatya? You are losing your touch,' Raja Sarvarthasiddhi snarled, veins popping out on his forehead.

A tense silence filled the air.

'Jester,' Rakshash barked, 'entertain us.'

A short hunchback, pockmarks painted on his face and wearing ugly false teeth, tumbled into the center of the chamber, where he promptly tripped over his own foot. Against their will, a couple of younger Nanda brothers laughed, distracted by the familiar antics of the jester, who tumbled and acted foolish. It was one more day at camp. In the meantime, their quarry had sailed away.

The Maurya Base Camp

Sashigupta's troops and some civilian subjects reached a small uninhabited part of the Jhelum riverbank and set up camp at a small private river beach sheltered against rough water by a tiny island. And on land, dense green forest cover and two streams. The men gave their horses a much-needed walk on firm terrain. Ramagupta had disappeared for three nights and two days without telling anybody, but Digvijay the Kushan was still in control.

Three days later, when Sashigupta and Guruji landed at the beach from further east, all knew that Prince Sashi's Patala speech had had veiled instructions for their commanders to confuse any double agent. No one questioned why their plans had changed suddenly.

A tall *kapata sanyasi*, a spy disguised as a holy man, dismounted from his horse and approached the boat on which Guruji was tottering.

'Patala, Sire,' the kapata sanyasi said grimly to the unasked question.

'Spit it out,' Prince Sashigupta growled.

'Patala has been demolished, except for the three gateways and the booby-trapped royal residence,' he said, hesitantly.

'Everything gone, Prince Sashi,' the kapata sanyasi said. 'They gutted the place within an hour after you abandoned it. The double agents on the Nanda payroll were informed almost immediately,' the spy informed them.

'How did the information reach them?' Prince Sashigupta demanded.

'A pigeon post was sent to the Nanda base camp in Gedrosia from Patala,' came the reply

'But our pigeon post man only sent ours. He packed all the rest of the pigeons for the river journey,' Sashi said concerned.

'No, Sire. Another pigeon from Patala was sent by god knows who,' the kapata sanyasi said.

Guruji and Sashigupta exchanged glances.

'The few priests left, escaped unscathed because Rakshash didn't want any Brahmin curses on him. He was warned by the king's black magic priests,' the kapata sanyasi said.

'Oh, good for us Dhanananda is superstitious. What exactly is the fool doing now?' Prince Sashigupta snapped.

Nanda Black Magic

Guruji was grimacing, making growling sounds in his throat, a sign that water journeys were not his favorite mode of travel.

'Prince Sashi, after the Commander-in-Chief died, your father's fear of ghosts and black magic has increased. He is spending panas after panas, to placate spirits before battle or to capture them in burial and cremation grounds,' the spy said.

'Explain,' the prince snapped.

'Dhanananda's daily wartime ritual includes animal sacrifice in the cremation grounds, to capture spirits to protect his wealth. He may perform sacrifices in Patala to capture some dead men's spirits. If you return, you will have trouble setting up an administrative post on the island,' the kapata sanyasi said.

'If only my father's fear of the dead translated into respect for the living,' Prince Sashigupta sounded cranky. 'How else has he ruined Patala?'

'Our agents informed us that everything of value has been looted from Patala, except the gateways. Even bricks on the jetties are being removed.'

'That's Dhanananda, my third-rate father. Those are special flood-proof kiln-baked bricks, they knew this,' Prince Sashigupta said furiously.

With much effort, Guruji raised his hand to calm him, the boat was still rocking.

'The news of making contact with the king of Kashmir and satrap Bessus has already reached Dhanananda,' the kapata sanyasi said.

Prince Sashi stretched out a second hand to steady his teacher, who was making incoherent sounds with the rocking of the boat. Seeing the old man struggling, a few soldiers waded into thigh deep water, grabbed the boat and dragged it almost vertically up the river beach. Guruji then stepped down gingerly on waterlogged sand.

Commanders at the Hut

The party reached a modest cottage on the bank of a backwater stream. Sashigupta stripped off his armor and clothes. The army washerman picked them up and disappeared. Guruji looked around the frugal hut.

'Where are our commanders?' Guruji asked.

As though he had summoned them, two tall men strode into the austere hut and touched the old man's feet.

'You men are on time for our next move,' Prince Sashigupta smiled. 'How are we placed for a raid?'

'Prince Sashi, except for one group stationed in Raja

Paurava's kingdom, another sent to Kashmir, and yet another to Parvataka Raja's kingdom, all my able-bodied men are here,' one of the tall men spoke. It was Digvijay, dressed as a cowherd.

'What is the advantage we have?' Guruji asked.

'Money is on their side, but a surprise raid will be a shock from our side,' the stable-hand spoke.

'Ah, Ramagupta! How was your journey?' Sashi was glad to see him.

'Message delivered to the Parvat, mountain. Answer affirmative, our men are safe,' Ramagupta grinned and handed over a small cylindrical metal box to Prince Sashigupta who read the message and handed it to Guruji.

'What are our plans?' Ramagupta asked.

'Tonight, three raiding parties will head south along the Jhelum riverside. Each party will raid 40 to 50 villages depending on the distance and return to base by early dawn' Sashi ordered.

'Who is the third raider, Sire?' Ramagupta wanted clarity.

'Me. I want to personally break the backbone of my father's subjects,' the prince said.

Guruji watched as Prince Sashigupta donned fresh clothes and wootz steel armor and nodded to the kapata sanyasi.

'First warning. After crossing into Nanda territory, the land between villages is occupied by *Svapaka*s, – dog breeders, *Svaganin* – hunters and *Lubdhaka*s – fowlers, who kill trespassers ruthlessly,' the kapata sanyasi said.

'Do not give these three lower castes any excuse to attack you. Ride only through the villages,' Guruji said.

'Sire, between villages is the best, as the Svapakas, Svaganin and Lubdhakas sleep at night. That's my humble opinion,' Digvijay interrupted politely.

'Ok' Guruji agreed. 'Let's do it two ways. Digvijay, you go the middle terrain, the other two parties will go through the villages. Do not forget. Our double agents are working overtime to update the Nandas. Return safely, no heroics from you three. Sashi, however furious you are with your father, now is no time for revenge,' Guruji cautioned them.

In the reddish glow of a flickering oil lamp, Sashigupta and his two commanders drew a sketch on the floor. Outside, the kapata sanyasi and squad commanders crammed the door of the hut to hear who was doing the talking. But there was no need. Being back on terra firma had improved Guruji's spirits. The sound of a distant rockfall meant Guruji was back in control.

The Code of Manu

'The Code of Manu,' Guruji's voice rumbled.

'As taught by western gurus of the Bharata tribe,' Prince Sashigupta added.

'...advocates poisoning an enemy king's subjects as a duty of a conquering king. The reason, once the enemy's loyal subjects are crushed, the kingdom is easy to conquer,' Guruji continued.

'Dhanananda is a king cobra immune to *beesh*, fire and deaths of subjects,' Prince Sashigupta argued.

'Beesh is the sign of a conquering king. Which king wants the Patala citadel reeking of poison?' Guruji answered.

'My father,' Prince Sashigupta countered drily. 'But I agree. My man, send for our *Rasada*, special poisoner, and *sattris*,' Prince Sashigupta told a young soldier.

'*Sattris*, Commander?' Ramagupta asked.

'Secret agents trained for ambush in wartime,' Prince Sashi explained.

'This time, fire is our ally. And poison,' Guruji was putting things in perspective.

Four Kinds of War, November 331 BC

'What type of war are we waging?' Ramagupta asked.

'Of the four kinds of war. *Mantra yuddha,* war by diplomacy, *Prakashayuddha,* open war…,' Guruji began.

'Yavanas, on Persians!' Sashigupta murmured.

'…*Kutayuddha,* secret war, which includes psychological warfare and *Gudayuddha,* undeclared war, with secret agents, black magic and covert tactics like assassinating enemy kings without outright warfare.'

'Like Dhanananda's death chamber. Our best bet, therefore, is secret war, Kutayuddha?' asked Sashigupta.

'On villages and tribes stubbornly loyal to Dhanananda. The sattris will brief you. Leave in an hour,' Guruji ordered.

'Men, we commanders will instruct you for night raids after meeting the sattris. Get your horses ready,' Ramagupta ordered his soldiers.

'Ditto!' Digvijay said.

The soldiers hissed, slashing the air with their swords. Soon it would be time to leave, the short period necessary so Nanda double agents would have no time to warn Nanda loyalists of the impending assault.

After the soldiers left, Prince Sashigupta instructed his two commanders to dress like him. The washerman had given him black oil. Now the two commanders looked like Prince Sashigupta's twins. Outside, the night raiders were ready, slippery with oil, black with dye. The three groups left together but parted at the fork of the jungle path.

Villagers Approach the Nandas

November, jungles, early winter rains. The chill damp breeze made the villagers shiver as they walked south. The Nanda western capital, Nandawati, was a three-and-a-half days' journey by foot through dense jungle or one-and-a-half days by a rocky boat ride from the farthest northern point of the kingdom, and thence land. Where the highway went in a different direction, village head Rama Murthy and his two nephews struggled through the thick thorn-ridden jungle asking tribes for directions when they were lost, determined to reach the Nanda capital. They were not the only ones. Further up the riverbank and landlocked northwest territory, entire villages and tribes had convened their *panchayat*s for a spokesperson to represent their village at court. The first two days were lonely, but by the third day, more and more villagers had joined Rama Murthy on the highway to Nandawati. Each village had an identical story, of night raiders. On the fourth day, Nandawati finally loomed on the horizon.

'Sir, as our most senior member, we request you to head the team,' the villagers requested Rama Murthy.

'Not me alone, two more men should represent us at the Nanda court,' he suggested.

The villagers agreed and picked two northerners.

'We must meet only the chief minister, Rakshash, who is a fair man,' Rama Murthy pronounced.

All three agreed.

At the Nanda Court

Getting into the palace was not straightforward. The gatemen at the moat refused to allow them in. The villagers put together some money, and after much negotiation and a couple of bribes, the three men walked with one set of weapons over the moat, towards the public court in session. Inside, there was no sign that the Nandas were in trouble. Caparisoned female elephants with fake jeweled tusks and horses with decorated heads, lined the way to the entrance to the public court. Under the sun image canopy slumped Raja Dhanananda, his chins merging into his neck. Around the king sat bejeweled princes and courtiers. Giant aromatic khuskhus fans drawn by unseen workers kept the air fragrant.

The Night Raiders

Accompanied by a gateman, Rama Murthy remained tongue-tied at the opulence until he stumbled on the rope fencing, off the king's throne.

A spokesman asked Rama Murthy, 'Why have you come to court?'

Incoherently, Rama Murthy narrated the entire sequence of the night raiders' surprise attacks. 'Village completely charred, youths who opposed them stabbed,' the village head mumbled.

'Do you have anything to help us identify the night raiders?' a middle-aged man with luxurious grey locks and sacred thread across his torso asked.

'We captured one man, stripped his armor and weapons, but he escaped. Here they are,' one of the trio held out a helmet, armor and rusty long blade, and set them down carefully.

A murmur of shock went through the court. Courtiers jostled each other to get a better view of the items. The armor was Nanda, down to the last bit of green copper coating on the sun emblem of the helmet.

'We killed one raider, but his companion picked up his body and disappeared into the jungle,' another villager said.

'How many villages were attacked?' the middle-aged Brahmin asked.

'Men from 70 villages are gathered outside. They chose me as spokesperson,' Rama Murthy said bewildered, searching for the chief minister in the court.

'This probably represents half to a third of the actual number attacked,' the grey-haired Brahmin said grimly.

'Our fodder and grain bins are now ash,' Rama Murthy choked, adding, 'our livestock are scattered.'

'How did they set fire?' the Brahmin asked.

'With flaming arrows.'

'Our cattle have come home to chew their cud,' the Brahmin said.

'Rakshash, what?' Prince Kaivarta snapped.

'We set fire to the whole of Patala with flaming arrows. They copied our move,' Rakshash, the grey-haired chief minister said calmly.

Sashigupta Lookalikes

Rama Murthy realized who the Brahmin was. The three villagers stared at Rakshash with hope.

'What about the raiders you caught?' Rakshash asked.

'With difficulty we caught one raider, all had oily skin that made them too slippery to grab. They were dressed in black, with black masks and were led by Prince Sashi,' Rama Murthy said.

'No!' the youngest villager raised his voice. 'Prince Sashi raided our village.'

'Our village too was raided by Prince Sashi,' the third villager, who had been quiet till then, protested.

All three men looked on the verge of an argument.

'Calm down,' Rakshash raised his hand. 'Can you

identify the armor, helmet and sword?' he asked one of his commanders.

'I can identify the helmet, it is from our river navigators of the first Patala raid,' the commander replied.

'Did any of you spot who or what caste they resembled?' the chief minister enquired.

'The one dead, the one we stripped, had the features of a man from Bahlika,' Rama Murthy said.

'Bah, Bahlika?' Raja Sarvarthasiddhi slurred, 'Ba, Bactria?'

'A Bactrian night raider?' Rakshash sounded shocked.

'Could Bessus, satrap of Bactria, raid our territories, siding with *ze* Prince of Patala?' Prince Kaivarta asked.

His brothers sniggered.

'What about you?' Rakshash focused on the second villager.

'Ours was a Pharsi Sashigupta, but our neighboring village was attacked by a Scythian, a Shaka Sashigupta,' the villager said.

'Scythians, Pharsis, Bactrians, Sashigupta lookalikes. Any other point?' Rakshash asked.

'The night raiders crossed tribal boundaries to attack us,' Rama Murthy said.

There was silence.

'You have come a great distance. We will recompense you. Go to the soldiers' mess hall and eat, all of you. Our intelligence agents will interview you later,' Rakshash dismissed them kindly.

With a wave of his hand, he motioned to two soldiers, one of whom left with Rama Murthy and his companions. The other soldier went to fetch the villagers camped outside the moat.

A buzz of conversation rose as the three villagers departed.

Counterattack

Rakhshash turned his chair around to face the king.

'We need an aggressive counterattack, to give them a taste of their own medicine,' Rakshash spoke.

'No counterattack means fewer territories,' Prince Kaivarta agreed.

'When?' General Bhadrasala asked incautiously.

'Today, with all possible speed, fool,' Prince Kaivarta snarled.

'Yes prince, we will send pigeon posts to our frontier commanders to bring back our troops,' General Bhadrasala replied, ignoring the rudeness.

He drew two rough maps of battle formations and held it up for Rakshash and Raja Sarvarthasiddhi for consent. Senior commanders crowded around to see the drawings. There was silence as Rakshash traced with the tip of his finger a possible assault strategy.

'Start here?' Rakshash's finger tapped the point to start the counterattack.

'Or will multiple attacks, on the north and northwest parts of our satrapy's borders, be a better strategy?' the chief minister asked.

General Bhadrasala made more markings showcasing infantry and cavalry moves. 'Multiple attacks. Elite night raiders will lead the assault,'

'Looks good. Move speedily,' Rakshash said.

General Bhadrasala departed for the pigeon cote and cavalry areas with his secretary, to take charge.

Damage Control

'*Whas* it, Amatya?' Raja Sarvarthasiddhi asked Rakshash who looked preoccupied after the General's departure.

'The law Code of Manu prescribes fire and poison to destroy the homes, food and fodder of a king's loyal subjects, to lower their morale,' Rakshash said. 'Where are our double agents?' he demanded.

He looked around the court.

'Come here, Hritik,' Rakshash beckoned to a young man in peasant's attire. 'I have a task for you. Go in mufti to ten villages in the north and find out if water sources were poisoned.'

'Yes, Amatya,' Hritik bowed and left the court.

Rakshash's secretary materialized next to him.

'I need six vaidyas and veterinarians for a cure for contaminated homes, a substitute for fodder and how to reverse effects of poison aconite on water,' he told them. 'Poison aconite?' Prince Kaivarta's voice rose, 'Rakshash, you believe poison aconite was used?'

'Yes Prince, it is the classic "scorched earth" policy, fire and poison to destroy citizen morale,' Rakshash said, nodding to the court trumpeter, who blew a long note to notify that the court was now closed.

'Call all senior commanders and chieftains to a meeting in half an hour's time. This is an emergency,' Rakshash gave more instructions to his secretary, who motioned to the court trumpeter and said, 'Blow a summoning note.'

The trumpet sound reverberated through the court.

'Commanders, chieftains, vaidyas, veterinarians stay back for a meeting,' the secretary announced loudly.

Courtiers not involved with military operations or medical interventions, left. The rope fence cordoned off Raja Sarvarthasiddhi, his secretary, brothers, royal vaid, and Rakshash. The general entered again midway through the discussions.

'Explain,' Rakshash said curtly. 'Why such an intelligence failure?'

'Our troops are busy with the famine on the western frontier in Arachosia.[1] And a few are still in Patala,' General Bhadrasala looked embarrassed.

'Looting bricks? Get them back,' Rakshash snapped.

'Immediately, chief minister,' the General said, leaving again to reorganize his troops.

Rakshash Meets the Vaids

Rakshash wasted no time. He not only met with pharmacist vaids, but also the palace soothsayer, intuitionist and omen reader.

'What do you know about this poison, beesh?' Rakshash growled at the royal vaidya.

'It is commonly used in the Northeast Mountains to kill big jungle cats that fall into traps. Each trap is rigged with arrow-like projectiles and when the big cat steps on a trigger, the projectile pierces its body, immobilizing it,' the royal vaidya began.

'Why target wild cats?' Rakshash asked.

'For powerful aphrodisiac. There is a huge market in China across the northeast mountains for wild cat body parts,' the royal vaidya began, with a not quite royal gleam in his eye. 'Rich old men pay vulgar sums for a mountain lion penis or testes with the hope it boosts their sexual ability…'

'How to reverse this beesh?' Rakshash rudely cut short this train of thought.

---

1 The Argandab valley in Kandahar. It did not reach the Hindu Kush, but it apparently extended east as far as the Indus River, although its exact extents are not yet clear.

'The remedy is expensive. Pure silver steeped for eight days in a classic decoction of herbs, is turned into *bhasma,* silver calx, and sprinkled on polluted water. After a day, the bhasma locks into the black membrane on the surface of the water and makes it sink to the bottom as sediment. The water above the sediment can then be strained and used for washing clothes, floors and bathing. But for cooking and drinking purposes, we need to import water from an uncontaminated source for a month.'

'We need to propitiate Varuna, god of the waters and River Saraswati to purify the waters,' the intuitionist added.

'Yes, only the gods can help us. Treasurer, give Vaid sir enough silver for calx,' Rakshash said brusquely, adding, 'and keep me informed about Prince Sashi. We cannot take him for granted anymore.'

'Nor the Persian satrapies,' the Governor General added.

'Keep us updated on both,' Rakshash ordered.

Curiosity for information on kings to the west was not limited to the Nandas. Prince Sashigupta and Guruji were also hungry for intelligence inputs.

Darius sends Alexander a Peace Offering

The rumblings of war were not restricted to India. In the far-off Persian Empire, Alexander was giving the Persians a bad headache.

Outside the hut, Xerxes was excited. 'What an update, Teacher, what an update!' he exclaimed.

'I can't wait,' Guruji smiled at the express man's enthusiasm.

Both were seated on a small platform around a peepal tree. Prince Sashigupta vaulted over a dead branch and sat down opposite Guruji.

'Start, man,' Prince Sashi said.

'News of Alexander's conquests has spread all over Asia. To stop him, King Emperor Darius sent Alexander a peace proposal offering *"concessions, 10,000 talents of money as ransom for the royal prisoners of Darius' household, and all territory west of the Euphrates up to the Aegean Sea"*. Emperor Darius also offered his daughter in marriage.

'Alexander's reply was a riposte, saying that he was "*uninterested in the money and would only accept the whole of Asia*", and if he wanted to marry Darius' daughter, he would do so without the emperor's permission.'

'Poor Darius,' Guruji tsk-tsked his tongue in sympathy.

'Then Alexander rode northwards with his nearly 50,000-strong army to Thapsacus, Syria. Hephaestion was busy constructing bridges for Alexander's army to cross the Euphrates River,' Xerxes continued, adding, 'Darius, informed about Alexander's departure to Nisibis, sent Mazaeus, the anything-but-brave satrap of Babylon, with 6,000 cavalry to stop Alexander's army crossing the Euphrates. Crediting Mazaeus with more guts than he actually had, Hephaestion left off the construction of the final bridge till Alexander returned.'

'And the King Emperor?' Guruji asked.

'After the riposte from Alexander, with a sinking heart, he sent posts to all his satraps, including Bessus of Bactria and Dhanananda of northwest India in a last-ditch attempt to save the empire.'

'Man!' Prince Sashigupta chuckled. 'Our problems are nothing compared to Emperor Darius' situation.'

'I wonder how these two cobras will respond to an emperor who has lost face publicly,' Guruji grunted ruminatively.

Darius Contacts Bessus

The combined court of Bactria and Sogdiana[2] was in session. From the back of the chamber, in the very center, was a view of the riding path through the outer and inner gates of the palace. The ornate gold throne of Prince Bessus had an eagle's eye view of both gates.

Prince Bessus' attention was on one of the riders, a pony express man in dark green livery who had dismounted at the outer gates and disappeared into the gatehouse to shed his weapons. That shade of green marked him as a messenger from the court of Emperor Darius.

The pony express man reappeared with a guard from the gatehouse who marched him to the entrance of the public audience chamber. The two doormen on either side of the court chamber checked the contents of the conical silver box. The pony express man then whispered something to the court horn-blower, who gave a long note and then announced at the top of his voice, '*Hail to the loyal prince Bessus, satrap and protector of Bactria and Sogdiana. A message is sent to Prince Bessus, from King Emperor Darius Codomannus.*'

Bessus stretched his hand for the missive, read the message and handed it to General Nabarzenes who read the content out loud, '*Dear Satrap Bessus, am currently near Arbela for the final battle stand against Accursed Alexander who has chased me from Media to Parthia. I require Bactrian troops. I have heard that General Nabarzenes has already met the Accursed.*'

Prince Bessus grunted as Nabarzenes finished reading the message. The courtiers looked warily at their monarch for his reaction.

---

2 Bactria was a province of the Persian empire located in modern Afghanistan, Uzbekistan, and Tajikistan. Sogdiana is in modern Uzbekistan, Turkmenistan, Tajikistan, Kazakhstan and Kyrgyzstan; the land between Amu Darya and Syr Darya. Arbela-Guagamela is Iraqui Kurdistan.

In Arbela-Guagamela

'So General, the King Emperor knows your moves already. Give me, postman, some background about the Accursed,' Bessus barked.

The pony express man cleared his throat.

'The Accursed is a fiend, winning both battles with the emperor at Granicus and Issus, and can overturn any battlefield with war strategy. There is rumor of a coming battle in Guagamela,' he disclosed.

'Guagamela or Arbela?' Bessus snapped.

'Both are almost the same, Prince,' he replied.

'What reply to give to Darius' request?' Bessus asked, his expression quelling any answer from his generals, a pack of yes-men.

There was silence from the assembly. Everyone stared at Prince Bessus, waiting for his cue. A tense silence enveloped the court.

'Let us join the King Emperor to destroy the Accursed. I will do everything possible to protect Bactria and Sogdiana. Dismiss the court, I need to meet my generals,' Prince Bessus said after a pause.

'And the answer I must give to the King Emperor, lordship?' the pony express man asked.

'My satrapies come first,' Prince Bessus said. 'I personally think Darius – I mean the King Emperor – must take his stand in Arbela so that the eastern satrapies are safe.'

'Can you give me a message to take back to the King Emperor, lordship?' the pony express man was politely insistent.

'Did you misunderstand my answer, you moron?' Prince Bessus raised his voice. 'I will ride to Arbela with Sarvarthasiddhi's Indian troops and my own Bactrians.'

The pony express man looked bewildered at this less-than-appropriate response. 'Okay, Sire, I will take leave,' he stammered, looking unhappy. He bowed low making a kissing gesture and left the chamber walking backwards.

Bessus contacts Sarvarthasiddhi

Bessus summoned the letter writer. 'This message is for the deva-worshipping Sarvarthasiddhi. "*Please send a contingent of crack Indian cavalry and infantry immediately to Bactria. We are having problems with Alexander Accursed.*" This message must leave by pony express and pigeon post to satrap Sarvarthasiddhi's court, immediately.'

'At once, Prince Bessus,' the letter writer made a copy, rolled it and put it into a small capsule. He gave one copy to a pony express man near the gatehouse and went to the pigeon post man with the second copy. The pony express man from Darius Codomannus' court heard the messenger and headed back to the King Emperor.

In Mesopotamia, the Court of Darius III

A string of pony express posts rode up the lane to the court of King Emperor Darius Codomannus. Huge white and gold human and flying horse figures lined both walls of the lane to the palace public audience chamber. On high platforms, bearded figures of Indra and Mithra, and Ahura Mazda with gold and silver workmanship interspersed the walkway. Pony expresses were tied to posts either side of the massive gates that started the lane. On the walkway to the open, public court, postmen held scrolls in cone-shaped silver and bronze boxes, depending on who the sender was. The gatemen checked to ensure their goods were post and nothing harmful, stripped them of weapons and then permitted each postman to go through to meet the King Emperor.

Darius sat at the end of a long hallway lined with courtiers, on an elevated gold throne under an ornamental white and gold brocade canopy. Above his throne was the emblem of the Zoroastrian god Ahura Mazda.

In sharp contrast to the grandeur of his surroundings, the King Emperor looked miserable, his lips drooping and bony wrists sticking out beneath opulent purple robes. A string of scouts and double agents had come with reports about Alexander, and the King Emperor's forehead was crisscrossed like a map of gullies and trenches.

'Any more information about the Accursed's latest movements?' King Emperor Darius asked tiredly of a scout, who filled in more disheartening details.

He was not the only one interested in Alexander's movements. Back in North India, Guruji and Prince Sashigupta were also taking a keen interest in Alexander.

Alexander in Guagamela

'Tell us more about Yavana Alexander,' Prince Sashigupta said.

A merchant from eastern Persia was seated in front of Guruji and the prince. His cart, laden with superior wine and winter-proof woolen garments, was parked under a banyan tree, and the bullocks were lazily chewing cud.

'After the Yavana thrashed the King Emperor in Issus, he spread out over the Mediterranean coast and Egypt. Going into Syria, he crossed the Euphrates and Tigris rivers. Darius' men gave him no opposition when he crossed the rivers with a force of 47,000 men, 8,000 of them cavalry. Satrap Mazaeus lived up to his well-deserved reputation as coward, he completely avoided engagement with Alexander's men.'

'What about Darius' superior navy?' Guruji asked.

'After Issus, Alexander spent a year seizing parts of the western Asiatic seaboard to neutralize the powerful Persian navy. Then, this year, Alexander again turned his attention to the Persian Empire,' Guruji and Sashigupta were informed.

Darius Fails to Placate Alexander

'Fill us in post-Issus,' Prince Sashigupta said.

The merchant nodded.

'In September, the forces of Darius and Alexander faced off.

'King Emperor Darius had not accepted Alexander's control of Persian dominions as permanent. A myopic man, unable to read the signs, he sent a letter through royal pony express to Alexander stating, "*You, Alexander have sent no representative to my court, to confirm the former friendship and alliance between the two kingdoms. On the contrary, you have crossed into Asia with your armed forces and done much damage to Persia. Now I, Darius the king, ask Alexander the king to restore from captivity my wife, my mother, and my children, and am willing to make friends with you and be your ally.*"

'Darius made Alexander this offer. Alexander rejected it.'

"I would have accepted these very generous terms," Parmenion, his second-in-command told Alexander.

'"If I were you, Parmenion, I would accept it too," the 25-year-old Alexander replied tartly.'

Alexander the Avenger

'Why was Alexander so…?' Sashigupta began.

'Stubborn? The reason was rooted in the past. Alexander's army was filled with Greek soldiers burning to avenge the insults Greece had borne at the hands of the Persians as long ago as 168 and a 117 years (499 and 448 BC).'

Catering to the Greek soldiers, Alexander's reply to Darius' request was a classic riposte, 'Let me recite it to you, "*O king! Your ancestors invaded Macedon and Greece, and caused havoc in our country, though we had done nothing to provoke them. As supreme commander of all Greece, I invaded Asia because I wished to punish Persia for this act, an act which must be laid wholly to your charge. My father was killed by assassins whom, as you openly boasted in your letters, you yourself hired to commit the crime. You unjustly and illegally seized the throne [of Persia], thereby committing a crime against your country. You sent the Greeks false information about me in the hope of making them my enemies; you attempted to supply the Greeks with money, your agents corrupted my friends and tried to wreck the peace which I had established in Greece. It was then that I took the field against you. By God's help, I am master of your country. Come to me, therefore, as you would come to the lord of the continent of Asia. Ask me for your mother, your wife and your children, and in the future let any communication you wish to make with me be addressed to the King of Asia. Do not write to me as an equal. Everything you possess is now mine. If, on the other hand, you wish to dispute your throne, stand and fight for it and do not run away. Wherever you may hide yourself, be sure I shall seek you out.*"'

'The pony express man looked down as King Emperor Darius read this out dejectedly,' the merchant informed them.

'Let me guess. The unwilling King Emperor was forced to get battle ready?' Sashigupta asked.

'He was and instructed his infantry head accordingly,' he replied.

'To?' Sashigupta was curious.

'Level the plain close to Arbela, near the Tigris River, "This will give our superior war chariots an advantage," Darius told his commanders.'

'How wrong he was became evident as the day progressed. Apart from the limited number of war elephants and the scythe-wheeled war chariots, Darius' men were armed with either javelins or bows and arrows.

'Alexander, however, was not an easy adversary. Scouts and double agents informed Alexander about Persian army statistics,' the merchant told them.

'Which were?' Prince Sashigupta probed.

History's Most Decisive Battle, October 331 BC

'Battle numbers and strategy!' the merchant rolled his eyes, outspread hands in the air.

'How did Alexander prepare?' Prince Sashigupta asked.

'On the day before the battle, with Alexander's full consent, his army enjoyed a good sleep through the night. Alexander himself overslept and when his generals went to wake him, he said confidently that he had "*already won the battle.*"'

'Before he even stepped on the battlefield?' Sashigupta sounded surprised.

'Correct. The entire Persian army tensely stayed awake the whole night in anticipation of a night assault, which never happened. This led them to becoming deeply exhausted and stressed by daytime,' he said.

'Can you help me draw the Persian battle formation?' Prince Sashigupta asked.

'Sure. Darius was in the center, midst of the elite infantry. Right center were Persian footguards, Indian cavalry and Mardia archers.

'On his right were Mazaeus the hero, with Syrian, Median, Mesopotamian, Parthian, Sacian, Tapurnan, Hycarnian, Albanian, Cappodochian, Carian and Armenian cavalry, and Greek mercenaries.

'On his left, Prince Bessus headed Bactrian, Dahae, Arachosian, Persian, Susian, Cadusian and Scythian cavalry. On both flanks, cavalry,' the merchant detailed out the position.

'Could you help me draw Alexander's position in the battlefield?' Sashigupta requested.

'On his left was Alexander's second-in-command, Parmenion. At the center was his sixteen-deep infantry phalanx armed with Sarissas. On the right, Alexander, his Companion Cavalry, with horses and specialized armor, in eight *Ilai* squadrons.'[3]

Battlefield Guagamela

'How did the battle start?' Sashigupta asked the merchant.

'With Alexander's classic strategy, the Macedonian infantry phalanx marched towards the center of the Persian formation, so that the Companion Cavalry could attack the enemy from the side and the back. On the left flank, the Macedonian army was angled backwards as a ruse to invite Persian cavalry to attack Parmenion's cavalry. On the right flank, Alexander stretched the Companion Cavalry to the outermost edge.'

'Thinning for what reason?' Sashigupta asked, drawing on a piece of dried parchment.

'His maneuver drew away most of the Persian cavalry to both flanks, creating a serious gap in the enemy's center, so the Persians could be struck in the middle,' he said, outlining Alexander's deft command over battle tactics.

'And Emperor Darius' opening assault?'

'Darius attacked the Macedonian front with 200 war chariots, scythe-like knives protruding from their wheels.

3 Territorial squadrons.

What he didn't realize was that this move had been anticipated by Alexander who had instructed his commanders on the counter move. The chariots met, as first line of defense, javelin throwers who stepped aside and let the chariots through. The war chariots were tricked into a circular trap, surrounded by Macedonian infantry and Sarissa troops. Every horse and its soldier in the Persian war chariot formation was brutally killed, those in front, flanks and rear,' he said.

'The scythe-armed war chariots failed as premium enemy destroyers?' Prince Sashigupta sounded shocked and awed at the same time.

'Failed? They were pulverized. Kings of the future may hesitate to use them in battle,' the merchant declared.

'Help me draw it, I want an accurate picture of battle progress,' Sashigupta made strokes with a piece of charcoal.

'While war chariots were being destroyed, Alexander organized the right flank into an arrow tip formation, moved parallel to the Persian front line and off the prepared battlefield. Darius ordered the Persian cavalry to thwart Alexander's men. But the Macedonian human arrow tip bored through the gap between Bessus and Darius in the diluted center, ripped Darius' elite guard, and the Greek mercenaries in the middle. Bessus the Bactrian, losing contact with the rest of Darius' army, retreated with his men. When Alexander punched holes in the Persian ranks, to directly attack Darius himself, the King Emperor pulled out too. Demoralized Persian cavalrymen, abandoned by the King Emperor and Bessus, fled the battlefield,' the merchant shook his head in condemnation.

Darius Escapes to Ecbatana, 330 BC

'So poor preparation led to the King Emperor's rout?' Sashigupta surmised.

'And lack of leadership. Alexander, spotting the fleeing Darius, was about to issue orders to pursue the dodgy King Emperor, when a messenger rode up to say that the Macedonian left flank under Parmenion was in trouble. Alexander had the option of capturing Darius, ending Persian domination once and for all, or helping his men.'

'But chose the latter. What was the reason for Parmenion's fiasco?' Prince Sashigupta asked.

'Alexander's strategy. When he stretched the Macedonian right flank thin to draw away Darius' army, a gap opened between the Macedonian left and right flanks. Darius' Persian and Indian cavalry broke through the sparse Macedonian center and galloped to Alexander's camp to loot. They asked Queen Mother Sisygambis to ride to liberation, but she flatly refused. Of course, Mazaeus lived up to his title of coward.'

'He pulled back again? A true hero!' Sashigupta whooped. 'And the Persians?'

'Totally collapsed. Post battle, Parmenion rounded up the Persian baggage train, captured four thousand talents, Darius' chariot, bow and arrows and fifteen war elephants.'

'What a disaster,' Sashigupta said.

'There is more,' the merchant responded.

'More? After Guagamela?'

The merchant laughed out loud.

'When Darius escaped to Ecbatana,[4] Alexander captured Babylon without battle. He took a break at the royal palace there, where beautiful prostitutes and high-born women entertained his men. And he also paid his soldiers for the first time in months, with monies from the Persian treasury.'

4 Hamadan Province, Iran.

'Sapta Sindhu, here comes the future,' Prince Sashigupta chortled.

Susa-Zagros Mountains, 330 BC

'Post the battle, what did the Yavana do?' Sashigupta asked.

'In autumn, Alexander captured Susa's fabled treasury of gold and silver, and became one of the richest men in the world. In a flush of generosity, he paid his men eight years salary in advance. He then sent most of his army via the Royal Road. Alexander himself, with a small contingent, went to the Persian Gates,[5] in the Zagros Mountains that were in Persian control. An old shepherd informed Alexander about a narrow alternate route, which Alexander used at night.'

'Intelligence gathering? Smart,' Prince Sashigupta said.

'He is. He snuck up behind and above the Persian Gates citadel, ripped the fortifications. Five thousand Persian soldiers luckily escaped, but the rest were butchered. There was another pitched battle with the Persians headed by Ariobarzanes.'

'Which the Yavana won of course,' Prince Sashigupta commented.

Epirus, Alexander's Family

There was a nip in the air, just right for some strong liquid nourishment.

Xerxes, visiting again, was getting out some fine alcohol from the merchant's stores, with his friend, the prince.

---

5 Persian Gate or the Susian Gate was the ancient name of the pass now known as Tang-e Meyran, connecting Yasuj with Sedeh Eghlid to the east, crossing the border of the modern Kohgiluyeh va Boyer Ahmad and Fars provinces of Iran.

'What are the latest developments in Alexander's life?' Sashigupta asked, after several thirsty swigs from a silver goblet. The day was chilly.

'His family has had a few tragedies. After his sister Cleopatra was widowed, when her husband, king of Epirus, was killed, she became regent for son Neoptolemus II,' Xerxes began.

'And Darius' family?' the prince enquired.

'In September, Queen Statira, pregnant through Alexander, died of childbirth in camp. Her newborn child died too.'

'A pity!' Sashigupta commented.

'It is, Sire,' he agreed. After a few more drinks, Xerxes took his payment, and left a thoughtful Sashigupta and Guruji behind.

Torture and the Sack of Persepolis

The merchant was back, and he was now talking about Alexander's moves to Persepolis, past the Persian Gates.

'Persepolis' turn was next. Eight hundred Greek prisoners, tortured by their Persian captors, came out miserable and mutilated,' he said.

'Tortured?' Prince Sashi asked.

'Badly. Some had no feet or hands, others, ears or noses or were branded with Persian letters on their bodies for the entertainment of their Persian captors. Alexander gave each man 3,000 denarii, and land with cattle, sheep and seeds to sustain themselves,' the merchant said.

'Horrible karma,' Guruji scowled.

'In revenge, Alexander allowed his men to loot the city and massacre or sell as slaves the Persepolians. He looted almost 3,500 tonnes of precious metals, carried by 5,000 camels and 20,000 mules. In addition, to avenge the Persian burning of Athens more than a century ago, a very drunk Alexander burnt the emperor's palaces in Persepolis goaded by Thais, a drunk Greek *hetaira.*'

'Ah women! His next move?' Sashi asked.

'Well, after this, the vengeful Greek troops were satiated and departed for Greece. This was a blessing in disguise for Alexander. He recruited young Persians in his conquered territories to replace the older Greeks.'

'Thanks for the update,' Prince Sashigupta dropped some coins into the outstretched hands of the merchant, who handed over flasks of premium harahura firewater, and left, grinning.

Darius is Assassinated, July 330 BC

A few months had passed.

'Yes?' Guruji asked the man in green western-style clothing who walked past his bodyguard. The old man was waiting almost all alone with only an old *Aghora* for company.

'Xerxes, Sire,' the young, bearded man said, bowed doubtfully to the sunburnt Aghora, and stooped to touch Guruji's feet, the Indian way. 'I come with tidings for Prince Sashi,' the young man said, peeling his beard, looking around hopefully for the prince who was a good drinking companion.

'Ah, Xerxes. I recognize you now. Prince Sashi is traveling, but I can take a message for him,' Guruji grunted.

The pony express man had a slight sinking of the heart, no diminishing the store of excellent harahura today. He stared perplexed at the old Aghora. There was something about the swarthy Aghora, feminine and familiar, but he couldn't place what. Probably an eunuch, he thought or Prince Sashigupta in appalling disguise.

'You are the right man to update us. We intend to send

our troops as mercenaries to Bactrian Bessus. How is Bactria?' the Aghora asked in a nasal twang.

'Messy, Sire. I came to warn you,' he addressed Guruji. 'The whole Achaemenid Empire is without any strong Persian ruler after King Emperor Darius was assassinated.'

'Assassinated?' Guruji's voice sounded like fracturing rock. 'Was the Yavana involved?'

'Let's see. After looting Persepolis, Alexander pursued the King Emperor to Ecbatana, Media, Parthia, Aria and lastly Bactria, where his cousin, satrap Bessus treacherously executed him.'

'Execution of the King Emperor?' Guruji's voice cracked with shock.

'When?' Aghora asked, his voice cracking too.

'Treachery, by his own cousin?' Guruji asked grimly.

'Why not? Dhanananda killed his own sons,' the Aghora growled.

Guruji gave the Aghora a sharp look, followed by a potent silence.

Persian Empire Ends with Bessus the Traitor

'How did Darius meet this fate?' Guruji broke the silence.

'The King Emperor was taken hostage by Bessus, Nabarzenes and Barsaentes, but assassinated by Bessus.'

'Did Darius have no warning about Bessus' evil designs?' Guruji asked.

'Some commanders warned Darius the day before he was taken prisoner, but the King Emperor seemed to have had a death wish. He made no attempt to save himself.'

'Why do you say that?' Guruji asked suspiciously.

'He stubbornly declined riding away on horseback, saying it was too demeaning for a man of his stature.'

'When was he killed?' the old man asked.

'Not even a month ago.'

For a few moments there were shocked groans from the old man, who was staring at the pony express man, speechless.

Polystratus witnesses Darius' Death

'But how?' the Aghora asked, waiting for Guruji to regain his composure.

'A very humiliating death, Sire,' Xerxes shook his head. 'The Macedonian troops were chasing Bactrian troops across the battlefield, between the Ahuran Pass and the city of Quse, when Polystratus, a Macedonian cavalry man, noticed a driverless bullock cart, meandering aimlessly off the battlefield, both oxen with spears sticking out of their ribs,' Xerxes narrated.

'Smart observer,' the Aghora commented.

'Investigating, he found the shackled, bleeding King Emperor on the floorboard, javelins protruding from the chest, accompanied by one faithful dog. He gave Darius a sip of water to drink, then the King Emperor thanked heaven for not being alone while he died, and breathed his last. Polystratus informed Alexander, who covered the King Emperor's body with his own royal cloak, had his corpse taken to Persepolis for a funeral worthy of his status next to his Achaemenid ancestors.'

Guruji grimaced and handed over coins to Xerxes, forcing him to leave.

'We cannot do anything to stop the course of history, however, we must act to control our own future history,' Guruji said.

The Aghora quietly unrolled a map to plan the next step. A spotted turban that looked like two amorous cuckoos embracing approached them.

'Dhoomal!' the Aghora exclaimed, adding, 'Message?'

The boy settled down with quill and parchment. Aghora hoped his instructions would bear fruit.

The Hut by the Riverside

The early morning sun was staining the Indus waters reddish gold, when the night raiders returned, tired but euphoric from their raid. As they tethered their horses to hitching posts, each of them took note of how many had returned unscathed.

The windows of Guruji's hut gave out an orange glow, which meant he had stayed awake the whole night to monitor the raiders' movements. Their commander knocked softly and entered. Guruji was in deep discussion with Prince Sashigupta, now as himself. Seated on the side was a man whose clean-shaven face and tonsured scalp, along with a flat wooden box full of potions in baked clay vials, proclaimed him to be the vaidya toxicologist.

'Sit down and tell me how many villages you raided, Ramagupta. Have all the men returned?' the old man asked with concern.

'About 80 new villages in Arachosia (Kandahar) were raided teacher, and many of them gave us a stiff fight. It seems like the Nanda High Command sent troops to defend their vassal villages. We got chased but eluded the enemy soldiers in the jungle – an advantage because our horses were used to night-time riding. Some of our men were wounded or killed by Nanda soldiers, we don't know the exact number.'

'But you completed your assignment, Ramagupta?'

'Yes, Guruji. It was quite an experience going on a night raid again, both for me and my men, I tell you,' Ramagupta began, preparatory to a long monologue.

330 BC
Poison comes into Play

Beesh

RAMAGUPTA, OTHERWISE A competent man, had developed a strong propensity for rambling. A sign of premature aging, Sashigupta secretly thought.

'Details, please,' Sashigupta said brusquely.

'We used beesh on all flowing and still water, wells, streams and agricultural ponds, irrigation canals and dams, plus bales of hay, public pathways, everything, except the residences,' Ramagupta said.

'Update us, how long will it take to show results, Vaid sir?' Sashigupta looked towards the vaid toxicologist.

'In three days to a week, the water will have a membrane-like skin on the surface, crisscrossed with black lines,' the toxicologist answered.

Sashigupta thanked the vaid who then departed.

'Any non-Nanda vassal territories covered?' he asked Ramagupta.

'Not that we know of,' the commander answered.

'Good, we don't want to violate Persian territory if we want a favor from them,' Sashi sounded relieved.

'Dhananada stays in the good books of the Persian empire with an annual payment of 360 talents of gold,' Ramagupta said, repeating the obvious.

'And we don't have that kind of money yet,' Sashigupta, the ever-practical man, said. 'So, we better be well behaved.'

Lookalike Confusion

Just then there were sounds of a horse being reined in outside the door and a minute later, a black-clad bearded man entered holding a teak leaf in his left hand. The old man raised his eyebrows. 'Yes?' he asked. 'Name?'

'Maraj, teacher,' the youngster said, peeling off his beard and whiskery eyebrows to reveal a familiar face. 'Bad news. We rode into a trap, Commander Digvijay has been captured,' he said.

'Captured?' Prince Sashigupta exclaimed.

'How?' Guruji asked.

'The village we went to had similarly dressed night raiders who attacked our men and were led by a lookalike Digvijay. Our next village had a Ramagupta lookalike attacking our troops. Both the fake and the genuine Digvijay had similar clothes and accents, we were a bit confused, but we completed the task of sprinkling beesh on all water bodies, public pathways, everything. The Nanda commander trapped me and commander Digvijay on our way back. Digvijay was interrogated in private. The Nanda commander sends this to you, Sire,' Maraj's voice cracked with pain as he handed a severed nose to Prince Sashigupta.

'If we don't retreat, they will cut his ears as well,' Maraj continued.

'Did you see him after he was tortured?' Sashigupta's voice cracked with stress.

'No. Commander Divijay was sent to prison after his

capture, I did not meet him then, or...' Maraj trailed off miserably.

Prince Sashi held out the blood-blackened nose on the piece of teak leaf to Guruji, who stared at it with blank shock.

'That's exceptionally generous of my father, only a nose,' Sashigupta said with no expression on his face. 'Alright men, go eat.'

The soldiers headed out for a well-deserved meal of wheat and meat porridge, and to set up their tents. Ramagupta stayed back.

Double Agents, the Jester

Guruji had gone quiet. His protégé realized the old man was too emotional to speak.

'Two raids and the Nandas have already become wise to us. It means that the Nanda double agents are just a day or two behind. Maybe even only an hour or two behind,' Sashigupta whispered.

There was a moment of silence.

'Where are our double agents in the Nanda court?' Sashigupta asked.

As if the gods had heard him, there was a hesitant knock on the door, and a short hunchbacked man with messy beard and a limp entered the hut, and prostrated to Guruji.

'Yes?' the old man barked.

'I am the jester from Raja Sarvarthasiddhi's court,' the hunchback peeled off his beard, showing a familiar visage. 'I took leave to visit my village, which is in the northwest.'

'Tell me, O jester, where is the biggest concentration of Nanda troops?' he asked.

'The riverside villages on the west bank of the Sindhu are well patrolled by Nanda agents and forest army corps.'

'How are they able to be on top so easily?'

'At least a quarter of your army has been infiltrated by double agents from villages,' the man disclosed.

'If new recruits are suspect, time to move northwest. I think we have done enough raids,' Guruji said.

'Thank you,' Sashigupta stretched his hand to drop a few coins into the jester's hands; and then the hunchback left for the military mess from where the aroma of a garlicky meat porridge wafted in the air.

Sashigupta and Guruji, both impervious to hunger due to their training, discussed in detail what needed to be done next.

Change of Plan

'Guruji, we need to re-strategize. Leave villages and townships alone, and target caravans with luxury goods, perfumes, sivi cloth with good resale value. If the caravan is herding well-bred cattle and horses, we capture them,' the prince suggested.

'Not to forget carts carrying ore, too,' Guruji added.

After a quarter of an hour when General Ramagupta, double agents, and other sundry commanders returned, the prince was ready.

'Okay men, a few tips for your next relocation. First, you will loot caravans with the following goods,' Sashigupta gave them the list.

'After the caravan raids, send your loot to the northwest dropoff so that Prince Sashi can maintain old and recruit new troops,' Guruji added.

'Your next move after the caravan raids, is relocation to the kingdom chosen for you as mercenaries. We will keep in touch through pigeon posts to Paurava country, Parvatakadesh, Kashmir and Gandhara. This camp will be abandoned before sunset today,' Sashigupta said firmly, squelching any arguments before they came up.

Guruji spoke next. 'During your travels, no matter how famished, do not eat or drink from public houses on the highway, they are crammed with Rasada agents, poisoners. As you travel north, you may poison Nanda food and drink sources with strychnine or poison aconite, keeping a couple secretly free. Ramagupta, Nanda double agents?'

Ramagupta cleared his throat. 'Suspect anyone from these professions who tries to befriend you, caravan trader, troubadour, palace dancer, snake catcher, kapata sanyasi, actor, roadside astrologer, bard, painter, sculptor, vintner, *madaari* and letter writer,' General Ramagupta concluded.

'In short, everybody,' Prince Sashigupta said with a straight face.

The hunchback did not move.

'Return to the court after a week, so that no one suspects you,' Guruji said kindly, wondering why the hunchback seemed reluctant to go.

The List

Prince Sashigupta stood up and ordered, 'Digvijay's brother Veervijay will take over his team. Is that clear, men? Veervijay, stay back, we will instruct you on what to do next.'

Looking flushed and excited, Veervijay stepped into the small hut. Guruji calmly instructed him and then sent him to Ramagupta for a pre-move briefing.

A quarter of an hour after he left, back in the hut, Guruji was frowning at Sashigupta. The place was empty except for the two of them, when the hunchbacked jester re-entered, looking worried.

'What is it, man?' Sashigupta asked.

'There are double agents who keep the Nandas informed about your every move,' he said, handing the old man a list of names. 'Traitors!' he whispered.

Guruji looked shocked. The list was headed by Digvijay and Veervijay. Sashigupta shut the door and windows as a precaution.

'Digvijay? Wasn't his nose chopped off?' Guruji whispered back.

'No, Sire, the nose belonged to a convict sentenced to death for murder. He was hanged after his nose was chopped off,' the hunchback said.

'Be careful!' Guruji warned him.

'I will, Guruji!' the jester prostrated to the old man and left.

Alone, both men scrutinized the list again.

'This list says that Digvijay was formerly working for Rakshash as a double agent and now we have made his brother commander. We need to re-strategize, immediately,' the extra rasp in Guruji's voice showed how angry he was.

River Jhelum, the Trap

Prince Sashigupta gave a low whistle.

'We know there are double agents. Finally, we have a list of the big names. One major flaw when we recruit villagers is we do not know how many were Dhananandа's men, prior to joining us. We need to set a trap,' Prince Sashigupta said.

'How about this? We send our dubious double agent, Veervijay, with inexperienced recruits to a dangerous armed village to check out the land. He should, as far as possible, have men from his own village. When his soldiers attack the village, the violent villagers must kill them all, first and foremost, the double-crosser,' Guruji whispered.

'Or, before the Nanda double agent Veervijay is sent out, we send first, a well-briefed double agent from our side. The Nandas should trap the second double agent Veervijay, and have his entire unit killed,' Prince Sashigupta said as he wet his finger and drew a rough map on the cow dung-smeared floor.

'Third scenario. Veervijay and men from his village can run into a trap, get cut off in a narrow gorge with steep unscalable rocks on either side,' Guruji drew another rough battle formation on the floor.

'I prefer my plan, Veervijay trap,' the Prince insisted.

'Okay!' Guruji whispered, adding, 'You talk.'

As the older man sprinkled water to wash out the drawings, Prince Sashigupta stepped out and hollered to a young recruit.

'Ask Commander Veervijay to report at once,' he ordered.

Ahrmoz, the Thal Desert

Minutes later, Veervijay knocked, took off his shabby white boots and entered.

'SHUT the door!' Prince Sashigupta said.

Veervijay did so, flushed, feeling important.

'Veervijay, we need you to go on a special mission, to Ahrmoz. Do you know where it is?' Sashigupta queried.

'The Thal Desert periphery of Dhanananda's kingdom in east Arachosia,'[1] Veervijay replied.

'Excellent! Do you know why it is important?' the prince asked in a commanding tone.

'A brother of Raja Dhanananda has a base camp there to mark the boundaries of their kingdom.'

1 In west Punjab, now in Pakistan.

'Correct. Your mission is to take a special force of dangerously-armed soldiers only from your village. Attack, loot Ahrmoz, kill or capture Dhanananda's brother, and then catch up with us as we travel.'

'Soldiers only from my village? We might have a smaller force,' Veervijay said reluctantly.

'But the advantage is those villagers from your home village will be extremely loyal to you and implicitly obey your commands, important in a fight,' Sashi goaded.

'You are right, Prince Sashi.'

'Go and instruct your men. Leave immediately at sundown. The night is your ally.'

'I will brief my men at once.'

'Send Maraj in,' the prince told him.

'I will,' the new commander said as he stepped out.

A few minutes later, Maraj, now clean-shaven, looking nineteen, and in a guildsman's green clothing, entered and touched Guruji's feet. Prince Sashigupta shut the door and leaned against it.

'We have a special task for you. Leave for Ahrmoz immediately, in complete secrecy. No one should guess you are riding to Ahrmoz. Here is what you have to do.' Prince Sashi's instructions were few but precise.

Ahrmoz village

A week later, in a new campsite, Guruji and Prince Sashigupta spotted a messy squirrel's drey loping towards the tent.

'Dhoomal!' Prince Sashigupta exclaimed.

The squirrel nest ducked down cautiously to touch Guruji's feet.

'Keep it short,' Prince Sashigupta growled, fearful someone would overhear them.

'Maraj rode into the moated camp of Prince Kaivarta in Ahrmoz two days after he left here. He told the prince about the arrival of traitor Veervijay, and his specially armed troops,' Dhoomal spoke fast.

'And then?'

'Prince Kaivarta waited for traitor Veervijay's arrival.'

'How long?'

'By next day. Veervijay confidently rode into Prince Kaivarta's camp, boldly entered his tent to inform him of Prince Sashigupta's next move. He was accompanied by heavily armed personal bodyguards. Just outside the prince's private chambers, the bodyguards were searched, and deadly, sophisticated weapons found in their possession. Assuming that Veervijay had come to kill him, Prince Kaivarta executed Veervijay. Veervijay's men, stripped of weapons, were killed viciously by Nanda soldiers,' Dhoomal informed.

'Is that all?' Sashi probed further.

'No. Without consulting you, Veervijay had sent a contingent of armed ex-convicts to join Prince Kaivarta's forces, but the prince was all suspicion.'

'He executed these ex-cons too?' Guruji smiled at the boy. 'Good account!' he told Dhoomal.

Sashigupta opened the flap for Dhoomal to go. 'Now our option is narrowed to the mountain kingdom of Parvataka desh,' he said.

'Can Raja Parvataka of Himavatkuta, the mountain kingdom, still be our savior?' the old man asked thoughtfully.

'Yes, but not to forget the king of Kashmir,' Prince Sashigupta said, pulling on knee-length white boots. 'And Gandhara.'

His bodyguard, who was standing outside, handed over the rest of his armor to him, piece by piece. When he was ready, Prince Sashigupta walked out to inspect his soldiers' readiness to leave for their different destinations. News of the after-effects of the beesh and the caravan attacks had not reached the camp. Not yet.

Nandawati, More Bad News

But less than a week later, outside Nandawati's palace gates, it was business as usual. Alternately bribing and begging the gatemen, a few tradesmen, including the now veteran Rama Murthy, got permission to enter the Nanda court. They were relieved to be finally able to meet Rakshash and all the Nanda siblings. Raja Sarvarthasiddhi who, true to form, had had several goblets of wine, gave them a baleful look.

'What is it now? I thought we solved your poisoned water problems,' Rakshash, usually the calm one in court, asked curtly on sighting Rama Murthy.

'This time it is different. Apart from water and fodder being poisoned, all caravans carrying perfume for the royal court were attacked and stripped,' the leader of the tradesmen spoke.

'General,' Rakshash barked, 'why is this happening again?'

His mouth dry, General Bhadrasala looked anxiously at the king. But there was no need. Dhanananda, eyelids drooping, was now emitting whistling sounds that ended in porcine grunts. He was snoring.

'What should we do to stop these attacks on Nanda territory?' Rakshash asked.

'A second line of defense. Or sham caravans with army troops in mufti?' Prince Kaivarta asked.

'Sham caravans to trick them into attacking us and getting the attackers killed,' General Bhadrasala agreed.

'Start immediately. No procrastination,' Rakshash snarled, harshly.

General Bhadrasala, accompanied by senior commanders, went to the barracks to brief his soldiers. Within two hours, the Nanda regiments had departed on various sorties, their role clear in the coming fight. Only time would tell if his ruse was successful, but General Bhadrasala visited at midnight, the tiny *Bhumi Devi* temple in the cremation grounds to offer *bali* of a dozen roosters, confident the goddess would take care of any lapse in the plan. Rakshash, though, was neither confident nor sure. Through long experience, he knew that the roosters as bali would work only if war strategy was fail-safe.

329 BC
In the Mauryan Hideout

Beautiful Eunuch Bagaos, Alexander's New Love

THOUGH WINTER HAD set in, it was a balmy day. The pony express man had returned to meet Guruji and Prince Sashigupta.

'Tell me, Xerxes, about the Yavana,' Guruji asked calmly. So calmly that no one except Sashigupta guessed how eager he was for news of Alexander.

'It was after the death of Darius that Alexander met the next love of his life, eunuch Bagaos,' Xerxes began.

'Another Bagaos? How did they meet?' Sashigupta asked.

'When Emperor Darius was on the run, his traitorous general Nabarzenes plied Alexander with expensive gifts, the most priceless being a stunning young eunuch named Bagaos. Darius had killed one Bagaos. He adored this new eunuch Bagaos, however. With Darius dead, it was Alexander's turn. Alexander developed a romantic sexual relationship with this Bagaos, approved by his army. Alexander kisses Bagaos on the lips publicly. The eunuch has coaxed Alexander to dress like a Persian Emperor in purple and white tunic, girdle and head ribbon,' Xerxes told them.

'That's sure to raise the hackles of his Greek soldiers, I can bet,' Prince Sashigupta grinned.

'Men, women, eunuchs. But no political marriage,' Guruji commented stonily.

Xerxes left after getting thoroughly drunk.

Bessus, Self-appointed King Emperor

It was freezing cold. Some weeks later.

'What happened after the King Emperor's assassination?' Guruji asked quietly. He was seated with the old Aghora for company. The question was addressed to Xerxes, who was visiting again.

'Bactrian Bessus has crowned himself King Emperor Artaxerxes V,' Xerxes began.

'What bloody cheek,' the Aghora sounded incensed.

'Hold on. In the hierarchy of satraps, the satrap of Bactria is called *Mathista* and is next in line of succession to the Persian throne,' Xerxes clarified.

'How did the Yavana react to Bessus crowning himself Artaxerxes V?' the Aghora asked.

'He thought Bessus was being impertinent. The Yavana feels he is Emperor of Asia setting up Alexandrias in Media, Parthia, Aria, Drangiana.'

'If Bessus is as malevolent as Dhanananda, that should put the relocation on hold,' the Aghora snorted.

Xerxes stared at the Aghora, recognition dawning on his face. Guruji tactfully stretched out his hand. The pony express man took the money and left.

'King Darius had *karmic* bad luck, routed by the Macedonian, betrayed by the Bactrian,' the Aghora sounded depressed. 'Let's focus on a successful transition,' he told the old man.

Guruji nodded his head, 'Yes, let's.' He wanted his protégé to forget his pain.

Ambhi of Taxila invades Paurava Territory

It was a cold, breath-freezing winter day. Guruji and Sashigupta seemed to have an almost infinite need for updates. In the new camp, Sashigupta's men were gathered around him chatting animatedly when a long-haired horseman, a wandering trader of children's toys, dismounted.

'Salutations, Prince Sashi! I come with tidings,' he greeted.

'Anything new?' Prince Sashigupta bowed to the trader.

'A new chapter in the old enmity of Ambhi of Taxila and Paurava,' the trader began to say.

'Background?' Prince Sashigupta asked.

'The first time Ambhi invaded Paurava's territory, he was captured, humiliated by Paurava, and vowed revenge,' he said.

'Why did he invade Paurava's territory?' the prince asked.

'For gain. Paurava's kingdom has fertile, saline-free, mosquito-swamp and desert-free territory on either side of River Jhelum,' the trader replied.

'The land around Taxila is also fertile,' Sashigupta argued.

'But prone to attack. And Ambhi is greedy, Sashi,' Guruji remarked.

'Exactly. He wanted the river tax on export goods in the Jhelum and Chenab traffic,' the long-haired horseman agreed.

'What did no-good Ambhi do?' Guruji asked.

'He captured two riverside citadels of Paurava, manned it with Taxila garrisons, making Paurava and his citizens furious. Villagers with farms, tribals whose forests were ransacked by Ambhi's army...'

'And Paurava hit back?' Sashi asked keenly.

'By liberating both citadels and capturing Ambhi. In their

military court, Ambhi in chains, was marched to Paurava's throne as the court horn blower denounced his crimes against them.'

'"What reason do you have to assault my kingdom?" Raja Paurava had growled.'

"I wanted virgin lands to settle, to expand my kingdom," Ambhi replied.

'There was a tense silence as the court digested this tactless answer.

"Virgin? Virgin lands? This is *our* land, Ambhi. It belongs to my people. Take your accursed face and never return," Raja Paurava snapped furiously,' the trader said, narrating what had happened in court.

'And?' Sashi asked.

'You should have seen Ambhi. His whiskers moved spasmodically, a mumbling sound emerged from beneath them, which everyone took as an apology. Then Ambhi, head shorn as punishment, left for Taxila on foot. Accompanied by Paurava's soldiers till the Jhelum bank, he then boarded a merchant ship that took him and his chained soldiers to the other bank and left free. Life is now normal for Paurava's river police and navy,' he added.

'So, peace reigns?' Sashigupta sounded doubtful.

'It does,' the trader replied.

Spitamenes

'Good update, trader. Any information on the Yavana?' Sashi said.

'Of course. To mark his territories, Alexander set up Alexandrias Arachoton, Ghazni and Nicaea, then crossed the Hindu Kush via the Khawak Pass, which took him behind Bessus.'

'No problems?'

'Actually, plenty. His army took 16 days to cross Khawak in the biting January cold. Food ran out, soldiers were forced to eat the pack animals, horses and donkeys raw with asafoetida,' he said.

'You have to do what you have to do,' Prince Sashigupta commented.

'But Alexander knew things,' the trader nodded meditatively.

'As in?' Sashi's curiosity was aroused even more.

'The Sogdian leader Spitamenes was a former commander in Bessus' army. "Bring him to me, I need information about Bessus," Alexander ordered.

When Spitamenes came, he prostrated in the Persian custom much to the disapproval of his European soldiers.

"Noble king Iskandar, Emperor Bessus has fled deep into Sogdiana," Spitamenes reported.

'Alexander set up an Alexandria and rode through Drapsaca to Bactria. Balkh, Bactria's principal city, accepted Alexander without fuss.'

A Greek Mistake

'His next move?' the prince asked.

'After leaving the bulk of his army with Hephaestion, Alexander took a small group beyond the Oxus river (Amu Darya), where there lay a city of Greeks, who made the fatal mistake of joyously welcoming Alexander.'

'Fatal?' Sashi asked.

'Alexander slaughtered these Greeks whose only fault was they were descendants of Greek priests who had given away their temple to Persian conquerors 150 years ago. Alexander's army and the locals were shocked,' the trader explained.

'Vindictive Yavana!' Guruji said somberly. 'Next?'

'Independent Sogdians annihilated a few garrisons of Macedonians. Alexander broke his leg, recuperated in Maracanda till the leg healed, and began his travels again, his army swollen with wives and children of the soldiers,' he continued.

Cross questioned till he had no more information to give, the trader left, his fist full of coins.

The Execution of Bessus

A few days later… The early morning chill had a couple of people huddled around a portable fireplace.

'Okay, Xerxes, spill!' A gravelly voice ordered. It was Guruji, alone except for a humble guildsman in a corner.

'News of Bessus… start at the beginning.'

'After he crowned himself King Emperor, Bessus was treacherously captured by his courtiers Spitamenes and Datames, and handed over to Alexander's general Ptolemy.'

'His punishment?' Guruji asked.

'For his treachery to Darius, Alexander ordered Bessus' nose and ears chopped off,' Xerxes said.

'Ah, nose cutting, the old Indo-Persian punishment!' Guruji nodded.

'And tied naked to a stake next to the highway with a slave collar. Alexander's army booed him as they marched past,' Xerxes continued.

'A fit reward for betrayal,' Guruji said grimly.

'After this humiliating ordeal, Bessus was sent to Ecbatana to Oxyathres, brother of the late King Emperor, where he was publicly decapitated. On Alexander's orders, Bessus was denied rites of a Zoroastrian funeral. No vultures would eat his body in a Zoroastrian Tower of Silence,' Xerxes informed.

'Humiliation in life and death!' Guruji sighed.

'Alexander killed traitor Barsaentes but pardoned Nabarzenes, though both had betrayed Darius. Right now, the Achaemenid empire has neither Persian ruler nor satrap. What will happen to leaderless soldiers on their way to become mercenaries in Bessus' defunct army?' the guildsman squeaked, his forehead furrowed with worry.

'Mercenaries are mercenaries. Let them join Alexander's army, it makes no difference who pays their salaries,' Guruji said.

'As long as they are employed,' the guildsman squeaked again.

Xerxes shoved Guruji's note into a brass cone and pocketed the coins.

'Keep us updated,' Guruji said as Xerxes bowed and left. After he departed, the old man and 'guildsman' spoke deep into the night, impervious to the cold.

Barsine and Alexander

A short time had elapsed. In the grassland campsite on no-man's land, Guruji and his men were seated around a bonfire that did double duty to keep away snakes, as well as aid their cook with the nourishing night broth of venison, rice and vegetables. Prince Sashigupta was dressed as himself, the weather being balmy. Next to Guruji was a traveling snake catcher. The coir lids were off and three cobras, hoods flared, rose out of the flat circular baskets, their scales gleaming in the firelight. Everyone's eyes were trained on their spectacled hoods.

'How is Darius' family?' Guruji asked the snake catcher.

'The King Emperor's eldest daughter is the beautiful Barsine, who was educated in Greek schools, making her a fit wife for Greek nobility. After capturing Darius' family,

Alexander gallantly instructed that all the women be protected.'

'So, she is fit for Alexander too?' Guruji asked.

'Evidently. The fact is Alexander made Barsine's mother, beautiful Statira, his mistress as a sign that he was the legitimate ruler of Asia. Statira died of childbirth, her baby died too. After her death, daughter Barsine became Alexander's mistress.'

'So, Alexander's family has increased in size?' Guruji asked.

'But only with locals,' the snake catcher reported.

'If you have any additional information?'

'No more, honored teacher, I need to hunt for food for my snakes.' He accepted some coins and departed with his slithery companions.

Hoodwinking Double Agents

After a few days, Prince Sashigupta, Guruji, their bodyguards and a few soldiers rode to a destination unknown to the rest of the troops. This, to make it difficult for Nanda double agents to inform their commanders. For two days, they rode through dense jungle, drinking water from streams and eating the occasional wild fruits that the vaid had told them were safe. They killed no wild animals, because the fire to cook the meat would be a dead giveaway, making the mess cook's job that much harder. Late one evening, Sashigupta's group came across an isolated hamlet and Guruji advised the party that they had to split up. Sashigupta, Guruji and a bodyguard stayed back, and the rest of the group rode into the thickets and disappeared. Sashigupta's bodyguard went searching for fodder, edible leaves from nearby trees. The prince took out his grey wig and snow-white beard, and secured them in place over head and face. Guruji too donned a wig of limp grey hair.

Digvijay Meets his Doom

In a few seconds, the sun set, and night descended all of a sudden. The bodyguard had managed some thin branches with enough leaves for the horses. In the fading light, they could spot, situated away from the village, a small thatched hut lit by a firewood stove, and quietly rode up to it.

'Mother,' Sashigupta called, 'Can we stay the night and indulge in your hospitality?'

A young married woman came out with a brass lantern in her hand, a small child clinging to her skirt. She stared at three old men on horseback. 'My husband is not home, but you may stay. Tie your horses next to the cowshed,' she said, gesturing towards a wall-less, thatched roof structure.

The three men dismounted and tethered their horses to a fence post for cattle. From the close by village, they heard the clinking of metal cymbals, as a singing male voice rose into the night.

The voice sang of 'Prince Sashigupta's forays into Nanda territory, the raids directed all over the north and the villagers evaded capture from the prince's raiders by migrating.'

Guruji and his protégé looked tensely in the direction of the sound, though nothing was visible. The young woman went in and returned with two brass pots of water for them to wash their faces and feet.

'Even though Prince Sashigupta's commander Digvijay was a Nanda double agent,' the voice continued, 'he was tortured by the Nanda high command for his brother Veervijay's suspected treachery, committed suicide and his body thrown into the cemetery for criminals.'

Sashigupta roared, but Guruji coughed loudly to cover up the sound.

A Mother's Advice

'Mother, who is singing in the village?' Sashigupta asked after he had regained control over his emotions.

The young woman laughed, 'That's the traveling balladeer, keeps us informed about kings and conquests.'

'So, what is the latest news, Mother?' Sashigupta asked.

'The latest news? Prince Sashi and his old guru are both on the run,' the woman replied.

She went in again and brought a large open pot of gruel for the horses that looked dehydrated. Sashigupta took it from her and set it between the three horses.

Then she made dinner – flat, thick wheat *roti*, bread, with some fresh butter to eat it with. The three men ate quietly, relishing the simple meal. Inside, they could overhear the young woman scolding her son.

'You are eating the way Prince Sashigupta and his guru attack the Nandas, going through the middle instead of from the side. If you eat from the center, it is too hot to eat, and the sides get too dry to eat later. If you and Sashigupta start from the sides, your *roti* would be easier to eat, and every conquest would be secure,' she scolded.

The tiredness the men were feeling disappeared. Sashigupta and Guruji stopped eating and looked at each other in the dim glow from the kitchen.

'I will always be grateful for this advice,' Sashigupta bowed in the direction of the voice, adding, 'Our moves are known already in these distant villages.'

'Yes,' Guruji spoke somberly. 'Thanks to the wandering balladeers, the villagers are more up to date than we are.'

The young woman came out again, with an iron fire pot, which she set between the three men and their horses. She put a large stem into the fire pot, angled such that it would last a long time.

'This is snake country, fire keeps them away,' she said in a matter-of-fact tone.

'Thank you for your kindness, Mother!' Prince Sashigupta said humbly, even though the young woman looked younger than him. He uncoiled his mongoose. All three men slept soundly in a triangle around the fire pot, waking only when the crows began to caw. They rode away from the hamlet before the young woman woke up, their disguises still in place.

Men with Wings at the Sogdian Rock, 328 BC

The long-haired trader was back. Not being an astute businessman (earlier he had plied Guruji with children's toys without much success), he now had a cartload of woolen clothes, it being summer and some farm implements (Guruji being a scholar) that he hoped would appeal to more adult tastes. But he was garrulous and for this helpful quality, Guruji encouraged his visits.

'In autumn,' he was chatting, 'Sogdiana and Bactria revolted. Alexander captured the Sogdian cities one by one. Commander Oxyartes had followed Bessus in his retreat across the Oxus River, and sent his wife and daughters to the impenetrable rock fortress in Sogdiana – the Sogdian Rock.'

'Impenetrable?' Guruji asked.

'The Sogdian Rock has long had a reputation for being invincible.... When Alexander reached the Rock, he asked the defenders to surrender. The cocksure Sogdians replied that only "men with wings" could capture the Rock. In pitch darkness, Alexander, who loved a challenge, sent 300 climbers up the steep rock face. Thirty men died in the attempt up the sheer cliff. After the rest of the men reached the top, Alexander, a master of psychological warfare, sent a taunting message to the defenders, that "men with wings" had arrived at the top of the Rock. Demoralized, the men defending the Rock gave up without a fight. However, Alexander's own men were fighting with their leader over a Persian practice.'

Opposition to Proskynesis

'Which was?' Guruji was curious.

'*Proskynesis,* the ritual of prostrating and kissing one's fingers to someone of higher rank. Like this,' the man got on his knees, kissed his fingertips and did a proskynesis to Guruji as a demo.

'One of those who detested proskynesis was Philotas, son of Parmenion, Alexander's second-in-command. Philotas hatched a plot to assassinate Alexander over the Persian influence in his personal life. Alexander found out about the plot through someone whose brother was a lover of the man who knew about it. Alexander conducted a public trial, found Philotas guilty and had him executed through stoning. Then, he hurriedly sent a posse of men to kill the trustworthy Parmenion, before he could hear of his son's execution.'

'So, the Yavana is vindictive,' Guruji said, his face expressionless. He filled the trader's cupped hands.

Cleitus the Black Killed

More than a month had passed traveling. Guruji, Prince Sashigupta and a small group of men were huddled together hungrily after sunset on the edge of a jungle. The mess cook was preparing dinner, the fragrance of frying garlic and charred wild boar filled the air. A horseman cantered slowly towards them, alighted and walked towards the group. Sashigupta's bodyguard stopped him and searched for hidden weapons.

'State who you are and your purpose?' the bodyguard

barked at the man.

'Cyrus, acrobat from Persia, sent by Xerxes with tidings of the Yavana.'

'Guruji!' the bodyguard waved at a pony-tailed old man and a long-haired younger man with a small drum who appeared to be an entertainer, in the center of the group. 'Message from Xerxes,' the bodyguard said.

'Update us,' the young man said as Cyrus joined them, 'What is Yavana Alexander up to?'

'Making enemies in his own army,' the acrobat replied.

'Enemies, in his army?' the young man sounded surprised.

'Shahenshah Alexander's alcoholism has led to a debacle.'

'Debacle? How?'

'Recently, Artabazus resigned as satrap of Bactria. Alexander then offered the satrapy to his savior, Cleitus the Black. The day before Cleitus' departure, Alexander held a banquet at Marakanda palace, where everyone got sloshed….'

'Including the Yavana?' the younger man demanded.

'Particularly him. A drunk Cleitus criticized Alexander for killing Parmenion and Philotas, and claiming to be son of God Ammon while denouncing his biological father, King Philip. At the height of the party, a thoroughly drunk Alexander announced that Cleitus would take 16,000 defeated Greek mercenaries to wage war against nomads of Central Asia,' the horseman continued.

'Cleitus objected?' It was Guruji.

'Acrimoniously. He rejected the offer, seeing this would distance him permanently from Alexander's close circle. The argument grew so violent that members of the banquet hustled a furious Cleitus out of the room, but he broke free and ran back inside to argue some more, when Alexander seized his bodyguard's spear and killed him, an act he bitterly regretted when sober.'

'He killed Cleitus, his savior?' the young man sounded horrified.

'He did. The whole party sobered when their supreme commander lost control.'

'How did Alexander's army react?'

'They are terrified. Many soldiers have become mutinous, though they outwardly keep quiet. Some think Alexander is blinded by his own success,' the man informed the small group on the edge of the jungle.

'And who does he have to fall back upon?' the younger man queried.

'Alexander trusts only his oldest companions like best friend Hephaestion,' Cyrus said.

The youth looked thoughtful, but the old man made a clicking sound of disapproval. After Cyrus departed, the younger man and the old man discussed the issue threadbare, most of the night.

The Messenger

Next morning, both men woke with the same thought, but Prince Sashigupta was the first to voice it. 'Bessus deserved assassination. But Cleitus?'

'I am worried,' Guruji sounded anxious for a change.

'I am not. What to do with troops sent to Bactria as mercenaries? Will the Yavana treat them right?' Prince Sashigupta asked.

'Let's think about an alternate king, like the man at Varana, who would value our superior horsemen. If their reputation precedes them, who knows, the Yavana himself will employ them.'

'Dhoomal!' Sashigupta gave a piercing whistle, and a spindly boy with a gypsy headdress came loping over. 'Take down a couple of messages to the independent pigeon post man at the highway pigeon cote.'

'Okay, boss,' the boy replied.

'And ask for updates on Bactria and Sogdiana,' Sashigupta added.

'Righto!' Dhoomal said, eagerly waiting for the messages.

'We may need to go in person and offer ourselves as mercenaries,' Guruji said. 'Write down,' Sashi said as he dictated messages.

A while later, after tucking the messages in his colorful headdress, Dhoomal rode towards the pigeon cote. Spotting a troubadour from the West, he guided him to the village outskirts where Prince Sashigupta had his roaming camp.

Balkh's 'little star' Roshanak, 327 BC

The sound of a fine small drum of the troubadour reached Sashigupta's village camp.

'The Yavana has fallen in love,' the troubadour mouthed mellifluously.

'Love? Again? Call that man here,' Prince Sashigupta told his bodyguard, who promptly yelled on top of his voice to summon the troubadour, who yelled back. After a confusing exchange of yells, the troubadour reached camp.

'Yes, Sire?' he said.

'You sang about the Yavana in love. Update us,' the prince said.

'This year, Barsine, Alexander's mistress, gave birth to Heracles, a son for Alexander. And this year, Alexander met a young girl whose father Oxyartes, a nobleman of Balkh, principal city of Bactria, headed the Sogdian Rock fortress.'

'How did they meet?' Sashi asked.

'After conquering the Sogdian Rock, Alexander met his

captives, Oxyartes' family, including 16-year-old Roxanne, who decided to make the best of the situation. During a wedding dance that Alexander attended, she presented herself and offered to become his wife. The Yavana, who treats his aristocratic captives with honor, fell in love with Roxanne who the Macedonians pronounced as the loveliest woman in Asia. Smitten by her beauty, Alexander accepted. Roxanne is his first legally-wedded wife. Roxanne's Persian name *Roshanak* means "Little Star,"' the troubadour said.

'Roshanak's star is in the ascendant,' Prince Sashigupta laughed. 'And Hephaestion?'

'Best man. After they wed, Oxyartes was made satrap of Paropamisadae,' the visitor said.

'A stroke of luck for Oxyartes, having a son-in-law like Alexander,' Sashigupta laughed.

'Alexander, his bride and army are right now in the western hinterlands of the Sapta Sindhu,' the troubadour continued.

'How is Roxanne in India?'

'Enchanted by India's plants, rare animals, religious practices. While Alexander and his army rest during the move through northwest India, she visits Aryan temples. Right now, she is more expert on the Aryan religion than Alexander's scholars.'

'A brilliant child,' said Guruji.

'And Alexander appreciates his teenage wife for being knowledgeable about India.'

'I wonder where the restless Yavana is heading now,' Sashi said thoughtfully.

News on that front would have to wait a few weeks. Guruji and Sashigupta were busy.

Raise an Army, Based on Merit

As Sashigupta's group rode away, they took particular care not to leave any traces behind.

'Visit different villages to rouse villagers into rebels to fight Dhanananda or his vassals, and live a better life,' Sashigupta instructed the soldiers.

Individual soldiers would go on sorties and report to Prince Sashigupta what percentage of villagers were keen on rebelling against the Nandas. Every few days, they set up camp on deserted grassland or jungles of the north, traveling northwestwards on the sort of land no king wanted to claim as his own except in extreme deprivation.

'What is the response?' Prince Sashigupta asked his commandant, Dhruv, who had ridden back from one such sortie.

'Many vassal villagers want to join our army in rebellion against hellish Nanda taxation,' Dhruv reported.

'Same old story,' Prince Sashigupta said disapprovingly.

Guruji too had visited several ashrams.

'I need to speak to gurus and their pupils, and raise an army based on merit, not caste or color or money,' Guruji said contemplatively.

'Alone, Guruji?' Sashi asked.

'I insist you do not accompany me. What if there are Nanda double agents in the villages I visit?' Guruji said firmly, adding, 'Better that only one of us gets caught rather than both of us.'

Sashigupta agreed. Knowing the danger that discovery would bring to the entire group, he stayed back in the austere campsites, sleeping during daytime for lack of anything to do.

The Lion King and the Lion Prince

Ten days had passed. Sashigupta's bodyguard had gone foraging for drinking water. Waiting for his men and Guruji to return, Prince Sashigupta fell asleep against a tree. Guruji very strictly made Sashigupta change his disguise often, so that any double agent who came across him would not recognize the prince. However, Sashigupta favored the Aghora disguise.

Vijayta was tethered nearby, his mongoose chained to Vijayta to avoid getting lost.

More than a mile around, bushy scrub and yellow dead grass speckled the landscape, ideal to hear any enemy soldiers riding up. Falling asleep with ennui, a sound roused him. Vijayta was neighing hysterically. Sashigupta woke to a hot fetid breath. He opened his eyes and his breath choked in his throat. Inches from his face was a massive battle-scarred lion, king of the Northwest jungle, sniffing him. His sword lay in its sheath, too far to be useful. For a long moment, both stared at each other, the lion and the prince. Then with infinite elegance, the lion swished his tail and disappeared into the yellow grass. In the distance, behind him, he could hear a sword being drawn and wished fervently his loyal bodyguard would not attack the lion.

'Hey Prince Sashi, are you okay?' his bodyguard called out.

More horses neighed in protest. The rest of the group had caught up.

'I am a bit shocked. I forgot that the lion's territory covers our troops' travel plans through the land of the Sapta Sindhu,' he admitted.

'It's a sign of good luck, the king of the jungle recognizing the future king of this territory,' Guruji looked elated, when he heard the story. He smoothed his ponytail and said, 'Soon, very soon, this will be knotted in a juttu.'

'I think the king of the jungle could occasionally brush his teeth,' Sashigupta grumbled.

The entire group, tethering their horses, laughed aloud, relieved.

A Poison Worse than Beesh

Moving to new places was the only way to throw the enemy off balance – of this both Guruji and Prince Sashigupta were in concurrence. And to do this, they needed information about the Nandas, more than they were currently getting. At a new camp, Sashigupta met horsemen and messengers who had information on brutal countermeasures by the Nandas.

'We need to send our people to safety,' Prince Sashigupta sounded stressed after one such meeting.

'Send our soldiers in different directions and in smaller groups,' Guruji said calmly. 'When the whole team scatters, they avoid capture and betrayal by double agents,' he advised.

'Yes, but smaller groups can be annihilated more easily. Ramagupta?' Sashi asked, looking towards his commander.

'To move on. Slain Nanda commanders and double agents' bodies are to be dumped into every water body around Nanda outposts in wells, ponds, dams, streams, canals to contaminate the water. The outpost and the surrounding villages will then be abandoned, and village supporters of the Nandas forced to migrate to virgin territories with unpolluted water,' Ramagupta said.

'Let us abandon camp,' Prince Sashi ordered Ramagupta.

Alexander and Hephaestion, Eternal Lovers

At the next stop, the circus acrobat had entertained them for nearly half an hour, when Guruji clapped his hands signaling an end to his antics. The man tethered his horse and came towards them.

'Bravo! Where are you from, my good man?' Guruji asked.

'I belong to the land of the Yavana,'

'You are the right man, then. Any personal intel about Alexander in childhood?' Prince Sashigupta asked lightly.

'Oh, lots. Alexander was an unusual child growing up. He preferred men, sexually. Both his parents were afraid that Alexander might live his life without contact with women. They set up Alexander's first encounter with Kallixenia, a professional Thessalian hetaira,'

'What's a hetaira again?' Sashigupta asked curiously.

'Courtesan.'

'To get used to women's bodies?'

'And also look outside his childhood love, Hephaestion. Alexander compares his love for Hephaestion to the love between Greek hero Achilles and his friend Patroclus. Alexander and Hephaestion stopped by Ilion on the ruins of Troy, where the king offered garlands and sacrifices to Achilles, and Hephaestion did the same at Patroclus' tomb. In keeping with an ancient rite, Alexander ran naked around the tomb of Achilles.'

'Evidence they love each other?' Prince Sashigupta sounded incredulous.

'No one can break up the love the two men have for each other, ever. Those who try, perish,' he said. The acrobat continued in this vein for a bit and left after payment.

Ambhi, 'the Enemy of an Enemy is a Friend'

The camp had a repeat visitor, midafternoon. The circus acrobat was rambling and Sashigupta, who for a change had gorged on jaggery and pepper-cooked goat meat, was listening to him with the half-asleep torpor of the well-fed.

'Now the Yavana is making new friends in India,' the

acrobat said, jogging the prince back into the conversation.

'So soon?' Prince Sashigupta asked.

'That's correct. Alexander had barely touched northwestern River Sindhu, when King Oomphis of Taxiles met him.'

'Oomphis? Taxiles?' Sashigupta sounded confused.

'Ambhi of Taxila,' Guruji explained.

'Ambhi the trickster?' Prince Sashigupta said to Guruji, 'He has his own agenda, I can bet.'

'At Taxiles, Oomphis sent an army expedition to meet Alexander. When a suspicious Alexander saw the forces of Oomphis, he ordered his own forces into a battle formation. But Oomphis responded with many gifts, offered him his army and agreed to surrender his prosperous dominions with this speech:

> *"To what purpose should we make war upon one another, if the design of your coming into these parts be not to rob us of our water or our necessary food, which are the only things that wise men are indispensably obliged to fight for? As for other riches and possessions, as they are accounted in the eye of the world, if I am better provided of them than you, I am ready to let you share with me; but if fortune has been more liberal to you than me, I have no objection to be obliged to you."*

Sensing no danger from Oomphis, Alexander reinstated him as king of Taxiles, and gifted him Persian robes, gold and silver ornaments, thirty horses and a 1,000 talents of gold.'

'Why did Ambhi befriend the first outsider who set foot in his territory?' Sashi asked searchingly.

'Because the enemy of an enemy is a friend,' Guruji grunted.

'So groveling works?'

'Clearly. Both royals are now good friends. Taxiles' military engineers aided Perdiccas and Hephaestion in building a pontoon bridge for Alexander's men to cross the Indus,' the acrobat said.

'Eat before you leave,' Prince Sashigupta said, showering coins into the acrobat's hand.

'The Yavana's military and personal life is so full of turns and angles, we will hear more soon,' Guruji said.

His intuition was right. Before long, more news on the Yavana came to them.

The End of Callisthenes, 326 BC

A Buddhist monk with an alms bowl, tonsured scalp and regulation robes of the Theravada school was seated in front of Guruji. When their argument on philosophy ended, Prince Sashigupta politely stepped in.

'So, can you tell us of Alexander's latest conquests, Holy Sir?' Sashigupta asked.

'In bits and pieces. To assimilate his conquests, Alexander adopts local customs. A custom that had dismayed European soldiers in his army was proskynesis...'

'The ritual of kissing their fingers to someone higher ranked?'

'Exactly. Another big critic was historian Callisthenes, Aristotle's grandnephew and Alexander's boyhood chum. In the beginning, Callisthenes had fawned upon Alexander, turning a blind eye to Alexander naming himself son of God Zeus. But Callisthenes, a harsh critic of proskynesis, was imprisoned, and died this year.'

'Died or killed?' Sashi asked with suspicion.

'Either or. Of disease or torture. Rumor is Alexander killed Callisthenes for conspiracy.'

'And Aristotle, how has he taken the death of Callisthenes?'

'The strong bond between Aristotle and Alexander has ended. His old teacher is now Alexander's implacable enemy,' the monk revealed.

'Bad karma, infuriating your own teacher,' Guruji shook his head.

'Alexander is least bothered. He returned to Balkh and spent nearly six months getting ready to invade India. He sent Hephaestion to India via the Khyber Pass, but himself marched up the Kunar Valley,' he said.

'And what exactly is Alexander up to in the Kunar Valley?'

Ashvakas of Massaga, Ora and Nysa

'Alexander has made inroads into northwest India. Massaga is his first big conquest,' the monk said.

'Massaga? In northwest India?' A manly voice beneath a green nest headdress asked.

'Mashkavati, the locals call it,' Guruji explained.

'The conquest of Massaga belongs in the annals of military history. The fort of Massaga was occupied by a free people, the Asskenoi.'

'Asskenoi?' the green nest asked again.

'*Ashvakas*, from *Ashva,* horse. Ashvakas are celebrated horse breeders,' Guruji said patiently.

'In the brutal siege, the leader of Massaga, a democratically elected king, was killed on the first day of the skirmish. The Massaga mercenaries pretended to give up the fort, kept under an unrelenting blockade by Alexander's men. Alexander himself had been wounded in the siege and was resting. The Asskenoi resisted Alexander's men with tens of thousands of cavalry and infantry.' the monk gave more details.

'They continued after their king's death…?' Sashi was

even more keen to know.

'Because Queen mother Cleophes led the army the next two days. The Massaga women warriors also took part in battle,' he was told.

'Good gender equality,' Prince Sashigupta said approvingly.

'Alexander was impressed, he made an impassioned speech to the Asskenoi. "*Stoic people of Massaga, I grant you your freedom if you give up the fight.*"

Alexander's messenger conveyed this. But the Massagans turned him down. At night, the 7,000 inhabitants of Massaga tried to escape stealthily, were spotted by Macedonian lookouts, and all men, women and children were butchered by Alexander's troops, over four days,' the monk told them of the carnage.

'That's genocide!' Guruji exclaimed.

'That doesn't worry Alexander. Next, Ora, and its Asskenoi were defeated.'

'Again?' Guruji said.

'Yes. But it was Nysa that Alexander valued.'

'Nysa of Dionysus, the drunkard god?' Guruji snapped.

'The same. When Nysa fell, Alexander's generals celebrated till the wee hours of the morning with Dionysian revelry.'

'That would have met with the god's approval,' Guruji grunted.

'Many small forts, 230,000 superior Zebu cattle, and thousands of invaluable battle horses were captured by Alexander. In desperation, some Eastern Asskenoi have run to Aornos.'

'Aornos?' the green nest queried.

'Varana, the invincible,' Guruji explained.

'Excellent rendition. All facts true?' Prince Sashigupta asked.

'Sir, I will grow hair on my head if I have erred,' the monk said, his scalp shining.

'Thank you, holy one, please take some food with you for tomorrow,' Sashigupta said humbly. 'And I request you to accept this payment as alms.'

Varana and the Yavana

Two boys departed with the monk to the distant mess.

'We need to move,' Guruji said as Sashigupta stretched lazily and stood up.

Both men, worried, knew what the other was thinking.

'What to do with our …?' Guruji began.

'Mercenaries? Seek a king who will value our superior horsemen. The commandant at Varana or Yavana Alexander himself?' Sashigupta asked. 'It is time we "offered" him our services in person.'

'Yes. Dhoomal!' Sashigupta yelled. 'Messages!'

Green Nest materialized.

'Messages for the pigeon post man in the north,' Prince Sashigupta said, handing over some parchment.

'Where next? And how many of us?' Guruji asked, watching Dhoomal depart with Prince Sashigupta's signet ring and messages tucked in the nest.

'To the Yavana's path. One-third cavalry,' Sashigupta said confidently.

'Are our soldiers battle-ready?' Guruji asked.

'Well, we have spent quality time training them to eat united in a common kitchen, and become excellent military engineers,' the prince informed his teacher.

'When it is time to use cavalry and military engineers, it is also time for *Yana,*' Guruji declared.

'Yana?' Sashigupta asked.

'Foreign policy that covers marching on a military campaign.'

'I will brief cavalry commanders on the route. The Yavana will appreciate our potent cavalry,' Prince Sashigupta said. 'Base camp should be close enough for our cavalry to be absorbed by the Yavana,' he added.

Preoccupied, he went to meet his commanders and to check if he had missed pigeon posts.

When he returned, he had a question for Guruji. 'Tell me something I can use with the Yavana,' he said.

Guruji smiled. He knew just the thing.

April 326 BC
The Yavana at Aornos

At the Nanda Court, Again

BACK AT THE Nanda high command, Rakshash and the Nandas were following every move of Prince Sashigupta with something bordering on obsession. This included any enemy Sashigupta could befriend, and news from any source was eagerly awaited. And so it was, into the noon time private court of the Nandas, traipsed in a creature festooned with an enormous number of colored shawls and jangly beads. The transgender settled down in front of the younger Nandas, Amatya Rakshash and the C-in-C, his jeweled hands gesticulating effeminately as he began to speak of this and that. Rakshash, who thought gossip couldn't be news, switched off, and came back just in time to hear the creature launch into Sashigupta and Alexander's meeting.

'At the Indus river, Alexander's army crossed over on a pontoon bridge of boats, rafts, barges and canoes. As the army marched towards Aornos, Prince Sashigupta's scout informed him about Alexander's army on the move,' the Nandas were informed.

'And?' Rakshash asked, now paying full attention.

'Prince Sashigupta rode up to Alexander, whose huge army

moves like a giant spider around him, and offered his soldiers,' the transgender continued.

'Bastard opportunist,' Prince Kaivarta scowled as he flung away his alcohol goblet furiously. The king snored loudly in irritation at being disturbed in his drunken siesta.

'The first meeting between Alexander and Sashigupta had Bactrian and Indian Aryans translating for the two men. Prince Sashigupta greeted Alexander and said, "My name is Sashigupta Maurya, formerly a prince, now homeless. I come to offer you my best horsemen, veterans in battle."

'To which Alexander responded, "Okay, let's test their mettle first in Aornos, and then maybe they can be hired."

'Prince Sashigupta went to instruct his men and told them that they "would be on trial before being absorbed in Alexander's army. I will remain your commander," he said.

'Sashigupta's soldiers looked relieved to still be with their chief.

"Tell me about Aornos," Alexander said to Sashigupta as they rode side by side.

"The Rock of Aornos, Varana, defeated Heracles, your ancient kinsman," he told the Macedonian king.

"Heracles? My mother's ancestor?" Alexander looked elated. "This challenge I cannot ignore," he laughed. "Conquering Aornos is a priority. Call my generals," he instructed Eumenes.'

The Rock of Aornos

'The same evening, Alexander, Sashigupta and a few commanders rode up to the Rock of Aornos for an advance recce. A deep ravine surrounded Aornos,[1] which was on top

1 Pir Sar, border of Swat valley.

of an extremely steep hill. Fog and dense jungle on the outer edge of the ravine obscured their vision.

"What do you think of my plan?" Alexander asked Sashigupta.

'Sashigupta nodded assent. Though Alexander's methods to conquer Aornos would lead to an ecological disaster, Sashigupta listened patiently as Alexander ordered all trees in the jungle be cut and thrown in the ravine. Sashigupta's men axed the trees, matched energetically by Persian and Macedonian soldiers. As more trees were cut and thrown in, the ravine filled up and became level with the ground they were standing on. Then, the soldiers clawed up the steep hill and attacked the Rock on which people from surrounding areas had taken refuge, fooled by its invincible reputation. Single files of soldiers climbed steadily up the sides of the Rock and crowded out the refugees.

'After Aornos succumbed, King Alexander called Prince Sashigupta to his tent.

"I leave you, Prince Sisicottus, in charge. Pay me a satrap's tribute," Alexander offered.

"I will be forever in your debt," Sashigupta was grateful.'

'Before leaving, Alexander built a royal residence in the fort.' This last fact brought a frown to the faces of the Nandas and their Amatya.

'So, that upstart Sashigupta has inveigled another place to govern?' Prince Kaivarta was irate, reacting for their king, elder brother Dhanananda whose eyes were shut and lower jaw, shiny with drool.

Rakshash was silent, thoughtful, as the transgender departed.

Sashigupta's Palace at Varana, May 326 BC

Weeks later...

The seller of bangles and beads was announcing his wares outside the walled royal apartment of Prince Sashigupta.

'Beads from the Indus river valley, superior beads for the special women of this charming land. Beads, beads, beads,' he was heard shouting.

Guruji looked up midway dictating a letter to Prince Sashigupta's secretary and asked his day bodyguard Gautami to bring in the bangle seller.

In minutes, the colorfully-dressed vendor with his wares had come to the balcony.

'What have you here?' Guruji asked.

'Best quality beads made with Indus clay and Arya technology. See these, fit for a queen…'

'…which we don't have,' Guruji croaked calmly.

There was a bewildered silence.

'What wares can you offer Sashigupta, our bachelor prince?'

The bangle seller looked even more confused.

'How is our benefactor, the Yavana faring?' Guruji broke his silence.

'I have information on the family life of the Yavana.'

'Prince Sashigupta should hear this. Call him,' Guruji said to Gautami, who promptly fetched the prince.

'Please begin,' Guruji growled.

'Traveling through northwest India with her husband, Queen Roxanne gave birth to a son who died. King Alexander captured Glausae territory (the Mallois) and is now marching east with a big contingent of Taxila's army,' he told his audience.

'Raja Ambhi's troops are now part of Alexander's army?' Prince Sashigupta sounded incredulous.

'Yes!'

'Why?'

'Their next objective probably is to conquer King Paurava.'

'Ah, got it,' Sashigupta knew his next move.

The bangle-seller departed; right hand clenched.

Prince Sashigupta was not pleased. He sent Dhoomal to warn Paurava the Elder, who ruled between the rivers Jhelum and Chenab (in Indian Punjab) about Ambhi Raja pairing with Alexander. Dhoomal returned with the monk.

Porus and Monsoon Fury, June 326

'What else is my lord Alexander up to?' Prince Sashigupta asked.

'Well, to save his army from more pitched battles, Alexander sent messages to Prince Abhisares and Paurava the Elder,' the monk said.

'Both accepted Alexander's offer?' a perplexed Sashigupta asked.

'Not both, Sire. Abhisares, prince of Kashmir, sent gifts and a welcoming message stating, "I accept your overlordship of Kashmir, King Alexander."

'And Paurava?'

'Sent a curt message to Alexander, "Let's meet in battle."'

'And he is battle ready?' the prince sounded worried.

'Well, Paurava immediately sent pigeon posts to his friend Abhisares "for your mercenaries stationed there to defeat the combined armies of Alexander and Raja Ambhi." But there is an unstoppable delay in Kashmiri aid, the whole territory is being ripped apart by the monsoon,' the monk said. 'So, Abhisares unhappily sent a pigeon post to Paurava the same day. It read: *"My mercenary army is slowed down due to floods and landslides in the Kashmir valley. We are still coming to your aid, but our army is delayed as many bridges have been washed away, and the highways are threatened by flash floods."'*

'Poor man!' Sashigupta said.

'Yes, Sir. Paurava is desperate. The monsoons are violent. All over his kingdom, otherwise helpful streams are overflowing their banks, flash floods are washing away entire villages. Village panchayat heads come daily to the Paurava court to complain of homes being inundated, livestock being washed away, croplands swamped by flood waters.'

'So, Paurava is struggling with civil calamities?' Sashi asked.

'Among other things,' the visitor said.

'Guruji, I need to go to my friend Paurava's aid right away,' Prince Sashigupta announced to Guruji, who looked thoughtful.

'Go incognito,' Guruji spoke with caution. The prince left.

Alexander and the Indian Monsoon

A couple of days later, the monk was back.

'Update me,' Guruji said.

'While Raja Paurava's state machinery struggles to help his citizens, his latest enemy, Alexander, a master in riverside strategy,' the monk began to say…

'All his big Asian victories being river-related,' the old man remarked.

'Alexander reached the territory of Paurava on the west bank of the Jhelum. On the way, he recruited 5,000 Indian soldiers to boost the numbers in his army.'

'Other preparations?' Guruji asked.

'Like Prince Sashi, Alexander uses lookalikes. To deceive the Paurava army, an Alexander lookalike prowled up and down the camp to fool Paurava's men into thinking he, Alexander, was camped on the upper banks of the flooded river. The real Alexander strategized with his generals in a small, dry camp clad in ordinary soldier's attire. Being of average height, a bare five foot and five inches, no one in the Paurava camp guessed the Yavana chief was disguised as a common infantry man', the monk explained.

'His strategy?' Guruji asked.

'Across the swollen river, opposite the Paurava military camp, Macedonian troops would holler and thrash about on the west bank. The first ten days of noisy provocation made Paurava's troops alert for a fight on the banks. Every time this happened, the generals of Paurava would get their men alert, but the tension would soon dissipate as the Yavana soldiers never crossed over.'

'But King Paurava knew better. "Be careful, they might fool us into thinking they will not attack, but do it when our guard is down," Paurava wisely instructed his generals after being briefed by his spies.

'But by the eleventh day, Paurava's generals had forgotten the king's advice. They barely looked up at the soldiers who were parading and making a ruckus on the opposite bank, a sign Alexander, adept at military tactics, was waiting for.

'Alexander called his generals to strategize in his modest tent. The Alexander look-alike prowled among the Macedonians exhorting them loudly to fight the enemy.

'Early tomorrow, ride downriver, cross over to the island midriver, then ride upriver again and fight like you did at Guagamela and Massaga. In self-belief, we meet victory," Alexander raised his sword in the air.

'His men yelled Alala and slashed their swords in the air. A young man stepped forward, clad in guildsman's clothing, a double agent.

"King Alexander, the prized post of guarding the territory downriver has been given to Paurava Putra, the eldest son of King Porus. He can be easily defeated as he has no experience."

"How come Porus made such a foolish decision?" Alexander asked.

"That Indian bane – nepotism. King Paurava is blind to his two sons' ineptitude, especially Paurava Putra," the spy told Alexander, who, calling Eumenes, said cheerfully, "Reward him."'

Paurava Putra Dies

'Days later, Alexander's men crossed into Porus' territory downriver where no assault was expected, his Indian vassal an hour behind.

"Why not build a bridge over the water, Sire?" Eumenes had asked Alexander.

"The deep river water is monsoon-rough and the bridge will alert the scouts of Porus of our attack plans," Alexander replied.

'It was early in the morning, dark, drizzling, the air damp and chilly. Alexander's commanders and half the cavalry rode by the riverside till they spotted a shallow part in the riverbed, a small island, and carefully, without much noise, crossed the river where they were spotted.

'Paurava's spies, alert for this kind of engagement, rode to the king's tent, which Paurava shared with his 21-year-old son, Paurava Putra.

"Raja Paurava, an attack is expected downriver near the rocks. The Yavana have crossed over," the alarmed spy informed Paurava.

"I will take on the Yavana army with cavalry, father,"

Paurava Putra said confidently.

"Spoken like a true Kshatriya," Raja Paurava looked on approvingly as his cocky son began to don his armor.

'Paurava Putra's offer to attack the enemy met with authorization from his father, Raja Paurava, who did not think senior generals were required as backup for his inexperienced son. But he sent a 10-strong team of bodyguards with the boy,' the monk told them.

'Was that useful?' Guruji asked.

'Well, one arm of the cavalry headed by Paurava Putra was woken up early and asked to be ready for battle. The soldiers knew that Paurava's son was inexperienced unlike his generals but given that prized role as eldest son of the king. With the Paurava heir at the helm of this mission, the cavalry scrambled hurriedly to mount their horses. The immature Paurava Putra, in his excitement, incautiously rode far ahead of his bodyguards and troops, some of whom were struggling in the monsoon slush,' the monk continued.

'Suicidal!' Guruji exclaimed.

'Very. In the dim early morning light obscured by steely gray monsoon clouds, the Paurava double agent pointed out the prince to the Macedonian cavalry who immediately surrounded him. As the first spears punched the boy's armor, he died before his men could reach him. Paurava's cavalry was demoralized. As the dead prince collapsed on his horse, the mounted soldiers fled, abandoning their leader.'

'Abandoned by all?'

'No, the bodyguards stuck around, tied the prince's body to the horse and led the horse with its dead rider back to the Paurava camp,' Guruji was told.

'Ahead of them, one lone loyal rider galloped speedily with the prince's sword and handed it over to King Paurava.

"Paurava Putra was attacked by a large group and died fighting, Sire," the rider said.

"What do we wait for?" Raja Paurava said harshly. "Let's meet the Yavana in battle," he declared. Raja Paurava donned his armor, met his generals for war strategy and ordered his war elephant readied for a long fight.'

Porus, Alexander's Battle of the Hydaspes

'Do you have statistics for the battle, venerable Sir?' Guruji asked the wizened monk politely.

'I do. Paurava instructed his 30,000 soldiers, 2,000 cavalry and 300 war elephants to adopt a classical battle formation. But Mother Nature played spoilsport. Stinging rain, deafening thunder and lightning strikes added mayhem.'

'Paurava's infantrymen did not know where to take refuge. Their commanders instructed them to keep their shod feet on dry ground to avoid being struck by lightning. But heavy rain made this impossible. The famed archers of Paurava, equipped with special six-foot high bows, could not set their bows down on wet slippery mud,' he said, describing the chaotic battlefield.

'The monsoons are an enemy like no other,' Guruji grunted.

'Nature sided with the Yavana. And to confuse Porus and his scouts, Alexander, who remained in disguise, spread his army over several miles along the banks of the Jhelum while his look-alike strutted around in one of the bigger camps,' the monk said.

Alexander's Army Face War Elephants

'Alexander was still dressed in a common soldier's livery, but his men made no mistake in identifying him. The Paurava double agent also knew this well.

'After the Porus heir was killed in battle, Alexander's Paurava agent informed him, "their cavalry fled from the battlefield. But Porus the Elder has now come on his war elephant to fight. His second son commands a regiment, far away from his father, but near you, the real Alexander."

"I think the time is right to cross over the river," Alexander said, his face flushed, as always before a battle. Alexander then commanded the rest of the cavalry and infantry to swim across the shallow part of the river.'

'The generals and commanders went out to brief the men.

'The downriver banks of the Jhelum bore witness to probably one of the worst battles Alexander's army has ever faced,' the monk explained.

'Why do you say that?' Guruji asked.

'Well, Alexander's men, led by an inexperienced Seleucus Nikator, had to face Paurava's raging elephant troops which gored, trampled, and wreaked unimaginable havoc on the unfortunate Yavana soldiers and terrified the horses. When inexpert Yavana soldiers foolishly shot arrows or hacked the war elephants with spears and swords, the furious pachyderms stampeded both Paurava's and the enemy's soldiers, equally destructive for both sides.'

'"This is the mother of all battlefields – so many out-of-control pachyderms," Seleucus swore under his breath, saying, "our horses bolt at the mere sight of an elephant."'

'A double agent rode up.

"General, King Alexander's horse Bucephalus has been mortally wounded by King Porus' second son," the spy informed Seleucus, who promptly reported the culprit to Alexander, who vengefully chased and killed the young prince.'

'Both kings lost something dear in battle that day.

Alexander, Bucephalus and, Paurava, his two sons,' the monk told Guruji.

Oomphis Fails to Negotiate

Hours later. The battle had raged for a while and was going nowhere near an easy victory.

Keeping tabs on the Yavana movement by pigeon post and double agents, and riding a couple of hours behind the Macedonians, Prince Sashigupta followed Alexander's route.

The bodies of men and horses littered the battlefield as far as the eye could see. Nearby, the water ran red with the blood of corpses. More than half the day was over, and the Paurava army showed signs of exhaustion. Thousands had died in battle, several thousand of Paurava's army, and more than 900 of Alexander's men. Neither side looked like they were going to stop before complete annihilation.

"Negotiate for a truce, Oomphis," Alexander told Ambhi.

This instruction touched Ambhi at the right spot. Thrilled at the chance to impress his new friend, he omitted to tell Alexander of his prior fiasco with Paurava. Looking much like a wily cat that had spotted lunch, a slow bandicoot, Ambhi rode confidently towards Paurava's bull elephant. But his attempt to look heroic failed when Paurava, spotting his old enemy, threw a spear that missed Ambhi by the narrowest of margins. Ambhi scurried back in undignified haste.

Alexander saw this and became thoughtful. He did not want a brave adversary like Porus to die and it looked like Porus would not submit to defeat.

But help was nearby.

Meroes and Porus

Agents of Guruji rode to inform Prince Sashigupta, 'Your

friend Paurava the Elder is in grave danger of being killed in battle.'

Hitherto, Sashigupta Maurya had followed the Yavana at a discreet distance, and stayed away from the battlefield. Now, Vijayta had caught up with Alexander. On Guruji's advice ('No bahirika knows that you are the illegitimate son of Dhanananda'), Sashigupta was disguised convincingly as his own fake, pony-tailed elderly father, Ramagupta Meroes. The grey-haired 'elderly' man rode up alone to Alexander and introduced himself.

'I am Ramagupta Meroes, father of Sisicottus. Do you want any service from me, esteemed Yavana?' he spoke in a quavery voice.

He was taken to the real Alexander in a few minutes.

'I do! Porus is a brave man, I do not want to kill him. Can you help me, Prince Meroes?' Alexander asked the 'old' man.

'He is my friend, I will convince him to surrender,' the 'elderly' Meroes promised.

Disguised as he was, Sashigupta dismounted, and holding aloft a gold-colored pennant, walked towards the massive elephant of Porus, easily the largest on the battlefield.

'Stop! I come with an offer,' Sashigupta said in his quavery voice.

King Paurava atop his beloved elephant, stopped shooting arrows and waited for the Maurya Prince to reach him.

'Who are you?' King Paurava asked gruffly.

'Come on, do you not recognize your friend under the wig? I am Sashi from Patala,' Sashigupta said in his normal voice.

'Prince Sashi, I trust you come with a proposal?' Paurava said.

'Your two sons are dead, dear Paurava. Make peace with Yavana Alexander. Ambhi's treachery can't get worse than this,' Sashigupta told his friend.

'Valid point. I trust the Yavana more than that old goat,' the king said.

King Paurava had sustained nine wounds. When he stepped down, his bull elephant tenderly pulled out the arrows, one by one. The 'elderly' Maurya prince handed over his leather canteen to King Paurava who drank some water, and then, Paurava limped across the battlefield to meet the real Alexander, who had changed back to his king's livery, with the telltale plumed helmet of a Macedonian conqueror.

'Like a King...'

Handsome, rugged, the seven-and-a half foot Paurava walked over to Alexander, who, seated on a new horse, accepted Paurava's surrender. Even in defeat, blood-stained, limping, armor ripped, Paurava looked regal. Alexander was impressed.

'How would you like to be treated, O King?' Alexander asked.

Paurava answered, 'Like a King.'

'Don't you want anything for yourself?' Alexander said.

'Everything is included in what I said,' Paurava replied.

'Sire, don't trust him,' Ambhi moaned, his visage crumpling like a desiccated gourd, at the thought that not only would Paurava escape annihilation, but worse, gain Alexander's friendship.

Alexander, however, raised a hand to stop any dissent. King Paurava stood, royal, fearless.

'I restore your kingdom to you, for a nominal tribute, Porus,' Alexander said, waving his hand at the flooded river plain behind Paurava. 'I also grant you land from the Glausea as a gift and make you my satrap,' he announced.

'Thank you, Yavana Alexander, I will remain your friend

lifelong,' Porus bowed.

A crestfallen Ambhi looked on, muttering to himself. The 'elderly' Maurya prince, humbly thankful, wished Alexander and Paurava goodbye, and rode back to Varana.

June-end 326 BC
River Jhelum

Alexandria, Bucephala and Nicaea

'HOW WAS IT?' Guruji asked. The grey-haired man in front of him first wrestled with a mass of hair on his face, and then a grizzly wig, both being stuck with a glue resin to stop them from sliding off.

'I nearly made a mistake, I rode straight to the real Alexander even though his lookalike headed a small arm of crack infantry troops. At the last moment, I swerved and went to the fake Alexander and asked him if he needed a go-between to speak to Paurava. Fortunately, the Yavana did not suspect my proposal and took me to the real one. And luckily Paurava recognized me at once,' Prince Sashigupta said.

'So, success?'

'A win-win. Paurava surrendered. He lives. The Yavana forgave him… gains a friend,' Sashi replied

'Losses?' Guruji wanted details.

'Paurava lost several thousand men, two sons and the battle. Alexander lost 990 men and his horse,' the prince said.

'Exceptional. No outcome from the battle could be better. But why so many casualties?' Guruji asked.

'I guess the Paurava army was unprepared and uninspired, not battle ready,' Sashigupta shrugged.

'Lesson learned. So, is the Yavana moving?'

'No, Teacher, right now, the Yavana is devastated as his horse Bucephalus was killed by a Paurava prince, so his general, Craterus, is building Alexandria Bucephala, named after his horse.'

'Where is Bucephala located?' Guruji asked.

'On one bank of the Jhelum. On the opposite bank, where he battled Paurava, Craterus will set up Alexandria Nicaea, which means victory. Alexander will move once Bucephala is ready.'

Sashigupta's information was right. As weeks went by, Alexandria Bucephala shaped into a military garrison town under Craterus' supervision.

At Varana: Snakes of the Subcontinent

Days later…

A man in dusty riding boots carrying several circular metal scrolls tied with leather string around his torso, dismounted. Sashigupta, Guruji and their men became quiet as they acknowledged the pony express man's greeting.

'Xerxes, what is happening with the Yavana?' Guruji asked.

'The monsoon. He has moved his army to higher ground to keep dry till his next sortie,' Xerxes informed.

'And are they dry?' Guruji sounded amused.

'Not much. Bhumi Devi, Mother Earth, seems to have connived with the monsoons to stop Alexander from marching further into Indika,' the express man hazarded.

'How so?'

'The Yavana army is coping poorly with rain, thunder and lightning,' Xerxes told them.

'Typical monsoon.'

'And snakes, massive king cobras and kraits are leaving soggy river-level ground for the higher, drier ground the Yavana army camps are occupying, and democratically biting anything on dry land. Horses, men, dogs. Macedonian doctors are helpless with the scale of the snakebites. And if this was not enough, gigantic scorpions, also seeking dry ground, are upping their misery.

"Sire, we do not know how to treat venomous Indian snake bites," the Macedonian royal physician and the army physicians repeatedly complain to King Alexander,' Xerxes said.

'Alexander then gave a directive, "Ask King Porus or Sissicottus to send snake bite physicians. After all, snakes must be biting Indians too."

'Alexander's secretary Eumenes messaged Paurava for doctors to treat venomous snakebites. Paurava immediately sent poison experts, toxicologists, to meet Alexander in his tent.

"Tell me about the venomous snake situation," Alexander asked.

"There are 65 varieties of poisonous snakes here out of a count of 275 species. But we have to worry about only six, both deadly and dangerous. Three types of vipers, one krait and two kinds of cobras. These six are both venomous and aggressive."

The vaid opened a pouch and pompously handed six stuffed snakes to an unimpressed Alexander, who commented, "My mom sleeps with them. What else?"

"Some snake bites are 'dry' bites, meaning the snakes bite without injecting poison. For the poison bites, we have medication."

"Excellent!" Alexander handed back the stuffed snakes. "Snakebite experts can man my tent. Inform all soldiers to go to the King's tent for snakebite medical aid," he informed Eumenes.

"We will proclaim this through the trumpeter, Sire," Eumenes said.

"Right away!" Alexander nodded.

'The vaids went to Alexander's tent to attend to their first batch of patients as the trumpeter blew a long, attention-getting note,' Xerxes concluded.

'Good update,' Guruji looked approvingly at the pony express man, saluting as he left.

The Two Vaidyas, July 326 BC

The message from Eumenes arrived in Varana. In the light of an evening fire on the terrace, Guruji, head and face covered as protection from vile monsoon winds, interviewed two attractive young vaids. One aged 28 and the other 25, the first a son and the other a nephew of Sashigupta's royal vaidya. Both were expert toxicologists.

'Keep in mind that Alexander cannot resist handsome young men. He may expect favors from you both. Become Alexander's lovers, only to further our cause,' Guruji briefed them.

'I need to bid goodbye to my wife, Guruji' the older vaidya said.

'Return soon. We need a few of our men on the inside, beyond suspicion.'

'Yes, Guruji!'

Both young men touched Guruji's feet. They would depart for Alexander's camp the following day.

The Guru-Shishya Story

Night time in Varana.

Guruji and Prince Sashigupta relaxed under a clear star-sprinkled sky, miraculous during monsoon. In front of them was the young acrobat from the West.

'I am intrigued with Alexander,' Guruji said, warming his cold hands above a crackling bonfire. 'He honors Paurava, dedicates a city to his horse, brutalizes Bessus for assassinating Darius,' Guruji said thoughtfully.

'And gifts me Varana for helping to defeat its inhabitants,' Prince Sashigupta added.

'Tell me, what air did he breathe, what soil grew his food, whose voices he heard growing up,' Guruji's intrigue was quite evident.

He smiled encouragingly at the acrobat who was contorted into a scorpion-shape, legs curved backward over his head like a double sting.

'What is the unstoppable Yavana made of? A man who demolished the more than 200-year-old Acheamenid Empire?' Prince Sashigupta asked.

The acrobat carefully eased his head out from under his legs, not an easy feat, and sat up.

'Alexander's first influences were his parents, Olympias and Philip. When Alexander was born, General Parmenion defeated the Illyrian and Paeonian armies. As a child, Alexander was nursed by Lanike, sister of Cleitus the Black.'

'Who Alexander killed while drunk?'

'Who else. As Macedonian nobility, Alexander trained in reading, playing the lyre, riding, fighting and hunting. And he was coached in Mieza by scholar Aristotle.'

'The great man himself? Tell me more,' Guruji slapped his thigh enthusiastically.

'When Alexander turned 14, Philip appointed Aristotle as his son's tutor, which he remained until the prince turned 20.'

'What did Aristotle teach?' Guruji asked.

'Logic, nature, ethics and politics. The latter two, Aristotle believes, covered practical knowledge to live happily. Aristotle considers happiness as man's goal, achieved with what a man does best. And that life should be governed by reason.'

'He sounds like a good teacher. Alexander lost a good mentor by killing his teacher's nephew,' Guruji gave a gusty sigh, adding, 'What topics, I ponder, Aristotle taught his students.'

'Very soon, your juttu will be knotted again and you will have an ashram brimming with students,' Prince Sashigupta said consolingly.

The Making of Alexander – His Heroes

'Tell us about Alexander's idols,' Prince Sashigupta turned to the acrobat, who had, in a few seconds, done somewhat a *padmasan* and was now swinging on both palms, body in the air.

'Alexander idolizes Persian emperor Cyrus the Great,' the acrobat said.

'Founder of the Persian Empire?' he asked.

'The same. Cyrus' grandfather Astyages tried to kill his grandson because of a prophecy that Cyrus would overthrow him. But Cyrus, protected by a shepherd as a baby and later restored to his parents, raised an army, overthrew his granddad, ruled Media, Persia, Lydia and Babylon, and called himself "King of the World."'

'And Alexander wants to better his record,' Guruji said shrewdly.

'Alexander is inspired by the *Iliad,*' the visitor said.

'The saga of the Trojan War with heroes like Achilles!' Guruji exclaimed.

'Alexander also looks up to Heracles (Hercules), son of God Zeus and Princess Alcmene. Hercules died when he wore a poisoned robe, mistakenly given by wife, Deianira.'

'Anything else?' Guruji asked encouragingly.

'Alexander thinks he is on par with Heracles, because Olympias has dinned into him that he is the son of God Zeus.'

'But poison can kill even the sons of gods,' Prince Sashigupta said.

'Past, present and future.'

Guruji dropped some coins in the acrobat's palm and all three hurried inside as a roll of lightning lit the landscape, followed by deafening thunder. The monsoon had returned to her ornery self.

River Beas: An Enemy Like No Other

Thanks to Varana's location, weekly visitors were aplenty. Now, a bald-pated visitor was updating teacher and prince.

'I think our Yavana is up to something.' Guruji's intuition was again on the mark. 'Please update us.'

The monk smiled.

'After the dirty battle fought with Porus, Alexander's demoralized army has had to face all the travails of an Indian monsoon.'

'An enemy like no other,' Prince Sashigupta chortled.

'All around the army's march path, rivers overflowed and flooded the plains. Meltwater from Himalayan snowfalls swelled rivers, worsening floods. Soldiers had to cope with insect infestations and tropical illnesses in damp weather. The damp rotted their food supplies. The rain corroded weapons, buckles, belts. Their boots leaked. Their wagons were useless on land that became swamps overnight.'

'The Indian monsoon is thrashing the Yavana's men,' Guruji chuckled.

'And, after the loss-heavy victory with Porus, the weary Macedonian troops had to next face the ordeal of Sangala.'

Sangala: Everyone... an Alexander

'Background?' Prince Sashigupta asked.

'Sangala, southeast of the Jhelum, was the principal city of the Kathoians.[1] They chose a low hill with a defensive line of "carts" near their capital from which they hurled missiles at Alexander's army. Alexander led the first cavalry attack himself, then realized that the cavalry was no use, since the average ratio of cavalry against infantry was roughly 1 to 10. He replaced them with infantry for assault,' the monk said.

'Smart move,' Prince Sashigupta said, 'Then next?'

'Alexander sent mounted archers to the front, to fire long range to prevent an enemy sortie. He positioned Agema cavalry, Agrians and Companions to the right. The Silver Shields were placed close to Companions of Perdiccas and infantry phalanxes of Meleager, Attalus and Gorgias. Alexander was assisted by Ptolemy.'

'And this worked well?' Prince Sashigupta asked.

'Barely. The Kathoians fought with such fury that Alexander sought reinforcement from Paurava, who arrived with 5,000 soldiers and a few elephants, but too late to participate,' he said.

'And the Kathoians?'

'When the Kathoians felt pressured by veteran

---

1 Modern Sialkot.

Macedonian footmen, they abandoned their positions and fled back within their city walls. After a four-day siege, Sangala fell. Eight thousand Kathoians died, another 9,000 perished when the Macedonians razed Sangala to the ground and 70,000 Kathoians were taken prisoner. The raids continued into the surrounding countryside, and systematically, the old, wounded and sick were slaughtered. Alexander's army witnessed a unique custom in Sangala. It was the first time they saw the practice of *Sati,* women immolating themselves on their dead husband's pyre.

'So moved was Alexander by the fierce Kathoians that he wrote to Olympias, "*I am involved in the land of a leonine and brave people, where every foot of the ground is like a wall of steel, confronting my soldier(s). You have brought only one son into the world, but everyone in this land can be called an Alexander.*"'

'Sangala demoralized the already disheartened Macedonian army, Macedonians wounded were exceptionally high. It turned out for Alexander, a psychological defeat,' the monk added.

The River Ocean – the End of the World

'Alexandria Bucephala is shaping into a classic citadel, with features like archer lookout points, and a moat occupied with medium sized mugger crocodiles. So, Alexander stopped thinking about it and made plans for his next strategic incursion into India.'

'South or east?' Prince Sashigupta asked immediately.

'Reports from the east of India told of unimaginable riches.'

'Some part of the Nanda Empire and the Gangaridae lie east, Alexander's scouts have told him. So, Alexander moved east – towards meltwater swollen River Beas, and met with his generals. "Listen men, if we travel east, we will come to the river called Ocean that is the End of the World,"' the monk reported.

Guruji snorted. It was a mere snort, but Guruji managed to put a lot of meaning into it.

The monk grinned and said, 'Loyally, the generals went to their men and announced that they would start a new conquest into eastern India. But the worn out, elderly soldiers rebelled. They squatted in front of Alexander's tent and did not stand up when he came out to check the commotion.'

Coenus Confronts Alexander

'A revolt?' Sashigupta asked.

'Totally. Infantry commander Coenus met Alexander near the bank of the swollen Beas, to convey how his troops felt.'

The monk continued, '"Commander, it has rained continuously for 70 days, the Beas is in constant flooded state. The soldiers are fed up with Indika," Coenus began.

"They will get over it," Alexander cut in, nonchalant.

"And demoralized with elephant attacks, snake bites," Coenus said.

"That's temporary," Alexander said impatiently.

"Tropical diseases have killed veterans who survived an 11,000-mile march. Their wounds don't heal in Indika. They will mutiny, they want to return home," Coenus continued obstinately.

"Memnon will bring 6,000 cavalry and 7,000 infantry from Thrace," Alxander's optimism was missing the point.

"The men oppose further fight with elephants. All of the Gangaridae combined have a deadly war elephant corps that defeats every enemy. A successful man knows *when to stop*," Coenus added bravely.

'This statement finally went home.

"How dare you? How dare you all? I want my conquests to extend to the end of the earth, to the River called Ocean," Alexander was livid. He disappeared into his tent, and remained two days, sulking. Coenus and the army top brass remained quiet.'

The Seers and Soothsayers

'On the third day, Eumenes entered the tent to see his boss shedding unladylike tears.

"The army is holding me to ransom," Alexander wept, adding, "They are forcing me to call off further plans to invade the rest of Indika."

"Sire, speak to your seers," Eumenes cautiously suggested.

'Alexander called a meeting with his intuitionists and astrologers, soothsayers and diviners. All were of the same mind.

"The signs are ominous, nothing good will come of this sortie to the east," the astrologer forecast. The intuitionist and soothsayer vigorously nodded their heads in agreement. This prophecy finally changed his mind.'

'And gave Alexander a way to save face,' Sashigupta commented.

'He called in the generals. "Commanders," he addressed them, "Change of plan, we will travel south towards the Sea."

'Coenus went out and addressed the army, which cheered loudly at the prospect of leaving snake-ridden, rain-soaked Indika for healthier and "easier" conquests.

"The conquered territories, Lord Alexander?" Eumenes asked.

"Divide them between Oomphis and Porus. Let them have a truce, maybe an exchange of brides, before we travel towards the sea. Let Oomphis have the land between the Indus and Jhelum, while Porus can have the land between Jhelum and Beas."'

'Good account!' Guruji exclaimed.

A few coins changed hands.

Between Chenab and Ravi: Porus the Younger

The acrobat was visiting Guruji again. The old man liked to gossip with youngsters, the more chatterbox the better.

'Just as soon as Alexander announced to his army that he would abandon the assault into the east of India, Memnon brought reinforcements. But they were too late. Alexander had already given his word that he would travel down the Jhelum,' the acrobat said.

'The Yavana left other Indian kingdoms in peace?' Guruji asked.

'Not Alexander. He sent sorties to kingdoms that had not accepted him as their king. He sent east across the Chenab a contingent to attack Porus the Younger, nephew of his friend, Porus the Elder, who hated each other. Porus the Younger's kingdom lay between the Chenab and Ravi rivers. Alexander's military reputation intimidated many rulers, including Porus the Younger. The day after the sortie, a scout met Alexander.

"Commander, Porus the Younger has fled east," he informed.

"Hand over his territory to my friend Porus the Elder," Alexander instructed Eumenes.

'Loyal Porus was grateful. He wrote to Alexander about Dhanananda, "whose kingdom lay eastwards, southwards and westwards," saying, "the Nanda king was a man of low origins, obsessed with wealth,"' the acrobat told his audience.

Alexander Seeks a Philosopher, September 326 BC

All the gossip said that Alexander was moving in a different direction. Now that conquering the rest of India was no longer an option, he decided on a new kind of conquest, his own self. News of this reached Guruji and Sashigupta through their double agents.

'And what military quest is the Yavana up to now?' Prince Sashigupta asked.

In front of him was a seller of illegal wild meats, himself looking like a wild creature with long nails, unwashed beard and bits of dead leaf sticking to his body. Earthen pots filled with animal carcasses, with a stray horn and hoof sticking out, were stacked outside.

'Non-military,' the meat seller corrected him, adding, 'Alexander wants to add an Indian philosopher to his entourage.'

'Hindu or Buddhist or Jain?' Prince Sashigupta asked, dragging his eyes away from a tell-tale antler peeping out from under a banana leaf.

'The monk called Calanos[2] by the bahirikas,' he replied. 'Alexander approached the white-haired old man. After earnest pleading, the old man agreed to accompany Alexander to teach him,' the meat seller said.

'Oh, oh! Calanos is Alexander's new preceptor?' Guruji stretched out his hand.

'Yes, Guruji,' the meat seller humbly cupped his hands to receive his payment.

---

2 Believed to be a gymnosophist from a Hindu sect in Taxila. Hermits of this sect wore very few clothes and adopted a very frugal lifestyle.

'I wonder what our next bit of information will be,' Guruji spoke his mind out loud. He didn't have to wait long.

A familiar visitor arrived with a few small companions, some weeks later.

November 326 BC
Warring Republics

The Salt Range, Gandhara and Thal Desert

THE MADAARI WAS half-heartedly restraining a black-faced mischievous *langur*,[1] who had taken a liking to the prince.

'How is the Yavana spending his time?' Sashigupta asked, firmly holding the langur's thieving paws from stealing his ornaments.

'Offering goats to the gods.'

'Oh, bali! Divine interventions for the Yavana's military life?' Sashigupta chuckled.

'Everyone believes so,' the madaari said.

'What is he up to now?' Sashi prodded.

'A small contingent of Alexander's men crossed the Ravi and received the surrender of Pimprana from the Adraistai,' the madaari said.

'Smart Adraistai!' Sashigupta smiled, extending one hand

1 Semnopithecus is a genus of Old World monkeys native to the Indian subcontinent.

to pet the wrinkly black face. It was a mistake; the langur took this as encouragement. 'Next?' the prince prompted.

'Alexander then went on a sortie to the southern Salt Range, a hill system bordering western Kashmir and River Jhelum, the Thal Desert, the kingdom of the Sophytes,' the madaari replied.

'The Saubhuti?'

'Yes. After subduing them, he sent a party of raiders cross-country to Gandhara, which had escaped his attention when Ambhi befriended him. The ruler of Gandhara did a bunk and Alexander took over without trouble.'

'Why go back towards Gandhara? Why is inter-nation contact between India and Macedonia so important?' Sashigupta asked the old man, who was listening in silence.

'The Yavana probably has good reason,' Guruji said thoughtfully.

'After which, Alexander crossed the Thal Desert overnight, surprised the aggressive chieftains west of the Jhelum, and won the battle,' the madaari said.

The Warships Change Route

'His next move?' Sashigupta checked the langur's tiny paws from exploring his ponytail for a snack.

'For several months, on the banks of the Beas, Alexander built a flotilla of 1,000 warships and appropriated another 800 merchant ships and barges. Dragging the collapsible warships from the Beas, across the Ravi and Chenab, to the Jhelum, was a task. The original purpose of these ships had been to sail down the River Ganga for Alexander's failed military pursuit,' the langur's handler explained.

'But the army mutinied,' Sashigupta reminded him.

'So, Alexander was forced to move his army three ways,

starting November. One part travelled down the Jhelum in warships. The second part on the east bank under Hephaestion and the third down the west bank with Craterus, Hephaestion's arch enemy,' he told them.

'They don't get on?' Sashigupta asked, pulling out the langur, who had managed to get under his civilian armor when his attention had wandered a bit.

'Not in the least,' the madaari said.

After a bit of chitchat, the madaari chained his monkeys and left, his fist full.

The Malloi Ally with Kshudraka and Siboi

The next day, in the cool afternoon, a kapata sanyasi, a fake holy man visited. Guruji and his protégé, squatting on the floor cleaning his swords with blackened fingernails and an assortment of oil cloths, were paying him full attention.

'What's the latest on the Yavana?' Guruji had asked.

'This month, Alexander began his voyage down the Jhelum towards the sea. The rivercrafts were laden with medical supplies and clothing. The Jhelum was about two and a half miles wide at that point and 40 oared galleys sailed side by side. Alexander was moving down Jhelum towards Chenab when a scout came on board.

"Updates?" Alexander asked.

'The scout informed him about the warring republics.

"On the banks of the Beas are the Kshudraka. Down the Ravi lie the war-loving Malloi, who rule over lush croplands both sides of the river. Their traditional enemies are the Kshudraka. But now, to rout your army, the two enemies have united to prevent you traveling through their territories, after exchanging prisoners. The jungly Siboi also decided to join in", Alexander was informed.'

'Fearless warriors, all. I wonder how the Yavana will deal with them,' Sashigupta murmured.

'Dealt with, like only the Yavana knows how,' the kapata sanyasi chortled. He added, 'when news spread that the Malloi were uniting with Kshudraka and Siboi to attack them, the exhausted Macedonian army was demoralized. Alexander had to use his damnedest best as a leader to rally them around. To prevent the tribes merging, Alexander raced down the Jhelum in five days.'

'That fast?' Sashigupta was surprised.

'And that too, after the fleet ran into trouble at the spot the unruly Jhelum met the volatile Chenab,' he replied.

'What kind of trouble?' Sashigupta asked.

'Designed by Greek and Macedonian engineers, the warships had double rows of oars. The bottom row of oars got stuck or snapped like twigs in the swampy banks of the Sapta Sindhu rivers. Some soldiers died in accidents,' he explained to them.

'Foreign technology,' Guruji commented.

'Indian rivers!' Prince Sashigupta countered, adding, 'No other problems?'

'There were plenty. The lead ship carrying Alexander had a close disaster and Alexander, who can't swim, nearly drowned when his ship almost sank,' he said.

'But he escaped?' Guruji murmured worriedly.

'He did,' the kapata sanyasi said.

Why the Siboi had to be Defeated

'While the ships were being repaired, Alexander split his army, crossed to the Jhelum west bank. He attacked the Siboi, who, clad in animal skins and armed with crude wooden clubs, were easily captured. But their chief delayed meeting

Alexander's general. After the Macedonian soldiers destroyed their rudimentary power center, burnt their crops, killed the men, and sold women and children into slavery, the Siboi chief met Alexander's general,' the visitor said.

'Why did Alexander care to subdue a small uncouth jungle tribe like the Siboi?' Guruji was curious.

'He needs the line of communication from Babylon to the Sapta Sindhu river system open at all times. And trade routes from India to other lands needed to be free of tribal interference,' he explained to them.

'Got it,' Guruji growled in approval, 'Communication and trade rule during peace or war. Darius I built the 2,500 km Royal Road from Susa to Sardis, Turkey, for the same purpose.'

A Sangala Disaster, from the Agalossoi

'Alexander's Indian spies informed him that some free Siboi and Agalossoi had united, and were about to ally with the rowdy Malloi near the confluence of the Chenab and Jhelum. Alexander massed his flotilla and spearheaded his men into an arrow-tip formation to split the three forces,'

'His trademark!' Guruji commented.

'The Agalossoi mustered 40,000 infantry and 3,000 horses, but in a bitter battle, were annihilated by Alexander's troops, and their two citadels captured. The second citadel was a vitiating Sangala-type disaster. The Macedonians suffered huge casualties and war-wounded.'

'Did Alexander build his usual trophy?' Guruji asked.

'Alexandria in the second citadel. Yes, but in a tearing hurry,' he said.

Knowing that no more infomation was forthcoming, Guruji handed over some coins and said hospitably, as the smell of roasted wild fowl wafted towards them, 'Eat before you leave.'

The Malloi and the Kshudraka Fallout

The young acrobat from the West was visiting Guruji and Prince Sashigupta again. After an almost impossible set of maneuvers, he lowered himself into a sitting position, sweaty all over.

'Can you tell us about Alexander's latest battles?' Prince Sashigupta asked.

'In small pieces. Alexander's spies informed him about the Malloi and the Kshudraka rallying at the confluence of Jhelum and Chenab. Admiral Nearchus and the repaired warships established a base at the confluence to capture escaping Malloi or Kshudraka. Alexander recalled Polyperchon's brigade, horse bowmen, Philip's corps, cavalry and a limited number of elephants to aid Craterus on the west bank,' the acrobat said.

'How many Malloi and Kshudraka troops?' Sashigupta inquired.

'Eighty thousand infantry, 10,000 cavalry, and 200 war chariots.'

'Did they succeed?'

'How could they? Reflecting a peculiar Indian ego problem over who was to lead the combined forces, the alliance between the Malloi and Kshudraka broke down, and both groups retreated to their own citadels.'

'How did Alexander take advantage of this?' Sashi asked.

'Two days later, Alexander asked both Craterus, on the west bank and Hephaestion, on the east, to surprise the Malloi,' he replied.

'That was Alexander's countermove?' Sashi was surprised.

'Yes,' the visitor said.

Coenus Dies

'He is lucky that the army follows him without hassles,' Guruji said ruminatively, with evident admiration for Alexander's leadership abilities.

'On the contrary, infantry veteran Coenus, who had represented mutinous soldiers when they resisted travel into eastern Indika, died mysteriously. Rumor is he was finished off for giving voice to the malcontents in the army,' the acrobat revealed.

'The Yavana trusts very few people?'

'Not even a handful,' the acrobat said.

'And the Yavana now?' Guruji asked.

'Has begun intense battles with the Malloi again,' the acrobat said dolefully.

Torsion Catapults

'When the infantry arrived, Alexander sent Perdiccas and his own cavalry to besiege a second Malloi stronghold, but asked them to desist from attacking it, and wait for him to get there,' the acrobat continued.

'King Alexander does not trust his veterans to complete a task without his personal supervision?'

'Correct. Alexander attacked the first citadel with Torsion Catapults, special siege equipment invented by his father Philip,' the visitor informed them.

'How do they work?' Prince Sashigupta, ever the weapons man, asked.

'Torsion catapults use torsion springs, which work by torsion or twisting through a flexible elastic object that stores mechanical energy. When twisted, it exerts a force in the opposite direction in proportion to the angle twisted,' he explained.

'Were the catapults effective?'

'With them, Alexander's army overcame the city's defenses, killing nearly all the 2,000-strong Malloi garrison,' he said.

'The Malloi are kaput, then?' Sashigupta asked.

'Not them, not yet!'

The Second Malloi Stronghold

'What happened next?' Guruji asked.

'Alexander gave his tired veterans a rest before his next move on the Malloi, who were showing no signs of giving in.

'The Malloi decided to fight Alexander in the mountain range on the west bank of the Ravi, but as Alexander approached, they bolted. When the fleeing Malloi realized how small the contingent of Alexander's soldiers was, they decided to fight the Macedonians. But after Alexander's men surrounded them, they fled precipitately into their citadel, which had two sets of walls,' he explained to Guruji.

'His next move?'

'Alexander followed them with half his force of soldiers. The citadel had thick, difficult to-ascend walls. Alexander crashed through one of the gates and then decided to destroy the inner walls. He ordered scaling ladders be brought to the wall. Impatient with his tardy men, Alexander climbed a ladder, followed by three bodyguards. When the excited Malloi realized who had come into the citadel almost single-handed, they attacked Alexander from all sides,'

'Foolhardy, very foolhardy,' Guruji grunted gravely.

'With adroit fencing, Alexander mortally wounded their leader, but he himself was struck by a leaf-shaped arrowhead in the left lung. He fought furiously till he fainted. Bleeding profusely and unconscious, he was protected by his ferocious bodyguards.'

'Then bodyguards are the key,' Sashigupta interjected.

'To keep safe. When his abashed men entered the citadel, they placed him on a shield and speedily took him to a tent where Perdiccas removed the arrowhead, no surgeon being anywhere nearby. In revenge, every human in the citadel was massacred.'

'Poor Malloi. Is King Alexander okay?' Guruji asked.

'For a few days, Alexander hovered between life and death, surrounded by highly anxious soldiers.'

'Anxious?' Guruji asked.

'… because they believed only Alexander could take them home. A rumor that he had died spread like wildfire. To prove he was alive, Alexander, still feverish, hopped on his horse and rode amidst his men, who touched him as he rode through. The Yavana took some time to recover,' the visitor concluded.

'Abandon Territory, Avoid Alexander', January 325 BC

Winter rains had frozen the land. Huddled around a smoky bonfire of moist aromatic leaves, prince and guru were questioning the young acrobat, who was now balanced on one palm, while the rest of his body stayed at a crazy 60-degree angle to the ground.

'And how are the Nandas coping with these offensives on their vassal territories?' Prince Sashigupta asked.

'Well, after the first Malloi stronghold's destruction, chief minister Rakshash met with a double agent, a wandering salesman, who was full of news about Alexander's ruthlessness. "He uniformly annihilates all enemy citizens, killing men, and selling women and children", he informed Rakshash.

'Rakshash sensibly sent out orders via pigeon posts to all heads of Nanda villages and townships to "abandon territory and hide".

'The nagariks, citizens, lost no time obeying the order.

'Aiding the nagariks was the fact that Alexander had given his men a day's rest. When Perdiccas arrived at a Nanda township in the southeast, below the Jhelum-Ravi confluence, he found it abandoned. He furiously killed the few nagariks outside. Many townships Alexander attacked, Nanda vassal strongholds, were completely abandoned with the nagariks having taken refuge in the countryside. These included vast areas downriver of the Jhelum-Ravi-Chenab-Beas-Sutlej confluences, and parts of Arachosia too,' the duo was informed.

More abandoned Nanda lands, February 325 BC

'Alexander was at a loss with the large number of abandoned territories. A scout brought a shepherd to meet him.'

'Alexander had only one question, "Why?"

'"The nagariks followed Nanda chief minister Rakshash's directive", he was informed.'

'More scouts came to tell Alexander that Raja Dhanananda's other townships and citadels were also empty of people and wealth, the nagariks being forewarned by Rakshash. Alexander took a dim view of the situation. Before the next attack on the Malloi, he met with Peithon and Demetrius.'

"March towards the rivers, forests and deserts of Nanda territory, and decimate those citizens who think they escaped me", he ordered.

'However, it didn't quite work out the way he wanted.'

'Why not?' Sashigupta asked.

'Because four days later, Alexander reached a rich, fertile administrative center devoid of people, horses, cattle and wealth. Plus their king, chief minister, generals and viceroy too.'

'Alexander did not have the dubious pleasure of subjugating Raja Dhanananda or his brothers. Rakshash had seen to it.'

"Whose capital is this, abandoned of all people?" Alexander asked.

"West Nandawati, Sire," the scout replied through the interpreter.

"And why pray…?" the king said.

"The old story repeated, Sire. The crafty Nanda chief minister Rakshash sent the army, courtiers and common citizens east to the badlands on the edge of the Indian Desert, and west to the Thal Desert beyond the River Jhelum", the scout informed Alexander.

"Makes it easy for us!" Alexander exclaimed, giving in to the inevitable. "Let's rest", he ordered.

'His aging army was glad.'

'While the army took a break, Alexander constructed Alexandria Ucch,[2] near west Nandawati and turned to the Malloi, still in fight mode.'

The Malloi Again, and Again, February 325 BC

A circle of men in battledress, his senior commanders, met Alexander on the warship's deck.

"How do we surprise this many-headed Hydra, the Malloi, Generals?" Alexander asked.

"Cross-country infantry ambushes should do the trick," one of them suggested.

'"Tell me a place no one thinks is a battlefield," Alexander asked his Indian spies.'

"The Bar is a deserted plain between Chenab and Ravi," said an animal catcher, who doubled as an intelligence officer.

"Ok! The Bar then," Alexander declared.

---

2 Uch Sharīf, southern Pakistan.

More Malloi, trapped at a ford across the Ravi and attacked from all sides, with no escape, were annihilated.

Alexander's assaults on the Malloi met with total success, since his intelligence gathering was thorough.

This was reported at Varana to Guruji and the prince.

'A point we should make our own,' Prince Sashigupta said.

The Sabarcae Tribe, February 325 BC

'Give me more intel about King Alexander,' Prince Sashigupta said.

In front of him, the woman mendicant was calmly rubbing a narcotic herb between her palm and thumb.

'Marking his route, Alexander set up Alexandria Opiana. Below were independent republican tribes, Abastonoi, Xathroi, Ossadoi. And more Malloi. All of them, except the Malloi, submitted to him.

'After that, Alexander advanced on the Sabarcae, a leader-free democratic republic, with 66,000 warriors and 500 chariots.'

"What is wrong with these people? No one wants to surrender," Alexander said in wonder to Hephaestion and their Indian interpreter.

"King Alexander, for millennia, India has been ruled by democratic republics, tribes and confederacies. Have a treaty with the Sabarcae," the interpreter suggested cautiously,'

'He took the advice?' Guruji asked.

'Conveniently. His elderly veterans need rest,' she replied.

Sword-wielding Brahmins of Atari, March 325 BC

Keeping a keen eye on the Yavana had become second nature to Prince Sashigupta. A trained intelligence officer, an ash-smeared kapata sanyasi, visited Varana to update Sashi on Alexander's travel itinerary.

'Alexander's army in the boats resumed their journey south, towards the sea. They have massacred 80,000 nagariks and sold prisoners into slavery,' the officer informed.

'Unafraid of bad karma,' Guruji grunted.

'It gets worse. Downriver, west of the Indian desert, the citadel of Atari ruled by a brotherhood of equals, martial, sword-wielding Brahmins, revolted against Alexander's foray into their lands. Alexander stormed Atari and burnt it. Five thousand Malloi were eliminated. All 17,000 sword-wielders were annihilated including, Prince Sashi, including..,' the kapata sanyasi stammered.

'My acharya too?' Prince Sashigupta looked upset.

'A knife blow! Dronacharya-type warrior acharyas are now extinct. Can no one stop him?' Guruji growled.

'Actually, Calanos, his new mentor, tried to restrain Alexander. "Warrior Brahmins must not be attacked. Each Brahmin warrior carries a curse if you kill him. It is bad karma", Alexander was advised.

'Did Lord Alexander listen?'

'No, he chose to turn a deaf ear to the old man,' came the reply.

'We need a message to be sent to our two vaidyas, verbally,' Guruji grunted.

'Which is?' Sashi asked.

'Befriend Iollas, Alexander's wine pourer, discreetly. God knows if the Yavana decides that we are expendable too.'

'I will need to travel a bit. The Yavana has resumed his journey downriver to the sea,' their intelligence officer responded.

'Thanks! We wait breathlessly for the Yavana's next move,' a grim Guruji said as he handed over some coins to the kapata sanyasi, who took some instructions from Sashigupta.

325 BC The Hindush

Mousikanous, Oxykanos: brothers in foolishness

IT WAS A full moon night, a *poornima*, and Varana palace gave off a ghostly blue glow. Guruji and Prince Sashigupta were talking to a late-night visitor, the jester, now updating them about the affairs in the south, and King Alexander.

'Dhananandaʼs former vassal, King Mousikanous (Sishunag) first submitted, changed his mind and then attacked Alexander, making him more intolerant,' the jester said.

'He slew Mousikanous?' Sashi asked.

'He then explored the area, whose people live for 130 years, and never use gold or silver though the area abounds with gold and silver mines. This territory, part of the Hindush satrapy, sent the maximum gold to the Persian empire as tribute via Raja Dhanananda,' the jester said.

'But became independent after the underground chamber calamity,' Guruji pointed out.

'And foolish. No one learnt from Mousikanous,' the jester continued.

'No one?'

'There were repeats. The kingdom of Oxykanos (Oxycanus whose king was Porticanus)[1] accepted and then opposed Alexander, who impatiently sacked these two cities. Tribal chief Sambo submitted and then attacked the Yavana, who less than thrilled with such copycat behavior, killed Sambo and sacked his citadel Sindhimana.'

'A good report. Please continue with updates,' Guruji yawned. The jester left.

Truce with the Malloi

A skinny young acolyte in saffron clothes and headgear a tad too stylish for his kind, was fiddling with some lengths of colored cloth.

'The latest on Yavana face-offs, Dhoomal?' Guruji asked.

'The Malloi campaign lasted till March. They had a last, fortified city. When Alexander captured the Malloi citadel, they and a few Kshudrakas, came to a truce. The Malloi gifted him 1,030 four-horse chariots, a thousand Indian shields, tame Asiatic lions and tigers, cotton goods, tortoise shells, skins of large lizards and 100 talents of gold. After the truce, the Yavna turned liberal with his men,' Dhoomal informed his audience.

'How so?' Guruji asked.

'Philip was made satrap of territories next to Porus, below the Jhelum-Chenab confluence. Peithon, who had expertly commanded infantry phalanxes, was rewarded with a satrapy around the Indus river, which included Sindhimana. For Seleucus Nikator's aid in defeating the Malloi, he was put in charge of a complete regiment,' the young agent briefed prince and teacher.

---

1 Mousikanous: Ref Strabo. Oxykanos: Ref Arrian

'We heard he is liberal with his soldiers too, giving them advance salaries equal to months and even years' pay,' Guruji remarked.

'Oh yes, he's a generous man, the Yavana,' Prince Sashigupta laughed.

Patala Citadel and Harbor, April 325 BC

'Where is King Alexander now?' Prince Sashigupta asked the ash-smeared kapata sanyasi, who was visiting again.

'At your old home, Patala. He has docked there as his translator pointed out to him, "Sissicotus' river citadel, King Alexander. That solitary well-preserved building was his royal residence, completely booby trapped."

"O Zeus! This badly-damaged wreck was Prince Sissicottus' citadel?" Alexander was surprised.

"And destroyed by none other than his biological father, the crass Dhanananda."

"The one who Porus wrote about? Not surprising. My biological father also lacked in paternal love," Alexander commented.'

'King Alexander then built a harbor at Patala, where his navy docked, rebuilt it into a citadel. Admiral Nearchus and the navy will sail around the coast to the Persian Gulf. Alexander himself will march through Gedrosia with the bulk of his army towards Babylon,' the visitor informed Guruji and Sashi.

'So, the chances of him returning are?' Prince Sashi thought aloud.

Both Guruji and the kapata sanyasi shrugged.

The Four-fold Army, April 325 BC

Some months had passed. A few townships under Sashigupta's satraphood had refused to send tribute. In Varana, Prince

Sashigupta, Guruji and the all-purpose Dhoomal were deep in discussion with the woman mendicant who was summing up the latest on the Yavana. 'On the way to Babylon, the Yavana constructed Alexandrias Pertus and Khambakia. When Alexander left his territories in the possession of his satraps and moved west, many defeated kings rejected his orders,' she said.

'Dhanananda?' Guruji asked.

'Has returned to Nandawati, and under orders from Rakshash, the Nanda high command will once again attack lands now beyond Alexander's reach,' the mendicant responded.

'A good king needs to keep foreign aggression in check with a well-equipped army. And internal dissension with a special covert field force,' Guruji pointed out.

'Hah! My father is now the "good king?"' Prince Sashigupta mockingly said.

'Thanks to Rakshash, he can be anything,' Guruji said drily.

'Right now, I worry more about my father's external army than internal dissension. What is the strength of the Nanda army?' Prince Sashigupta asked.

'The Nandas are nearly 20 times our number,' Dhoomal replied.

'Correct,' the mendicant nodded her head.

'What formation can "subdue" Dhanananda's army?' the prince asked.

'All kings in India use the four-fold elephants, chariots, cavalry, infantry formation. Each chariot or elephant has five horse units. And each horse rider commands six foot-soldiers,' Guruji explained.

'To defeat the Nandas with a fraction of the manpower, we need to re-strategize,' Prince Sashigupta concluded and told his secretary, 'Call my commanders.'

'And the treasurer,' Guruji added. He bowed apologetically to the mendicant, who took her payment and left.

Commanders and the treasurer arrived together.

'What is the state of our internal revenue?' Prince Sashigupta asked the treasurer, who looked grim.

'Some townships have stopped paying tribute to Varana. Now that Yavana Alexander has moved a safe distance away, his Indian territories have risen in revolt. The territory around Varana is no exception,' he was briefed.

'I see. How is our army faring?' Sashigupta asked the infantry commandant.

'Let me see. Up and down the land, new regiments need to be raised, infantry battalions, military engineering units, mule supply trains. The best men were recruited as mercenaries by the Yavana, so our troops are mainly non-Kshatriya,' Ramagupta began, taking off his sword and gauntlets, preparatory to starting a monologue.

'Non-Kshatriya?' Sashigupta cut in, adding, 'That's bad news. How are our ordnance depots?'

'Ordnance is the only thing going smoothly as they report directly to you, Prince Sashi,' the commander said.

'Five hundred warships...'

'What about our waterside situation?' Prince Sashigupta asked naval commandant, Commander Muthu.

'Not good. Either pirates or Nanda naval craft have begun to attack our solitary craft in the dead of night.'

'Naval night raiders?' Sashi was surprised.

'Yes, Sire,' Commander Muthu replied.

Prince Sashigupta said, 'Any Nanda intel?'

A young man clad in the livery of a humble Nanda stable

cleaner, bowed and spoke. 'I was removing horse dung outside the private court a couple of days ago, when the Nanda admiral announced to the Nandas that their navy had "damaged 500 enemy Varana warships and merchant vessels", he said.

Prince Sashigupta roared and slapped his knee. 'And the Nanda reaction to this bilge?' he asked.

'Raja Nanda and the whole court bellowed with approval,' the stable hand replied.

'And then?' Sashi asked angrily.

'Rakshash spoke, "Let's decide on our next strategy. Sashigupta is too far off to help his navy,"' he informed the prince.

'Okay, if Rakshash has commented, then it is noteworthy,' Prince Sashigupta said. 'I need backup for this information,' he whispered to Guruji.

Guruji cleared his throat and said nothing. He agreed. Backup came in the form of a pigeon post.

The Sashigupta high command read in court, '*five hundred warships of Prince Sashigupta....*'

Commander Muthu chortled, 'We have just over 200 warships and barges, three dozen catamarans with the self-protective plava and 20 merchant vessels. The Nanda navy has more than doubled the number destroyed to scare coastal townships.'

'Or boasted to get honors from king and Amatya,' Guruji said shrewdly. 'Tell us about our navy.'

Sashigupta's Naval Fleet

'Our ships are either merchant vessels or fishermen's boats plying up and down the river. We need escorts as deterrent to the Nandas' open piracy,' the naval commander said.

'Before we invest in more ships, fill us in on what our

ships are bringing us, other than fish,' Guruji asked.

'Essential cargo like rice, cooking oil, etc. are being shipped to key transshipment ports along the Sapta Sindhu,' he was informed.

'Ship building for internal trade must be converted to ship building for military use,' Commander Muthu said.

'Justify,' Guruji snapped.

'In packs of five warships, the Nandas are attacking our poorly escorted convoys. We are losing not just food but also imported goods shipped from the west to upriver Indus. And several tons of our cargo have been lost within days to Nanda-financed pirates,' Commander Muthu explained.

'Commander, a way out?' Sashi asked.

'Our navy craft are being decimated or captured faster than we build them. I think we should contact our allies for aid. If the warships are made away from our soil, maybe the ships might be saved,' he proposed.

'That's a good idea. Who do we contact for a joint venture?' Prince Sashigupta said.

'Paurava the Elder?'

'Ideal! Paurava is dependable in emergencies,' the prince sounded optimistic.

'And he owes us. Dhoomal!' he yelled. 'Send the pigeon post man,' the prince ordered.

A man covered in pigeon droppings entered in minutes and Guruji dictated a message for Paurava the Elder.

What Not To Do with Your Army...

'Fill us in about Nanda army stats,' Prince Sashigupta said to General Ramagupta, who was unrolling a piece of parchment.

'We need to consolidate all our newly acquired territories for a strong kingdom. Our army should be well-trained, well-paid, honored and united, not like the Nanda army, who are usually paid only after a victory or tax raid.'

'Okay! Lessons from the Nandas, what not to do with your army,' Sashigupta said aloud.

'The Nandas do not honor bravery in battle,' the General said.

'And?'

'They do not rest their army after Acts-of-God disasters,' Ramagupta continued.

'Plus?' Sashi probed.

'Their army is forced to fight even after battlefield loss or after their commanders flee the battlefield,' he added.

'Bad for morale! Besides this?'

'Untrained Nanda soldiers have to fight on hilly, jungle or desert terrain.'

'Disadvantage?' Sashigupta asked.

'Though a larger army than ours, the Nandas have caste-based army units and commanders, something we do not tolerate,' Ramagupta remarked.

'And?'

'The Nandas have a vast network of double agents in and outside Nanda territory.'

'That's bad?' Sashi was confused.

'Nanda covert operatives feed the enemy wrong news, and also their own commanders so that they get paid well by both sides,' Ramagupta revealed.

'Double agents that do double espionage!' Prince Sashi chortled. 'Call my agents. I need backup intelligence reports on Dhanananda.'

Prince Sashigupta's secretary returned with two young widows, both cooks.

'Tell us the latest about the Nanda army,'

'After the Yavana left, the Nanda C-in-C disbanded some garrisons and sent them to the interior, near the mosquito-ridden marshland, causing an epidemic of water-borne diseases. Many troops are down with uncontrolled diarrhea,' the first cook said.

'Good! A sick army cannot fight as equals with a healthy army,' Sashigupta commented.

'Horses are down too with worm infection; veterinarians are working round-the-clock to cure them. For some reason, elephants are unaffected, but the *mahouts,* elephant minders, are ill,' the other cook added.

'Excellent. A sick army will not fight when men and animals are both ill. Gives us time.'

Sashigupta's Army, May 325 BC

Varana palace. A week later.

Seated around an immense table covered with maps, the commanders, the treasurer, prince and Guruji were in an impromptu meeting.

'Army stats?' Prince Sashigupta asked.

'Crack cavalry bowmen are being trained, and small numbers of horse, elephant and camel troops are also being taught to take on any terrain, desert, river and seaside, jungle, and plains. No war chariots, though,' General Ramagupta began.

'Army morale?' the prince asked.

'Good, but we need to pay them,' the General said.

'I agree. An unpaid army fights well if we pay them before battle,' Guruji's voice rasped out. 'An un-honored army fights better if honored and incentivized,' he advised.

'How are we paying the army?' Prince Sashigupta turned to the treasurer.

'Revenue comes in through fines, levies, taxes, leasing

out difficult crown land to farmers and crown water rights for fishing. Irregular revenue through ambushing luxury caravans,' the treasurer said.

'Is the revenue enough?' Sashigupta asked.

'No, Prince,' the treasurer admitted miserably.

'Tribute from surrounding townships?' Sashi continued to ask.

'Dhanananda has arm-twisted townships to pay him tribute, instead.'

'Treasurer, any other means to make more money?'

'Well, during wartime, our agents can sell goods on credit at twice the price to make extra money. That can recruit more soldiers. And sell honors to the newly-wealthy who have no status,' the treasurer said.

'Brilliant!' Prince Sashigupta said, 'Start ASAP.'

Everybody, except the guru and the prince, rose and left the room.

Paurava to the Rescue

It was mid-afternoon. Outside, the sun burnt the treetops mercilessly. Guruji was interrogating his naval commandant, Commander Muthu. A few senior commanders were seated near the old man. Prince Sashigupta lounged on the wall, looking down at pedestrians outside the palace walls.

'What is the latest?' Guruji asked.

'Guruji, Paurava the Elder has sent 1,000 naval troops and 50 warships that will accompany our merchant ships in convoys of five. Paurava's special archers with six-foot bows man the ships. Paurava's biggest ship, named *Paurava Putra* after his late son, heads the convoy. Paurava has also sent a cargo of foodgrains and other supplies for Prince Sashigupta,' the Commander briefed Guruji.

'Our merchant navy can now export superior quality beads, khuskhus and sandalwood perfume (from the South), and gold and silver jewelry,' he added.

'Import goods?' Guruji asked.

'Fur and horses from Bactria, and excellent harahura wine, Guruji.'

'Hah! When drunk, we can blame the *Shaka* for harahura. What about our superior iron ore?'

'Guruji, thanks to our war requirements, the ordnance factories use up our entire weapons grade wootz steel. None is exported any more to Damascus for their famed blades,' Prince Sashigupta said.

'Excellent!' Guruji noted.

'How are former territories of the Yavana, Nandas and our own faring?'

'Prince Sashigupta, you have a loyal following in the interior and your former territories. However, many kings and republicans have increasingly begun to rear a defiant head, we suspect with Rakshash's help,' he was informed.

'Any good news?'

'Maybe. Each former Nanda village has orders to send five young men for Dhananandas army, but recruitment is limited to criminals on the run or low caste Chandala, Lubdhakas or Svapakas. Dhananandas commandants promised each man that joined the army an acre of free land.'

'So, try as they might with all the bribes, the Nandas are unable to get quality soldiers to man their army,' Prince Sashigupta laughed. 'Bad news?'

'Ashrams from villages that opposed vexatious Nanda taxes have been razed to the ground, scattering gurus and students. All schooling is shut, as teachers taught students to question repressive economic measures, including poverty-inducing

Nanda taxation.'

'Guruji, don't take this badly,' Prince Sashigupta said.

'Well, what can you expect from the Nandas?' Guruji grimaced.

Both guru and prince hunkered down to discuss damage control.

The Good Military Psychologist, June end 325 BC

As a method to consolidate territory, Prince Sashigupta would take small sorties through his territories and head back to Varana. This was one such incursion.

'What is your Yavana boss-friend doing? I need details, more details,' Guruji spoke to Sashigupta, who had just arrived, dressed as a court messenger for a fictitious kingdom.

They were in luck, news of Alexander's travels came from a passing letter writer.

'Updates on the Yavana?' Guruji asked.

'Alexander's army marched to Turbat and replenished supplies. Then he split the army, the fleet going to the Persian Gulf. The rest of the army went through Makran Desert adjoining Gedrosia, marching through sand dunes, their boots crammed with sand, their wagons, sinking. Water was a serious problem, and the army abandoned their route many times for drinking water. Plus, there was a plethora of poisonous snakes and plants, one type of poisonous cucumber squirted juice that blinded whoever's eyes it hit.'

'And how did Alexander keep up army morale?' Guruji asked.

'Well, when the thirsty soldiers gave Alexander a helmet full of water, he poured the water on the sand… an inspirational gesture that filled his soldiers with the feeling that their boss was their equal in war or peace, hunger or thirst.'

'Alexander is a good military psychologist, like you, Sashi,' Guruji nodded in approval. 'And then?'

Gedrosia, July-August 325 BC

'After a 100 miles and 60 days through Makran, Alexander marched to Salmous, where he met his army contingent that had taken the northerly route from the Indus Valley,' the letter writer said.

'Smooth journey?'

'Anything but. While traveling through the Kech river valley, flash floods from rainstorms in the mountains washed away the supply train. It carried food, water, and equipment, as well as weak soldiers, women and children. The 85,000-strong army shrank to 25,000.'

'And how did our Yavana react?'

'Alexander questioned why his carefully planned supply trains gave him the slip, the last moment. His spies reported to him that some satraps had become disloyal and corrupt. Enraged, Alexander killed Appolophanes, the newly-appointed satrap of Gedrosia without giving him a chance to explain why the supply trains failed.'

'He killed his own satrap?' Sashigupta croaked, looking aghast. Guruji gave him a warning look, saying, 'Then no one is safe.'

'That was just the start. Alexander executed five more satraps who had defied him. The result, the executions scared other satraps who then obeyed Alexander's orders to offload their mercenary forces.'

'Punishment, danda niti, works where virtuous conduct, dharma, is lacking,' Guruji summed up.

...we ate our own camels, December 325 BC

'After punishment, what did the Yavana do?' Sashigupta asked as he undid sticky white boots.

'From Salmous, Alexander went to the Strait of Hormuz to meet his wornout fleet under the command of Admiral Nearchus. When he met Alexander, the admiral had an unkempt beard, torn Indian clothes, and was badly sun burned.

"Nearchus, old friend, what happened?" Alexander asked emotionally.

"Our fleet sailed to the Persian Gulf, survived a school of whales that rammed our ships, unfriendly coastal tribes and a lack of food, that forced us to eat our own camels", the admiral replied.

"You okay, Nearchus?" Alexander's voice cracked.

'But the admiral consoled Alexander, saying, "The fleet is secure."

'Alexander was so relieved, he ordered athletic and musical fests to celebrate their safe return.

"Our next stop is Persepolis," Alexander announced at the end of the fests.

'After a march of 800 kms, Alexander reached Persepolis. When Alexander saw the burnt ruins of the Persepolis palace, he regretted torching it. From Persepolis, he left for Susa.'

There was a silence as this news was digested by the listeners.

'But before that, the 30,000 Persian boys sent some years ago to Macedonia for training, returned, making old veterans miserable and fearful that newcomers could now discipline them,' the letter writer concluded.

'Very good rendition,' Guruji said, dropping some coins into the letter writer's palms. 'I wonder what happens next in our unpredictable Yavana's life.'

Several months later, they got their answer.

Bahirika Marry Local Women, March 324 BC

Summer was showing signs of arriving early, everyone was thirsty.

'Can you tell us about the Yavana's political *shtrategies*?' Prince Sashigupta asked, his speech slightly slurred.

In front of him was an inebriated Xerxes, taking swigs of premium harahura alcohol.

'Kind of. The Yavana believes in symbolic gestures,' Xerxes said.

'As in?'

'The Yavana is no *shettler,* the locals know *dis,*' Xerxes was also slurring.

'What did he do now?' Sashigupta asked.

'To build trust between locals and conquerors, in March, six years after his last trip to Susa, King Alexander and his officers married local noblewomen in a five-day mass marriage between Persian women and 91 of his men, to blend Persian and Macedonian cultures,' the express man said.

'Alexander married Barsine, Darius' eldest daughter, mother of his first-born son Heracles. Alexander then married Parysatis, daughter of Artaxerxes III Ochus.'

'Why marry two royals?' Sashigupta was curious.

'By marrying the daughters of two consecutive Persian kings, Alexander broadcast that he was now rightful ruler of his conquered Persian territories.'

'Continue!'

'He gave Hyphaestion, Drypetis, sister of Barsine, so their children would be cousins. Seleucus Nikator married Apama, daughter of Bactrian Spitamenes. Alexander's secretary

Eumenes and Ptolemy, his bodyguard, married daughters of Artabazus. Nearchus married the daughter of Barsine and Mentor,' Xerxes said.

'So inter-nation weddings are the way forward,' Guruji chuckled.

'After the weddings, each man took his bride home, each woman endowed with a huge dowry from Alexander. Five days of celebration followed these weddings.'

'For the regulars, army numbers were swelled by 10,000 children of the soldiers, who by Alexander's orders, were trained in Macedonian ways,' the express man added.

'Maybe he wants to incorporate them into his army,' Guruji growled.

'Wait, Guruji, I haven't finished,' Xerxes interjected.

'Hold on, I am going to draw a map,' Prince Sashigupta unrolled a piece of parchment and started to mark it.

Recognition as a God..., May 324 BC

'Continue,' Guruji said nodding to Xerxes.

'Alexander and a few soldiers sailed upstream along Tigris, to prepare to invade Arabia. Wherever he found irrigation dams, he smashed them, as the agricultural activities of the area had no importance for him.'

'Our Yavana is eco-destructive,' Prince Sashigupta recollected. 'Remember Varana?'

'He also announced that his old, weary veterans, who had opposed his venture into eastern India, would be retired, sent home to Macedonia and replaced with new recruits.'

'The reason?'

'Many veterans were critical of Alexander's acceptance of proskynesis and the increasingly Persian style of administration. At a public meeting, Alexander jumped into the crowd, pulled out mutinous group leaders and ordered them to be executed. With the worst offenders killed, the remaining Macedonian commanders were demoted and replaced by Persians. This last move crumpled Macedonian revolt and after much groveling they were reinstated.'

'So, our Yavana can't endure even the slightest insubordination?' Guruji commented.

'The Yavana demands blind loyalty, like the kind he has for his own friends.'

'Example?' Prince Sashigupta asked puzzled.

'Hephaestion was made Grand Vizier, an office he abused with favoritism, bribery and corruption. In a short time, Hephaestion managed to become so hated by his veterans that Alexander was forced to send home 10,000 Macedonians under Craterus, so the rest of the army was not tainted by their anger.'

'Smart move. Getting rid of people who outlived their loyalty,' Guruji said calmly.

'That was just the start.'

'There's more?' Sashi was surprised.

'You bet. Alexander has sent a letter to the Greek states asking to be recognized as a god,' Xerxes said.

'God?' Guruji's grainy voice was in danger of chipping the walls. 'Mad man!'

'The letter provoked loathing and resentment in Athens. But Alexander was undeterred, he left Susa, near the mouth of the Tigris.'

'For another Alexandria! Thank you, Xerxes.'

Xerxes left, nursing a small, welcome flask of harahura booze and a thoughtful silence behind.

The Oath at Opis, May 324 BC

The traveling balladeer in court was immersed in his own song.

'Where have you come from, my good man?' Prince Sashigupta hurriedly asked the balladeer, when he paused for breath.

'From the former Persian kingdom.'

'Excellent! Please update us about our Yavana lord,' Prince Sashigupta said.

'Though Alexander killed those who opposed proskynesis, he has had a change of heart.'

'What change?' Sashigupta sneered.

'He has become a champion of the brotherhood of man, coached by Calanos.'

'How do you conclude this?' Guruji asked.

'Through the oath at Opis,[2] which tried to unite his conquered territories from Egypt to Macedon to Indo-Persian territory into one whole. I can reproduce his lofty speech, I wrote it down,' the balladeer offered.

'Nothing could please us more,' Guruji grunted encouragingly.

The balladeer solemnly read, '*I wish all of you, now that the wars are coming to an end, to live happily, in peace. All mortals from now on will live like one people, united and peacefully working towards a common prosperity.*

You should regard the whole world as your country, with

2 http://profgvk.weebly.com/alexander-the-greats-oath.html#:~:text=(OPIS%2C%20324%20BC)&text=From%20now%20on%2C%20may%20all,for%20the%20good%20of%20all.&text=will%20govern%20regardless%20of%20their,into%20which%20they%20were%20born.

common laws, a country where the best and brightest rule, regardless of race.

I do not separate people, as do the narrow minded, into Greeks and Barbarians. I am not interested in the origin or race of citizens. I only distinguish them on the basis of their virtue. For me each foreigner is a Greek, and each bad Greek is worse than a Barbarian.

If ever differences arise, never resort to arms, but resolve them peacefully. If need be, I will serve as your arbitrator. Do not consider God as a dictatorial Ruler, but as the Father of all, so that your conduct would resemble the cohabitation of siblings of one family.

On my part, I consider all of you equal, white or dark, I would like you not to be only plain subjects of my commonwealth, but all shareholders, all partners.

To the extent it is in my power, I shall try to accomplish all that I promise, keep the oath we are taking with the libation tonight like a contract of love.'

'The oath at Opis combines Greek and Indian influences,' Guruji said reflectively.

'The Yavana filled with late regret?' Prince Sashigupta sounded unconvinced. 'Over the decimation of more than 80,000 men, women, and children?'

'The east-living Greeks, 17,000 sword-wielding Brahmins?'

'Towns razed, cities sacked?'

'Can it snow in summer? Doubtful!' Guruji summed up tersely.

Prince Sashigupta asked cautiously, 'Have you told this news to anybody?'

'Everybody, Sire. Meat-food courts on the highway, Nanda soldiers.'

Though Prince Sashigupta and Guruji did not exchange glances, both knew what the other person had concluded. The Nandas were waiting to pounce on conquered territories of the Yavana.

The balladeer was quiet and taking this as a cue he had no more information to give, Sashigupta stretched out his hand, murmuring, 'Thank you, my good man.'

Both guru and prince were silent after he left.

324 BC Sapta Sindhu Mauryan Moves

Nanda Overtaxation, May 324 BC

THOUGH BUSY WITH plans for the invasion of Arabia, and other related activities, Alexander too got regular updates on Indika, this time from a wandering love expert.

'In Northwest India, change after change is convulsing your conquered territories, King Alexander. Prince Sashigupta is fighting a fierce battle for survival against militant republicans and his deadly father Dhanananda....'

'The reason?'

'There is no fear of you returning, so Dhanananda, back in Nandawati, has ordered assaults on all former Nanda vassals and satraps. Nanda regiments are ripping the countryside to shreds. And villagers are being severely overtaxed, when they have no money or grains to give, their cattle and sheep are confiscated.'

'My satraps?' Alexander asked, surprised.

'Weak and fearful.'

'Same old!...' Alexander was laconic.

Meeting Parvataka Raja

Back in Varana, scouts and double agents brought news that 'border villages were willing to enlist in Prince Sashigupta's army and take on the Nandas'.

Guruji and Sashigupta were elated.

'Good news. So many villagers enlisted into our army, without payroll. They must have reached the limits of their patience long ago,' Sashigupta sounded cheerful. 'If we have just one powerful ally, we can defeat my father's army. Parvataka Raja, whose territory lies between Ambhi and Kashmir?' he looked at Guruji.

'Yes, let us fix a meeting with him. I will leave early tomorrow,' Guruji said. 'Secretary!' he shouted.

A skinny young man with a long ponytail came running up.

'Arrange for my immediate departure to Parvataka Raja's capital, gifts and all.'

'At once, Guruji,' the secretary took out his scroll.

Northwest India, June 324 BC

In Himavatkuta[1], a small hill fort in the Himalayas, Guruji met Parvataka Raja three days later. He took a suit of wootz iron ring armor, special tri-blade swords and iron gauntlets, all three lightweight battle kit fit for a king.

---

1 Parvata Kingdom refers to the territory of a tribe known as Parvatas (Mountaineers), mentioned in the epic Mahabharata. Most of the descriptions of Parvata kingdom in the epic refer to a mountainous country in the Himalayas. Modern-day Himachal Pradesh, perhaps. Tribes belonging to other mountainous regions in the northwest, west and the east of the Indo-Gangetic Plain were also known as Parvatas, when used as a collective name. Parvataka Raja was how the chieftain here was called. Modern-day Nepal too was known as Parvatakadesh.

'I come with a message from Prince Sashigupta,' the old man said, as his bodyguard handed over the gifts to the king's secretary in the gaudy gilt colored public court. 'I request a private meeting with you, O noble king Parvataka,' Guruji said politely.

'Dismiss the court, we can have the meeting immediately,' Parvataka Raja waved towards the horn blower who sounded a long, low note of dismissal for the entire court. Parvataka Raja had no chief minister, Guruji observed, but he had a deputy, his porcine brother Vairochaka.

'Honorable Raja Parvataka, Prince Sashigupta requests you to ally with him and if our combined forces win, you get half the conquered territory for your participation.'

'Very good,' Parvataka Raja slapped his thigh in excitement. 'I value a friendship like this.'

Vairochaka smirked in agreement.

Guruji nodded silently. He knew greed, not friendship, motivated kings like Parvataka Raja. And he was aware that the Nandas would be informed by double agents very soon.

The Fight on Indian Land and Water

Guruji returned after five days with special turbans and jeweled shoes fit for a king. Both Guru and prince didn't need to talk. They already knew the next step without discussing it. The courtiers were curious, but neither the old man nor the prince said a word out loud, an agreement both had made to stymie double agents.

But the next day, 'Call the commanders to a meeting,' Guruji said curtly to the horn blower, who sounded a long, attention-capturing note.

This, and the roaring horn blower's oral command, informed everyone present of an important military meeting.

Several men in regimental livery vaulted over the tasseled rope in front of Prince Sashigupta's throne and seated themselves on ornate chairs in front of their boss.

'General Ramagupta, what is the state of our army vis-à-vis the Nanda forces?' the Prince enquired.

'Badly outnumbered.'

'By how much?' Sashigupta asked.

'A worse ratio than Patala, one to 20 or 25,' Ramagupta submitted.

'Excellent!', to everyone's surprise, Prince Sashigupta punched the side of the wooden throne with energy. 'Compactness is strength. Remember Guagamela where King Alexander's men won against the Persians due to high morale and military strategy,' the prince said.

Guruji smiled grimly at his protégé's enthusiasm.

Double Agents Do Their Work

'Send in our double agents,' Prince Sashigupta said.

Within an hour, two *vrshalas*, tonsured nuns, were ushered in.

'What news of the Nandas?' Prince Sashigupta asked them directly.

'When the Yavana traveled through our land, Amatya Rakshash ordered all nagariks to abandon the citadels. Neither army nor common citizens could be captured by Alexander's army. But, in the aftermath, many Nanda citizens are as homeless as our people after the Patala battle,' they informed the Prince.

'Where are the Nanda citizens?' Sashigupta asked.

'In no-man's land, barren territory beneath even low caste Chandala and Svapaka.'

'And the Nanda army?'

'The army crossed the Indus and captured forts from

forest tribals and republicans in the anarchic East bank, which anyway was so-called Nanda territory. Other forts either side of the Sapta Sindhu rivers, former Nanda or vassal territory, are occupied by Yavana garrisons,' they briefed the prince.

'Learn from the unconquerable Yavana. Lay siege to every Nanda fort on the way to Nandawati and take them one by one,' Guruji said.

'What about forts occupied by the Yavana's men?'

'As satrap to the Yavana, respect his Alexandrias,' Guruji said.

'And the riverfronts?' Prince Sashigupta asked.

'The Nanda navy is a bunch of pirates,' a vrshala said contemptuously.

'We know. So the way forward, establish two lines of defense, land and water. Either capture Nanda warships or sink them. There should be a sizable gap between destruction and production, the less ships produced by the Nandas, the better control we have of the waterways,' Guruji said.

'We lost about 1,000 tons of allied shipping craft pre-Paurava.'

'Right now, we do not know whether the Nandas are quiet because they sank our local watercraft before Paurava aid....'

'Or because our few warships have superior capability or the torrential rains,' Guruji added.

'What about the land?'

'Our night raiders, caravan raiders, guerillas are doing smash-and-retreat sorties on all road traffic in present Nanda territories,' he was told.

This conversation was overheard by a Nanda double agent, a fan-puller agitating khuskhus fans behind the audience court wall, who promptly faked a bad cough, and traveled overnight to Nandawati.

Prince Sashigupta's Army

Six days later, in Nandawati, the open court of the Nandas overflowed with foreigners and locals. In front of the king's throne, the fan-puller from Prince Sashigupta's court was bowed almost double, giving Rakshash and the army Commander-in-Chief information on the two lines of defense. The king himself was not made by nature or heredity to be an all-seeing administrator. This was Rakshash's job and now the Amatya was quizzing the general.

'General Bhadrasala?' Rakshash barked.

'Our navy is better equipped than Prince Sashigupta's naval squad. But right now, it is scattered. Yavana Alexander captured or sank several hundred tons of our warships,' General Bhadrasala said.

'Next move?' Rakshash asked.

'We need to free our merchant ships from the job of carrying cargo for export revenue. And we need to ally with pirates who terrorize rivers.'

'Prince Sashigupta's navy does double duty as merchant navy too,' the fan-puller added.

'Pull back our forces from the borders, which they were guarding against the possible return of the Yavana, and concentrate them where our kingdom is vulnerable to attack on all sides,' the chief minister instructed.

'I need an intelligence report about *zat* bastard, Sashigupta,' Raja Sarvarthasiddhi slurred, irritably aimed some betel juice at the spittoon, missed it altogether, splashing Rakshash and Prince Kaivarta.

'Prince Sashigupta plans to capture our abandoned citadels with his army garrisons,' General Bhadrasala said.

'How?' Rakshash demanded.

'Intelligence reports tell us that Prince Sashigupta has

contacted the tribal conclave around the citadels.'

'And?'

'Prince Sashigupta's army, wanting the support of warring jungle tribes, has assured them all military measures are only against our army. No tribals are in danger. Prince Sashigupta has warned the tribals that our army loots forest produces to enrich Nanda coffers,' Bhadrasala said referring to his intel.

'True. What is the composition of his army?' the shrewd chief minister enquired.

'Prince Sashigupta's army numbers are boosted by villagers and forest tribals, not too much of a threat. The best soldiers, Kshatriyas, were recruited by the Yavana. Guru Chanakya though, has recruited small numbers of Kushan, Bahlika, Shaka, Ashvaka, Gandharva and Persian mercenaries. With his key ally Parvataka Raja's help, a bilateral strike from two different places is possible.'

The king's younger brothers groaned out loud.

Covert Battles

'Where do we do battle?' Prince Kaivarta, more sober than the king, asked Rakshash, ignoring the groaning.

'Well, our citizens are still scattered, and we lack forts,' Rakshash said. 'Conquest of our old territories and settlement of virgin lands are needed to strengthen the kingdom. General?'

'Our war tactics will be *Gudayuddha,* covert war off the battlefield. Our *guda*, secret agents, will stay at important sites in occupations to fool the enemy. In each place, an undercover Intelligence Officer disguised as an ascetic will run covert operations,' General Bhadrasala said. 'And we must recruit jungle tribes.'

'Why jungle tribes, General?' Kaivarta asked.

'Advantageous, Sire. For instance, the jungle tribe Siboi,

bare-chested, clad in animal skins and armed with crude wooden clubs, are dangerous as they fear no one. They kill trespassers and owe allegiance to no king. Again, as the Yavana cannot return in a hurry… the "scorched earth" policy and tie-ups with jungle tribes are our way forward.'

The commanders agreed, drawing maps to plot further.

The fan-puller was given instructions in a roll of parchment. No one noticed the pockmarked hunchbacked jester in the Nanda court, taking "permission to visit my sick mother" since he did this all the time.

Tough Citizens

The hunchbacked jester landed at Varana a week later. Guruji and Prince Sashigupta were in a meeting with a few scouts and spies, along with the army commanders when he came limping in.

When Prince Sashigupta said, 'Speak!' the jester related all that he knew.

'The Nanda army has taken a leaf from our book. Nearly endless night sorties are being carried out against villages loyal to you, Prince Sashigupta,' the jester concluded.

'How many sorties, Commander Ramagupta?' Sashigupta asked.

'A few hundred,' he replied.

'That's seriously detrimental to our citizens' health and wealth,' the prince sounded worried.

'Moreover, Sire, villages are being abandoned by villagers loyal to you, some of whom have taken refuge in the jungles. Their animals have been scattered over a wide area to stop Nanda soldiers plundering livestock. Each abandoned village is being burnt by the Nandas as revenge for your past water-polluting activities,' Ramagupta said.

'Safe passages?' Sashigupta wanted to know.

'Stone citadels on hills are best resistant to fire. Homeless villagers are sleeping in rock tunnels at night-time.'

'General Bhadrasala deems hill forts *of very high nuisance value*,' the jester added.

'Hill forts are not easy conquests. How are the plains' villagers reacting?' Sashigupta asked.

'Bravely! The nagariks, citizens, are a tough lot, even though riverside villages are a mess,' he was informed.

Though they did not know it, news of Sashigupta's moves was being broadcast far and wide.

Sashigupta, the Ordnance Man

The restless Xerxes was wandering again, this time reaching Alexander's tent, somewhere in the foothills of the Zagros mountains near the border of Babylon.

'How does Sissicottus fare with his father?' Alexander asked Xerxes, still keen on keeping abreast of his old allies and satraps.

'Prince Sissicottus' war preparedness has reached a new high to win battles with his vile father,' Xerxes said.

'Explain!' Alexander said impatiently.

'To equip his army against the Nandas, Prince Sissicottus set up five below-ground ordnance factories, for army boots, gauntlets, shields, helmets with wootz steel and cow leather. Swords, daggers, arrow tips, spearheads are also manufactured.'

'That's it?' the king asked.

'No, King Alexander! Stand-alone machines that throw stones, and shoot arrows, flame throwers, fire dampers, and two-pillar *Bahu* are assembled too,'

'Indian stuff! Anything new that I could use?' Alexander, also a weapons man, enquired.

'There is *Sakthi,* a leaf-shaped spear, *Kunta,* a lance for horsemen, *Hataka,* a three-pointed weapon, and broad-blade sword *Bhindipala* for cavalry. Metal ring armor, sheet metal or cotton, wool or hair stuffed fabric as well as neck guards, breast and back plates, knee or ankle length coats, and thigh guards are also being manufactured.'

'These sound like infantry weapons.'

'The furnaces also churn out superior weapons for horses, elephants and chariots,' Xerxes added.

'"Superior" weapons are not enough. Darius and Guagamela are proof. What else?'

'Sisicottus is facing a blockade from superior Nanda numbers. Neither his, nor the Nanda troops or civilians can move back or forth. To keep out infiltrators, no new passports are being issued.'

'Oh, a stalemate!' Alexander exclaimed.

'And there is a food shortage. To overcome this, Prince Sisicottus transports food via convoys of ships plying between different river ports which he controls. Besides this, Sisicottus' army is training in offensive and defensive battle tactics.'

'With Sisicottus' battle preparedness, I wager it could go either way,' Alexander said. 'His biological father must be sore,' he smirked.

Xerxes laughed. He agreed.

'...Our Superior Naval Fleet', June 324 BC

How sore, it was visible in the Nanda court. The normally clear-headed Rakshash was aggrieved.

'Sashigupta's villagers are being supplied food. What happened to our superior naval fleet?' Rakshash asked the naval commandant sharply.

The commandant coughed and looked at the fan puller.

'The enemy have copied us. Our ships are being scuttled night-time by Prince Sashigupta's river troops, in ships flying the flag of King Paurava's navy. At night, Prince Sashigupta's merchant ships do double duty as war ships. Coracles and catamarans are docked on the north jetty at Patala on the Indus at night-time,' the fan puller said.

'Has Patala been salvaged?'

'Alexander constructed a harbor,'

'What is Sashigupta's intention?'

'The prince is seeking four kinds of forts, river, jungle, desert and mountain. His first river fort was Patala on the Indus. His mountain fort is Varana. He doesn't have desert forts, yet. But he is moving strongly in that direction.'

Let Diamond Cut Diamond... June 324 BC

Rakshash's temple began to pulse suddenly. 'What do you mean?' he snapped.

'Desert tribes come to Varana to be briefed by Prince Sashigupta,' an officer said.

'What for?' Rakshash barked.

'Varana is proxy headquarters for desert warfare.'

'Impossible,' a livid chief minister said.

'On the contrary, Sire. To train desert tribes in desert warfare, Sashigupta's men ride south to the Thal desert to train them in their own terrain. Prince Sashigupta has recruited camel troops.'

'Okay, let diamond cut diamond,' Rakshash said harshly. 'General?'

News of the Nanda countermeasure reached Sashigupta's court via the hunchbacked jester.

'With advanced intelligence from his covert operatives, Rakshash has also recruited desert tribes, so in a face-off, both communities of desert troops would attack each other,' he said.

'A deadly move for us, Prince Sashigupta.'

'Nothing we can't cope with. Take our camel troops out of the equation with Nanda camel troops. Instead, our camel troops will cross the desert to face the Nanda horse cavalry,' Sashi said cannily.

The Desert and Plains Battle, July 324 BC

In the middle of the ruckus of war, Rakshash was visited by a double agent, a Scythian importer of wine.

'I have information for your ears only, Amatya,' he said.

'Begin,' Rakshash instructed.

'Some border desert tribes have joined Sashigupta's army. Since fighting their own compatriots would be counter-productive for the desert warriors, Prince Sashigupta sent them to attack Nanda horse cavalry and plains' warriors,' the double agent informed him.

'Send in General Bhadrasala,' Rakshash growled at his secretary.

Once the general had walked in, 'Repeat what you told me,' Rakshash barked at the Scythian.

When the Scythian left, both men had a detailed meeting.

Gedrosia-Ahrmoz, July-August 324 BC

A few weeks later…

The Scythian had been busy. He had an audience with King Alexander and after proskynesis, was verbally vomiting everything about the fracas between Dhanananda and Prince Sashigupta.

'On the western borders of Dhanananda's kingdom lay the strategically important desert fort of Ahrmoz. You, King

Alexander captured Ahrmoz from the west Malloi, who had taken over from the Nandas. Ahrmoz is now under Sissicottus' control.'

'Why has Ahrmoz citadel such strategic importance?' Alexander asked.

'Ahrmoz splits desert from well-watered plains, keeps troops safe from flash floods and is perfect for desert or plains warfare. Besides, the tactical worth of Ahrmoz fort is immense. It is a watering hole for horses, camels and bullocks, as without water, the troops are stuck.'

'Who is Sissicottus' commandant?' Alexander asked.

'Commander Ramagupta, he briefs the desert tribal chiefs twice a day,' he replied.

'The outcome?' King Alexander asked.

'Inspired by you, King Alexander, Prince Sissicottus directed the camel desert warriors to travel overnight across the desert and attack the Nanda cavalry in plains, off the desert. Taken by surprise, the Nandas had no time to retreat into their citadel. About 5,000 Nanda foot soldiers were supposedly attacked by 1,000 desert warriors who surrounded and slaughtered them, and the Nanda cavalry in battle. No prisoners,' the Scythian explained.

'Post-Ahrmoz?' Alexander asked.

'Detachment after detachment of camel troops from Ahrmoz, backed by crack horse cavalry from Varana and foot soldiers on the flanks, chased Nanda cavalry off all land around Ahrmoz. Many villages and townships were captured by Sashigupta's men without effort. The villagers indifferent to who conquered them, yourself, Nanda or Maurya,' he informed the king.

'Good for my old friend,' Alexander said.

Prince Sashigupta Wins, September 324 BC

Disguised during the entire time, reaching Varana, Prince Sashigupta immediately went to Guruji and prostrated at his feet.

'We have won, thanks to your able guidance, Guruji.'

Raising both hands, the old man blessed Sashigupta. 'You fought valiantly, and the Gods were on our side.'

'However,' Guruji solemnly added, 'never underestimate a wounded and defeated enemy. Dhanananda has enough gold to buy up mercenaries of five kingdoms if he chooses and he has many kings as friends who escaped death in the underground chamber. Some of them actually admire your father for getting rid of so many opponents so easily. Dhanananda will fight again.'

'Our men need a break, Guruji,' Prince Sashigupta said quietly. 'We need to re-strategize.'

'You know best.'

Hephaestion's Death, Ecbatana, October 324 BC

Both Guruji and Prince Sashigupta had discussed their war strategy threadbare, when Xerxes dropped in to see them. 'What is it,' Prince Sashigupta asked Xerxes, who looked serious.

'I have some shocking news from your two vaidyas. From Opis, to recover the bulk of his Persian war loot, King Alexander took his army to Ecbatana, where the army went on an unrestrained alcohol bender.'

'The whole army?'

'The entire lot. Alexander and Hephaestion binged like famished alcoholics. Hephaestion died of alcohol poisoning this month.'

'Hephaestion dead? Actually dead?' Both Guruji and

Prince Sashigupta were staring at each other, aghast.

'Yes, Prince. When his Macedonian physician, Glaucios, failed to save Hephaestion, Alexander crucified him.'

'Poor man!' Guruji shook his head.

'Then, Alexander decided to punish the gods for their non-involvement in saving Hephaestion. He destroyed physician god Asclepius' Ecbatana temple,' Xerxes said.

'Seriously, punishing the gods?' Guruji's voice grated so badly, the walls were in danger of getting chipped.

'Yes, Guruji!'

'Only a megalomaniac…,' Guruji regained his composure. 'Next?'

'After Hephaestion died, Alexander lay on the body for a day and a night, his friends had to pull him off. He fasted three days and shaved his head. He ordered all ornaments of the city broken, and manes and tails of horses sheared. Banned music and ordered his conquered territories to take up mourning. You must have heard too. Alexander sent envoys to Ammon's Oracle in Egypt to request divine honors for Hephaestion, but there was no response.'

'The gods didn't approve,' Guruji said somberly.

'Alexander embalmed Hephaestion's body and sent it to Babylon. The funeral cost more than 10,000 talents.'

'And the effect on the Yavana?' Guruji asked soberly.

'Hephaestion's death crippled Alexander, he began to believe the gods had deserted him,' the express man said.

'Bad karma always catches up,' Guruji said thoughtfully. 'The curses of the massacred Brahmins, innocent Greeks, and multiple women and children returned to haunt him,' Guruji said, looking pensive.

'But he never learnt. A short time later, Alexander went

to the country of the Cossaeans[2] and massacred the lot as a sacrifice to his friend's ghost.'

There was a long silence, then seeing his friend in no mood for a drink, Xerxes tactfully left, his fist full.

Porus writes to Alexander, December 324 BC

Battles between Prince Sashigupta and his father Dhanananda were being seriously followed by kings and republicans all around the Sapta Sindhu, the land of seven rivers, and beyond.

News of the battlefronts reached Alexander too. Porus the Elder sent a note via pony express man Xerxes, who opened a silver cylinder and handed over the missive, a contemptuous assessment of Dhanananda, to King Alexander, who had sought an update.

It read, '*Dhanananda is not merely a man originally of no distinction but even of the very meanest condition. His father was in fact a barber. He lives for wealth alone.*'

'How does my trusty satrap Sissicottus fare with his father, Xerxes?' Alexander was curious. 'He pays monthly tribute without fail.'

'Sisicottus and Dhanananda are in a fight to death over territory. Sisicottus' military engineers and toxicologists have poisoned all water sources,' Xerxes said.

'The Indian way!' Alexander commented.

'The Nandas, under siege, are succumbing to poisoning of water reserves. Without drinking water, Nanda soldiers were routed. No prisoners.'

---

2 A tribe of mountain people settled in western Iran; their land was called Cossaea/Kossaîa. Ref: Diodorus.

'Sisicottus is winning battles?'

'Savagely!' Xerxes exclaimed.

'That's my man!' King Alexander sounded happy.

Women who Changed the Status Quo

Varana, December 324 BC

PRINCE SASHIGUPTA AND Guruji were seated in a large tent outside Varana, with commanders, double agents, secretaries and aides. A cooked-meat seller reeking of stale spices was standing in front of Sashigupta.

'What news of the Nandas?' Prince Sashigupta asked the meat seller directly.

'They are preparing to wage war, in the northwest from river banks to the mountainous north,' the meat-seller, also a double agent, spoke.

'Too many wars and battles undermine the peace of the countryside,' Prince Sashigupta said thoughtfully to Guruji.

'Our troops will have burnout. Let's discuss this in the evening.'

'I want victory with the least bloodshed,' Sashigupta said. 'All of you, meeting over. Let the army rest for the next two days. We will meet again before battle,' Prince Sashigupta said, certain the double agents in his company would head straight back to the Nandas with this news.

Guruji blessed the men as they left, raising his right hand.

As soon as the men left, Guruji called the meat-seller, double agent Tejas, again.

'It is now time for woman power, change tactics,' Guruji advised Sashi.

Dhara, the *Vishkanya*

'Women?'

'We must send our prettiest *ganika*s, courtesans, to kings who have switched loyalties to Dhanananda, especially the ones who implement Nanda war taxation policy,' Guruji began on the new strategy.

'Call the ganikas, they need to infiltrate the Nanda king's private chambers,' Guruji said. 'For this job, I need someone with loads of attitude.'

'Guruji, one of the ganikas was fined 5,000 panas by Raja Ambhi of Taxila for refusing to entertain a visiting general, the Nanda infantry chief.'

'Bring them all, let me interview them,' Guruji said calmly.

Tejas went to round up a few young ganikas. Sashigupta's secretary interviewed each one, one at a time in Guruji's private chamber. Guruji sat silent as each girl was interviewed. The last one in, was incredibly graceful.

'Ambhi Raja,' the secretary whispered.

Guruji sent the secretary to summon Prince Sashigupta who was training with his favorite tri-blade against two of his star warriors.

Guruji then turned his attention to the girl. Her faintly green skin at fingertips and toes screamed *vish kanya*, poison (beesh) damsel, a girl who had had exposure to poison from early childhood. She looked a mere teenager but turned out to be Sashigupta's age. Prince Sashigupta walked in silently.

The meeting between Guruji and the ganika went on for

nearly an hour. 'My daughter,' Guruji said after a lengthy discussion, 'We have an assignment for you. Your target is king Dhanananda himself....'

'But the Nanda infantry chief, General Bhadrasala, knows my face from the past,' she said.

'Don't worry, we will take care of it,' Prince Sashigupta assured.

At the end of the meeting, the ganika, her common name Dhara, pledged to work with the Nanda cohort. She would be paid a salary of 3,000 panas a year for attending to Dhanananda and the money would be paid clandestinely. She left the room after prostrating on Guruji's sandalwood *paduka*, footwear.

'Can we trust her? What if she spurns the king himself?' Sashigupta asked quietly.

'She wants to get even with the general and Ambhi for humiliating and fining her in open court. She will deliver,' Guruji sounded confident.

'Humiliation and fines?'

'Ganikas are subject to the biggest fines if they do not entertain a client sent by the king. This girl was insulted and fined 5,000 gold panas for refusing to entertain the Nanda army chief, who complained bitterly to Ambhi Raja. This ganika has an axe to grind with the Nandas, she will take special care,' Guruji said.

'I want someone who has had recent contact with the Nandas,' Prince Sashigupta told his secretary, who hurried to arrange it.

A Kushan Double Agent

Late in the day, Tan Mei, a Kushan double agent came to meet Guruji and Prince Sashigupta, who was being attended to by the royal vaidya. The prince had scratches on his arms beyond the gauntlet, where he had failed to protect them. The royal vaidya was pouring fresh neem leaf juice and dusting turmeric powder on the cuts when the Kushan entered.

'What do you know about the Nanda infantry chief? Is he in Nandawati?' Guruji asked.

'No, he is traveling south to recruit specialists in rust-proof iron-sword manufacture, basically to see that their weapons are a match for Prince Sashigupta's,' Tan Mei said.

'And when will he be back, precisely?' Guruji asked.

'In a month.'

'He must be delayed from returning to the capital,' Prince Sashigupta said.

'That will be taken care of.'

'Do you have any promising contacts in the royal household of the Nandas?' Guruji asked.

'I do, Guruji,' Tan Mei said. 'Nanda's favorite maidservant has an ailing mother in her village, it is common knowledge, and everyone knows this. She wants to head home to take care of her mother and will do anything, I mean anything, to go home soon. Dhanananda loathes giving any holidays for her to go nurse her mother.'

'She seems to be our card to defeat the Nandas without warfare. Very cautiously, contact the maidservant,' Guruji said. 'Collect some money from the treasury. Return once you have accomplished your tasks. Let me brief you on what steps to take,' Guruji outlined in minute detail what to do.

Guruji sent his secretary to collect some money. Tan Mei left.

'I was instructed by one of my early teachers that one lethal assassin can accomplish more disaster than a regiment full of crack soldiers,' Prince Sashigupta said calmly.

'Bank on her,' Guruji said.

Guru Chanakya had briefed the vishkanya well. She left for the court of Dhananananda, with an impressive escort dressed as men from the kingdom of Lampaka.[1]

The Poison Damsel in Court, January 323 BC

Some time had passed. Guruji had a garrulous visitor at noon, the pockmarked hunchbacked jester from the Nanda court. Prince Sashigupta was silently sharpening one of his favorite swords.

'Just the details,' Guruji cut in before the hunchback could drone on.

'Well, Dhara arrived at Nandawati with your impressive "Lampaka" escort. When she entered, she introduced herself as Nartaka, dancer, Dhara to Raja Sarvarthasiddhi, who is an expert in dance. The king, who had just begun to drink, immediately ordered, "Show us your favorite dance, nartaka".

'Your girl was ready, and instructed the court musicians and her elderly *vadaka*, musician.

'Her dance so mesmerized all, that when it finished, the courtiers and the king's brothers stomped their feet in appreciation. Raja Sarvarthasiddhi held out a lapis chain, an approval, and when she came towards him, pulled her on to his lap. Glimpses of Dhara's dark skin could be seen through the sandalwood paste.'

'Was she discovered?' Guruji sounded concerned.

'On the contrary, Raja Sarvarthasiddhi asked for a duet, and then the corpulent Dhanananda and Dhara danced, an obese Krishna to her slender Radha, matching eachother step for step.'

---

1 Afghans from Laghman province.

'As soon as the dance finished, Dhanananda roared crudely, "What next?"

'Rakshash answered, "The royal music room."

'The old vadaka was sent off to another part of the palace compound.'

'This music room, is it special?' Guruji asked the hunchback.

'It is connected by a permanently locked wooden door to the king's day suite,' he replied.

Chief Controller of Alcoholic Beverages

'Your girl Dhara lost no time in making important contacts,' the hunchback continued.

'How did she start?'

'She noticed during her court performance that Dhanananda loved his booze, and so she went to the Chief Controller of Alcoholic Beverages for a permit to buy alcohol.'

'Why is the Chief Controller a big deal?' Prince Sashigupta looked up from his sword.

'Alcohol sales, licenses and manufacture are state monopolies. The Chief Controller and a food taster – both certify whether a type of alcohol can be served or not.'

'Alcohol control is important?' Prince Sashigupta asked.

'Definitely,' Guruji said. 'Booze kills in wartime or peace because soldiers frequent drinking houses.'

'Dhara bought good-quality *Prasanna*, mixed it with the Vacha alcohol which the Chief Controller sampled and then approved as safe for the king. Dhara can now ply Dhanananda with alcohol whenever she wants.'

'Good progress,' Prince Sashigupta said.

'Her visit nearly got derailed when she returned to the music room on her first day. The two guards at the door refused to let her in as she was late, curfew being one hour after sunset. But when Dhara displayed the Prasanna booze in leather pouches, and begged them, she was allowed back in with a warning,' he said about her escapade.

'That was a close call,' Prince Sashigupta said. 'And then?'

Bali at the Temple

'Next day, after sunset, Dhara visited a tiny Devi, goddess, temple that would admit ganikas. A motley group was assembled.

'A young woman in green palace livery began to speak tearfully to the priest just after Dhara entered. "My mother is ailing and coughing blood. Give me some remedy to send to her," she pleaded.'

'The priest was instructing the young woman to break a coconut, when a palanquin suddenly appeared. The crowd melted away as the priest shut the outer sanctum door. Dhara too was about to follow the departing crowd, when she spotted the royal priest getting down from the palanquin. She hid behind a pillar and overheard snatches of conversation as the royal priest said authoritatively to the temple priest, "Midnight when the full moon is out, in the cremation grounds". Wondering what the priests were talking about, she noticed under the peepal tree, a turmeric-smeared lamb tethered to a stone with black smears on it. The lamb would be sacrificed,' the jester narrated.

'And this is significant, how?' Guruji asked.

'Dhara has accidentally stumbled on the royal experts on bali, the court and temple priests.'

'Does my father stick to animal sacrifice or…?' Prince Sashigupta asked.

'Rumor goes that before battle, a captured prince or high-born noble is sacrificed to Kartikeya, god of war,' the jester said.

'Human sacrifice for what unholy purpose?' Prince Sashigupta was aghast.

'To capture power over Earth, Heaven and *Patal*, the underworld,' Guruji explained.

'Power over the three worlds? On top of being the richest man in the country? Greedy bastard!'

'You need to return speedily, so your absence is not noted,' Guruji sent the jester out, after generously filling his fist.

The Veena in the Music Room

Back in the music room, Dhara set up her tabla, special flutes and the gold vessel of Vacha alcohol. A dusty, ivory-inlaid double bulb veena was also displayed. When Dhara tried to play the double bulb veena, it was hopelessly out of tune.

'The veena is off tune,' Dhara shook her head in frustration. 'Where is my vadaka quartered?' she asked the maid.

'I will take you there.'

The maid and Dhara left with the veena for the stark quarters outside the palace, a contrast to the sumptuous private and public areas within. The old vadaka was happy to get an unscheduled visit from Dhara. No one was talking to him, and he was lonely. After much string-pulling and tightening, the veena became well-tuned.

Dhara returned to the music room, settled down and started plucking the strings. It was back, the veena was out of tune.

This time, Dhara went without help to the old man.

'But I just now repaired it,' the vadaka looked puzzled. He again plucked and tightened the strings till they were in tune. Dhara thanked him and returned to her chambers, where she set the troublesome instrument back in its case and practiced singing instead. After a dinner of ash gourd cooked in yogurt, rice tempered with melted butter and mustard seeds, and honey bananas, Dhara went to bed.

Early next morning she did her daily ablutions, yoga, sang with the tabla, then danced to its beat through memory. Lastly, she pulled out the veena, positioned one bulb on the curved sole of her foot and the other over her shoulder. The veena played beautifully for a while, then turned off tune again. Dhara felt a tinge of irritation. The first three strings played well, but the fourth string had a flat note.

Patiently, she put her slim, small hand inside the veena and groped for the hinge inside. Her fingertips brushed against a lump. Carefully, she worked the lump loose, and brought it out. A small square of turmeric cloth wrapped around a brass stick figure of a king embedded with deep cuts. Black magic! The truth shone at her from the metal image, others had wanted Raja Sarvarthasiddhi dead as did his son Sashigupta. And the black magic had failed.

The maid yelled that snacks were ready, and she quickly hid the metal piece in one of the leather straps of the container that carried Vacha alcohol. She placed the veena on its stand knowing that from now onwards, the instrument would give no trouble.

The Tryst with Raja Sarvarthasiddhi

There was a knock on the door. A palace spokesman opened the door and stepped in.

'Any message?' Dhara asked.

'Raja Sarvarthasiddhi expects you at the morning bedroom within an hour,' he said.

Dhara thanked him. She would go to the royal bedroom

dressed in pure white.

Dousing Khuskhus perfume on important *mrus,* acupoints, all over her frame, Dhara walked to the king's morning bedroom, and knocked on the door.

A girl opened it.

'You must be Dhara,' she said, pointing towards a muslin curtain. The fragrance of southern sandalwood filled the air. Khuskhus fans worked by unseen fan pullers behind the wall kept the room cool and fragrant. Behind the curtain, Raja Sarvarthasiddhi sprawled uncouthly on a vermillion-colored bed, which heightened his blotchy skin. Jewels of all descriptions covered his torso. A girl next to him was holding a jug, Dhara guessed it had alcohol, imbibed liberally by the king, whose jaw was sagging.

'White, the color of an Apsara's clothes,' the king leered, waving his hand.

The girl left, bowing backwards and shut the door.

Dhara took the jug, smelt it and poured its contents into a gold wine glass.

'Sit on my lap,' the corpulent king said.

'Why not, your Highness,' Dhara gracefully lowered herself on his right thigh.

'Song and dance. Who was your guru?' Raja Sarvarthasiddhi asked, his breath smelling of cloves and alcohol, his hairy hand tracing patterns on her right breast.

'Acharya Vardhraj, your Mightiness,' Dhara smoothly interspersed her hand between the king's hand and her chest, some kind of warning telling her to do so, and slid off his lap to reach for the jug.

'Is your guru from Palani? Our court percussionist trained under Acharya Vardhraj of the Palani court.'

Dhara's heart gave a thud of fright. Whoever was the

double agent in the Nanda court, the jackass had forgotten this important little nugget of information, Dhara thought.

She slid back on to his lap.

'No, Your Highness, I first trained in a *tapovana,* in the north mountain foothills. A Guru-pupil school,' she said without hesitation.

'Who chose you, when the northern mountains are so far off?'

'My mother's family are court dancers for generations, my aunt danced for your late father,' she said.

Raja Sarvarthasiddhi lowered his face towards her neck, where he tasted a slight bit of salt.

'Your Highness is a good dancer, too,' Dhara heard a faint clink of metal anklet behind the bed, and alertly turned her head.

'Bodyguards.'

'Your first performance?'

'The late prince of Sirsanagar came hunting to our forest and got lost.'

'Late? His late father came to Nandawati for a free lunch – his last,' the king roared with laughter at the memory.

'That evening, in the temple, was my first public performance,' Dhara continued. 'The prince sent for me, and I became a taxpayer from then on.' 'And when did you go to Lampaka Raja?'

'After the Sirsanagar prince died, I was sent to Lampaka Raja, Sire.'

'And what other arts are you trained in?'

'Six string, astrology, romantic poetry, palmistry,' Dhara replied.

A Born Murderer

'Read my hands,' Raja Sarvarthasiddhi stretched his coarse hairy hands towards her, palms upward.

Dhara raised herself gracefully on one elbow and 'read' the hands.

'Animal strong,' Dhara said, as she stroked the rough skin of his wrist. 'Stubborn as wootz steel,' she flexed the rigid thumbs.

'Tell me stronger stuff,' Raja Sarvarthasiddhi sounded like an impatient little boy. 'How will I die, in battle, of old age or disease?'

'Your Mightiness will die in your own bed in sleep.'

'Alone or with a woman?'

She stroked the unnaturally cushiony Mount of Venus.

'Your Highness will never lack for love.'

'To die in my beloved's arms, paradise,' Raja Sarvarthasiddhi cackled sarcastically. Beyond the latticed screen, a woman's snicker came loud and clear, either a female bodyguard or a member of his huge female entourage, Dhara thought.

Dhara frowned at the lifeline curving deep and strong towards the wrist on the right palm. A small dark dot marred the line near its end.

'Anything unpleasant, Dhara?' the king asked.

'No, Your Highness,' Dhara said doubtfully. 'May be one small incident towards the end, but nothing for immediate worry,' Dhara said as the king raised his eyebrows.

'I have the right to know, what evil is in store for me,' he said gruffly.

'No evil, Your Majesty, just that your heartline is very short,' Dhara said.

'And?'

'It means you have no regret,' Dhara was suddenly

nervous. The extreme shortness of the heartline was sending out alarm bells, the king not only had no remorse, he was also a born murderer.

Sarvarthasiddhi smiled slyly at Dhara, watching her like a cat stalking a small bird prior to attack.

Dhara smiled.

'Your Excellency is a terrific artiste too. With whom did you train?' she kept her composure.

'A guru from the north mountains. I was surprised your Radha style was so different to my Krishna,' he said slyly.

'My mother's sisters trained me in the basics, then sent me for advanced training to the tapovana,' she said.

'I see, maybe my old guru and you should duet as Nataraja and Parvati, the styles will be a contrast,' the king's tone had changed.

Dhara leaned forward to reach for the jug, but Raja Sarvarthasiddhi grabbed Dhara's long hair roughly, saying, 'Bed now.'

The girl winced. The king smirked.

Dressing like a Bahirika

There was a cautious cough at the door just as Dhara began to undress.

'Who dares disturb me?' Raja Sarvarthasiddhi snarled.

'My Lordship,' a woman's voice said hesitantly, 'The military court is in session and awaits you.'

'What do you do after sunset?' Raja Sarvarthasddhi impatiently pulled Dhara's hair again, as she grimaced with pain, the king leered cruelly.

'I practice song and the flute. I will come tonight if you wish,' Dhara said.

'Good, we will continue where we left off. Vasuki will

fetch you,' the king said.

'Vasuki?'

'My maidservant,' he said.

'I can come on my own.'

'You can't. My night bedroom changes daily to confound would-be assassins,' he tittered.

There was another hesitant knock and two young women entered with scented clothing.

'What are you staring at, Dhara?' Raja Sarvarthasiddhi demanded, as Dhara looking slightly dazed, righted her clothes.

'You dress like a bahirika, O King!' Dhara handed over the king's court ornaments, one by one to the women as they dressed the king.

'Only for today. The Yavana replaced our old masters, the Persians. The day a Yavana ambassador visits, our senior military commanders dress like their military top brass,' he disclosed more information.

'Which military, Gracious King?'

'Macedonian, ignorant female,' Raja Sarvarthsiddhi snapped, putting on a plumed helmet and preening in front of a polished brass mirror.

Indian or Yavana clothing, the king had taken ugly to a whole new level, Dhara thought, as she set her hair in order, smiling sweetly at him.

'Now, entertain the visitor and earn your keep,' the king snarled as though he could read her mind.

Today, Dhara thought, would be one long day. Dance, sing to an audience wearing appalling disguises or the real thing.

Vasuki

As the sun set, the king returned drunk and reeking, and summoned Dhara to finish his incomplete exertion with her. Dhara performed admirably in bed, considering she had spent half the time holding her breath to avoid the stale odor from the king's mouth. Dhara was escorted back after a couple of hours by a girl in green livery.

'Thank you.'

The girl nodded her acknowledgement.

'Your name?'

'Vasuki,' the girl replied.

Dhara recognized her as the young woman at the temple asking the priest to help her ailing mother.

'You must instruct me about the king's likes and dislikes,' Dhara said.

'I will, on my half-day off,' Vasuki said.

Dhara returned to the music room and picked up the double bulb veena. After a couple of hours of practice and her night meal, she went to bed.

The Maid from Morvati, February 323 BC

The next few days were lazy. Raja Sarvarthsiddhi and his siblings had gone to a nearby forest to hunt. Vasuki came to meet Dhara after lunch while she was practicing different dance steps.

Dhara greeted her gladly.

The nartaka asked, 'Why did the last dancer before me leave?'

'We don't know. She vanished on a *Poornima*, a special full moon night. No one saw her next day,' Vasuki said.

'So how is it to be the favorite maidservant of the king's household?'

'Mostly okay, but right now my mother is seriously ill and none of the brothers will give me even a couple of days off,' Vasuki's eyes filled with tears.

'Where do you come from?' Dhara asked.

'Morvati.'

'Isn't Morvati Prince Sashigupta's mother's village?' she attempted again.

'Morvati supplies many maids to the Nanda palace. I am chief maid. How do you know Prince Sashigupta?' Vasuki's question put Dhara on her guard.

'I don't. But the mountains are full of stories of his tryst with the Yavana at Varana. Tell me about Raja Sarvarthasiddhi's penchants,' Dhara changed the direction the talk was going.

'All female bodyguards and maidservants must be of "use" to Raja Sarvarthasiddhi. When he loses interest, usually within three months, he needs a new person. Then his brothers take over.'

'Thanks for the tip,' Dhara said.

The Nanda General is No More

In Varana, Prince Sashigupta and Guruji were getting an update from Tan Mei.

'Guruji,' Tan Mei said, 'General Bhadrasala has been neutralized, and left for wild animals to eat.'

'Good! Our work must have no obstacles,' Guruji reached out and dropped a generous handful of coins into Tan Mei's palm. 'Any news of vishkanya, Dhara?'

'Dhara has found many black magic idols of Dhanananda, none affect the king,' Tan Mei said.

'Is that because he, weekly or daily, does bali, animal sacrifice, to defuse the black magic?' Prince Sashigupta asked.

'Probably!' Tan Mei laughed.

'Dhara must move to the next level,' Guruji stated thoughtfully.

Message from Guruji

A communication reached Dhara within days, hidden in a garland of jasmine given by an 'admirer'.

The hunchbacked jester from the court of Raja Sarvarthasiddhi was seated in front of Guruji and Prince Sashigupta, with his latest reports on the Nanda court.

'Dhanananda is very generous to all the women, except his favorite maid, Vasuki, who wants to go home and take care of her ailing mother.'

'In desperation, Vasuki comes to Dhara's quarters on Fridays, and both women go to the temple of Bhumi Devi, the Earth Mother.'

"I need out," Vasuki has been crying every Friday. "Give me a way out, Devi!"'

Dhara carefully sent the news of Vasuki's misery via a snake charmer who frequented the temple when Vasuki couldn't come due to her monthly periods. The snake charmer, in turn, gave Dhara an easy message from Guruji. Dhara decided to act on it.

The Poison Damsel and the Maidservant

On the next Friday, Dhara spoke softly to Vasuki as she cried on the way back from the temple.

'If you follow what I tell you, you may get liberated from the Nanda palace,' she said.

'I will do anything,' Vasuki wept.

'Okay. Just do something simple, but keep it to yourself,' Dhara said.

'What?' Vasuki was anxious.

'I will give you a powder. Lace Raja Sarvarthasiddhi's drink with it, one small pinch at a time. Ditto for the Nanda brothers' drinks. They will change, I guarantee,' Dhara said confidently

Vasuki followed Dhara to the music room, where Dhara gave her some powdered root she had stored in a leather gourd, which Vasuki tied to one corner of her *vastra*.

'Remember, gradually,' Dhara warned Vasuki, who departed before Dhara's maid came with dinner.

The Lampaka Message

'In the days that followed, Vasuki has become a regular at Dhara's music room,' the *vrshala* nun updated Guruji.

'Two weeks later, Dhara instructed Vasuki, "Increase the dose gradually so that the king accepts the difference in taste. Same for the Nanda nephews and brothers."'

Raja Sarvarthasiddhi was now consuming copious amounts of Vacha alcohol, a fresh batch of which Dhara had imported, and thirstily drinking a lot of water, too. The weather was balmy, and naturally, all men of the royal household were thirsty.

The snake charmer handed over instructions for Dhara, who the following day, sent a message by pigeon post to an agent in the kingdom of Lampaka. The pigeon post man secretly took a copy of the message to Rakshash. It read,

> *'The Chief Controller of State Trading controls distribution of local and imported goods. He fixes prices, hires agents for sale of goods that are sold at fixed prices or through state owned retail outlets. He also checks weights and measures, and controls hoarding, and inflation, and bans adulteration.'*

'Why would the king of Lampaka be interested in Nanda

trade administration? Keep an eye on her, she might be a *guda*, a covert operative, giving vital information for conquest,' Rakshash instructed his secretary.

The answer to the note came within a week from the Lampaka kingdom.

'Good, we will install the best administration features of the Nandas, and the Acheamenid Empire.'

Rakshash read the answer quietly.

'Secretary, I think there's more to her than just her ganika avtar. Monitor her movements. Update me on Raja Lampaka, keep him under covert surveillance,' he instructed.

'Shall we get rid of her?' the secretary asked.

'No. We need to see what hand she plays but double the security around her.'

The Temple in the Fortress, April 323 BC

Thanks to her hectic schedule with morning dances in the court and the king's apartments in the evenings, it was nearly two months later, on a Friday, when Dhara made her next visit to the Devi temple, before sunset.

Dhara humbly asked the priest if she could dance as devotion to the goddess.

'By the peepal tree,' was the terse answer.

Dhara tied her dancing bells around her ankles and danced without music, the anklets making up the beat. Several men, soldiers and civilians, slapped their thighs in appreciation. As Dhara ended the dance, a palanquin stopped at the door and the royal priest got out. The temple priest roughly shooed everyone out and the soldiers shut the doors.

As Dhara untied her dance anklets, she overheard a familiar voice say, 'In the common cremation grounds tonight as the full moon rises, all of you.'

The priest's acolyte brought two lambs to be tethered to the stone under the peepal tree, where Dhara was struggling to untie a difficult knot.

The acolyte looked taken aback at her presence, but shouted out a warning,

'Your lordship, there is a devotee present.'

The two priests stopped talking till Dhara packed her dance anklets and left. Taking the circuitous route so she could think, Dhara puzzled over the choice of venue, until it dawned on her that the fortress inhabitants dreaded the cremation grounds which doubled as hanging grounds for criminals, for centuries. No decent person would venture there at night unless they were a night sorcerer or necromancer. And she had to see what the priests were up to, if it was a war homa cum bali, it could mean a vicious battle for Prince Sashigupta or any other king.

An Admirer

Dhara prepared for the night by giving her maid the evening off, saying she needed to practice without disturbance. But man (or woman) proposes, and fate disposes.

Today, of all days, Dhara's unusual beauty had netted its first non-royal admirer. A knock on the door opened to admit the Governor General of the citadel.

The old man took off his sword, dagger and tiger claws, and handed them to four armed bodyguards outside. Dhara welcomed the Governor General by pouring water on his feet to freshen them.

After he settled down, Dhara poured hallucinogenic mushroom alcohol into a bell metal, silver filigree tumbler.

'What brings you here, My Lord?'

'Whenever I walk past the music room, I hear divine

music. Today, I came for a sample,' he leered.

'You came on the right day, I was going to practice the Thandava.'

'Who trained you in dance?' the official asked.

Dhara smiled. She knew she was being tested. 'Acharya Vardhraj, Gracious Lord.'

Dhara's dance that evening was a muted version she had danced in court, partly because there were no accompanying musicians and also because her audience was an amorous soldier getting drunk.

The full moon shone bright through the latticed windows, reminding the girl of her task. The old man was drunk but still alert. Desperately, she poured some Prasanna, mixed with her precious gold-stewed Vacha, the king had kindly allowed her a big gold vessel to brew it in, and more hallucinogenic mushroom paste.

'What's that in your hand, girl?' the Governor General asked.

'Vacha,' Dhara replied softly. 'I dance better on lubricants.'

'Like me,' the Governor General laughed hoarsely.

Three tumblers later, when the Governor General began to snore, Dhara covered him with a blanket and bolted the door so no one could come in. She donned black clothes and rubbed special oily black ash on her exposed face, midriff, arms and neck. Packing some lightweight goods, carefully, she tiptoed over the red tiled roof, and from there through trees and roofs towards the cremation ground outside the fort to observe what the three men were doing, and destroy the homa, fire ritual, if it was that. She was in for a shock.

The Cremation Grounds

From a treetop, she had a bird's eye view of the cremation

ground situated midway between the fort, forest and a small stream that supplied water. The whole cremation ground glowed with the light of many fires. Beyond the cremation ground lived the lowest castes, Chandalas and Svapakas, who were notorious for robbing the more expensive pyres of their precious scented wood. But tonight, no thieving was possible, the ground was ringed by armed soldiers.

Innumerable homa fires in square metal containers made the cremation ground glow blood red. Dhara counted nearly 200 fires burning simultaneously, each attended by a bare-chested, ash smeared acolyte with a priest. And in the middle of them, was the biggest homa attended by palace and temple priests, and an acolyte.

Something big was on the cards. Raja Sarvarthasiddhi was planning not merely an invasion but something huge, the scale of the homas boded no good. Prince Sashigupta had to be warned right away.

As each small homa got completed, the priests and their acolytes got up and left through the main exit patrolled by guards. The place was nearly empty. But the main homa was still on and had to be sabotaged. She climbed slowly, very slowly, one move at a time, through the treetops, till she was directly above the main homa, the smoke being a good cover. Carefully plucking some dry leaves, she smeared them with hallucinogenic paste, and dropped them one by one, into the fire below. Within half an hour, as each leaf turned into smoke, all three men dozed off.

Climbing down, Dhara hurriedly tied each man's mouth with his own shoulder cloth so he couldn't yell and attract attention. Then quietly, scooping concentrated poison from her body, she smeared the three men. She climbed the tree, and waited for the poison to take effect, an hour. After each man's body twitched in death throes, and fell quiet, she climbed the trees and crawled back to her apartment.

Brahma Muhurtha

When she reached the music room, Dhara checked if all the guards, and the maid and her son were in deep slumber. They were. Her uninvited guest, the Governor General, was still snoring. Gratefully, she scrubbed her skin clean in silence, and washed metal tumbler and alcohol mixing vessel with aromatic mud. After leaving a coded message in the dead flowers she used for her hair, in the auspicious time called the brahma muhurtha – too charged to sleep, she practiced on the veena before the maid came to give her breakfast. The Governor General woke up as she ate. Looking foolish, he left after mumbling goodbye.

Deaths of the Three Priests, the Aftermath

Dressed in her normal attire, Dhara attended court, determinedly awake. A soldier blew a horn to make an announcement in the audience chamber that turned the court chaotic.

'Three men's bodies, including Pujari Rayade, our court priest, have been recovered from the common cremation grounds.'

'Dead bodies in the main homa, that's inauspicious,' Rakshash snapped tensely.

The court astrologer said, 'No auspicious work can be undertaken till purificatory rites have cancelled the pollution from the priests' deaths.'

Rakshash agreed. 'How many days before the pollution goes?' he asked.

'Eleven days, Sire.'

'Okay general, the army will not march till day twelve starting today,' he declared.

Dhara glanced at Raja Sarvarthasiddhi, who was frowning irritably. His brothers looked stressed. The Governor General looked through Dhara, as though she was invisible.

The royal vaid, a trained toxicologist, came in looking grave. He had checked the three corpses. 'Your Highness,' he said, 'the three men were killed by beesh, a common wartime poison, administered through the skin.'

'Ah! The poison used by Sashigupta to cripple subjects of enemy kings was used here?' Rakshash growled

'Yes, Your Majesty, but different modus operandi.'

'Summon the chief guard in charge of security outside the cremation ground. The Chandalas too,' Rakshash said curtly, a vein beginning to tic on his forehead.

'A Black Woman'

The chief guard had no answer, he had only kept people from entering through the gate. But the Chandalas, questioned in court, said that 'a black skinned woman came late at night over the fort wall and left alone.'

The Governor General lined up all dark-skinned women in the palace for the Chandalas but they were indecisive, – 'The woman came at midnight and the pyres in the cremation ground made the woman look red and black. The three men were alone doing the homa for quite some time before the woman came,' head Chandala, Lallu said.

'Palace astrologer and intuitionist?' Rakshash barked. 'Who is this "black" woman?' he demanded.

'She is not "black", probably someone in the king's coterie of servants,' the intuitionist said.

'She is close to the king,' the astrologer added.

'Close to the king? Call the king's favorite maidservant immediately.'

Vasuki was hauled in for interrogation.

'Where were you last night?'

'Sleeping in my room,' she replied.

'Anyone to vouch for you?'

'No, I am sorry. Can I have two weeks off to see my dying mother, Sire?' Vasuki interjected, trembling.

'No leave will be sanctioned. You will attend to me and my brothers too,' Raja Sarvarthasiddhi snarled at her.

Vasuki left, crying piteously. Dhara, on the way back with the double bulb veena (Rakshash had asked for calming music), gave her an awkward hug.

'The king's brothers will make my life hell with their demands,' Vasuki sobbed.

'All this is short-lived,' Dhara consoled her, adding, 'Trust me!'

Next, it was Dhara's turn.

'Where were you last night?' Rakshash growled.

'I was sleeping in the music room. My maid, guards and a visitor will vouch for me,' she replied confidently.

'Visitor?' Rakshash asked sharply.

Dhara looked anxiously at the Governor General who cleared his throat and waved his hand vaguely as if to ward her off.

'So, you visited Raja Sarvarthasiddhi's current concubine?' Prince Kaivarta turned to the old man.

'I was not alone,' the Governor General said defensively. 'My bodyguards were present.'

Prince Kaivarta snapped, 'Did you see or hear anything?'

'I was drunk, Sire,' he stammered.

'On what?' the prince asked.

'Mushroom hallucinogenic alcohol.'

'Drunkard!' Kaivarta spat a mouthful of alcohol with fury.

'Dhara, vadaka, some soothing music, please!' Rakshash said loudly to nip the potential for a full-on fight. 'Ask the intuitionist and the astrologer for an expert on Bali,' Rakshash whispered to the Governor General who barked an order to his secretary.

The same day, a pigeon post arrived at Varana.

'Thanks to Dhara's interference, Dhanananda's invasion is on hold,' Guruji handed over the post to Sashigupta who read and burnt it.

Vasuki, the Agent, May 323 BC

Rakshash was not the only one to want surveillance of neighboring kings. Prince Sashigupta had also doubled the surveillance on Dhanananda for many months.

In Guruji's austere chamber, Prince Sashigupta, sipping a smelly combination of poisons given by the old teacher, was a worried man.

'It is taking some time, Guruji. Vasuki's mother is still critical, I worry about Dhara.'

'Uprooting Dhanananda, the malady, will result in a just kingdom,' Guruji said.

'Justice is not enough,' Sashi replied.

'I agree. To be a good king, one should learn at every opportunity, have national and global viewpoints, and be an able commander-in-chief of army, navy, and law and order in the kingdom.'

'Or have a Rakshash?'

'Yes, a Rakshash, who single-handedly mans the show for Dhanananda,' the old man agreed.

'Rakshash's only failing is his ignorance that the rural

population chokes with taxes by a cohort of corrupt ministers,' Prince Sashigupta said.

'They increase taxes during natural calamities, and no one can bypass high officials and complain to him. Furious villagers are your strength.'

'My boys are on it, Guruji. They meet gramikas all over the countryside to recruit villagers, to fight the Nandas.'

As though he could read their minds, Dhoomal dropped in.

'What's up in the villages, young man?' Prince Sashigupta asked, grinning at the fur-topped headgear, with one wilting feather.

'All peasants that join up to fight are frustrated with Dhananandа's taxes. Every war, the Nandas' new taxes fund battles, but choke the villagers,' Dhoomal said.

As he spoke, two vrshala nuns came to meet Guruji and Prince Sashigupta. As soon as the boy left, they spoke.

'We have important information. Vasuki the maid was an orphan before she joined the Nanda household. She is a plant and so is Dhara's maid,' they informed.

'What? How do we warn Dhara?' Guruji sounded tense.

'We wait for the right opportunity.' Prince Sashigupta was worried too.

'ASAP!'

Calanos Speaks, *'...our farewells in Babylon'*

Tan Mei, the Kushan, came with a disquieting message of a different sort.

'Yavana Alexander was facing a tough time with his spiritual mentor. The army knew about it. Seventy-three-year-old Calanos, the holy one, was ill in Susa and did not want to travel any farther. He announced that he wished to die on an Indian-style funeral pyre, which Alexander instructed

Ptolemy to build. Calanos gave away his royal Nasaean horse to Lysimachus, and distributed his gold cups and ornaments to common soldiers. The whole army gathered around the enormous pyre. As the Macedonian commanders and soldiers watched, Calanos sprinkled libation on himself, finished his prayers, calmly stepped on the pyre and immolated himself. Trumpeters blew long and loud, joined by elephants whose furious trumpeting sounded like battleground commotion. Before stepping on the pyre, Calanos curtly told Alexander that "*we will say our farewells in Babylon.*"'

'And how did our Yavana take it?' Prince Sashigupta asked.

'This terse goodbye mentally crippled Alexander who now suspects that all luck has deserted him.'

The Chaldean Magi warn Alexander, May 323 BC

Guruji and Sashigupta were in court handling land disputes, when a friendly visitor dropped in. When the prince raised an eyebrow, Xerxes said, 'Alexander!'

This got them a break from court proceedings.

'King Alexander traveled to Babylon with Roxanne, pregnant with their second child. He was joined by his friend, Admiral Nearchus on the journey.

"The Chaldean Magi have advised you, King Alexander, not to visit Babylon, or if visiting it, to avoid the Eastern gates", Nearchus told Alexander.

'He listened to Nearchus apathetically. When the army approached Babylon, extensive swamps blocked the northern and southern gates. The Royal Gate on the western wall could not be approached,' Xerxes said.

'Did Alexander take Nearchus seriously?' Guruji asked quietly.

'Not at all. Though Alexander has brilliant military

engineers, it did not occur to him to clear the swamps. In a hurry, Alexander was forced to enter through the malevolent Eastern gates.'

'Didn't his coterie of intuitionists and astrologers warn him?'

'They did, but their words fell on deaf ears. Alexander suspects everybody. And he was spooked by ill omens,' the express man said.

Fighting Ravens and Other Omens

'Ill omens!' Guruji exclaimed. 'Like what?'

'When Alexander arrived at the Eastern walls, he witnessed a vicious fight between numerous ravens and one raven fell dead in front of him,' Xerxes continued.

'For the superstitious Macedonians, birds fighting is an ill omen?' Guruji asked.

'It is. But that was just the beginning. Governor Apollodorus offered a human sacrifice for Alexander's well-being. The reader of omens, Pythogoras, said the sacrificed man had no lobe in the liver, another bad omen.'

'Next, a tame donkey kicked to death the most powerful Asiatic lion in Alexander's menagerie,' Xerxes added.

'A portent that the powerless overthrow the mighty,' Guruji sounded cranky.

'And then there was the incident with the mad stranger….'

'Mad?'

'Crazy! Loopy! Mad! One day, Alexander stripped off his clothes and went to exercise, to find a stranger clad in his clothes and crown seated on his throne. He who told Alexander that he was a common prisoner and that a god had commanded him to wear Alexander's clothes. This last incident tipped the scales. Alexander had the man executed.'

'So, Alexander is losing it?' Guruji sounded depressed.

'His morale is leaning south, he suspects his friends, men, everybody. In Susa, he purged the Macedonian infantry for their rebellion in India, disbanded and sent home half the Macedonian infantry, and replaced them with young Persians. When a few Macedonian troops protested, he threatened to set the Persians on them, and executed thirteen Greek officers for leading the mutiny.'

But the Macedonians troops were not the only ones who opposed him.

Iollas and the Vaidyas

It was mid-afternoon, and Guruji was gazing at the royal vaid's handsome son and nephew. Both had come on a short leave to meet Sashigupta's vaidya.

'What message have you?' Guruji asked.

'Alexander's teacher Aristotle has been secretly sending alcohol from Macedonia, we suspect poison,' the older vaidya said.

'To whom?'

'Iollas, the wine pourer. His father Antipater sent Iollas a unique "gift,"' the younger vaidya said.

'Gift, as in?'

'Poison in the hoof of a mule, in turn packed in an iron box, probable destination Alexander.'

'There must be a conspiracy by many to hit Alexander. We have received anonymous messages, maybe from Aristotle himself,' Guruji handed pieces of parchment to them.

Both vaidyas read the messages and then Guruji threw the parchments into a firepot that smoked away mosquitoes. The smell of foreign burning parchment was the only proof that Aristotle had contacted Guruji. No double agent could cross-verify the details from the ashes.

'One more thing. Alexander's drinking companion Medius is Iollas' lover.'

'Our people cannot endure another decimation of women, children, sword-wielding Brahmins. Should the Yavana decide to return, do whatever is needed, far from Indian soil. Alexander must not suspect any Indian hand in his illness.'

Both toxicologists bowed in agreement.

Alexander Dies in Babylon, June 323 BC

In the sweltering summer, Xerxes visited again.

'Alexander is dead!' he said to Guruji, who stared at him with the cold cynicism he might have accorded another chopped off ear. The old man was mulling over the information and not liking it one bit.

Prince Sashigupta, hurriedly summoned, blurted out, 'Details, please!'

'The palace of Nebuchadnezzar II, where Alexander was put up, is crowded with intuitionists, soothsayers, diviners, astrologers. Every day, Alexander offered the gods his usual sacrifice. But one fateful time, after a sacrifice, he got drunk and much after the party broke up, he continued drinking with his friend Medius, who invited him to join a *comus*,'

'A *comus*?' Sashigupta asked.

'A private drinking party. The next day, after offering his usual sacrifice to the gods, he settled down again to drink through the night with Medius. Wine pourer Iollas[2] silently served his master, noting that Alexander was drinking way

2 Iollas was son of Antepater. Last he was heard of historically was in 322, when he accompanied his sister Nicaea to Asia, where she was married to Perdiccas.

more than any time in the past. Though the food tasters had passed the wine that Alexander was served, Medius personally poured wine laced with, we suspect, poisoned hoof contents into the "Cup of Heracles."'

'So, Alexander could not escape?'

'Not when his inner circle were traitors. This time Alexander developed a fever, he believed, was a carry-over of an old malarial infection from the battle of Issus. Doctors came to attend to him, without success. Sensing his time had come, Alexander gave his signet ring to Perdiccas. The day after, he was carried on a stretcher to conduct his usual sacrifice to the gods. There he lay in the men's quarters and continued to give orders for the planned foray into Arabia.'

'Dying but still desirous of conquest?'

'That's the man. A day later, still feverish, he was helped on to a stretcher to conduct the sacrifice and rattled off instructions to Nearchus. The next day, even more feverish, he instructed his officers, but by now everyone realized he was seriously ill,' Xerxes continued.

'For the next two days, he remained critical. When the Companion Cavalry tried to stop soldiers from meeting him, there was a near rebellion. Given permission, Alexander's worried officers and soldiers filed past their supreme commander, where he feebly raised his hand in acknowledgement, unable to speak.

'Anxious about Alexander, Peithon and Seleucus went to the temple of a local god. They asked if the Yavana would heal better in the temple premises, but the god, speaking through the oracle, said he was better off where he was,' the express man said.

'The gods did abandon him! When exactly did he pass away?'

'The 13th of June. His death triggered by drinking suspect

wine at a comus.'

'How old was he?' Guruji wanted to know.

'Alexander was 32 years and eight months when he died, and had been king and Commander-in-Chief for 12 years and seven months.'

Xerxes left early, leaving behind two silent men, digesting this life-altering news.

'Alexander's Symptoms?'

Prince Sashigupta was pacing up and down, eager for more details of his late friend and boss.

'What happened at the banquet?' Guruji asked.

In front of him was the royal vaidya's son.

'Alexander was invited by Medius to a comus in honor of Hephaestion. When Alexander sat down with trembling hands beside Medius, he complained that he felt a heavy yoke around his neck. When he stood to drink in one gulp a toast to the hero Heracles (whose birthday is on 1 June), he shouted with pain, as if struck through the stomach with an arrow.'

'Alexander's symptoms?' Guruji asked.

'Five people at the banquet chronicled symptoms and sequence leading to his death. Bodyguard Ptolemy, Admiral Nearchus, secretary Eumenes, chamberlain Chares and military engineer Aristobulus.'

'Which included?'

'Agitation, tremors, restlessness, aching or stiffness in the neck followed by a sharp, sudden pain in the stomach. He then collapsed and suffered excruciating agony when touched. He also manifested extreme thirst, fever, delirium, and through the night experienced convulsions and hallucinations, followed by periods of calm. In the final stages, he could not talk, but could move his head and arms. Ultimately, his breathing became difficult, he fell into coma and died,' the vaidya said describing Alexander's last moments.

'Poor, poor man!' Guruji spoke mournfully.

'To the Strongest.'

'Before his death, Alexander's friends and generals asked him to whom he was leaving his kingdom. With his last breath, he struggled to reply, "*To the strongest. For I foresee that a great combat between my friends will be my funeral games.*"'

'These were his last words, Guruji,' the younger vaidya said.

'Shortly after his death, we destroyed all evidence that Aristotle and Alexander's wine pourer, Iollas, had colluded to poison the king. All the king's wine was poured into the narrow sewage channel that flowed out of the king's bathtub. But people know this, though.'

'We heard wine-pourer Iollas was honored after Alexander died. The whole of Greece knew of his hand in Alexander's death. Athens erupted with celebrations on hearing of Alexander's demise. The almost stab-in-the-back from us, Indian-origin toxicologists, remained a secret, as Guruji and you, Prince Sashigupta had desired. We neither did, nor stopped the poisoning,' the other vaidya said.

'One more thing. *Alexander's body did not decompose during the six days after his death, in spite of the scorching heat.* His body, embalmed with many perfumes, was placed in a gold coffin, hijacked and taken to Egypt, and put in a beautiful tomb in Alexandria, Egypt,' the vaidya added.

'A beautiful man in a beautiful tomb,' Prince Sashigupta said, eyes shining with pain.

Arrhidaeus, July 323 BC

In Macedonia, Alexander's illegitimate half-brother, Philip Arrhidaeus was made King, with Perdiccas as regent. This news was imparted by the visiting Xerxes.

After Alexander's Death

'What were the fallouts of Alexander's death?' Guruji asked Xerxes.

'Talk of loyalty,' Xerxes remarked drily. 'In Susa, Sisygambis, mother of late Darius Codomannus, was informed of Alexander's death. Whereupon she stopped eating and drinking, and died five days after Alexander, like a true mother mourning her son,' Xerxes said.

Guruji laughed. 'I am guessing his biological mother was different?' he was curious.

'Dear Olympias. When Alexander died, she was living in Epirus, with her daughter, the widow queen Cleopatra. As an alternative to combat, to win power, Alexander's generals scrambled to propose to his sister, Queen Cleopatra,' Xerxes said.

'But it was a disaster?' Guruji asked.

'And how! Alexander had made old Antipater viceroy of Macedonia. Antipater has two sons, Cassander, who had pleaded for his father to continue as viceroy, and Iollas, Alexander's wine pourer. Daughter Nicaea was married to Perdiccas. Alexander, who was very astute, had requested Antipater who was causing mischief, to meet him but instead he sent son Cassander,' the express man explained.

'And how did Olympias react to this?' Guruji wondered.

'Olympias got Queen Cleopatra engaged to Perdiccas, Antipater's son-in-law. When troublemaker Antipater heard this, he began to prepare for war, there being no Alexander to deter him.'

'Barsine's daughter had married Admiral Nearchus. The Admiral tried unsuccessfully to push forth Heracles' claim to Alexander's throne after the king's death, but failed,' Xerxes chuckled, evidently amused with royal intrigue.

THE ASCENT OF **CHANDRAGUPTA**

January 322 BC at Varana

The Vishkanya in Trouble

ALEXANDER'S DEATH LED to frenetic activity in the subcontinent too. In late January, a snakecharmer was heard shouting outside the Varana citadel to get an audience for his pets.

'Trained snakes, dangerous and deadly snakes! Who wants to see excellent snakes?' his singsong voice reached into the citadel.

Guruji's sharp ears picked up the sound and his body guard Gautami ushered the snakecharmer to the chamber.

'So, how many snakes do you have?' Guruji asked kindly.

'Several, and all at least seven years old,' the snake charmer replied.

He opened one of the baskets, and took out a silver-grey king cobra.

'See how long it is. He eats other snakes for dinner, so I keep him separate from the others,' the serpent tamer was flaunting his skill.

'Show me the others,' Guruji gave a coin to the man who replaced the snake in its circular coir basket. 'You may leave me now.' Guruji nodded at Gautami, who left.

'You have to pay more than that to see what else is new,' the snakecharmer said.

'Ah, sometimes, hearing is more important than seeing,' Guruji quipped.

'True. If my snakes hiss, their hiss has more meaning than just the sight of them,' he agreed.

'Of course!' Guruji laughed. 'If a human hissed, what would it tell me, say?' the seasoned teacher asked.

'That women are more venomous than snakes,' the man replied.

'Where precisely?' Guruji got curious.

'In Nandawati palace, Dhanananda's favorite maidservant, Vasuki, was planted by Rakshash to betray an unsuspecting Dhara, who had patiently listened to the maid's woes about her "dying" mother. Vasuki reported to Rakshash that Dhara had been giving her poison to kill the king, his upper caste son, brothers and nephews,' the snakecharmer told Guruji.

'Our girl betrayed?' Guruji sounded anxious.

'No, Guruji. Dhara had been giving Vasuki Brahmi calx to soothe the Nandas, so that they would permit her to visit her mother. The court vaidya vouched the powder was brain-calming Brahmi calx,' Guruji was informed.

'How did Dhara suspect the maid?' the old man asked.

'Dhara realized Vasuki was lying because her mother had been on her "deathbed" for a long time, but not yet dead,' he replied.

'Intelligent child!' Guruji exclaimed.

'But the best part is that after Dhara was cleared, Dhanananda trusts her,' the snakecharmer said.

'So Rakshash's plan backfired? Any message?' Guruji wanted to ensure Dhara's safety.

'She says Rakshash has increased surveillance on her. She is being stalked, followed, eves-dropped on,' he continued.

'Thank you!' Guruji thoughtfully handed over coin money, panas.

Dhanananda's End, February 322 BC

Hardly had the month gotten over, when more news came their way. The hunchback jester was back.

'Dhanananda is dead, and his brothers, son and nephews are dying or dead,' the jester said, seated on the floor in front of Guruji.

'And this happened, when?' Guruji asked, curious.

'After an epic dance and drink session by your ganika,' the jester replied.

'How?' Guruji sounded a bit impatient for more details.

'After being accused of poisoning the king's family, Dhara, knowing time was running out, waited for…' the jester was saying when Guruji interjected with

'The right time to strike?'

'And for Rakshash to move out of the citadel. Knowing that she could neither serve alcohol nor food to the king and being watched closely no matter what she did, Dhara upped her game during the weekend when Rakshash was called away for a family emergency.

'She massaged her body and the thick, wavy hair the king was so fond of hurting, and filled her mouth, fingernails and precious stone rings with poison. When Dhanananda was served alcohol by his maid, Dhara would sip his drink and feed the king with her mouth. An amorous and drunk Dhanananda took several mouthfuls of poisoned alcohol from Dhara before his mouth became paralyzed and he collapsed,' the jester described.

'Proof?' Guruji was not convinced yet.

The hunchback jester dropped Raja Sarvarthasiddhi's signet ring into Guruji's palm. The old man stared at it.

'Why are there no pigeon posts? How is the death being treated?' Guruji asked gravely.

'Deaths, Guruji. Deaths! All Nanda men have succumbed. Dhara powdered all precious stones from her rings and necklaces, and added them to the palace alcohol stores. The antapura is terrified. All women servants including the conniving Vasuki have vanished. All are suspect,' the jester hesitated.

'Any bad news?' Guruji asked sharply, walking towards Prince Sashigupta's favorite chair to look behind it.

'Rakshash escaped being poisoned due to the fake family emergency (Guruji's face became blank) he was called away for. When he returned overnight, he forbade any public talk of the deaths, so the palace media is completely silent,' he informed him.

'Why?' Guruji asked.

'He reportedly said in a closed-door meeting, that "power is not constant, shifts over time and that death comes as the end. Silence would confuse the enemy into thinking nothing had happened."'

'A lesson he learnt the painful way,' Guruji commented.

'But, after the cremations, he left for Parvataka Raja's court,' the jester added.

Parvataka Raja

'Doing what?' Guruji checked behind the thick drapes.

'Making mischief, offering his services as Amatya,' the jester said.

'Continue,' Guruji gestured with his hand.

'At the first meeting, he told Parvataka Raja that he should have acquired more conquered territory. And he offered the Nanda army,' the jester informed him.

'That's a dangerous alliance. And my ganika?' Guruji was still concerned.

'Vanished,' he replied.

'I need to update Prince Sashigupta with this news. Thank you!' Guruji handed over some panas to the hunchback, who left.

Guruji walked into the crowded audience chamber with a grave look, nodded to the prince who turned serious. Both walked back to Guruji's room after dismissing the court, the old man updating him on the way.

'Parvataka Raja's volte face. Getting more territory than he deserved, but still discontented,' Prince Sashigupta said angrily.

Guruji barked at his secretary, 'Ramagupta!'

The general entered in minutes. 'Guruji, Prince, have you heard?' Ramagupta sounded flustered.

'That our army faces battle in the coming months?' Sashigupta said gravely.

'With the combined forces of Raja Parvataka and the Nanda army,' Guruji added.

'Let's set up a tactical meet now,' Sashigupta ordered.

In the small private informal court of Guruji, a motley group met.

'Ramagupta, is Rakshash beyond our reach?' Guruji asked.

'No, Gurudev. His family is hiding outside our fort, in a walled house with his wife's parents. The Nandas had a jungle lodge nearby,' he said.

Guruji clapped his hands and a young woman in armor, Gautami, materialized swiftly.

'Summon Maraj. I need to instruct him to keep an eye on Rakshash's family,' Guruji instructed.

The bodyguard left.

Fiscal Health of the Kingdom

It was midday.

Both Guruji and Prince Sashigupta were taking a leisurely walk through the meditation garden facing the east.

'We need to raise money for the coming military operations,' Prince Sashigupta broke the silence.

'What exactly are we doing for fiscal health?' Guruji asked.

'Our two sources of revenue include mandatory services to the public like passports, police escorts to caravans of luxury goods, making standard weights and measures,' Sashi began.

'And?' Guruji asked.

'Second, a four-fold revenue. Income from state-controlled production and recreational activities, agricultural taxes and, trade and commerce,' Prince Sashigupta added.

'These public works give just enough revenue for basic maintenance of the state,' Guruji said.

'For warfare we need extra cash. I suggest special taxes, a country-wide lottery, an extra crop, and selling expensive honors to traders and artistes, the more expensive the better,' Prince Sashigupta said.

'Dhanananda sold even village names to prospective wannabes who had wealth but no respect from the general populace,' Guruji mentioned.

'We should be battle-ready, but a little indirect war, secretly waged, would serve us well,' Prince Sashigupta said.

'I agree,' the teacher replied.

'Let's do the secret war first and meet my double agents immediately,' Prince Sashigupta said.

That night, Guruji's man rode away towards the Parvataka capital.

Rakshash and the Ganika, March 322 BC

The deaths of Dhanananda and his brothers had left Rakshash grief ridden and devastated. Though he knew that Dhanananda had been a fiendish monarch, he felt badly for his death.

Rakshash met Parvataka Raja, who having no chief minister, welcomed him gladly. Rakshash called the late Nanda king's secretary, a learned man, to a secret meeting at his new home.

'Dhanananda was my master and I should have done more to protect his family. I want revenge for the deaths of my late king and his brothers,' he said.

'How can I help?' the secretary offered.

'Tell me a good way to hit back at Sashigupta,' Rakshash said.

'Our sources tell me he likes his women,' the officer revealed.

'Like father, like son,' Rakshash thought.

'Have a secret meeting with the guild of the nine grades of ganika', the secretary suggested.

'Can established prostitutes who pay heavy taxes be entirely trusted?' Rakshash looked dubious.

'Definitely, Sire! They make the best spies, the ganika in the music room played an important part in Dhanananda's death,' he revealed.

'True, by the time I suspected her, she had done the damage. It is time Sashigupta was paid back in the same coin. Send me your three best,' the scheming chief minister said.

The secretary returned with three graceful young women. Rakshash interviewed all three.

'Wash your faces and show me how you look without makeup,' Rakshash ordered at the end of the interviews.

The girls went to the bath house and washed away their makeup with beauty mud. When they came back, the youngest turned out to be the most dark-skinned of the three. The girl's faint greenish tinge previously camouflaged with turmeric facials screamed vishkanya. Court rumor had it that the greener the extremities, the more the poison exposure. This was the time to find out if it was true or not, Rakshash thought wryly. He dismissed the other two.

The Vishkanya from Taxila

As Rakshash had guessed, the vishkanya excelled in poison through alcohol, and in all forms of the poison, Beesh.

'How old are you?' Rakshash asked.

'I am thirty,' she replied.

'You look like a teenager!' Rakshash hid his surprise.

'I keep my youth with *rasayana,* mercury,' she told him.

Rakshash approved, he spent more than an hour briefing her.

'You will go first to Prince Sashigupta with gifts in red brocade, including sivi cloth for the king and a special double-bladed iron sword made only for kings, or their gurus. Bachelor Sashigupta cannot resist pretty women,' he told her.

The ganika smiled. She would leave the next day as a 'gift' from King Ambhi of Taxila, to reward Prince Sashigupta after hectic conquests.

The aide who accompanied the vishkanya, rode with his mount to the rather bare court of Prince Sashigupta. The vishkanya looked out of place in the sparse audience chamber. However, the girl was up to it.

'What do we have here?' Guruji asked. 'Where are you

from, child?' he grunted politely.

'I come as a gift from Ambhi Raja,' she started to say.

'Of Taxila?' Guruji asked.

'Yes. I offer to dance for you whenever you like. I am not tired, I can dance even now if you wish,' the vishkanya said, her voice deep and sexy.

'Well, this is as good a time as later. We would like to see the caliber of Raja Ambhi's gift,' Prince Sashigupta said, looking lewdly at her.

In approval, some of the courtiers tapped the carved arms of their chairs with fingers crowded with thick gold rings.

'As you wish, Your Majesty,' the ganika obeyed as she went up to the court musicians and gave them instructions.

The musicians began the slow unfolding of a classic dance tune and the ganika sinuously started her dance like a cobra swaying to the music of a snakecharmer. Each courtier present gazed hungrily at her, she had their attention completely. The vishkanya was so beautiful, her dancing so exquisite, that here and there, the courtiers sighed with envy. Guruji glanced indifferently at her arms and feet, the toes had a telltale green tinge where the sandalwood paste had rubbed off during the dance.

Exchanging Gifts

Guruji looked expressionless. 'Show me the other gifts,' he told the aide, who carefully unwrapped the rest of the gifts. With hands covered by his shoulder cloth he revealed a double-blade sword, a vastra and special sivi cloth for a kingly robe.

With his two hands under his own shoulder cloth, the old man picked up the sword, held it up to his face and smelt it. 'Just made, I see,' he nodded approvingly to the aide. 'Show me the cloth,' he said.

The aide held up the gold and silver sivi cloth for Guruji's approval, which had a strong perfume of khuskhus. Guruji held it up to his face and briefly, passed it by his nose, eyes closed in appreciation. Prince Sashigupta, who was looking lecherously at the dancing girl, noticed the old man's handling of the gifts.

'Excellent,' Guruji said approvingly to the aide, handing it over to his secretary.

For less than a second, there was a look of relief on the aide's face, something both, the old man and prince, noted.

'Take them to the gift room,' he barked at the secretary who left with the gifts.

Sashigupta, lecherous look plastered on his face, mouth covered with his hand, bent towards the old man and asked in a low voice only Guruji could hear, 'What are you looking for, Guruji?'

'Beyond the khuskhus perfume, there is an organic smell from the iron and cloth. Both have been treated with powerful poison, so that when you wear it your skin will absorb the poison,' Guruji whispered back, covering his mouth with his shoulder cloth.

'Same old, same old,' Sashigupta drawled.

He turned to the girl, who was staring at him, and winked amorously. The courtiers roared.

'Tell Raja Ambhi that the gifts are well appreciated. Accept from us jewel-encrusted shoes for a king, and special wootz iron armor,' the prince said.

Sashigupta's secretary returned with the items.

Guruji dictated a letter thanking Ambhi Raja for the gifts, inviting him to visit, and sealed it with Prince Sashigupta's signet ring.

With the gifts, the aide departed hurriedly. He was followed at a discreet distance by Dhoomal in mufti, sporting a big farmer's turban, swirling mustache, who had been tasked to see which highway the aide would take. The aide rode up to a fork in the highway with his men, and then took the left turn, the way to Rakshash's wife's family manor.

More Gifts

When Dhoomal returned, the vishkanya had started another sinuous dance, the courtiers devouring her with their eyes.

Guruji, however, looked preoccupied.

'What's on your mind, Guruji?' Prince Sashigupta asked quietly, amorous smile in no way giving away his thoughts.

'Her toes have a green tinge, and she smells divine, like khuskhus perfume,' the teacher noted.

'And?' Sashi was curious.

'Don't touch her even by mistake,' Guruji instructed the prince.

'You feel she could be coated in Beesh, to which she is immune, but I am not,' Prince Sashigupta said reflectively.

'We will send her back to that cheat Parvataka Raja as a gift from you,' Guruji said in an expressionless voice.

Sashigupta raised his eyebrows. 'But, Guruji, won't Rakshash stop the girl from going to Parvataka Raja?' he wondered.

'Let's ask our double agents for intel on Rakshash's schedule,' Guruji said quietly.

He instructed his secretary and within a couple of hours, two tonsured vrshala nuns came to meet him privately.

'Rakshash takes the day off on Saturday and then is going on a recce to the border. We will see she reaches the court on a Saturday, when Parvataka Raja gets her all to himself,' Guruji said.

'How?' Prince Sashigupta asked.

'Send a message purportedly from Rakshash's household to reach him late Thursday that his mother-in-law is ill and wants to see him. Rakshash will depart hurriedly to his family manor and that will give us time. I don't want a pretty-faced ganika breaking up our fledgling court,' Guruji said coldly.

Sashigupta was non-committal, for he too had recognized who she was.

'Pity, we cannot bank on Parvataka Raja anymore,' Guruji added.

'He has shifted allegiance,' Sashigupta said bitterly.

'Any man who is bought so easily is not a trustworthy ally. But no unnecessary bloodshed,' Guruji concluded.

The Vishkanya Again

A day later, Guruji met the vishkanya. A small bag of gold changed hands. Neither of them mentioned what was discussed. But, after three whole days of entertaining Sashigupta's court, the fourth day, the vishkanya left for Parvataka Raja's kingdom with an impressive escort dressed as mountain tribesmen. They were warned not to talk in her presence or become friendly. The party arrived on a Saturday morning, and as Guruji had predicted, Rakshash was not there to see her enter the Parvataka court.

Parvataka Raja was thrilled when he saw the ganika. Her dancing was exquisite and her fragrance, irresistible. Parvataka could barely control himself. He spent the night with her the day she arrived, the ganika was femineity itself.

The Mother-Son Pair of Monkeys, April 322 BC

'So, what is the news? Any progress?' Sashigupta asked the agents from Parvataka Raja's court. They were in the private chamber adjoining the king's bedroom and the prince was examining a new sword that ended in three sharp double-edged blades, which only an expert fencer could handle.

Guruji was in court, handling land dispute cases.

'Commander, Rakshash is even more firmly entrenched as Parvataka Raja's right-hand man. Rakshash has completely convinced the king that he should have acquired more than half the conquered territory, as without Parvataka's army, you would not have had such a decisive win,' they informed him.

'The vishkanya?' Sashi was curious.

'Rakshash tried to wean the king off the vishkanya. When that didn't work, he warned him not to take any food or fluid from the girl. He has appointed a food taster and a mother-son pair of monkeys who taste all the king's food and drink first,' the prince was briefed.

'Guruji was right, Parvataka Raja has changed loyalties with the speed of a hunter's steed,' Prince Sashigupta thought as he feinted at one of the men, who immediately drew his sword at lightning speed and parried. For a few moments, prince and man fought all around the chamber, the rest of the men moved out of the way. Finally, both men called it off.

'Rakshash and Parvataka Raja, let's break up this happy duo,' Prince Sashigupta said grimly. 'Dhoomal and Maraj, we have a special, difficult, mission for you,' Sashigupta listed a set of instructions for them.

Parvataka Raja Dies, June 322 BC

Guruji and Prince Sashigupta, as usual, were on track. Barely a month later, they had a visitor, the kapata sanyasi, who informed them that Parvataka Raja was severely ill, with a suspected overdose of Beesh.

'The king has severe diarrhea and vomiting, and stomach and chest pains,' the double agent informed.

'How did the vishkanya manage to poison Parvataka Raja, when she could neither feed nor give him any drink?' Prince Sashigupta asked curiously.

'When he slept with her, through her skin and clothes, camouflaged by khuskhus perfume,' he replied.

'Where there is a will, there is a way,' Guruji grunted.

'And Parvataka absorbed it when he touched her, they must have touched each other a lot.... When do you expect him to die?' Sashigupta asked.

'Any day now,' the kapata sanyasi revealed.

'And our girl?' both Guruji and prince were worried.

'The vishkanya, knowing her life was in danger, vanished when the king fell seriously ill, before Rakshash returned to the capital from his forays to the restive borders,' The man told them.

Guruji poured some panas into the man's hands, happy with the news.

In a week's time, another pigeon post informed them of Parvataka Raja's death. Rakshash, enraged that a vishkanya of his choosing had poisoned the king in his absence, set out to trap and bring her to justice.

The girl made contact through Dhoomal, who came to meet his beloved Guruji. In Dhoomal's enormous trader's turban, was a small note addressed to both men asking for refuge. Her message by pigeon post arrived at the same time, '*Parvataka Raja is no longer a parvat. The mountain has crumbled.*'

'Reward her with income from a village within Varana dominion,' Guruji said gratefully to the secretary.

The old man himself went into the private audience chamber to inform Sashigupta, the faithful Dhoomal following him like a pet dog.

Malayaketu becomes King, July 322 BC

Ten days later…

Dhoomal was back.

'Sir, bad news. The persistent Rakshash is not one to give up. He attended the coronation of Parvataka Raja's legitimate son Malayaketu,' Dhoomal reported.

'Our true enemy is not Malayaketu, but Rakshash,' Prince Sashigupta said.

'Malayaketu had barely ascended the throne, when Rakshash had a secret meeting with him and a few trusted double agents.

"Sashigupta cheated on sharing the conquered territory with your late father, Parvataka Raja. He, and now you, deserved a larger share of the territory, O Raja," Rakshash advised the young king.

"What should we do?" King Malayaketu asked eagerly.

"To get your rightful share, we need more alliances", the chief minister told him.

"Like?", the youth asked.

"Chiravarma Raja, Megaksha Raja of Parasika, Narasimha, the Malloi princeling on River Ravi, Raja Pushkaraksha of Kashmir and Raja Sindhusena from River Sindhu", Raksash replied.

"Will they ally with us?" Malayaketu asked doubtfully.

"The enemies of our enemy are our friends", the shrewd chief minister commented.

"Ah! The latest on the vile Sashigupta?" Prince Malayaketu asked.

"Sashigupta has been renovating Dhanananda's northwestern summer palace, and will move in there in three months' time", a court musician, a double agent, informed him.

"Excellent news! I know that palace better than anyone", Rakshash nodded, eyes gleaming.

"One more good news, Sire. Sashigupta is seriously ill", another double agent, a traveling wine seller, filled in the details.

"Great!" Rakshash said and in a sinister tone added, "We can send our special vaidya to take 'care' of him."

"Do that!" Malayaketu said malevolently.

"I'll instruct the vaidya on how to conduct himself. He will go as a vaidya from the court of Lampaka Raja, that convenient king", Rakshash had an evil smile,' Dhoomal briefed Guruji and the prince.

The 'Lampaka' Vaidya and Vacha

Many soldiers and courtiers were waiting outside the palace apartments for news of Prince Sashigupta. When the royal vaidya from 'Lampaka' entered Sashigupta's modest bedroom, the prince lay ill in bed. Two people seated on either side of him were quizzing him about his symptoms, the royal vaidya and Guruji.

The new vaidya came with terrific references, Lampaka Raja, Ambhi of Taxila, Abhisares of Kashmir, Malloi princes, and he had treated members of different royal families. An hour after he entered, he touched the acupoints of Sashigupta's feet, and pressed the pain out of his soles. Prince Sashigupta was impressed.

Not Guruji though. 'No golden needle therapy,' he snapped when the vaidya unrolled a leather pouch, lined with gold needles shaped like tiny spears, and swords and daggers.

The Lampaka vaidya shrugged. 'I am an expert,' he said in his soothing voice, 'skilled in all 108 *mrus*, acupoints, for relief in any ailment.'

'No!' Guruji roared.

But the vaidya was very persevering. When Guruji was away, he spent his time with Prince Sashigupta talking about the various cases he had solved through golden needle acupuncture.

A week later, the vaidya offered Sashigupta a vial full of medicated alcohol from a lidded gold jug. Guruji was not in the room, nor were the royal vaidya and food taster.

'Let's take your treatment to the next level,' he spoke in a coaxing tone, as though the prince was a small child. 'This medicine stewed only in gold vessels, has Vacha and black pepper. Black pepper in food kills any form of food poison. And in medicated alcohol there is no substitute for Vacha alcohol,' the vaidya stretched out a vial to Sashigupta's mouth.

'The foodtaster,' Prince Sashigupta said feebly.

'The foodtaster has already sampled this,' the vaidya said, persuading the prince to consume it.

'I need to consult Guruji,' Sashigupta sounded apologetic, not wanting to offend the nice vaidya.

'What does the old man know about medicine? He is a scholar, not a doctor,' the vaidya spoke scathingly.

This was the wrong thing to say.

'Please summon Guruji,' Prince Sashigupta spoke weakly to one of his bodyguards who promptly went to Guruji's quarters to fetch him.

The old man rushed to Sashigupta's bedroom, alarmed the prince was in danger. He was just in time. The vaidya had the vial next to the prince's lips.

'Wait a moment!' Guruji gasped to the vaidya, out of breath. 'Drink half the medicine yourself,' he commanded.

The vaidya blanched for a moment, smiled superiorly, and then took a small sip. 'Really, do you doubt my prescription?'

he asked in a patronizing tone.

This irritated the old man. 'Drink the whole vial now, "noble" vaidya!' Guruji ordered curtly.

'But this is Vacha alcohol meant only for the king,' the vaidya protested, rolling his eyes at Prince Sashigupta. Guruji glared at him. The vaidya drank the whole vial and smiled confidently at Prince Sashigupta, who was looking at Guruji for clues to this rude behavior. The room fell silent. Guruji's breathing gradually stopped being hoarse.

'Fetch the royal vaidya,' Guruji ordered one of the guards, when he regained his breath.

The royal vaidya came rushing in, in fear for his young master. An hour passed. Guruji and the royal vaidya were making small talk, after examining the gold vessel and feeling Sashigupta's forehead and pulse, when the Lampaka vaidya interrupted them again.

Ativisha

'Look, nothing has happened to me,' the vaidya said. He poured out another vial with frothy smelly fluid for Prince Sashigupta. The prince trustingly reached for the vial, looking for Guruji's approval, when the old man scowled. Sashigupta feigned weakness and hurriedly set the vial on the lion feet-carved table next to the bed.

'Drink up!' Guruji snarled at the Lampaka vaidya.

'Don't you trust me?' the vaidya asked with a condescending smile.

'Drink!' Guruji ordered again sharply.

Warned by Guruji's tone, one of the bodyguards moved towards the Lampaka vaidya to see that he had complied.

Within moments of drinking the second draught, the vaidya's face became stiff, and his legs and hands began to tremble violently. He dropped on his knees clutching his stomach.

'Water!' the vaidya wheezed.

A bodyguard gave him a copper tumbler with cumin water, which he drank in a gulp.

'Bathroom,' he gasped, vomiting smelly fluid like a projectile on the polished black eggshell floor. Everyone backed away from the splash of puke.

The royal vaidya pointed towards the royal toilet. Struggling to stand up, shivering uncontrollably, the vaidya collapsed on the floor clutching his chest and stomach. As the small group stared, he clawed his stomach with both hands, sweat pouring from his skin, writhed in pain, and finally became quiet and still.

Like Bagaos Again

The nauseating smell of medicated vomit filled the room.

'Examine him!' Guruji ordered the royal vaidya, pointing at the prone man, whose mouth was open and eyes, staring. The royal vaidya checked the three pulses on the wrist, briefly bent to smell the dead man's mouth, and shook his head.

'He is dead from a strong dose of *ativisha,* poison aconite root,' the royal vaidya said, straightening up.

'Beesh? How did you diagnose that?' Guruji's gravelly voice was in danger of making rock crumble.

'Mouth odor, waxy skin, stiffness of face, simultaneous chest and stomach pains, weakness in legs and hands, lip and nail color changes, vomiting. These are key symptoms of Beesh, which attacks different systems simultaneously. And he gulped water, as if his mouth was on fire,' the royal vaidya explained.

'A powerful poison, fit for a king,' Guruji quipped.

Sashigupta weakly sat up and looked down at the corpse.

'How did you guess, Guruji?' he asked in a feeble tone.

'Well, I thought of Bagaos the eunuch, trying to poison emperor Darius,' Guruji said looking coldly at the dead man. 'Remember, Sashi, a king should never trust anyone until he is completely sure of his loyalty,' Guruji sounded furious. He knew that as they spoke, thanks to double agents, news of the vaidya's death would reach Rakshash by pigeon post within a day, maybe within hours.

He clapped his hands and gestured towards the dead man. 'Guards, burn the body in the hanging ground for criminals,' he growled. 'Dispose the remains in the sewage canal that empties into the moat. Let his funeral be the ultimate insult,' a livid Guruji snarled.

Dhanananda's Coterie

The same day at sunset…

'I think we need to give Rakshash a taste of his own medicine,' Prince Sashigupta said, adding, 'Dhanananda always had a coterie of *kartantika*, soothsayer, *naimittika,* reader of omens, *mauhurtika,* astrologers, and *ikshanika,* intuitionists.'

'If Rakshash is involved, Malayaketu has a copycat coterie,' Guruji growled.

'However, they could not predict the deaths of Dhanananda and his male family members,' Prince Sashigupta scoffed.

'…Whose deaths were linked to their past karma of murder. We need to put some bad omens in the path of our illustrious colleagues, scare them some,' Guruji said.

'What do you have in mind, Guruji?' Sashigupta asked curiously.

'Dhanananda's personal purohita is expert in black magic and omens. Send the zookeeper,' Guruji ordered his secretary.

The Zookeeper

'Only I can give you poison,' Guruji was coaxing his protégé to drink some foul black liquid when the reek of animal feces announced the approach of the zookeeper. His nails were mucky, the heels of his feet cracked and filthy. But his expertise in his work made people trust him.

'I need white crows urgently, either dyed or naturally white, trained to fight black crows to the death,' Guruji said, making a valiant effort to stop breathing as long as possible.

'It will take a couple of days to train crows to fight each other,' the zookeeper replied.

'Do that and get back to me,' Guruji instructed him, waiting to breathe freely.

The Old Nanda Palace

Evening. The next day. The military attaché walked in to meet Rakshash in the private court.

'Bad news, Sire. Our poison vaidya was forced to drink two powerful doses of toxin poisons and died immediately. The old man was wise to him,' he informed the chief minister.

Rakshash was stunned into silence.

The attaché added reflectively, 'Killing Chanakya would serve the Nanda cause better than killing Sashigupta.'

'I agree, but Prince Sashigupta is fiercely possessive of his guru. He guards the old man better than he does his own family. Any attack on the old man would invite a fight-to-the-death assault on us. What else?' Rakshash felt helpless.

'Prince Sashigupta's royal quarters has developed leaking roofs with the monsoons. Snakes and scorpions are entering through the windows. He plans to relocate to the northern-most Nanda palace after renovation,' the officer informed the chief minister.

'Keep me posted,' Rakshash said grimly, 'about what work it needs.'

Bali, August 322 BC

A few weeks later, the attaché walked in to meet Rakshash in the audience chambers at noon when the king had gone for a siesta.

'Sire!' the attaché was hesitant, 'There is a bad omen.'

'Spit it out,' Rakshash growled.

'At the gates of the fort, four white crows were attacked by four black crows, and the white crows died. The black crows then flew to the forest, so we couldn't catch them,' the officer said dejectedly.

'That is a bad omen. Purohita! The white crows that died…' Rakshash began.

'…can be turned to our advantage,' the Purohita finished.

'By?' Rakshash asked immediately.

'Bali, an animal sacrifice,' came the reply.

'So, bali is the only way out?' Rakshash asked.

'Yes, bali is the only way,' the Purohita submitted.

'Okay, how?' Rakshash asked.

'Son, pick up the dead white crows, feed them to a rooster, the rooster to a puppy in the cremation grounds, and take an unblemished five-year old boy. Then wait for me,' the Purohita instructed one of two young acolytes who accompanied him everywhere.

'I will, Purohita!' the teenager nodded and left.

The Purohita ordered the other acolyte next. 'Take firewood, sandalwood, frankincense, raw eggs, black threads, and anything else needed for bali,' he instructed.

The second acolyte too left. The Purohita barked at his palanquin carriers, 'To the cremation grounds.'

Rakshash regretted asking the Purohita. Through long experience with the Nandas he knew what the boy child meant, human bali.

Nanda Palace Renamed, September 322 BC

Back in the northwest, a couple of hours from Varana, late King Sarvarthsiddhi's royal residence, formerly called Nandawati, was being spruced up. Giant statues of lions, bulls and sun images decorated the path to the palace. The royal pathway décor copied the Achaemenid palaces of the Persians. Peacocks flew peacefully across the road, making high-pitched cries, giving the new name to the citadel palace, Morvati, according to common rumor.

Only Guruji knew why.

Prince Sashigupta had insisted, 'Nandawati must be renamed Morvati after my late mother, Mura.'

Morvati Palace, December 322 BC

The palace was under extensive renovation. Booby-trapped parts like the throne and the king's bedrooms were completely rehauled. Four months had gone by, and the palace was taking shape, making Sashigupta impatient. Every day, Guruji's agents would inform him of the secret staircase under the dining room floor, the trap that rained spiked metal balls in the dressing area, the bathing tank that filled up with 'medicated' water from nowhere.

End of the fourth month, the royal architect came to inform Prince Sashigupta and Guruji that the restoration was completed.

'I have covered all your points, Guruji, a small homa can be done now, before our noble king enters the palace. I have brought the key to the palace for your entry, Prince Sashi,' the architect said.

A massive bronze key on a red and gold tasseled cushion on a silver tray was offered to the prince. 'You can move in tomorrow, if you wish,' the royal architect bowed, holding his turban in both hands.

'Homa first,' Guruji snarled.

'As you desire, Guruji,' the architect bowed again.

'The palace may be ready to move in, but I want to inspect the palace prior to King Sashigupta's housewarming homa,' the shrewd teacher declared.

The architect bowed in acknowledgement, but his smile seemed to falter for a second, 'As you say, Guruji.'

The old man looked stonily at the architect, wondering.

'Tomorrow, we will set out during the time of the Brahma muhurtha so that inspection is over before sunset,' the old man said.

The architect left the court.

'Secretary, get an elite troupe of bodyguards to accompany Guruji, tomorrow,' Prince Sashigupta said. 'He should be well-guarded at all times,' he ordered them.

The secretary left for the guard house to organize a posse of elite bodyguards.

Bodyguards at the Former Nanda Palace

The next day, a palanquin accompanied by elite bodyguards set off long before sunrise. When Guruji arrived at the renovated palace early in the morning, there was a large group of attendants eager to show him around. Guruji's own eight formidable bodyguards accompanied him just two steps behind.

Guruji stepped out of his sandalwood paduka, washed his feet and put his right foot on the first step.

'Let us bow to Brihaspati and Sukra, the gurus of the gods

and anti-gods, who devised the art of politics. Let us bow to both,' Guruji intoned, pouring holy Sindhu river water on the ground as he spoke.

There was silence till he finished praying. Guruji looked around and then nodded to the architect.

'Snacks are ready, if you would prefer to eat,' the architect said, bowing to the old man from the head of the crowd.

'Let's see the public quarters first,' Guruji said to the architect, dismissing all plans for breakfast.

The Lac Flowers

Both men entered through the high, carved wooden palace doors, which opened into public and private areas, and went left to the public areas. Bodyguards kept people from reaching the old man. The first room they entered had a floor made of differently textured tiles.

'This is the dance chamber, its special floor tiles make music with different sounds when danced upon,' the architect began to brief him.

With childlike fun, Guruji knocked on different tiles with his sword disguised as a wood walking stick to hear the sound effects. He nodded in approval. The architect looked pleased.

'Next, in the music room, is a brand new, double bulb veena and new tablas, for the king to practice,' he continued.

Guruji walked in, picked up a flute, and blew into it carefully, his lips cushioned by his shoulder cloth. A familiar organic smell and a puff of powder came out of the blown flute.

'What wood is it made of?' Guruji asked, suspicious.

'I … uh…don't know, Guruji,' the man stuttered, at a loss for an answer.

'Hmm, continue,' Guruji waved his hand.

'Here are the two royal treasuries,' the architect nervously opened the double doors of the first treasury. He added, 'They have 8-foot-thick walls, and tunnel proof floors.'

Guruji nodded in approval as he tapped the black stone flooring with his walking stick.

'Next, the public audience chamber,' the architect showed signs of nervousness.

They had entered a room with ornate sandalwood carvings on walls and roof.

'Off the room, are the chambers for secretaries, lawyers and lower functionaries. Then we have the royal kitchen and food storage areas,' the architect resumed his briefing. Guruji's entourage went from room to room.

'These are the animal rooms that will be filled with animals of the king's choosing,' the architect pointed out to huge empty cages in a room that had a tree growing out of the ground and whose large windows looked out at an expanse of skillfully laid, wild garden.

It was now noon. The architect's stomach rumbled loudly. But he dared not ask Guruji to break for lunch, as the old man moved briskly forward.

'...as busy as ants'

'Now the private rooms of the king,' the architect bowed towards the main door. The chamber reeked of strong perfume.

'Why so much lac used for décor? Every flower, every leaf is lac,' Guruji looked around. 'You will make the royal housekeeper lazy by using artificial flowers everywhere,' he said.

'Guruji,' the royal architect looked ashen, 'we were informed Prince Sashigupta is allergic to pollen.'

'Who told you this?' Guruji snapped.

'Er... the royal vaidya's assistant,' the architect lied, a

trickle of sweat dripping down his cheek.

Guruji looked stone-faced, pretending he hadn't detected the lie about the assistant. 'So, this is a royal bedroom?', he played along.

'The main one,' the architect wiped his forehead with the fine luxury cloth on his shoulder.

Guruji silently noted more sweat snaking down the architect's neck in spite of the cotton turban. Then he turned his attention to the bed chamber, the sandalwood carving of the king's four poster bed reminded one of burning incense in a temple homa, fire ritual.

Off the bedroom, the royal weapon storage area had brocade curtains, with walls lined with exquisite lac flowers.

Guruji went to one of the flower vases on a windowsill, plucked a lac flower, smelt it and reached down to pluck a wax leaf. Behind the vases, a row of industrious ants in single file tidily took away their booty, grains of cooked rice, going from a hole in the floor to window and outside.

Guruji's face turned mask-like. The architect fidgeted with his shoulder cloth, now openly wiping sweat from his forehead. He gave Guruji a nervous smile.

'The royal baths are this way, Guruji,' the architect pointed to a door behind the royal four-poster.

'Let's first check the garden outside the king's private quarters,' Guruji turned abruptly and strode through the doors to the palace entrance.

'But Guruji, there are guest bedrooms to be seen, and courtesans' quarters,' the architect ran behind to implore the old man to check out the rest of the palace.

But Guruji had marched through the garden walkway as far away as possible from the palace and was thoughtfully surveying the landscaped garden.

'How is it, Guruji?' the architect asked, eagerly, two steps behind the old man.

'Call the rest of my men,' Guruji snarled.

Looking confused, the royal architect sent two men to call Guruji's palanquin bearers, and other bodyguards who had remained at the back of the crowd. There was no need, hearing his stentorian voice, Guruji's men came rushing up.

The Palace on Fire

'Yes, sire?' the head bodyguard Magai asked.

'Clear the palace of all people and set it on fire,' Guruji said.

'Are you sure, Guruji?' Magai sounded puzzled.

'Do as I say,' Guruji snapped.

Leaving one massive, dangerously-armed bodyguard with the old man, the rest sped to the kitchen, piled firewood methodically, setting fire to the palace doors, audience chambers, the king's private quarters, other areas and lastly the servant quarters at the back.

The architect smacked his forehead desperately. He ran around the palace like a madman from the kitchen to the bodyguards who were systematically setting piles of wood on fire. Guruji's bodyguard barred access to the old man. As flames licked the wood and stone walls, the wax and the lac, the brocades and the carved wood melted into one huge blistering mass of flame. The exquisite fragrance of burning sandalwood filled the air.

'But why, Guruji? It is a splendid palace, fit for a king,' the architect clawed his turban, rivulets of sweat now pouring down his nose and cheeks.

Just then, above the explosive sounds of bursting flame, came the wrenching screams of more than 100 men, trapped by fire. Ignoring the sounds, from a safe distance, Guruji supervised setting fire to parts of the palace not yet aflame.

Continuous high-pitched screams competed with bursting fired wood.

The palace had burnt for three and a half hours when the screaming stopped. As the sun sank low on the horizon, Guruji patiently waited to check areas that resisted fire and saw carved stone walls or metal doorframes.

After nothing but ash and blackened stone rubble remained, an occasional wood burst interrupting the silence, Guruji asked for his palanquin. Overheated stones in disorderly heaps and the still smoking landscaped garden remained as mute witnesses to the inferno.

When Guruji's palanquin was brought, several men ran forward, but crashed into the wall of bodyguards surrounding the old man.

The architect wormed his way through and fell at the old man's feet.

'Mercy, Guruji, mercy!' he cried.

The old man remained impassive. A bodyguard tied the architect's hands and led him away.

The Mahabharata Again

When Guruji entered the modest abode that Sashigupta called home, he had the painful duty of informing the prince that his future royal residence was now ash.

'It was a trap fit for a king. The cellar was full of Rakshash's men waiting to ambush and burn you to cinders. I saw the ants with cooked rice grains coming out of a small crack in the floor, and recognized the trap,' Guruji said in a composed tone.

Sashigupta looked livid.

'I waited so long to enter my father's north-most abode,' Sashigupta snapped in anger.

Guruji looked thoughtfully at Sashigupta. 'The decorations were all fire friendly, the fools replicated the Mahabharata trap, where the Pandavas were supposed to be burnt to death. Tomorrow, my son, you will understand what was in store for you,' Guruji looked unforgiving at the memory.

'...a Grand Achaemenid Palace'

Very early the next morning, Prince Sashigupta and Guruji departed for the palace, with an even larger force of elite bodyguards. When they reached the palace, a few parts were still smoldering. An aura of blistering heat radiated from the entire structure. Aromatic sandalwood smoke competed with the nauseating smell of burnt human flesh.

Prince Sashigupta and Guruji walked carefully towards the king's private quarters. Instructed by the old man, soldiers hacked away at the king's bedroom floor, fire blackened, dangerously fragile. Under the spot where the royal four poster bed had been, a gaping hole gave a clear view of burnt corpses and their soot blackened weaponry in the secret chamber below.

Sashigupta stared silently at the charred bodies.

'Your master bedroom!' Guruji said.

'Guruji, you are right, always. Let's meet the architect on our return,' Prince Sashigupta's voice was low and humble.

'We will build you a better palace,' Guruji said quietly, patting the prince on his shoulder, adding, 'An Achaemenid-style palace as grand as the ones King Emperor Darius Codomannus had in Persepolis and Susa, with Persian architecture.'

'I would like my palace to have a 100-pillared façade,'

Sashigupta sounded like an enthusiastic boy.

Guruji smiled. His protégé had learned his lesson and moved on.

Sashigupta's Court

But closure was necessary. As soon as Prince Sashigupta reached his residence, he asked for the general in charge of homeland security.

'General, send for the architect first thing tomorrow, and tell him he needs to tell the truth otherwise his family will be hanged,' Prince Sashigupta's face was expressionless.

Next morning, the imprisoned architect was brought to court. Within two days, minus his ornate turban, his lined face covered in grey stubble, he looked twenty years older. Tears rolled down his cheeks as he tried to touch Guruji's feet.

Guruji moved his paduka away, repulsed. 'Start with your real name and connection to the Nandas,' he snapped.

'I am Rakshit, architect of Rakshash's family residence,' he began.

'Are you related to Rakshash or employed by him?' Guruji growled.

'Both. My hand was forced. Rakshash promised my wife's useless father and three brothers, jobs in King Malayaketu's treasury if I agreed to this,' he confessed. He twisted his hands wretchedly, saying, 'Now no one will give them jobs.'

'A fair exchange, four jobs traded for the life of your king,' Guruji said.

'Who sent the soldiers in the basement?' Prince Sashigupta asked coldly.

'Rakshash chose each man personally. He will be bereft,' the traitor said.

'Forgive us, if we feel no sympathy,' Guruji's voice was low with cold fury.

'Forgive me!' the man fell at Guruji's feet and moaned.

'We spare you as a Brahmin,' Guruji said unfeelingly, 'although your treachery makes even a corpse-carrying Chandala your superior. We also strip you off your Brahmin status,' Guruji growled.

'Leave the kingdom today in permanent exile. If we find any member of your family here tomorrow, we will imprison them and behead you,' Prince Sashigupta scowled.

A palace guard cut the ropes binding the man's hands to his feet, and escorted him out of a side exit, which clanged shut.

Both Guruji and Prince Sashigupta looked at each other in silence.

Then Prince Sashigupta whispered the one name on both their minds,

'Malayaketu!'

The Nandadurga Fortress

News of Malayaketu reached them through a new double agent from Malayaketu's kingdom. The over-painted brothel owner, squashy bosom sloping like overripe watermelons, was gossiping non-stop with Prince Sashigupta, General Ramagupta and Guruji in his austere suite.

'Where is King Malayaketu now?' Guruji interjected when the woman paused for breath.

'He is in his summer capital, Nandadurga hill fortress in mountain terrain,' she said.

'Near our north border?' Guruji asked.

'The same,' she replied.

'And Rakshash?' Guruji wanted to know his whereabouts.

'Traveling the length and breadth of Malayaketu's kingdom

to nip insurgencies,' the brothel owner said.

'No Rakshash? Great! Time to capture the fort?' Sashigupta said looking at Guruji.

'That's a tough job,' the visitor told them.

'Why?' Sashi asked.

'The fortress is surrounded by dense forest, a haven for poisonous snakes,' she began to say.

'We can kill the snakes. Or pray to the God of snakes. How else is Nandadurga vulnerable?' Sashigupta wanted more details.

'Wooden houses. The whole fortress has a strict fire code. Craftwork and public cooking are done away from residential and governing areas, like the palace. The Governor General maintains law and order, and imposes night curfews two hours after sunset,' the brothel owner explained.

'But the biggest hazard, fire, is difficult to control?' the prince asked, curious.

'Quite,' the woman paused.

Food, Fodder and Alcohol

'What else can you tell us?' Guruji asked her.

'Nandadurga is a few miles from the highway,' she replied.

'The Royal Road. And?' Guruji nodded.

'Outside Nandadurga is an influx of beggars; cripples with missing limbs beg at the citadel's elephant gateway across the moat…' she began to describe.

'These beggars are important, why?' Guruji was curious.

'They are friendly with the gatekeepers who supply them drinking water,' the brothel owner continued.

'Okay, so?' Sashigupta too was curious now.

'They have all the news. Occasionally, a seller of wild meats comes to meet the food manager, then a toxicologist and trained dogs test for poison. In return for buying his food, the seller informs fort security about the location of roaming bandit gangs who prey on forest villages for grain and fodder, which otherwise must go to the king. Malayaketu's men are unable to control bandits,' she explained.

'Ah, a parallel mafia outside the fort! And then?' Sashigupta queried.

'The king has to send his troops out,' she began to resume.

'To police the highway?' came another question.

'No, for food. Fort staff with armed escorts seize provisions left over by the bandits. Milk, vegetables, fodder and firewood; the villagers next to the highway are starving,' she informed them.

'Copycat Nanda behavior! Supply trains?' Guruji asked.

'They take difficult hill terrain routes far from the fort. Rumor is provisions are going to Nandadurga via a secret tunnel,' she told them.

'Perhaps we can flood tunnels, cut supply trains of food and fodder to Nandadurga,' Prince Sashigupta thought aloud.

'Another point, sellers know good provisions are going to the fortress. Poor quality provisions for the locals are routine,' the visitor disclosed.

'Is that all we can do to cripple the fort? Stopping the food supply?' the old man asked keenly.

'No, Guruji. Highway vintners can poison wine and Prasanna,' General Ramagupta added.

'Let's strangulate Nandadurga, no more convoys of food and fodder,' Guruji declared.

'And I want some psychological tension to ruin morale, give me some ideas,' Prince Sashigupta said looking at his teacher and the senior military officer.

Guruji and Ramagupta nodded.

A Demon outside Nandadurga, January 321 BC

What Prince Sashigupta had requested, came true within a month. The highway was a desolate road. The fort dwellers and surrounding villages were scared sick. Rumors of an evil monster or *Naga,* a human shape-shifter in cobra form on the prowl, were scaring everybody. Chief minister Rakshash was still on tour.

King Malayaketu ordered his double agents to bring him a reliable informer, who turned out to be an excited forest tribal.

'Tell me!' King Malayaketu barked at the tribal whose wilted feathery headdress obscured his face.

'Highness, a demon with black face, hairy body like a bear, went three times around the fort last full moon. Howling dogs and jackals accompanied him,' he blurted out.

'This demon is eating men alive in the cremation ground, honorable king,' the tribal said.

'Call my coterie,' King Malayaketu said to his secretary, who returned with a gaggle of people, soothsayer, intuitionist, a bali expert, astrologer and reader of omens.

'What must we to do to stop the demon from eating humans?' Malayaketu sought their counsel.

'Sire, only a king like you can stop attacks by personally offering bali, animal sacrifice, in the cremation grounds,' the omen reader said.

The remaining men nodded in agreement, bali was the only answer.

'I need you,' read King Malayaketu's pigeon post to Rakshash. 'Please come immediately to Nandadurga,' he instructed.

This message was also relayed to Prince Sashigupta and Guruji.

'Where is Rakshash?' Prince Sashigupta asked his double agent, a seller of wild meats.

'Recceing in the middle of the kingdom, to stop warring republicans declare independence since…' he began to brief the prince.

'Since the Nanda deterrent is nonexistent now,' Prince Sashigupta finished.

More news came shortly after. Dhoomal dropped in next day, in a fur hat, that was for a change, quite appropriate for the weather.

'Rakshash has reached the fort with a large retinue of men, much to King Malayaketu's relief. Governor General and double agents have briefed the Amatya about the demon and the fact that the fort food supply was under siege by night raiders and poisoners. The Governor General is full of complaints, "Who would have thought, procuring food, such a commonplace activity, would turn into such a blister for our army boys?"

'All of them are guessing that, "Prince Sashigupta may be the mastermind behind the night raids, it sounds like his strategy, and he may himself be stationed in the jungle as the demon,"' the double agent informed them.

'And why are they saying that?' Sashigupta asked.

'Well, for months, there has been no news of you,' Dhoomal replied. 'So, Rakshash has asked the assembled military commanders to smoke you out,' he added.

Double Agent Vijay

The first one to react, the military attaché, was especially furious. He waited till the rest had left and then, in private, he and his most trusted agent, Vijay, met Rakshash.

'I want a full intelligence report. Who is the brain behind this increasing low public morale, Prince Sashigupta or…?'

the chief minister demanded.

'I will return within a week, Sire!' he replied.

Double agent Vijay sallied forth disguised as a deformed beggar. For one week, he spoke to other beggars, forest tribes, *Atavi* jungle troops, highway vintners, hunters, and low caste Chandalas and Svapakas. Carefully, he gathered information and once he was sure, discarded his rags, saddled a horse, and rode back to the public court.

'The forest is full of demonic spirits according to superstitious tribals who go for protection to a 400-year-old holy man, who claims that he has lived through different monarchs' reign, many who honored him through the centuries,' Vijay informed Rakshash.

'And what are we supposed to do?' he asked, irritably.

'The holy man has told his disciples that only the king can save his people from the shapeshifter, by doing bali, animal sacrifice, for a week outside the fort to save his subjects,' the agent apprised them.

Rakshash looked grim. 'So, the king himself must do the sacrifice?' he asked sullenly.

'Yes, Amatya,' the agent replied.

There was silence for a few minutes.

'King Malayaketu, you are required to do bali outside the citadel. We start tomorrow,' Rakshash informed the king.

The king nodded assent.

Malayaketu Performs Sacrifices

A week later, King Malayaketu, with an impressive escort, rode through forest paths to the 400-year-old holy man. Smelling of ash and old age, with a face wrinkled like a pickled mango, the holy man accepted all the gifts the king offered him. And every night, in a makeshift cremation ground near the forest cave, King Malayaketu sacrificed several sheep, goats and chickens.

On the last night, which was a Poornima, a full moon, a large number of animals, both wild and domesticated, were to be sacrificed. The small cremation ground was ringed by tribal chieftains, Chandalas, eager for fresh meat, and Malayaketu's soldiers.

The holy man asked the king, dressed in ceremonial robes, to bow down to the resident goddess of the cremation ground. As the king bowed his head down to the stone altar lit by the full moon, the holy man raised a trident and brought it down with force. As the trident passed through the neck of King Malayaketu, the royal turban fell off the king's head, which was bald. As the body became limp and slumped sideways, the posse of soldiers sheathed their swords, and disappeared.

The holy man flipped the turban, which had a thick wig attached to it, and shrieked, 'Ai, ai, ai! A false king!'

The Attacks Increase

The court was full, and Rakshash was seated next to Malayaketu.

'So, this old man was not Sashigupta?' Rakshash asked, elated that King Malayaketu had escaped a trap.

'No,' Vijay said, adding, 'He is not the 400-year-old fake. He is an elderly fraud, not Prince Sashigupta. Both he and the cannibal Naga have disappeared.'

Rakshash was cheerful, but the young king himself was seething mad, pacing up and down.

'Forget my head… food and supply convoys are being attacked, and taken over on the highway, a short distance from the fort,' King Malayaketu snarled.

'These extra assaults are masterminded by Sashigupta for

sure. The forest raiders are well trained and fearless probably because Sashigupta is their *de facto* leader,' Vijay said.

'He is a master in guerilla warfare on hill forts,' the Governor General spoke. 'He probably controls the forests,' he added.

'So, you suspect that he could be here as someone else? If so, we need to smoke him out,' Rakshash said grimly. 'Our last bit of information, more than a couple of months old, was that he was in Varana, with his guru,' he recalled.

Getting Rakshash as Amatya

The Aghora

'HAS SASHIGUPTA RELOCATED?' Rakshash asked the Governor General. 'He is missing from the circuit of village, fort, and forest tribes,' he was curious.

'Our double agents mention an old Aghora, who has recently made a jungle cave his home,' an officer said.

'And you conclude, again without proof, this is Sashigupta in disguise?' the chief minister demanded to know.

'Well Sire, this Aghora's body glows as if on fire at night, he is too attention-seeking,' he added.

'Does the Aghora have a large number of disciples?' Rakshash asked.

'Yes, all rough looking chaps,' was the reply.

'That's the clue, soldiers in mufti,' Rakshash muttered.

'Intelligence reports say that Guru Chanakya is in Varana, and so if Prince Sashigupta is the Aghora, he is in the forest alone. There is a black horse, – maybe Vijayta, outside the Aghora's cave,' he was informed.

'The horse and the "disciples" are the convincing evidence. Send for our trickster agents, we need ideas,' Rakshash was desperate to counter Sashigupta.

Tricksters to the Rescue

A metallurgist and a madaari, both tricksters, entered the private chambers of King Malayaketu. The madaari left outside his snakes in coir baskets, three monkeys and one sloth bear in chains. His voice was squeaky.

The Governor General's heart sank. How could someone so lacking in personality be of any help? But his face was expressionless, after all he needed an important service. And chief minister Rakshash's icy presence was a deterrent.

'What can you tell me about Prince Sashigupta that can trap him?' the Governor General asked the metallurgist first.

'Prince Sashigupta is a master of wootz steel work, he makes his own weapons and oversees that of his army too,' the metallurgist said.

'Okay… madaari?' the official looked towards him.

'He loves animals,' the man replied.

'Animals?' the Governor General was a bit puzzled.

'Prince Sashigupta is partial to lions, has a pet mongoose and adores his horse Vijayta. We could have a horse trade fair,' the madaari said.

Rakshash looked reflective and said, 'This may work, Governor.'

Dvarabahirika Tax

The Governor General sent for his best jobber, and then with his special agents and Rakshash, went into a huddle for days and nights, planning their strategy.

Within one hectic week, the plan was ready.

'Send forth trumpeters to announce to the surrounding villagers and forest tribes that there is a big reward for whoever cracks this puzzle from the land west of the Sindhu. Inform the troubadors too,' Rakshash said instructing his secretary.

'Anything else?' the secretary asked.

'Let us make the toll for Bahirika very high. Only someone with money should be able to enter the fort and pay the *Dvarabahirika,* entrance toll tax for outsiders,' he instructed.

'Yes, Sire!' the secretary replied.

'One more thing, Vijayta has a white diamond on his black chest. Keep an eye out for black horses tethered near the fort,' he alerted them.

'Will do, Amatya,' he replied.

Reward for the Lion Puzzle

The next day, by sunrise, horsemen with scrolls, and men on foot, tapping drums, went up and down the highway.

'Reward, reward, reward! For the one who solves the puzzle of the lion. Inside the fort is a lion in a cage. The cage has no doors. How did the lion get in? Solve the puzzle and win 800 panas as reward,' the announcement was made.

The madaari, dressed in the dark blue clothes and flat cone-shaped turban of a westerner, also yelled out loud near any gathering, 'Live animal show for the brave of heart, the strong of mind.'

A stream of men and women from the surrounding forest came into the fort, paying a token amount to the lion man to solve the puzzle. All of them failed and were publicly insulted by the lion man to the jeers of the crowd.

Back in a secluded part of the forest, an old Aghora was informed by a youngster in a beehive-shaped turban about the lion in the cage in Nandadurga. And the challenge that King Malayaketu's men had set forth, about the manliness of the man who could solve the puzzle.

The old Aghora could hardly ignore such a challenge. 'I must go,' he said.

The turbaned youngster cautioned him, 'It is a ruse to trap you, Sire.'

'Turban man, I know that and will wait for a reply. Send a pigeon post saying that the Aghora would attempt to solve the puzzle after three days.'

Four days passed.

'Is there no answer?' the Aghora asked his pigeon post man.

'No, Sire!' he replied.

'Our Guru maybe traveling and therefore hasn't received the communiqué yet,' the Aghora reasoned.

The Bahirika

After three more days, an old Bahirika decided it was time to check out the lion in the cage. It was a challenge he could not resist. Dressed in shabby green western-style clothes, with straggly grey hair, the Bahirika rode to the fort on a white horse.

The Bahirika noticed that curfew around the fort was relaxed. Cows, horses, mules, goats and donkeys left outside the fort, made for a kind of smelly chaos. A trickle of villagers and forest tribesmen had been allowed inside to solve the puzzle of the caged lion.

After dismounting, the Bahirika carefully stepped over different types of poo, crossed the moat to the check-post, where he was divested of his weapons. In the distance, the Bahirika could hear the lion man exhorting the public to solve the riddle – 'Do any of you dare risk your reputation to solve this puzzle?'

The Bahirika frowned.

'Why have you come, Sir? State your purpose,' the sentry was curt. He never trusted foreigners, and this specimen was shabby and old, and had a limp.

'I am from the western hills, and I come here intrigued with your caged lion,' the Bahirika replied in a shaky voice.

'You need to pay the *Dvarabahirika* entry fee here and then once again before you enter the fort area to see the lion. Do you have enough money?' the sentry asked.

'I do,' the Bahirika counted out money from a dilapidated cloth bag and handed it to the sentry who checked the silver coins were genuine, and then made a green mark on the Bahirika's right wrist.

'For payment received,' he said to the Bahirika's unasked question. 'What do you have in your left hand?' he asked.

'A gift for the lion,' the Bahirika said.

The sentry opened the parcel, and he and his fellow sentries shrugged their shoulders.

'Alright Sir, beyond the marketplace through the wrought iron gate is the lion in the cage,' the sentry said patronizingly to the old man.

The Bahirika thanked him in a trembly voice, and entered the covered market at the end of which a narrow, metal gate with spikes admitted people who wanted to solve the lion puzzle. Wide, barred windows in the brick wall either side of the gate allowed spectators to watch the fun without admission fees. The Bahirika paid up and was let through.

The Lion in the Cage

In the middle of a large open ground, the Bahirika saw people gathered around a majestic Asiatic lion in a cage, the lion was ignoring the crowd.

'You have optical rectalitis…'

'Your brain is in your bum,'the lion man hollered.

After the lion man insulted the few people who made

bad guesses, the Bahirika went up to him, and silently gave him the money to make a couple of bids. His left hand held a wrapped parcel still dripping blood, the head of a freshly beheaded goat.

First, walking to the front of the cage, the Bahirika bellowed like a donkey, the lion neither blinked an eyelid nor swished his tail. Then the Bahirika took the goat head slimy with fresh blood and approached the cage from the side, but the lion ignored the food, not even twitching his nose.

Puzzled, the Bahirika went to the sparse elephant stable, paid a bribe, and brought a blindfolded elephant with its mahout, to the cage. Again, the lion regally ignored the elephant.

However, when the lion man went near with his thick staff, the lion growled fiercely and jumped at the cage bars.

'See how ferocious the lion is, now predict how he came to be in the cage,' he teased.

The Bahirika stood apart observing the lion, which only became ferocious when the lion man neared it with his staff.

The Bahirika broke off a dead branch from a nearby tree and waved it in front of the lion. The lion took no notice. This puzzled the Bahirika for a moment. He looked around at the staff held by the lion man, and noticed how straight and symmetrical it was, almost like a metal rod in a wooden cover.

'Can you give me your stick, Sire?' the Bahirika requested politely, trembling all over.

'Which stick?' the lion man winked at the sentry.

'He actually wants your staff,' the sentry smirked.

The old Bahirika ignored their jokes, intuition telling him things were not as they appeared.

Slowly, the old man limped to a wall bracket, which had a lit torch, set fire to the branch in his hand, and waved it in front of the lion, which ignored him again.

'The lion only listens to me,' the lion man began in a superior tone, not realizing what the Bahirika was up to.

The old man limped full circle around the cage and realized that the lion was blind, it could neither see him, nor acknowledge the burning brand in his hand. But the feral smell from the cage was of a real lion, probably its hide, the Bahirika guessed.

Moving away from the lion man to the far side of the cage, the Bahirika suddenly thrust the burning brand through the bars of the cage into the torso of the lion before either lion man or sentry could stop him.

'Hoi, you will burn my lion!' the lion man shrieked, sprinting towards the cage.

The Bahirika deftly blocked him, tripping him with his lame foot. In the few seconds the lion man took to get back on his feet, the lion and cage were aflame. As the lion man rushed to the cage, staff still in hand, the burning lion leapt up and roared. Desperately, the lion man and sentry wrestled with a barrel of water towards the cage and threw the water on the lion, but the burn had done its damage. The iron framework at the core of the lion became visible through the flames, the lion man moaned loudly.

The crowd was in uproar, yelling and jeering the lion man for being a cheat. Villagers, who had lost money, removed slush-caked footwear and smacked the lion man for duping them. Soldiers rushed in to form a barrier in front of the excited crowd.

The Bahirika Speaks

'Now, you have your answer, the lion was placed in the cage and then the bars were built around,' the Bahirika walked up to the lion man behind the wall of sentries, and spoke in his normal voice.

'Who are you, Sir?' the lion man asked humbly, all bravado gone.

'I am a westerner,' the Bahirika said.

The lion man looked piercingly at the Bahirika, waved his right hand at one of the palace windows that overlooked the grounds, where a sentry stood at attention, and yelled, and pointed to the Bahirika. There was a shouted command to capture the Bahirika who was immediately surrounded by soldiers in mufti, who had mingled with the crowd. The old man seized the sword of the man nearest to him and began to fence though he was outnumbered. He fought furiously moving backwards towards the moat gateway.

There was a thundering of hooves from behind the soldiers, 'Quick! Let us flee!'

The Beggar

The Bahirika vaulted on to the horse of the unknown rider, and before the moat guards were alerted, galloped out of the fort, frantically followed by Malayaketu's soldiers who lost valuable time scrambling for horses tethered near the elephant stable. Outside the fort, several leprous beggars picked up staves and tripped the soldiers' horses giving the two men time to escape.

Down the highway, forest tribals formed a barrier, not letting any of Malayaketu's men through. Then they charged, the counter-attack was led by an elderly leathery skinned tribal chief with a stringy ponytail hanging down his back.

The Bahirika dismounted and looked at his rescuer, a man with pockmarks, repulsive tumors and filthy clothing, a mere beggar.

'Thank you for saving my life,' he said to the beggar, who had dismounted and was humbly prostrating to the tribal chief.

'Guruji!' The Bahirika bent low and touched his mentor's feet. 'You sent my savior?' he said.

'The beggar is Preran, the double agent I sent without informing anyone else, in case of an intelligence leak,' the familiar rough voice was balm to the Bahirika.

'Reward him with the revenue of one forest village,' the Bahirika spoke, in his normal Sashigupta voice, removing his wig.

The 'beggar' humbly bowed to Prince Sashigupta, peeled off his tumors, and touched his feet.

Malayaketu's troops barred by forest tribals and Sashigupta's infantry galloped back, the moat gateway pulled up, and the huge wood and metal gates shut.

Rakshash's double agents met King Malayaketu and the Amatya immediately.

'It was Prince Sashigupta, who solved the puzzle. His men were waiting for the prince where Guru Chanakya had organized the blockade. We were forced to return as the counter-attack was vicious,' they informed the chief minister.

'You did what was appropriate, we finally smoked out the real Sashigupta,' Rakshash said calmly.

At the Forest Camp

Back in the forest camp, Guruji and Prince Sashigupta met their commanders.

'Send our orphans to villages paying King Malayaketu taxes,' Guruji said. 'It is time the villagers made up their minds whose side they are on,' he added.

'Contact the chiefs of the *Sreni,* the native militia,' Prince Sashigupta said.

Sashigupta's secretary did both, he called for a meeting with jungle tribal chiefs not affiliated to King Malayaketu, and the Sreni chiefs. After a one-hour briefing, he concluded, saying, 'Follow my orders.'

The meeting ended on a positive note.

'The Atavi, jungle tribe militia, will obey their chiefs,' Guruji said.

The Atavi and Sreni spread out to do Sashigupta's bidding. Outside Nandadurga, climbing the nearest trees, the Atavi and Sreni shot fire arrows into the trees around the perimeter of the fort. Thousands of rock bees that built hives only atop high places filled the air in a black buzzing cloud, stinging anybody who came their way within the fort.

'We need more intel…' February 321 BC

Inside the fort, screams of people running helter-skelter stressed the Governor General.

'Light wet haystacks,' he shouted.

The resulting smoke choked people and animals, and disturbed the bees further. Unable to breathe, people were forced indoors.

A few burning branches broke off and fell on wooden houses. The Governor General worked overtime to keep both bees and fires under control.

Prince Sashigupta was not one to rest, however.

'Burn all grass and trees for a distance of several meters around the periphery of the fort,' Sashigupta instructed the Sreni and Atavi.

'Our Rasada, poisoners, have already poisoned the water around the fort, putting Beesh into wells and streams next to the fort, the people in the fortress will slowly dehydrate,' they informed him.

King Malayaketu and Rakshash had a meeting with the generals. They could no longer stay in the fort without fighting, food, fodder and drinking water were running out.

Keeping up the pressure, supply trains for Nandadurga fort were being captured and rerouted to Sashigupta's camps.

'There is a black market for daily provisions,' the Governor General complained petulantly to Rakshash. 'We are paying huge amounts for provisions for the fort's inmates,' he said.

'It is time we fought those bastards,' King Malayaketu sounded pissed.

'First,' Rakshash cautioned, 'we need outside intel.'

Two tribal chiefs rode in over the moat, during the battle strategy meeting. They went in to meet King Malayaketu and Rakshash.

'Tell me about Prince Sashigupta's war preparedness,' Rakshash said.

'The militias of villages who pay Sashigupta tribute are being trained by the prince,' they informed the chief minister.

'What else?' he asked.

'He has turned a few villages into ordnance factories for war boots, saddlery, and gauntlets, and daggers, plus swords, and arrow heads using looted wootz steel,' Rakshash was apprised.

'And?' the chief minister sought more information.

'A couple of villages into road constructors for cavalry and infantry passage,' one of them said.

The commanders of infantry, and cavalry troops and the general were in a bit of an uproar.

'We have no choice, Amatya,' the general said. 'War it is. Battle formation will copy the horseshoe of the Yavana,' he stated.

'I agree,' the military attaché added.

'Cavalry to the right and left, infantry in the middle, mercenaries and elephant troops to reinforce the back,' the general continued.

'Battle it will be,' Rakshash replied patiently, 'but, the land being uneven, no Yavana battle formation can be followed here. Let's just do an infantry charge backed by cavalry. Contact our allies.'

Pigeon posts were sent to various 'allies', who politely declined. As ex-satraps, they were bogged down with post-Alexander problems of their own.

'Guru Chanakya has probably flooded the tunnels, there is a lot of digging around the fort, we have no escape route,' Rakshash was cautioned.

Double Agents, Again

News of the inner workings of Malayaketu's court came to Sashigupta and Guruji via a perfume seller, a favorite of Malayaketu's antapura.

'When he heard about the flooded tunnels, Rakshash suddenly looked stone-faced,' the perfume seller said to Guruji and Prince Sashigupta.

'And then, as emergency supplies ran out, Rakshash and Malayaketu decided the only way out is combat,' he added.

'We will wait for them to make the first move,' Prince Sashigupta said.

The move came sooner than expected. Malayaketu's army came out of the fort on to the highway, and battled Sashigupta's troops. Pulverized badly, they retreated into the fort, followed by a prolonged silence. Prince Sashigupta's camp was silent too, in fear of a trap. For two days, there was silence on both sides.

Two recently-arrived double agents, tonsured widows, hairdressers for the antapura, updated them on the third day.

'As the siege continued, King Malayaketu, Rakshash, top officials and handpicked contingents of soldiers have escaped through a newly-dug tunnel under the fort wall last night,' the younger widow said. 'We were watched, so we could not come earlier,' she said apologetically.

'Where exactly did the cohort go to?' Prince Sashigupta asked tensely.

'They supposedly raced across the land to freedom in the northwest.'

'To stop fort dwellers escaping, my men filled every known tunnel with poisonous gas. But these tunnels are new,' Sashigupta said.

'Has everybody left?' Guruji asked.

'No, Sire,' one of the widows said. 'Left behind are women of the royal antapura, confident that they are safe… uh… with rumors of Prince Sashigupta's libido,' one of them said, hesitating.

This was all the confirmation they needed. Prince Sashigupta's face was expressionless.

He ordered his army to enter the fort by breaking down the elephant door across the moat. At the first meeting in Malayaketu's court, a spokeswoman from the antapura came to meet Prince Sashigupta, who declined taking over the women.

'Some of them may be vishkanyas,' Guruji warned his protégé, so he would not have a change of heart.

'Yeah! We have enough poisoned food and water and air, don't need poison damsels in the mix,' the prince agreed.

The Hidden Kosa

The battle had cost money, there was no revenue thanks to the exploitative greed of their former rulers, and Guruji and

Sashigupta met on the urgent need for finance.

'We can't tax our villages and forests any more, Guruji. Where is the kosa, hidden treasuries, of King Malayaketu?' Sashigupta asked his double agents.

No one knew.

'I want to meet prisoners on death row,' Guruji said shrewdly. He patiently interviewed one-on-one, each prisoner.

Finally, they sent in the last one – a Chandala rapist sentenced to death for violating an Arya, upper class lady. He was a runt of a man with tufts of hair sprouting from his ears. He told Guruji about two hidden treasuries he had helped build, one within the fort under the elephant stable, and the other outside the fort where the escape tunnel, now flooded completely, ended within dense forest.

In return for help in draining the water and digging out pots of treasure, the rapist was pardoned and exiled to the west, with a small bag of money.

The gold in the kosa could now be used.

Parvatakadesh Virgin Lands

Back in Malayaketu's tent, Rakshash looked agitated. In front of him were two roaming actors who were giving information about the situation post-Nandadurga.

'Slowly, Prince Sashigupta has taken over leaderless forts that King Malayaketu abandoned in the eastern half of his mountain kingdom while escaping to the western border,' they informed.

'Is that the only bad news?' Rakshash asked.

'No Sire, Prince Sashigupta is settling virgin lands around Nandadurga with tribals and farming communities. There is enough rainfall, the soil is easy to till, and they can get good revenue from crop rotation,' he added.

'Anything else?' the chief minister enquired.

'Guru Chanakya has given strict instructions to cultivate Brahmin good wishes.'

'He says, "Let's reserve fertile land with fruits, flowers and water for religious rituals of *Srotriyas,* high-born Brahmins, who will not be taxed. By propitiating God and the scholarly Srotriyas, calamities like floods, epidemics and drought can be controlled," Guruji sent out this command.'

'Prince Sashigupta has agreed, "...and, the Yavana generals will not return to India in a hurry. We can rule as we like for our citizens' prosperity" he said,' Rakshash was apprised.

'Besides this?' Rakshash asked.

'Guruji sent a message to his spies, asking for an update on the Yavana's aftermath,' one of them said.

'We need the same update,' Rakshash added.

Perdiccas dies in Macedonia, March 321 BC

Very soon, Xerxes dropped by.

'Can you update us on the Yavana's family and former colonies,' Guruji asked.

'Alexander had given his signet ring to Perdiccas, his trusted friend, with the order to send Alexander's mortal remains to the temple of Zeus Ammon. This never happened... becoming Perdiccas' first failure,' Xerxes began.

'There are more, Xerxes?' Guruji asked.

'Many more. Six months after Alexander's death, when his son Alexander IV Aegus through Roxanne was born, Perdiccas supported the baby boy as heir to the throne.He was also regent for Alexander's mentally-deficient brother Philip Arrhidaeus,' he continued.

'So much power?' Prince Sashi asked.

'But to no use. The Asian-Greek syndicate was, as usual,

full of intrigue. Perdiccas and Roxanne connived to kill Alexander's wife, Parysatis, suspecting she was pregnant,' the express man informed.

'So, no obstacles for the future ruler, Aha!' Sashigupta thought.

'But Perdiccas' perfidy soon came to a sticky end. Peithon, Seleucus and Antigonos together murdered him. After his death, senior Macedonian army commanders appointed as regent, old Antipater, who then exiled Roxanne and Alexander Aegus to the small town of Amphipolis,' Xerxes explained.

'So, Alexander's inheritors are in dire straits?' Guruji asked.

'Not all. General Seleucus Nikator was appointed satrap of Babylon by Antipater, but this was followed by the Wars of the *Diadochi*, where he barely escaped with his life,' he said.

'Alexander's successors!' sighed Guruji.

After a couple of hours, Xerxes left, his pocket full, his stomach sated with pork and rice gruel, a specialty of the mess cook.

King Malayaketu's Five Allies

A bare-headed Dhoomal was visiting when Xerxes dropped by again.

'Any news about Rakshash's latest tricks?' Prince Sashigupta asked Xerxes, pouring out a new brew.

'There is. The troubadours sing of an alliance between Malayaketu and five princes, Chiravarma of Kaulutu, Megaksha of Parasika, Narasimha of the Mallas from the Ravi, Pushkaraksha of Kashmir, and Sindhusena of Saindara on the Sindhu. Rakshash forged this alliance,' Xerxes said.

'He personally got the princes to join in,' Dhoomal added.

'That's so Rakshash,' Guruji said.

A few drinks later, Xerxes left, and then Prince Sashigupta

and Guruji had a pow wow.

'Rakshash and Malayaketu are becoming a serious headache, I think this happy couple should break up,' the prince said.

'How many of Rakshash's close associates have we captured?' Guruji asked Dhoomal, who was silently rolling strips of colored cloth around his head for a new style of turban.

'Several, but the most important is the jeweler cum financier, Seth Chandanadasa,' Dhoomal said, his voice muffled with a fold of cloth across his face.

'Excellent! Accuse Chandanadasa of adulterating precious metals with copper,' Prince Sashigupta said to his secretary.

'How, sire?' he asked, confused.

'The usual. Plant his smithy with copper, chemicals, bellows, anvils, chisels, moulds, dig an extra deep furnace for the making of bronze, rather than gold or silver. This will earn him exile,' the prince instructed.

'Also accuse him of funding the Malayaketu war machine with untaxed black money. This will earn him a death sentence,' Guruji added.

'Send him and a couple of bonafide criminals after a couple of weeks to the municipal hanging and cremation grounds. Wait a while before you strike. You know what to do,' Sashigupta winked.

'I will contact you after the Seth is sentenced to death,' Dhoomal said.

Rakshash' Signet Ring, April 321 BC

A week later, Rakshash's wife dropped his signet ring in the garden, where the new gardener with his huge turban was sweeping out dead leaves. The ever-sharp Dhoomal brought it hidden in his turban to the old man.

'Aha, Rakshash, I now have you in my fist,' Guruji chortled.

'Send someone you could trust with your life, but is unknown to Rakshash,' Prince Sashigupta spoke to Dhoomal, who sent one of his comrades to the duo.

Together, Guruji and Prince Sashigupta instructed Dvived, a trusted orphan, on the steps to take. Little did prince and Guru know that their enviable camaraderie was about to be tested.

Prince Sashigupta and Guruji Fall Out

Next day at court…

Prince Sashigupta had just returned from the front, after annexing a small republic.

'I not only annexed the republic, I defeated their *Kulamsamgha* too,' he boasted to his secretary in court.

'Which Kulamsamgha, Sire?' the man asked.

'A clan oligarchy of Kshatriyas. I want whole Varana citadel to celebrate the next two days, with actors, dancers, musicians, mimics, storytellers, acrobats, jugglers, magicians, the works,' Sashigupta announced, bragging over his latest conquest.

'I will organize it immediately after consulting Guruji,' the secretary replied.

'Do that,' Prince Sashigupta smiled cheerfully.

The next day, Prince Sashigupta went to the terrace to see how his citizens were celebrating his victory. The citadel was quiet. No ropes of jasmine flowers decorated the gateway to the royal residence, the temples of protective deities on either side of the gates or anywhere in the palace. In the distance as though to mock him, a flower seller shouted aloud his wares, 'Kanakambara, jasmine, red roses! Flowers for your hair, flowers for your prayers! Kanakambara, jasmine, roses!'

The prince walked into the audience chamber, where his ministers and courtiers were assembled.

'No music, no flowers, no procession, no floats. Why is there no celebration?' Prince Sashigupta asked furiously of the minister closest to his throne.

'Guruji cancelled them,' the minister said awkwardly.

'Summon Guruji!' he barked at his secretary, who ran to call the old man, trembling.

Shortly, Guruji came to the court, swinging his vastra over his shoulder.

'What is the matter?' Guruji grunted casually.

'The celebrations to mark my victory were cancelled. By whose authority was this done?' Sashigupta snapped.

'My authority! We have work to do, this is no time to celebrate,' Guruji said sternly.

'Do not forget that I am the king,' Sashigupta roared.

'Do not forget that I made you the king,' the old man snapped. 'Learn gratitude!' he added.

'Earn it. Don't tell me how to behave,' Sashigupta snarled.

'No, I am telling you about protocol, which you flout every chance you get,' Guruji replied, irritation evident in his tone.

'I am trying to make a point, but as usual, you misunderstand,' a vein in Sashigupta's forehead was pulsing badly.

'As USUAL? What do you mean "as usual"? Until you apologize properly, I will not return to court,' the old man stomped out.

'Do not return. I wish a mature man like Rakshash was my Amatya,' Sashigupta shouted at Guruji's retreating back.

Prince Sashigupta's courtiers gazed at the floor in shock

rather than look at both their leaders squabbling.

By next day, pigeon posts reached all enemies of Sashigupta with the news that he and his guru had had a falling out. Malayaketu and his allies were elated, without the scheming Chanakya, the army of Sashigupta could be easily vanquished. After a huge meeting, all the armies from the respective kingdoms marched for a whole day towards Sashigupta's territory and camped together at base camp.

The Savior of the Evening...

Late evening, the same day, on the outskirts of Varana citadel, agent Dvived rescued one of Rakshash's closest friends, the goldsmith Chandanadasa, from being hanged in the local cremation grounds. He was just in time.

For several generations of kings, this ground had served as the place to hang or behead criminals dangerous for the state. Now, two slave-rapist murderers were already swinging from a tall tamarind tree.

But the third man being strung up was not a criminal, but Chandanadasa, a goldsmith being punished for funding Rakshash and the wars fought by the Nandas. Dvived, riding by, drew his double-edged sword and fought all three hangmen who fled the expert assault.

After cutting the ropes that bound the Seth, when he tried to thank his benefactor, Dvived broke down and confessed, 'Chanakya killed my father and brother and I have no home. I am in danger of imprisonment for supporting the Nandas.'

'I know how you feel because I too was a supporter of the Nandas. I can offer you a place in the camp where Rakshash is staying,' Chandanadasa said appreciatively.

'A job for me?' Dvived looked grateful.

'Oh, it's a mega camp with regiments of six kings, making

it battle-ready to wage war on Sashigupta. The combined might will crush Sashigupta in no time, they are all moving northward,' Seth gave out details unwittingly.

'I cannot thank you enough,' Dvived bowed, accepting the offer.

Malayaketu's Base Camp

King Malayaketu's base camp was an overnight journey. The two men , now good friends, rode non-stop to the camp. The campsite was on one bank of a swiftly flowing stream, which had been diverted to form a moat on the other three sides of the square-shaped camp. On the southern end, elephants and horses were stabled. The five kings' men were put up on the eastern and western ends, with each king's tent in the dead center of their troops. Malayaketu's tent and soldiers were northside. With some difficulty, they located Rakshash's tent.

'I am grateful you saved Chandanadasa's life,' Rakshash responded after the goldsmith explained how he had been rescued at the last moment by Dvived.

'We can only offer you the position as cook's helper in the kitchens for common soldiers,' he added.

'I will do anything to have regular employment,' Dvived said, his eyes filling with tears. He knew that nothing conveyed gratitude like copious tears.

However, Dvived's gratitude did not last, he was immediately put to work cutting what felt like an endless supply of vegetables – garlic, carrot, greens, and soaking turmeric root, tamarind in water for gravies to accompany the rice, and, chopping wood for the ovens, sweeping out food debris after the meals several times a day, and helping to serve several thousand soldiers who queued up for their daily meals.

Overwhelmed with work, Dvived had to fight the sleep

of exhaustion. He went on sorties every night after work to get acquainted with the layout of the sprawling camp. With difficulty, via a snake charmer, Dvived sent a note to Guruji, who silently read it to himself. 'The six combined armies of Prince Malayaketu and his allies will encircle Prince Sashigupta's soldiers in a semicircle formation, pressing them towards the Indus riverbank, where it would be a fight to the death,' he informed the teacher.

Guruji's orders were explicit, Dvived had to recce only after nightfall, and on his special day, the day before the battle march, well after Rakshash the disciplined Brahmin, went to bed.

Because Guruji and Sashigupta continued to ignore each other, the old man sent a message through the kapata sanyasi, who also doubled as a cattle trader with access to the kitchens. The message was brief, 'After He sleeps.'

The Night before Battle

Dvived was sleepless after he received the message. Tomorrow, the troops would march towards Sashigupta's forces. He waited patiently for Rakshash to go to sleep early as was his habit. Everything had to go according to plan.

Dvived was captured prowling in a suspicious manner next to Malayketu's tent late the night before battle. By then most of the camp were asleep in preparation for the early morning march.

The night watchman, bodyguards and soldiers dragged Dvived to the opulent tent of King Malayaketu who was about to go to sleep after drinking steadily for a couple of hours.

'Sire, this man was skulking near your tent,' they said.

The soldiers pushed Dvived on to his knees in front of King Malayaketu.

'What were you doing?' Malayaketu snarled at Dvived.

'I lost my way, O Raja,' Dvived smiled weakly at the young king.

'Who do you work for?' Malayaketu asked.

'I am... am from Rakshash's camp,' Dvived stammered.

'Search him!' Malayaketu barked.

A soldier stripped Dvived naked and found a sealed letter.

'What is this?' the young king demanded.

'I... I... was given this,' Dvived stammered again, trembling. He futilely tried to wrest the letter from the soldier, who then hit Dvived's head with his shield. Dvived fell face down, blood dripping down his neck.

'By whom?' Malayaketu snarled.

'I cannot say, O Raja, forgive me,' Dvived lay groveling at Malayaketu's feet.

'Break it open,' Malayaketu snapped, kicking Dvived viciously with a metal-tipped white boot, more blood flowed down Dvived's face.

The soldier sliced open the package with his dagger, to reveal a communiqué wrapped around a signet ring.

'Sire, the letter is addressed to Prince Sashigupta by Rakshash,' the soldier said.

'And the ring?' Malayaketu stretched his palm out for the ornament. 'Rakshash!' Malayaketu looked at it for a long moment, a vein in his temple started to pulse visibly.

'Read the letter out loud,' Malayaketu snapped.

Malayaketu's secretary, Yadava, read out the letter:

Dear Prince Sashigupta Maurya,

Now that you have removed Chanakya, I accept your offer to be chief minister. I will help you win the battle against Prince Malayaketu. The five kings are our allies now. They will betray Malayaketu on the battlefield as agreed. Killing Malayaketu is the key to the distribution of his kingdom. I will aid you in its proper division after you win the battle. Gratefully yours, Rakshash.

'These kings are cheats,' Prince Malayaketu furiously threw his unsheathed sword towards the flap of his tent, his bodyguards jumped out of the way. He raised Dvived to his feet and slapped him hard on the face.

'Behead him,' Malayaketu screamed. 'I have enough traitors in my camp,' he snapped at his secretary, 'send my best men immediately to the tents of the five kings, and decapitate them. **Do not** inform Rakshash.' He held out his right hand, palm upwards.

The secretary's fist tightened around Malayaketu's signet ring.

'As you wish, Sire,' he went to Malayaketu's C-in-C's tent, entered, and clapped just loud enough to wake the general.

'General, get your best men to execute the five kings silently, with all possible speed. I have the signet ring of King Malayaketu to back me,' he whispered.

The general inspected the signet ring, nodded his head, and grunted at his aide to summon 60 of his crack warriors.

Within minutes, 60 men, armed, muscular, came to his tent. The general snapped: 'Divide yourselves into five groups. These are your orders.'

He drew a map on the mud floor with instructions for each king in different parts of the camp. After he drilled them on how to complete their missions with least opposition, the general went to a vantage point to oversee that all took place according to Malayaketu's orders. The five groups crept to the tents of the five kings, and after half of each group immobilized the bodyguards by beheading them, the other half stormed each tent and executed the kings, each taken by surprise, the lateness of the hour being an ally.

The skirmish was not silent. The yells of defending bodyguards and the sword fights woke up the entire camp, including Rakshash, who had gone to sleep shortly after sunset as was his habit. Hearing noises from the tents of the five kings, Rakshas rushed to the tent nearest, Chiravarma Raja's, and was horrified to see the headless corpse of the king.

Shocked, he raced to the tents of kings Meghaksha, Narasimha, Pushkaraksha and Sindhusena – each crowded with soldiers still fencing and saw each king's head parted from its torso. To add to the confusion, the cattle trader's animals, cattle, aggressive and unfettered, went barreling through the camp, butting and goring everyone who came their way.

Rakshash is Confounded

Rakshash rushed to Malayaketu's tent, stepping over a headless, naked dead body.

'Your highness, what happened? We were supposed to go to battle tomorrow,' Rakshash said, bewildered at this shocking turn of events.

A sweaty-faced Malayaketu screamed with unsuppressed rage, 'Traitor, you allied with the five kings to destroy me, but I came to know your plot on time and sabotaged your plan.'

'What are you…?' Rakshash sounded dazed. 'What did I…I do wrong?' he tried to say.

'Don't act innocent,' Malayaketu threw both letter and signet ring at Rakshash, who caught the letter first and then picked up his signet ring.

Rakshash gazed at the signet ring and understanding dawned. 'This is the signet ring I keep with my wife, King Malayaketu,' he explained.

'So?' the young king was blinded by fury.

He read the letter silently, 'My letter writer makes a mark in the middle of the letter, a swastika. This letter is a fake, there is no swastika.'

'You liar,' Malayaketu screamed again, outraged. 'You poison my father by sending a vishkanya to him, next, you target me, and no doubt, you had plans for my five foolish allies too, to become chief minister to Sashigupta. Be gone, do not show your face to me again,' he yelled.

'Prince Malayaketu, please hear me out,' Rakshash begged. 'This is Prince Sashigupta's trick. No one approached me for post of chief minister.'

'Enough! I have listened to your rubbish too long,' an enraged Malayaketu shouted.

'O King, let us at least question the letter carrier to ascertain the actual mastermind of this plot', Rakshash pleaded.

'He's dead!' Malayaketu crudely spat at the headless body on the tent floor. 'Leave, now! I spare you because you are a Brahmin. Secretary, assassinate commanders-in-chief and generals of each king,' he ordered.

The secretary left the tent to brief Malayaketu's commander-in-chief again. Everyone ignored Rakshash who was standing with a defeated look waiting for someone to tell him what had gone wrong.

After an hour of futile waiting, completely overlooked, Rakshash departed on horseback, shocked, miserable. His goldsmith friend Chandanadasa, riding side by side, confided to him about the way that he had been rescued by Dvived.

'It was planned from the very beginning,' Rakshash said, still dazed.

On the highway, a day later, the goldsmith parted company with Rakshash, saying he would travel to his wife's father's house, where his family was. Rakshash was inconsolable. Riding along the small townships that bordered Prince Sashigupta's kingdom, he failed to observe the men who followed him. Finally, while resting against a tree on the highway, a passing troubadour walked up to him.

'What news of the city of, of…I forgot? How is my… the… the family of Rakshash?' Rakshash asked faintly.

'All prisoners in the family ward of the prison,' the troubadour said.

Rakshash buried his head in his hands. 'My king dead, friends scattered, our kingdom lost, family in prison. What have I to live for?' he looked crushed. 'What would I not do to have my family safe? Our kingdom safe?' he wailed.

Rakshash spent three more days, without food and water beside the highway, miserable and depressed. On the fourth day, time passed slowly; a sortie of soldiers with a palanquin stopped by the other side of the highway. Two soldiers dismounted and came cautiously to him.

A Chief Minister, Again

'Rakshash, Sir!' the soldiers spoke in low voices of respect.

'What is it?' Rakshash asked wearily, raising his head.

'Prince Sashigupta has sent you a message', the senior soldier handed him a silver cone.

Rakshash read its message and looked up in surprise. He said, 'My friends are freed, and my family lives in their old home again. What manner of miracle is this? And how can I repay it?'

'Very easily,' a gravelly voice spoke from the palanquin. The curtains parted, Guruji alighted and walked towards Rakshash, who stared at him, stunned.

'Guru Chanakya, your eminence! What must I do to deserve this good luck, plus a visit from you in person?'

Rakshash said, his voice breaking.

'Become Amatya and bring justice and peace back to the land,' Guruji said in his usual tone.

'But Guruji, what about the fight between you and Prince Sashigupta?' Rakshash sounded confused.

'A drama to fool spies and double agents. Help my prince to achieve his goal of a prosperous democratic society, beyond caste or creed, color or nationality,' Guruji spoke calmly.

Rakshash stared at Guruji with awe, 'Your hair is tied once more, Guruji!'

'Yes, my work is over. Will you take over now, Rakshash?' Guruji offered.

'Why are you giving up your position as chief minister?' Rakshasha asked, still dazed by the latest events.

'I am old and want my ashram *gurukula* to coach future leaders.That has always been my passion. So could you step in now and help forge these principalities into the greatest *mahajanapada,* nation state, ever?' Guruji said.

'I will. I cannot thank you enough for saving my friends and family from destitution,' Rakshash said with gratitude.

Rakshash mounted the dark brown horse saddled for him, and gratefully accompanied Guruji back to Sashigupta's court, where he was warmly welcomed by Prince Sashigupta.

A week later, Rakshash was anointed Amatya, chief minister, in a small ceremony by Prince Sashigupta and Guruji.

'Ha, the missive came true! I have become your chief minister,' Rakshash quipped.

Guruji and Prince Sashigupta smiled, both concealing the pain of Dvived's death.

The Inheritors

Sashigupta expires, Chandragupta is born

TWO YEARS AFTER the poisoning of Alexander, Sissicottus' identity as the satrap prince, a.k.a. Sashigupta, died.

King Chandragupta Maurya, Sandracottus, emerged as king of the Indian northwest. Alexander's conquered eastern territories, absorbed by Seleucus Nikator, included areas the Persians and Macedonians (and Dhananda) had conquered, taxed, and taken tribute from. Back in the Seleucide camp, many rumors were attracting attention from Seleucus himself.

'Who is this new king Sandracottus of the Indian border territories?' Seleucus asked his Indian double agents, a madaari and a kapata sanyasi.

'From the name *Sashi* (which refers to the "moon"), it is the same Sissicottus, now renamed *Chandra* (which also refers to the "moon"), during his coronation. Sissicotos is Sandracottus,' the madaari answered.

'Is it a custom for an Indian monarch to change his name during coronation?' Seleucus asked.

'Yes, Lordship!' the kapata sanyasi replied.

'Strange are the Indians!' Seleucus thought.

Bindusara is born, January 320 BC

A few months had passed. Back in the palace inner quarters, Rakshash and the king were whiling away their time with a game of chess.

'My Durdhara, due next week,' Chandragupta said, smiling at his new wife, who was munching on honey-flavored bananas. 'I see, Guruji has sent another drink,' he smiled at the attendant, who handed him a gold goblet, with two handles.

'Can I have a taste?' Durdhara asked.

'You may, my queen,' he said.

The attendant handed over the goblet, Durdhara gulped half the drink in one go, gave a sigh and sank to the floor. The attendant shouted out, and the king and Rakshash ran towards the queen, whose face had frozen. Both Rakshash and the king waved their hands in front of her eyes, which remained unmoving.

'Call Guruji and the vaidya,' Chandragupta shouted anxiously.

Both men came running at full speed.

'Guruji, Durdhara is unconscious, she drank,' Chandragupta gestured at the goblet.

The vaidya felt her pulses, and shook his head. 'Nay, dead, just seven days from delivery,' he said gravely.

'Oh, gods, the drink had new poisons to immunize you, Chandra,' Guruji hit his forehead repeatedly. He had stayed back only to take care of his protégé.

'I fed her by mistake,' Chandragupta said wretchedly.

'Leave the room, Chandra. The vaidya will cut open the queen and extract the baby.'

The king left with Rakshash protectively beside him. A few minutes later, Guruji called out, 'Chandra, you may come in now.'

'How is the baby, with all that poison?' the king was concerned.

'Motherless, your first child, will be named Bindusara because he was touched by a drop (*bindu*) of his mother's poisoned blood,' Guruji pronounced.

King Chandragupta held out his hands, tears trickling down his cheeks, to carry his son and heir.

Sapta Sindhu: The Love Expert

The bitter chill of winter announced that the start of a new year had come. General Seleucus Nicator had just finished a rewarding chat with one of his favorite visitors, the love expert.

The tall man with toned physique and sweet breath checked the list of aphrodisiacs before handing it over. After checking it too, the general turned official.

'Any news of Sandracottus and Indika?' he asked.

'Sandracottus has started right,' Seleucus was told.

'How?' the king wanted to know.

'He has begun to implement a blueprint for diverse economic activities. Like horse breeding and cattle rearing,' the visitor added.

'King Alexander was so impressed with Ashvaka-bred superior cattle and horse breeds that he sent thousands of superior horses and 230,000 oxen to Macedonia,' he said.

'And?' the general sounded curious.

'Metal and mineral mining, and extraction are state activities,' he was briefed.

'Smart! No weapons and agricultural tools or surgical implements can be made without the king knowing,' Seleucus noted.

'The state also strictly controls all luxury cotton weaves. If any kingly cotton is caught secretly leaving the kingdom, the perpetrators are put to death,' the visitor continued.

'Ah! Greek and Persian women love Indian luxury cotton, and the treasuries of Persia and Greece pay huge import fees for the ladies' sartorial elegance,' the general mused.

The love expert smiled, tucked his fees into a leather pouch and left.

Antipater Dies in Macedonia, March 319 BC

In the war room, King Chandragupta was bent over a long table on which a detailed map of Alexander's conquests was spread out. Other people surrounded the table.

Tan Mei, the Kushan, tapped on the map. To Chandragupta's unasked question, he said, 'Macedonia, Sir! Antipater is dead.'

'That troublemaker?' Guruji asked. 'What was he up to?' he wondered.

'Antipater had divided Alexander's conquests in the following manner: he gave Ptolemy, Egypt, Antigonos Asia, and Seleucus, Babylon. For himself, he kept Macedonia. As viceroy, he played political dice with his three children, Iollas, Alexander's treacherous wine pourer, daughter Nicaea wedded to Perdiccas, and Cassander, who will now become Macedonia's viceroy, while Arrhidaeus rules,' the king was informed.

'Cassander? Poor Macedonia!' King Chandragupta said.

'And poor Arrhidaeus!' Guruji grunted in agreement.

The Pony Express Man in Bactria

Xerxes had finished tying across his barrel chest a number of silver and brass cone-shaped message carriers. General Seleucus' replies were enclosed in the cones, and now he sat relaxed, with his feet on a silver lion-headed footstool.

'Tell me,' General Seleucus said, 'about Indika. What is Sandracottus, one of Alexander's most loyal Indian satraps, up to?'

'Evolving from satrap to king. He and his two Amatyas are organizing their territories into tax-paying districts,' Xerxes said.

'Two? Didn't the old man retire?' the general asked.

'He was supposed to, but can't stay away from his protégé,' Xerxes smiled.

'Pity! Continue,' Seleucus said.

'The Indians are organizing their territories into tax-paying districts,' he continued.

'How?' the general asked, intrigued.

'By consolidating different economic setups with individual tax structures,' the express man said.

'Oh, money gathering!' Seleucus was surprised.

'King Sandracottus has made standardized weights and measures mandatory for agriculture, industry, commerce, all subject to different taxes. Surplus monies are used for military upkeep,' Xerxes explained.

'Throughout?' the general asked.

'No, the tax exempt includes all manner of philosophers, Brahmin priests, Buddhist monks, Jain munis, religious scholars like Srotriyas etc.,' he replied.

'Even if some of them are spies?' Seleucus asked, smiling.

'Even if,' Xerxes shrugged. 'Indian kings need the blessings of holy men to keep power,' he added.

'I prefer animal sacrifice to holy men, at least the animals give no advice,' the general said cynically.

Xerxes left quietly.

The Guilds, May 319 BC

The non-stop notes of a falsetto from General Seleucus' private court announced to all who could hear them that the travelling balladeer was entertaining the general. After a couple of hours, the voice halted to ask for a drink of water.

In fear the voice would begin another onslaught of classical notes, the general asked kindly (and hurriedly): 'Where have you been last, singer?'

'In Indika, King Sandracottus' court,' he replied.

'And what is the Indian king doing?' the general asked.

'Job creation. Something called shreni,' the balladeer mentioned.

'And this…uh?' Seleucus' curiousity over Chandragupta was evident.

'Shreni are guilds of artisans and merchants, who protect from start to finish, all handmade goods,' he explained.

'So, they must have economic clout?' he asked.

'They do, but King Sandracottus keeps them subservient to Brahmanas, the priestly class, and Kshatriyas, the ruling warrior class,' Seleucus was told.

'So, economics is subservient to politics,' the Macedonian general commented.

'It is,' the visitor replied.

After a few more songs, the general's secretary dropped a stream of coins into the balladeer's outstretched hand, looking at his master, who nodded at him, when to stop the flow.

Queen Mother Olympias, May 318 BC

A year later… seasons had come and gone.

'I wonder how the Yavana's family fares without him,' Guruji said ruminatively. He was sitting relaxed in front of Xerxes, whose beard had grown salt and pepper.

'Guruji, the women in the Yavana's family are worse than any poisonous snake,' he told him.

'Who now?' Guruji asked.

'The queen mother!' Xerxes said.

'Oh, Olympias, what is she up to?' the teacher was eager to know.

'Conniving for power. Unluckily for Olympias, she no longer had the loyal support of Perdiccas. But luckily for her, after ancient Antipater died, Olympias was free to indulge in more intrigue for her grandson's sake,' Xerxes replied.

'Does Olympias still have power to do as she pleases?' Guruji asked.

'Oh, yes! Five years after Alexander's death, the Queen Mother had many men executed,' the seasoned express man mentioned.

'As revenge?' Guruji was intrigued.

'And how! She had the ashes of Iollas, the wine pourer, scattered in the wind for his part in poisoning Alexander,' he told Guruji.

'How did she conclude that?' the teacher questioned.

'Rumor goes that Aristotle had "encouraged" Antipater, Iollas being his son, to poison King Alexander,' Xerxes said.

'How did Alexander's mentor change into his enemy?' Guruji asked.

'In his defense for his part in the remote-controlled death of Alexander, Aristotle announced cryptically, "No one freely endures such a rule."'

'Thank the gods such perfidy has not yet entered India,' Xerxes said drily.

'Dhanananda was quite as bad, and he too came to a sticky end,' Guruji retorted.

Philip Arrhidaeus coinage in Mauryan India

The soft glop-glop sound of warm herbal oil being smacked on bare skin filled the room. The visitor in the room, Xerxes, was gossiping with General Seleucus, who now turned over, relaxed and oily.

'Tell me,' the general asked, 'what else is Sandracottus up to?' always curious of the affairs of Chandragupta.

'He has introduced high levels of standardization for economic activity throughout the kingdom. But he is stuck in one very important aspect,' Xerxes said.

'Stuck? Sandracottus?' Seleucus was curious.

'He does not mint his own coinage. He uses coins minted by Philip Arrhidaeus of Macedonia,' he replied.

'Half-brother to my late liege, Alexander?' the general asked, surprised.

'The same. Arrihidaeus coins are used all over Sandracottus territories,' Xerxes said.

This info was not received with enthusiasm and the general said, disgruntled, 'I am going for my bath.'

Xerxes took the hint, bowed and retreated backwards.

Arrhidaeus dies in Macedonia, May 317 BC

'Sire, you asked about Philip Arrhidaeus,' Tan Mei the Kushan said.

'Some background since I use his coinage in my kingdom, including my acquisition, Taxila, after I kicked out Eudemus. I need to know more,' King Chandragupta said.

'Alexander's father, King Philip, had a short affair with Thessalian dancer Philinna of Larissa. The son of this brief tryst was Philip Arrhidaeus,' the Kushan began.

'And did he have a claim to the throne?' the king asked.

'He did. This bastard son put dread into the heart of

Olympias, who feared the boy would claim her son's throne in the future. She poisoned the child, who did not die, but suffered lasting damage to his brain. In spite of this, Philip Arrhidaeus became king five years ago with Perdiccas as regent,' Tan Mei explained.

'And how did Olympias take it?' Chandragupta asked.

'Vengefully. Arrhidaeus died this year, and Olympias, tireless meddler, forced his wife Eurydice to hang herself,' he replied.

'Alexander's extended family is suffering?' the king wanted to know.

'Not all, Sire!' Tan Mei shrugged, saying, 'Eighteen-year-old Neoptolemus II, grandson of Olympias, has become king of Epirus.'

Porus, Eumenes, Eudemus Killed, June 316 BC

The Mauryan court was taking a break. An out-of-breath kapata sanyasi, who had hurriedly arrived in court, was talking in a rush, pigeon posts not yet having arrived for that day. The urgency of his visit was evident from the bits and pieces of holy ash falling off his forehead as he spoke. The 'holy' ash not being the regulation holy ash of a bona fide holy man.

'King Chandragupta, Guruji, bad news. Your ally and friend, King Paurava has been killed by Eudemus, Alexander's general, whom he made satrap of some Indian territories, and Paurava's elephant troops, captured,' he informed.

'Intrigue with elephants?' Guruji asked dryly.

'And Eumenes, Alexander's secretary, too,' he added.

'What went wrong?' Guruji asked.

'First, Eudemus betrayed Eumenes to Antigonos, and then Eumenes was executed by the Macedonian Silver Shields,' he replied.

'Why did the Silver Shields take this step?' Guruji shot another question.

'Eumenes was Greek, plus he was stupid enough to lose a baggage train with 30 years of their war loot,' the kapata sanyasi said.

'Ah, loot, the tipping point. Eudemus?' Guruji waved his hand to continue.

'Eudemus executed by Antigonos for betraying Eumenes, leading to the ongoing Third War of the Diadochi,' he replied.

'Diadochi?' Chandragupta asked.

The king and his two Amatyas looked confused with the fast flow of information.

'Daidoch means successor and refers to the first generation of military and political heads after Alexander's death,' explained their messenger.

'And who stands to profit from these grisly events?' Rakshash asked.

'General Seleucus. Rumor goes he is now marching to capture the eastern part of Alexander's empire next to your kingdom,' they were informed.

'Gandhara and Kambhoja?' the king asked.

'They call it Paropamisadae,' the visitor replied.

The kapata sanyasi departed, leaving the three men in a continuous discussion. All three agreed that good intel was key to better control of their fledgling kingdom.

Olympias Killed, July 316-March 315 BC

Back in his Sapta Sindhu court, General Seleucus Nikator was attentively listening to a double agent from the east, a wandering balladeer and another from the west, a trader of children's toys.

'In the Indian northwest, King Sandracottus defeated

a small force of the late general Eudemus. But attacks on Alexander's conquests are not restricted to India,' the balladeer said.

He was bowing low to Seleucus as he spoke, 'There is news from Macedonia too, Lordship.'

'Fire away!' Seleucus said.

'Prince Cassander, son of late Antipater, brother of late Iollas, has taken over Macedonia,' the trader said.

'And this is earthshaking, why?' the general asked.

'After Alexander's death, Queen Olympias' machinations tried to keep his empire for her grandson Alexander IV Aegus. She failed, and has been captured by Prince Cassander,' he informed.

'Captured? What political rot!' General Seleucus sounded peevish.

General Seleucus' comment on the continuing rot of political power-hustling came miserably true again within months. He had a familiar visitor with important news. The trader of children's toys was moving his hands and head preparatory to speech, overcome with emotion.

'What bad news have you for me today?' Seleucus asked in a resigned tone.

'Queen Olympias was assassinated by the families of her victims after her capture. Vengeful Cassander reportedly denied her body the rites of burial, still seething for her treatment of his brother Iollas,' the toy trader said.

'And the remaining women in Alexander's family?' the general inquired.

'Roxanne, along with her son, Alexander IV Aegus, was kept under the charge of Glaucias, in Amphipolis. Prince Cassander stripped all royal privileges from the boy,' he was informed.

'Shame on him, taking revenge on a little boy,' General Seleucus shook his head sadly. 'But Cassander is not done yet, I wager,' he glowered.

Meeting on the Achaemenids in Varana

Back in Varana, King Chandragupta and his two Amatyas were closeted in the war room. Guruji's voice getting hoarser by the minute signaled that the lesson on leadership was coming to a close.

'And so, a king can only reign with the help of others, one wheel does not move a chariot,' Guruji was explaining.

'But,' the king protested mildly, 'thanks to my two Amatyas, my state machinery moves itself smoothly.'

'We need to evolve, learn from the Achaemenid domination of Gandhara, Kambhoja and Sapta Sindhu territories for 200 years,' the old man noted.

Rakshash who was listening quietly, added, 'And adopt Achaemenid taxpaying, political structures like satrapies.'

'And don't forget the glorious architecture of Susa and Ecbatana for our future palaces, though I prefer sandalwood from South India, and local teak that they used in their palaces,' King Chandragupta said, now an expert on royal residences.

'Good point!' Guruji said, adding, 'The Achaemenid palaces used teak imported from Gandhara.'

'For official purposes, we use Kharoshthi script, which is derived from the Aramaic language and alphabet. Both were extensively continued to be used for Achaemenid admin purposes,' the king added.

His secretary noted everything at top speed, to avoid missing any details.

The Maurya War Machine, April 314 BC

They were back in the strategy room, the king and his two Amatyas, discussing the way forward, eastwards. General Ramagupta was there too.

Amatya Rakshash looking incensed, veins popping on his forehead, grey locks flying in all directions, growled, 'All former Nanda tax-paying territories have gone rogue after Dhananandaʼs death.'

In front of him, poring over the map which detailed former Nanda territories, rivers, and cities, were the king, the general, and Guruji. Behind them were many agents waiting to receive orders.

King Chandragupta spoke quietly, 'Ramagupta, take over.'

The general bowed and spoke.

'From the Sapta Sindhu to the Ganga ending in the sea in the east, the Nandas had tax-paying control. After their deaths, the lands have turned into kingdoms and republics. So, takeovers must be done,' he suggested.

'One by one eastward?' Chandragupta asked. 'Each territory completely consolidated?' he wanted to know.

'And with different types of warfare to confuse each enemy,' Guruji added.

'All our enemies know we use Rasada, poisoners, to get rid of the opposition. To keep the element of surprise, we need other means,' Rakshash said grimly, 'Ramagupta?'

'Our secret service already uses Sattri, secret agents and Tikshna, assassins, as regular or roving agents,' Ramagupta counted on his fingers.

'What can we add to the mix?' Chandragupta asked.

'Counter-espionage agents who can become householders or traders, or ascetics, who mingle unnoticed by the general populace,' the general proposed.

'Double agents?' Rakshash asked.

'We have a few high-ranking double agents, whose families and properties, we have kept hostage,' Ramagupta continued.

'Our women agents, especially poison damsels, are the best. What other women can complement them?' Chandragupta asked.

'We have top class entertainers, who can move in and out of every kingdom as actresses and musicians, and that special category for unhappy housewives, women love experts,' Ramagupta chipped in.

'The last category shows promise,' Chandragupta said. 'Choose a town or dense rural area, where important officials' wives are known to be suspicious of, and unhappy with, their husbands,' he added.

'Philanderers' wives are ideal for our lady love experts to pump news of their men, without suspicion,' one of them mentioned.

'Anything to avoid a divorce,' the king quipped.

'Wives with a grievance are a legit way to get info on a man's movements,' Guruji said grimly.

'My bachelor guru!' Chandragupta winked at Rakshash. 'He has a special feeling for the opposite sex,' he winked.

It was true. Guruji did have a special feeling for women, he feared them more than water travel. Guruji growled something in protest, sounding somewhat like distant thunder.

Eastward to the Kuru Lands, January 313 BC

Leaving Rakshash to manage the few very ornery criminal cases in court, King Chandragupta and General Ramagupta had gone to the strategy room for an update.

'So how is our intelligence activity progressing?' King Chandragupta asked, shutting the sound-proof door firmly.

'We have set up low-level attendants for all important persons, umbrella bearers, water vessel cleaners, fan-pullers or shoe polishers,' General Ramagupta began.

'Anyone who need not be suspected by the rich. How is the psychological warfare angle, like instigating treachery in enemy camps?' the king asked.

'Our holy men, camped in temples, are interpreting all omens to mean that your army, Raja, is unstoppable,' he replied.

'This takes time. We need to pressurize neighboring oligarchs, in this case the ancient race of the Kurus,' the king said impatiently.

The door opened. A messenger and a frowning Guruji entered.

'Ramagupta, any news of Maraj and my other pupils who have gone to entertain the Kuru army as actors?' Guruji sounded like a worried parent.

'Guruji, a pigeon post has just arrived, in code,' the messenger removed the sacred, silver amulet from his neck, thrust it into Ramagupta's hand and left.

'What are your boys up to?' General Ramagupta opened the missive and said out loud. 'They have picked up some toys from Kuru land,' he began chattily.

'How many?' the king snapped.

'The two most valuable ones, Governor General and Amatya,' he replied.

'Good, now we negotiate,' the king looked at Guruji, who gave a rare smile.

Neoptolemus II in Epirus

On a warm balmy day, two friends were settling down for a peaceful drinking session.

After a while, Xerxes informed King Chandragupta, 'The news is, the reign of Neoptolemus II, Alexander's nephew and Olympias' grandson in Epirus, has come to an end.'

'My late liege's family continues to go extinct,' the king sighed, pouring himself and Xerxes a drink each.

'Inexorably!' the visitor exclaimed.

Both men settled down to drink in silence.

In the Kuru Court, April 313 BC

It was a hot, dry summer day, dust whirlwinds obscuring the vision on all sides.

A brotherhood of equals, all Kuru princelings, noisily crammed the royal court of the Kurus. Into the noise, the court spokesman announced a messenger from King Chandragupta.

Dhoomal, in an eye-watering turban of chain mail and vivid cotton ropes, bowed low to the assembly, but not so low as to risk dropping his turban.

Noting the sparse hair on Dhoomal's upper lip struggling to be a mustache, the royal priest, also the de facto military advisor, asked curtly, 'What is your mission here, uh… boy?'

'King Chandragupta would like to sign a treaty for safe passage to the east with his army, with strategic benefit for both our kingdoms. The conditions,' Dhoomal extended a silver cone to the royal priest, his surprisingly deep voice at odds with his teen looks.

The royal priest took the cone and then waved dismissively towards the exit, saying, 'You may go. We will get in touch with your king about our final decision.'

After Dhoomal exited the court, a babble of sound filled the chamber.

'So, Chandragupta sends this multi-colored clown as his messenger…'

'He can't be serious...'

'He takes the Kurus for granted...'

'If Chandragupta wants a treaty, it could be a ruse to gain time...'

'Where is our Amatya when we need him most?'

Complaint after complaint, filled the chamber.

Into the center of the court entered a travelling trader for toys, widely renowned for being a double agent for various kings. He was wrestling violently with a baked clay bullock cart with two riders, evidence that toy sales were really not his main occupation. As the princes yelled impatiently, he crudely broke off the two riders, to reveal a secret compartment with parchment in the cavity.

This he handed over to the royal priest, who announced to the court, 'The mystery of our missing Amatya is solved. The Mauryas have our two most powerful men as hostages, Governor General and Amatya.'

The cohort erupted chaotically but stopped when they saw the royal priest putting up his hand.

'What do you say, you?' the royal priest growled at the trader, who was waving his hand to draw attention to himself.

'Chandragupta has sent two cavalry regiments to your west border,' he said.

'That low life, every passing week, he's turning into his dad Dhanananda,' the eldest Kuru prince snarled.

'We have no choice, we have to negotiate mutual conditions,' the royal priest said, trying to sound calm.

The cohort noisily made suggestions, which the royal priest listened to carefully. The Mauryas, he knew, were now unstoppable, only time would tell which suggestion was plausible.

Seleucus begins his Empire, March 312 BC

It was yet another warm and dehydrating day. In the private chambers of King Chandragupta, the pony postman was seated relaxed next to the king, having a drink like only two buddies could. Guruji was mixing Vacha alcohol with various tinctures of poisons. He intended to give his protégé one different poisoned drink a day for the next one week. Now he diluted one of them sufficiently so Chandragupta could swallow it with minimum fuss.

'Any news?' the king asked after downing one more bitter, smelly potion.

'Bad methinks! General Seleucus has taken over Persia, Gandhara, Kambhoja, territories west of the Indus, and a few coastal territories next to the southwestern sea,' he said.

'Bad, bad! He might come east of the Indus to try to conquer us again like my former liege, Alexander,' the king growled. 'I don't want distractions from my eastern conquests right now,' he said irritably.

'Let us wait and watch,' Guruji said pacifically.

The king's wine pourer, who also doubled as his bodyguard, refilled his wine goblet.

The Surasenas in Central India, July 312 BC

It was cool and dark in the long armory room. King Chandragupta was inspecting two pieces of improved armor, a breastplate reinforced with woven cotton that deflected normal arrows, and leather gauntlets that protected against minor cuts. Both were being fitted on a leather and wood model of a footsoldier, and arrowheads of bone, wood and iron were assembled for the king to attack the 'soldier'.

Guruji, General Ramagupta and Amatya Rakshash were also in the room looking at their hands-on king.

'Sire,' a young bodyguard entered as the king shot his arrows. 'The Kuru envoy!' he informed.

A young man with noble features entered and handed over a cone to General Ramagupta, who sent him away and read the message.

'The treaty is working!' the general said.

'Is it?' King Chandragupta threw a pike enthusiastically at the wooden soldier, which came crashing down. 'Conditions, Ramagupta?' he asked.

'Our army can march through their highway and build up on their east borders in exchange for high value prisoners,' the general said, propping up the 'soldier'.

'But we will continue to keep their families as hostage,' Guruji added. 'Summon my new agents from Surasena territory,' he added.

'Only one has returned, Guruji,' the bodyguard returned with a bejeweled smelly man.

The *sarpagraha*, snakecatcher, had fingers and throat crowded with black-magic silver amulets and tattoos as protection against poisonous snake bites.

'Surasenas?' Guruji asked.

'As the Kurus have warned the Surasenas about the Maurya war march, they are worried about our regiments permitted to park on their western border,' the snakecatcher said.

'Predictable!' King Chandragupta said.

'Let the enemy stew. Marching into battle during monsoon, all these floods and landslides, will demoralize our men,' General Ramagupta said firmly.

'Inaction is a psychological weapon, it leads to low enemy morale,' Guruji grunted.

'We negotiate again,' General Ramagupta beamed. 'And this time, we will,' the general went into some onerous detail on what the next steps could be.

Panchalas in Central India, April 311 BC

Several months had passed and the Surasenas had come to an amicable settlement with the Maurya war machine.

'What next?' King Chandragupta asked in the war room.

'Panchala[1], the natal abode of Panchali, Draupadi, wife of the five Pandava brothers, is next on the agenda,' the scholarly Guruji answered.

'Its important location is undeniable, between the upper Himalayas and the River Ganga, and from there to Vaishali and from thence to Magadha, the eastern stronghold of the Nandas,' General Ramagupta said.

'The governance model?' King Chandragupta asked.

'It moves from ancient monarchy to oligarchy to a king-and-Amatya administrative structure,' Rakshash answered.

'Which means being a satrapy might be new to them,' King Chandragupta said thoughtfully.

'Agents?' the general barked at the people behind him.

Maraj bowed slightly. 'Rumor goes that the Panchala army has not been paid, as there has been a crop failure for two seasons, and the kingdom is running out of revenue,' he said.

'Why?' Ramagupta asked.

'Insect invasions,' a vrshala widow spoke out loud.

---

1 The Panchala kingdom had two capitals: Kampilya for southern Panchala and Ahichchhatra for northern Panchala. The Panchala kingdom's territory included the present-day States of Uttar Pradesh and Uttarakhand.The Buddhist text *Anguttara Nikaya* mentions Panchala as one of the sixteen mahajanapadas of the 6th century BCE. The 3rd century BCE text *Arthashastra* also attests to the Panchalas as following the Rajashabdopajivin (king consul) constitution. Panchala was annexed into the Magadha empire during the reign of Mahapadma Nanda in the mid-4th century BCE.

'An unpaid army is an angry army, disunited. We march towards Panchala,' the general said.

'Good Ramagupta! You think on your feet,' Guruji ground out approvingly.

All those present hunkered down for the appropriate strategy to conquer Panchala, General Ramagupta in the lead.

Haihayas in Western India, June 310 BC

Panchala had fallen. Now, crowded around a map made with sand and pebbles, were King Chandragupta, his two Amatyas, General Ramagupta, and several double agents. Much to the relief of all his listeners, General Ramagupta, a man with the sterling trait of being very thorough, was now ending a rather long monologue on the Haihayas.[2] 'The Haihayas are spread over many tribal pockets and difficult to vanquish like a multi-headed cobra. If you cut off one head, another rears in its place,' the general said.

'Agents?' King Chandragupta asked.

'It is true, Sire,' Vijay, Rakshash's favorite agent, said. 'Plus, the Haihayas don't trust outsiders,' he added.

'General?' the king looked towards Ramagupta.

'The usual bribing and prostitution won't work. They are loyal to each other and also greedy,' General Ramagupta replied, adding, 'We need an alternate strategy.'

'Guruji, I prefer peace to war. No unnecessary bloodshed, but no spineless submission either,' the king said.

'What about vassal status or an offer of satraphood?' Rakshash asked, evidently thinking of Dhanananda's equation

2 The Haihayas were native to the present-day Malwa region of Western Madhya Pradesh.

with the Persian empire.

'Won't work, Sir. The Haihayas are tribesmen whose natural enemies are non-tribesmen,' Vijay said.

'We could comfortably ask the Panchalas and Surasenas to send some troops, since now they are our allies and friends,' Rakshash suggested.

'We could win, after a prolonged series of battles, but that would deplete our treasury and ruin our soldiers' morale. Guruji, give me a suggestion from your textbook,' the king looked at the old man with confidence.

'Well, we could fall back on secret war, undercut the enemy's economy, block all essentials from entering their kingdom, and stop all the waters. Without water and a viable economy, the Haihayas will be forced to consider a treaty,' Guruji grunted, his words the final word on the future course to take.

'This time, no poison of any sort will be used on the waters or soil, since after conquest, the enemy's subjects will become our people,' King Chandragupta added firmly. 'But divert the water in the irrigation canals and the water tanks built for rural usage. And dam the rivers,' he instructed them.

Rakshash thumped the table in approval for General Ramagupta to go forward. Several mountains and rivers changed location on the 'map'.

'Execute Roxanne...', 310 BC

Outside India, change convulsed Alexander's former territories. Within five years, Seleucus' depressing prophecy about Cassander's political treachery came true.

Tan Mei, the Kushan double agent, was updating the Maurya court.

'That Cassander had many strategic plans, soon became apparent.

"Didn't Alexander say that his funeral games would be the fight for supremacy by his generals? He forgot one important component", Prince Cassander said ruminatively in court to Glaucias.

"Who?" Glaucias asked curiously.

"Me! The way his father Philip took over the throne from his brother's son, I too will do the same, take away Macedonia and all Greece, right under Roxanne's nose, depriving her son of his birthright," the prince said.

'Prince Cassander then ordered Glaucias, "Execute Roxanne and her son, Alexander IV Aegus."'

"Get rid of the legitimate heir to Alexander's throne?" Glaucias looked shocked.

"Any more questions and you will be next", Prince Cassander snarled.

'Glaucias left to finish his task, he had no choice. He killed both, Alexander's son Aegus and Roxanne. Denying them the dignity of a funeral, Alexander's son's body was chopped into pieces and thrown into a well along with his mother's corpse. When informed, Prince Cassander was smug,' the Kushan briefed the court.

'Unfeeling bugger!' the king commented.

'He completely is,' Tan Mei agreed.

Alexander's Son Killed in Pergamon, 309 BC

Seasons changed fast, but not intentions. Months later at the private audience hall…

'Any update on the filthy Cassander?' King Chandragupta asked Tan Mei.

The Kushan cleared his throat and began, 'Oh, Prince Cassander always has more up his sleeve. It was Heracles's turn next. Prince Cassander ordered Polyperchon "to murder

Heracles and Barsine,"' Tan Mei informed.

'Did Polyperchon?' Chandragupta asked.

'He did. He had to travel a bit. Heracles, Alexander's firstborn and his mother Barsine lived in Pergamon,' he continued.

'And no one opposed him?' the king asked, surprised.

'No one. Polyperchon tricked Heracles into attending a dinner, where he was strangled, killed Barsine, and had both bodies buried secretly,' Tan Mei told Chandragupta.

'Poor Alexander! Any other offspring?' he asked.

'No. With Heracles' death, Alexander's lineage has come to an end. What could have possibly happened to his only daughter is a mystery lost to history,' the Kushan concluded.

Vitihotras Face Secret War, 309 BC

It was cool and dark in the room. General Ramagupta and Guruji were alone in the king's chambers. The king himself had gone on a hunting expedition and Rakshash had the tiring duty of being judge for some criminal cases.

'The Haihaya status?' Guruji asked.

'The Haihayas have crumbled due to lack of water and food,' General Ramagupta paused.

'But?' Guruji asked the unasked question.

'But the Vitihotras[3], the most violent Haihaya subsect, are far from vanquished. They take no prisoners and fight to death. It is difficult to penetrate their brotherhood,' the general said gloomily.

'Well, it is in the universal nature of men to be partial to a set of good curves. Many a Vitihotra will fall short of being

3 Tribes on the banks of the Narmada river.

a model husband when succumbing to this predilection,' Guruji intoned in his grainy voice.

When General Ramagupta continued to look grim, Guruji added, 'And it is in the universal nature of women to resist being replaced by one of her sex young enough to be her daughter.'

'Our women love experts can be placed in Vitihotra neighborhoods,' General Ramagupta looked slightly cheered.

'Send for Vijay and Dhara too,' the old man said.

A short time later, both agents entered. Guruji briefed them separately.

'Dhara will go as a brothel owner,' Guruji concluded.

'But I have no experience,' Dhara sounded dismayed.

'That's precisely what makes you a good fit. Our regular trained agents are falling prey to sabotage and treachery,' Guruji explained to her.

'We want an outsider, on the inside. Besides, any information from three kinds of agents will be considered true,' General Ramagupta said.

'And how do I…?' the agent began to ask.

'Keep note of everything and anything, do not confide in anybody,' the general warned and went into some detail on the next steps. 'Vijay,' the general took him aside to brief him as an entertainer for the Vitihotras.

In separate batches, Mauryan agents landed in Vitihotra territory.

Maithila is Next, 308 BC

Many 'servants' from Vitihotra territory had sent pigeon posts, each message saying the same thing, that the Vitihotras were down, subdued, defeated.

'What next?' Amatya Rakshash asked in the war room.

A profusion of pigeon posts lay on the table, each waiting its turn to be read and burnt to ashes in the fire pot.

'Maithila,[4] should be subject to water wars too. Capture dams, bifurcate rivers and canals away from farming land. Farms downstream should have no water for irrigation purposes, farmers should complain to the king,' Guruji said.

'How will we know we have succeeded?' Vijay asked, he headed the espionage group camped in Vitihotra lands.

'Simple! Pay attention to the servants' chatter. When the master of the house has to forego his bathtub and manage his daily ablutions with a mere bucket, the water war has succeeded,' came Guruji's witty reply.

Vijay left.

Cleopatra, Alexander's Sister, is Killed

Xerxes was having a drink with his friend – Chandragupta's laced with poison.

'And how are my former boss' family bearing up?' the king asked the express man.

'Anybody related to Alexander has bad luck coming to them in floods, and here I am talking of his only full blood sibling,' Xerxes began.

'Cleopatra?' Chandragupta asked.

'Used as a pawn by both her father and mother for political intrigue. Father Philip forced her to marry her uncle, king of Epirus who is her mother Olympias' brother, to appease his ex-brother-in-law after divorcing Olympias.

Years later, Olympias tried to manipulate Cleopatra to remarry when her husband died. After his death, Cleopatra

4 East of modern-day Nepal. Nepal finds mention in Vedic texts.

became regent for son Neoptolemus. But thanks to Olympias' ambition to capture power through her daughter, Cleopatra, former queen of Epirus, was kept captive and then assassinated by her suitor and that fraud Antigonos, who gave her a grand funeral afterwards,' Xerxes informed the king.

'Traitorous hypocrite!' Chandragupta said dismissively of Antigonos' antics. He looked preoccupied and the pony express man, sensitive to his friend's moods, left early as Guruji, Rakshash and General Ramagupta entered, preparatory to having a brainstorming meeting.

'Maithila has succumbed,' Guruji informed his protégé.

'Next on the agenda, Kashi Raja,' Chandragupta said.

The men talked late into the night with their agents, finally deciding that something never before done would be tried, with trusted old-timers. Intelligence gathering was important so the agents left for Kashi after being briefed.

Kashi Court, 307 BC

It had taken a while…

The hunchbacked jester was now a fixture in the Kashi court. He entered now through a narrow side entrance, stooping carefully beneath the court sentry's spear. But his turban, snagged by the spear, unraveled as he walked towards the king, until he was completely bare headed by the time he reached the throne. The court laughed. They were in pause mode, having heard from intelligence officials about unwelcome Mauryan incursions. Some lighthearted entertainment was welcome.

Behind him, permitted to enter for the first time, came an extraordinary creature, who tinkled musically at every step. The creature, resplendent with false hair and an attention-seeking, false chest, now signaled to the current court favorite, a dancer hired from the highway brothel, who took up the challenge in a competitive mood.

As the two vied with each other to get the most applause, an agent entered, and the king and his Amatya went into the private chambers to discuss the issue, the implacable Maurya war machine and the next step to take. The hunchback squatted down and made a play at both dancers, meeting with much sniggering from lowly court officials.

The hunchback was cautious of going too near the private chambers but snatches of conversation repeatedly mentioned the same thing.

'The power equation dictates the policy of one king with another. Whether equal, stronger than or weaker than, the king of the land...,' the Kashi top general was saying in a gruff tone.

'That low caste Maurya has won every battle fought, thanks to astute Amatyas, and a trustworthy general,' Kashi Raja growled.

'On the downside, they don't know Varanasi. And our army numbers are massive in comparison, whereas they have people of all races and tribes in their marching army,' his Amatya said.

'That makes them our equal. We need, though, to move the battlefield away from Kashi mainland,' the general said firmly.

'So set up a temporary army camp,' the general's second-in-command suggested.

This suggestion met with the king's approval and all the men hunkered down for a meeting that would decide the kingdom's fortunes.

Intelligence Gathering

The Maurya high command were soon informed about the temporariness of the army camp. The hunchback had sent a message via a guildsman wearing a green guild turban. Similar messages from the dancer of the brothel and the male impressionist confirmed the same.

In the war room, King Chandragupta was slapping the guildsman on the back for wearing such a restrained outfit. 'Good show, Dhoomal! Even I wouldn't have recognized you,' he lauded.

Then the king turned to his Amatyas.

'First things first, we need to penetrate this temporary army camp. And do something new. Weaknesses?' he said.

'Food is a problem in the new campsite,' the officer replied.

'It always is. What have we not done, and who have we not sent? Yet?' the king asked.

'Vijay, that master of disguise, can go to the camp as a trainer for horses and buffaloes with a large number of both types of animals,' Ramagupta suggested.

'Ideal! Call the vaidya and Vijay,' Rakshash snapped.

The Kashis Tumble

Ten days later, a humble cowherd wearing a sweaty head scarf and smelling of fermented milk, came to the gates of the Kashi camp with a herd.

'State your purpose!' a gateman growled.

'I heard that milk is in short supply and all my cows have recently calved, we have enough milk for at least half the soldiers,' he told him.

The gatemen had a brief pow wow, and went to meet the man in charge of food. 'We will ask the mess cook if it is acceptable to bring in the cows,' the gateman said.

The cowherd waited patiently.

'Permission granted,' a gateman said.

Two of the gatemen physically checked the cowherd for concealed weapons, and then allowed him in with his beautiful horned cows and some massive bulls.

Every day, the cowherd went on routine trips to procure cattle feed, loading it on his bullocks and bringing them back into camp for the next day's feed. Three days later, on an *Amavasya,* a cloudy moonless night, late in the evening, the cowherd quietly mixed some herbs in the feed. After all of the cattle had eaten and drunk water, he took the bulls and a few dried-up cows to the center of the camp, where the horses were tethered, and cut the cattle loose.

Screams and shouts filled the air. The realization that something beyond their control was happening took over the camp when frenzied cattle gored every horse that was tethered, and crashed through tents where unsuspecting soldiers were sleeping. As half-awake soldiers ran helter-skelter in almost pitch darkness to avoid being gored and trampled, the chief commander of elephants, horses and chariots rushed out of his tent to check what had upset the loudly whinnying horses. The humble cowherd who had taken shelter behind the commander's tent, stabbed him with a cow-horn accurately in the most vulnerable acupoint *mru*, killing him on the spot.

The pigeon post was read out to Guruji, the king, the general and Amatya Rakshash.

'The Kashi army is in full flight, disarray. Horses dead, soldiers missing, the camp, a mess. Kashi Raja, his Amatya, top generals and civic administrators, are meeting to see how to get out as best as they can,' the message read.

'There is only one way,' Guruji growled, and without saying much, the others agreed too.

Within a week, a shaken Kashi Raja sent a message: 'We accept a new overlord, the Maurya king.'

Pataliputra, the Eastern Capital, 306 BC

There was a slight lull in the marching. In the king's tent, a few men were gathered around their king. The gravelly voice, for the uninitiated, was Guruji speaking out loud to King Chandragupta.

'Many northern kings have at least one ancestor from ancient Magadha. In your case too, Chandra. Dhanananda's mother was a queen of the Shishunaga dynasty, who his father seduced. Mura's grandmother, the court dancer, was a Shaka, who originally resided near Kushinagar below Nepal,' Guruji said.

'Is Magadha then my birthright?' the king asked.

'Then and now. I don't want any unwanted violence,' Guruji said. He looked at Rakshash and asked, 'Do you still have pull in Magadha?'

'Do I?' Rakshash made an agreeable trumpeting sound like a baby elephant getting used to his grownup voice. 'Guruji, after my late master Dhanananda died, Magadha has a mixed bag of Kshatriya and Vaishya republicans, who came in and out of the Nanda court. I will do something,' he said.

'Do something' turned out to be an understatement.

Chandragupta's army walked into Pataliputra without any opposition. All Magadha seemed to have turned out to welcome King Chandragupta, Guruji, Amatya Rakshash and General Ramagupta. Magadha was now Maurya territory.

In the old Nanda palace, in a low-key ceremony, Rakshash coronated his king, witnessed by a silent Guruji, both overwhelmed.

'What are your thoughts, Guruji?' Chandragupta asked.

'Pataliputra, the son of Patala, is now the eastern, the second, capital of the kingdom, for strategic reasons,' Guruji said.

'We can now concentrate on Kalinga,' Rakshash, the futurist, announced.

Kalinga, a Complete Failure

An effeminate creature was sashying into the private chambers of King Chandragupta Maurya, who was poring over a map with General Ramagupta, the court having concluded its work for the day.

The king frowned trying to place the visitor. 'Messages?' he asked.

'The Kalingas are putting up a stiff resistance,' the effeminate creature, clad like a dancing eunuch, replied.

'Where exactly?' the king asked recognizing Vijay's voice.

'The area between the Mahanadi and Godavari rivers, adjoining the east coast next to the sea, is not giving us an inch,' he informed the king.

'Why is Kalinga so important?' Vijay was curious.

'It poses a threat to the safe passage of goods going south. And let's take a leaf out of our late lord Alexander's book on war, all routes for military and commercial movement should be kept free and unhampered,' the king explained to them.

'But the Kalingas are not giving us even a seer[5] of dry soil, they are fighting us something fierce,' the messenger sounded hesistant.

'General Ramagupta, what next?' Chandragupta asked.

'Sire, let us leave Kalinga alone, and march southwards

5 An Indian measure, 1 seer is equal to 1.25 kg.

towards Asmaka,' the general suggested.

'Enough said, I agree. Call both my Amatyas to the strategy room,' the king instructed.

The Vindhyas in Central India

In the new court's strategy room…

'General,' King Chandragupta looked at Ramagupta and asked, 'What progress with the Asmakas?'

'The Asmakas,[6] around the River Godavari, unprepared for war, were living under the false hope that the Maurya war machine was tied up with Kalinga, and not coming south,' Ramagupta began to brief the king.

'That's true. But our reason for not attacking the Asmakas is to give our army a break from marching on another exhausting conquest. What next?' the king said.

'We have sent our best lady agents to work, the woman mendicant and lady love experts. They are currently gaining the confidence of high officials' wives, several officials who have sullied the marital bed,' the general smirked.

'So, the way forward?' Chandragupta sounded curious.

'Love potions with undetectable poisons,' Ramagupta replied.

'Poisons to kill?' the king asked, concerned.

'No, Sire. These poisons will derange the officials mentally, making them unfit for work,' he said.

'But the king is not being administered the same poison?'

---

6 Asmaka Assaka was a Mahajanapada in ancient India which existed between 700 BCE and 425 or 345 BCE according to the Buddhist texts *Anguttara Nikaya* and Puranas. It was located around and between the Godavari river in present-day Telangana and Maharashtra.

Chandragupta wanted to know.

'No. Vijay, posing as a vaidya, has a different tale to tell. Vijay?' he looked towards him.

The effeminate creature now launched into a narrative about the doings in Asmaka's royal court.

'Two bribed servants from the king's inner circle informed me secretly about birthmarks, boils and moles on the king's body. As vaidya, in court I proclaimed to the king that people with such a combination of boils and birthmarks will go in for an incurable disease. The king realized that he had the exact same combination of body markings, so he took my medicine, which induced vomiting. The royal vaid then gave the king medicine to stop vomiting. Emetic and anti-emetic medicines are now playing havoc with the king's mental health, weakening him and making him unfit for ruling or waging war,' Vijay briefed them.

'Any other strategy?' the king asked.

'Our double agents disguised as bakers are set up in the marketplace. Should the Asmakas take too much time, the bakers will set fire to their shops, and destroy the entire marketplace,' the general gave more details of their strategy.

'When will Asmaka be ours, Vijay?' Chandragupta asked.

'The poison has done its job, wait for official confirmation,' Vijay replied.

'So, society and the day-to-day economy, great combination!' General Ramagupta said, looking pleased.

'Except for Kalinga, we have conquered most former Nanda colonies,' he added.

'Ah, Kalinga! A flea which never fails to aggravate. We'll get back to it later,' Chandragupta said.

Seleucus Mints Coins in His Name

Everybody, except Rakshash, was still getting used to the huge palace that the Nandas used in the eastern part of their former kingdom.

'How are the lands around Varana faring?' the king turned to Xerxes, who had entered with a slight limp.

'Right now, your western borders are threatened as General Seleucus has been unfailingly marching into Alexander's India, of former Nanda territories,' the pony expressman said.

'Specifics?' Chandragupta asked.

'With Ambhi dead, the territory around Taxila, southeast of Varana, is under attack. He has taken over land next to the Indus and is trying for the western sea. The general is establishing military strongholds like our late Yavana boss, Alexander. He's become superconfident,' Xerxes said.

'Super confident?' the king was curious.

'Minting coins in his name,' the expressman replied.

'Ah! A sign that he feels all conquered lands are now irretrievably his. How are our people faring?' Chandragupta asked.

'The viceroy is barely able to manage your capital Varana, and the governor general is struggling to control revenue collection, and the law-and-order situation,' he told the king.

'I think Varana needs us. We head back north,' King Chandragupta declared.

Guruji and Amatya Rakshash nodded in agreement.

Alexander's Empire Breaks up, 305 BC

It was a rare day. All four men, Guru Chanakya, Amatya Rakshash, General Ramagupta and King Chandragupta, were in Varana's war room taking a break as an old friend had dropped in to visit. The four men stared; Xerxes looked withered.

In answer to the king's question, 'How are our former boss Alexander's lands faring after his death?' Xerxes had launched into a long soliloquy. The king privately thought General Ramagupta must have infected Xerxes with his gift for monologues.

'Alexander's legacy to the peoples of Asia was that of "a long-haired demon of the race of wrath". His territories crumbled after his death, his subjects being indifferent to who ruled them.

'Alexander's dying declaration, "I foresee that a great combat between my friends will be my funeral games", became prophetic,' Xerxes said.

'How so?' King Chandragupta asked.

'Because, soon after his death, civil war broke out. Alexander was more conqueror, less settler. His generals had no training otherwise. They did not know how to settle the new lands they had conquered. The empire broke into pieces, each part ruled by a Diadochi, Alexander's successors,' the expressman explained.

'Good observation, Xerxes,' King Chandragupta said, waving at his bodyguard to pour Xerxes a drink, and settling down with a resigned sigh with a poison potion given by Guruji.

Indian Wars with Seleucus Nikator Begin

'King Chandragupta, we need to form plans to fight Seleucus,' General Ramagupta said thoughtfully. He was frowning as he spoke, stooped over a table spread with maps.

'Give me intel about General Seleucus, I need to understand my enemy before I engage in warfare with him,' King Chandragupta addressed Xerxes, who was also stooped over the maps.

'Seleucus went from humble soldier to general in Alexander's army. It was during the campaign against Bessus that Seleucus proved his mettle. When Alexander died, Seleucus captured territories of Asia, including the Indian ones, that the Macedonian king had conquered but is unable to enforce law and order in his conquered Asian territories. He took over Paropamisadae from Roxanne's father, Arachosia, Gedrosia, parts of Aria and many other former Alexandrian Indian territories with the help of satraps,' the expressman said.

'Before General Seleucus becomes entrenched in his new territories west of the Indus, we need to mass in Varana,' King Chandragupta turned towards General Ramagupta.

'The Kurus, Surasenas, Panchalas, Vitihotras and others east of the Sapta Sindhu will send men and elephants,' the general said. 'Infantry, horsemen, elephants, we need battle formations for maximum impact,' he added.

'Sire, I was also thinking of a gradual wearing down of the enemy,' the general said. 'A war of attrition,' he suggested.

Guruji agreed, 'A war by other means is good strategy.'

'Wearing down?' the king thought aloud. 'Let's count the ways. Geography, Xerxes?' he said, looking towards the expressman.

Satraps Philip and Peithon, 305 BC

Xerxes nodded and began another monologue.

He wound down saying, 'Before Alexander left the multi-river Indus area, he made Philip, son of Machatas, satrap south of the Jhelum-Chenab confluence and Thal Desert next to lands governed by Porus the Elder. Peithon was given a satrapy below Philip's around the same time, close to the Indus including Sindhimana near Patala,' he told the king.

Xerxes poked at various points in the maps.

'I forgot to add, after Porus was killed by Eudemus, Porus' territories were taken over by his killer till he was assassinated too, and now the territories are ruled by Philip,' he added.

'Relevant, how?' the king asked.

'Seleucus rules via vassals from Gandhara and Kambhoja, and the Sapta Sindhu to Aria, Arachosia and Gedrosia. Because Philip and Peithon are old friends, he takes advantage of this. His men have safe passage through rivers Jhelum, Chenab and Indus, and this enables open lines of communication right up to Gedrosian territory[7], which he annexed after Lord Alexander died,' Xerxes gave details.

'Let's stir the pot a bit,' the king sounded upbeat.

'By?' a curious General Ramagupta asked.

'Bunging some Yavana, Scythian and Persian mercenaries into the mix. Spice in the rice,' King Chandragupta said flippantly, getting a rare glare from Guruji. 'Please brief our double agents,' he added.

General Ramagupta gave some orders gruffly to his second-in command. 'Need intel on Philip. Send in our best jobbers.'

Within a few minutes, Maraj entered.

'What say you, boy, about Philip?' Maraj was asked.

'Politics, and some history, Sire! Eleven years ago, Eudemus assassinated Porus the Elder shortly before Antigonos assassinated him. After Eudemus died, Philip, whose satrapy bordered Porus' lands on the east, took over Porus' territory. Seleucus has Philip as friend, neighbor and satrap,' Maraj said.

'One, one at a time,' the king said quietly to Guruji and Rakshash after Xerxes departed.

7 The area referred to as Gedrosia runs from the Indus River to the north-eastern edge of the Strait of Hormuz.

Philip and the Athletes

The manly love expert had returned. All was quiet in court, the courtiers taking a break from proceedings.

'If it is about Philip, speak!' King Chandragupta said.

'Sire, Philip misses all things Greek, most of all the Olympics.'

'The Olympics?' the king exclaimed.

'Yes. Rumor goes, he misses his interactions with ah… ah… heavenly bodies,' the love expert sounded a tad embarrassed.

'Heavenly? Like stars and moon bodies?' the king sounded baffled at this sudden foray into astronomy.

Guruji raised an eyebrow.

'No, more like stars shining with oil and minus all clothing,' the love expert tried to explain.

'Got it! Ramagupta, do we have athletic Yavana mercenaries?' the king asked.

'And a few locals too,' the general replied.

'Good! Brief them and send them on,' Chandragupta ordered.

'Both groups separately,' Guruji growled.

It was a warm muggy day. Satrap Philip, clad in Greek clothing, sat slouched on the royal seat, looking on at some local entertainment, a wrestling bout. Two men, rippling muscles shiny with oil, were in a square ring, which had very fine mud packed into the ground. Both wrestlers grunted bad-temperedly as they circled each other, as if the more offensive the grunts, the easier to annihilate their opponent. This entire sequence was being repeated to King Chandragupta in his weapons room.

'Then Sire,' the agent with a ghastly Yavana-hybrid headdress spoke. 'After some vigorous action, one of the muddy wrestlers won. Philip rewarded him with a lapis chain,' he said.

'Onwards, Dhoomal!' the king nodded.

'Next, it was the Yavana athletes' turn. Philip moved out towards the mini temporary stadium near River Jhelum built for this sole purpose. The exceptional skills, attractive oily bodies, and entertaining nature of the games were so appreciated by the satrap, that he invited the whole lot to a comus,' Dhoomal was briefing when the king interjected with

'A drinking party!'

'Where, the "athletes" got Philip drunk, then strangled him, followed by a vicious fight to death with his bodyguards,' Dhoomal narrated the events.

'A satrap-free satrapy?' the general asked.

'Satrap-free anarchy, more like!' Guruji commented.

'Good for us, bad for Seleucus,' Chandragupta handed over some coins to the informer, who smiled and left.

Salt from the Salt Range

The hunchback was waiting patiently for the royal court of Varana to adjourn, before he could speak. Once the court was given a break, double agents, the king, his guru, Amatya, and general, all retired to the war room.

'Start!' Guruji growled with his characteristic brevity, 'What have you learnt?'

'A small observation, Sire!' the hunchback said. 'Peithon's army prefers inland salt from the Salt Range to sea salt. A lot of Salt Range salt from above the Thal Desert is imported through that route,' the jester informed them.

'And Peithon?' the king asked.

'A wino who likes his alcohol varied,' he replied.

'Excellent! Send veteran Persian and Kirata mercenaries, all new faces so no one can recognize them, as salt traders to infiltrate the soldiers' mess and officers' kitchens,' King

Chandragupta said. 'Our Scythian can import high quality wine from Harahura. Let him meet Dhara before he meets Peithon. For make-up tips,' King Chandragupta directed his officials.

The hunchback and general left together.

Crawling Villages, 304 BC

In the war room, Guruji was getting messages that confirmed how his strategies were working.

'News of the poisoning death of satrap Peithon has flooded different kingdoms, both sides of the Sapta Sindhu. General Seleucus is upset. With both Peithon and Philip dead, he is forced to send his own men to guard the borders, and river pathways so that roving bands of pirates and thugs can't loot food, tax payments, other necessities,' General Ramagupta said.

'General, one more stratagem. Farmers in border villages can stretch their fields into Seleucid territory, slowly, gradually,' King Chandragupta said ruminatively.

Guruji agreed. 'Our farmers are respected by both enemies and our people. Brief our gramikas of border villages to push the boundaries gradually, they will do the needful,' he said. 'Tell them there is no need to rush,' he added.

Double agents in charge of border rural areas immediately departed after being coached by Guruji and the general, this being a strategy that would take time.

Nikanor's Assassination

In the late afternoon, Guruji entered the war room, and stared grimly into the far side of the room, where two identical young men with headdresses large enough to clothe all the women of a respectable village, were bowing towards him.

'Two Dhoomals?' he asked grumpily as the king, Amatya

and General Ramagupta followed him.

'No, Sir! One of us is fake, but we look alike,' an unfamiliar voice spoke.

'Pray, why do we need to see two of you?' Guruji asked, impatient.

'To test if we could fool you,' the boy replied.

'You did. Purpose?' Guruji asked.

Amatya Rakshash now spoke. 'If you yourself can be misled, then so can the enemy,' he smiled.

'Target, Rakshash?' Guruji asked impatiently.

'Nikanor, Seleucus' friend!' he said, excited.

'The friend of an enemy being also an enemy,' Guruji nodded in agreement. 'Background?' he asked.

'Governor Nikanor became Macedonian satrap of Parthia, after the previous satrap, Eudemus, was betrayed by Antigonos, the "one-eyed". He is consolidating his satrapy and coming east with some vehemence. And Seleucus and he are getting cozy with each other with troop exchanges, etc.' the general briefed them.

'I still don't see the point of having lookalike agents,' Guruji asked oddly.

'Nikanor has a penchant for luxury goods, everyone knows this. Our Persian mercenaries disguised as Indian jewelry traders who already have safe passage from Seleucid to Nikanor territories, can fool Nikanor with lookalike disguises.'

'Smart! Send our best makeup artist Dhara to the "traders" at once,' Guruji ordered.

'And the treasurer too, he can add something "royal" from our own treasury, to gain entry into Nikanor's private chambers. And the love expert,' the king spoke.

'Thus chipping away at Seleucus and Nikanor. Are the "traders" briefed?' Guruji looked cheerful.

'Already done! With good makeup and disguises,' General Ramagupta interjected.

'And some royal jewelry,' the king added.

'We can direct them to work,' the general said.

Warfare without War – the Farmers

A couple of weeks later, a solitary pigeon post arrived at Varana with the message: 'Work completed. No more Nikanor.'

Vijay came to court a few days later with more heartening news, 'General Seleucus has been forced to send soldiers to guard the borders of late Nikanor's satrapy, now shorn of top generals who have died mysteriously through dehydration,' he told his listeners.

'O, Scythian alcohol! Guruji, our warfare without war should be taken up a notch,' King Chandragupta said.

'What do you have in mind? And where?' Guruji asked.

'Border disputes, starting outer Taxila which is satrap free after Ambhi's death. It is where a few Seleucid forces still man a garrison and keep a tenuous check on surrounding rural areas. Farms should be ransacked by responsible raiders, granaries looted, not destroyed. To increase farmer stress, our zookeeper can drive herds of wild pigs through farmland to damage standing crops. Seleucus will have to send soldiers to protect both,' the king elaborated.

'Call our zookeeper. He knows the capture and training needed for wild animals to do his bidding,' Guruji said, his eyes twinkling.

'Stretch Seleucus thin,' the king chortled.

Low-caste Chandalas, a New Irritant

In the war room, the king and his guru were chatting, Chandragupta trying a new pair of 'tiger claws' on an enemy, in this case a wooden dummy.

The king was repeatedly scratching the cotton armor-covered dummy soldier to see how deep the gashes could get.

'The stretch on Seleucus must be taken to its limits with yet another strategy for warfare without war,' the king said.

'Which is?' Guruji asked eagerly.

The dummy soldier (had it been alive), would now have been a veteran of several battles, so ripped was it.

'Sending low caste outcasts like Chandalas and excreta scavengers to upper caste wells, for bathing and other hygiene activities like washing blood, urine-stained clothes or baskets used to carry excreta, at the washing stones,' the king began to tell Guruji. 'Then these wells become tainted and impure. And many such polluted wells will make upper caste villagers complain to General Seleucus, who will be forced to send his men to protect wells and also arrange for decontamination. Even better, his soldiers will be detained away from battlefields to protect high caste wells from Chandala users,' Chandragupta added.

'And forced to stay on as guards. Secretary!' Guruji's growl had a faint air of contentment.

'The Chandalas succeeded, Guruji,' the filthily dressed, low caste scavenger, who came a week later, said.

He was in the old man's private quarters, and the bodyguards were looking askance at the excreta-smelling visitor.

Guruji, though holding his breath, calmly replied, 'You did good, Vijay!'

Drought as an Act of God, 303 BC

'Time is an unforgiving upsetter of power plays, and can turn a victory into defeat through "Acts of God."' Guruji droned, as he put away a chapter of the *Arthashastra.*

'There is one ongoing now, the hot season. Drought has been declared in the west of the Sindhu,' Amatya Rakshash said.

'Drought wreaks more havoc than rain,' the king spoke thoughtfully.

'Villagers have begun to fight over water sharing. Small village militias, some infiltrated by our mercenaries, are destroying the bunds of local check dams for water downstream. These skirmishes will last till the monsoon comes,' Rakshash murmured in a resigned tone.

'After which, half of the villages will be washed away,' Guruji added philosophically.

Water – the Sword that Slays

In the war room, the hunchback, Vijay and Dhoomal were all giving reports on weather systems in a query from the king. Guruji and Rakshash were tied up in court, trying criminal cases, where both criminals and victims were lying through their teeth, and needed two fine brains to sift out the truth. General Ramagupta was away on a secret sortie.

'Any good news?' the king asked.

The hunchback grinned.

'According to chatter on the highways, courtesy our double agents, Seleucus has been sending, partly via the Sapta Sindhu water route and partly through camel caravans via Thal Desert, a lot of medical men to his distressed satrap friends in Gedrosia,' Chandragupta was informed.

'Object?' the king asked.

'Soldiers are falling prey en mass to worms that tie up muscle, and cause itchy skin trouble,' the jester replied.

'How are these worms infecting them?' the king probed.

'Through drinking unfiltered contaminated water,' came the reply.

'Are the medical men Vaidyas or Greek physicians?' Chandragupta wanted to know.

'Both,' he was told.

'Treating?' the king was curious.

'Diarrhea!' Dhoomal piped up, with youthful glee, adding, 'Diarrhea is our friend when it happens to our enemy, our enemy when it happens to us.'

'True!' the king said. 'An army with diarrhea cannot march. In addition, no clean water for washing can try the olfactory patience of fellow soldiers, and may lead to rank mutiny,' King Chandragupta said.

'Diarrhea has dehydrated soldiers, making them unfit for battle,' Vijay added.

'Our Yavana mercenaries must replace Seleucus' doctors, our double-agent vaidyas, vaidyas in Seleucus' team, and Vijay, you too,' the king said.

'Mercenaries posing as laborers can contaminate drinking water storage structures,' Vijay added. 'More mercenaries can be sent when Gedrosian soldiers are completely down and out,' he added.

'Don't forget to keep a few wells uncontaminated for our soldiers,' Chandragupta reminded him.

After briefing from the king, all three agents left to do mayhem.

Gedrosia, Patala and Sauvira

In the war room, double agent Maraj, looking peaceful, his usual expression, after prostrating first to Guruji, and bowing head first on the ground to the king, threw a small pouch on Gedrosia, marked on the sand map. The Gedrosian desert flattened into a plain.

'Gold!' he said, in answer to Guruji's frown at this quick

change in geography. 'Gedrosia is now ours. The Makran yielded its treasures real easy. Their soldiers were no match for our mercenaries,' Maraj informed them.

'And they cannot fight for General Seleucus,' the king chuckled.

Next to Maraj, a mud-coated youngster, looking like something tat blown in from a duststorm, grinned, showing white even teeth. 'Patala is now yours again, O King, after the top-secret naval blockade. And Sauvira, east of Patala, is also yours, the Matsyas did a good job,' Dhoomal's familiar voice spoke.

'Sporadic warfare whittles, and our enemy is no wiser,' Guruji said gruffly.

Back in the Seleucid palace, this info was conveyed to General Seleucus and his commanders.

'Why did we not fight back?' the general asked, his face all red and blotchy.

'Our forces are spread thin all over your territories, general,' the double agent, an Indian weaver, replied.

'Where all?' the general barked at his commanders.

'Parthia border, Arachosia, Gedrosia, Patala, the Thal Desert, east of the River Indus, wherever your former liege Alexander had conquered the Indians,' the commander of his foot solders replied.

'Commandants, recall more of our men, we may need them in an emergency,' General Seleucus snapped at the senior commanders.

Monsoon – Divine Anger, June-July 303 BC

In court, King Chandragupta was gathering info from Vijay and Dhoomal.

'The drought in many parts of our kingdom has been

replaced overnight by a drown-everything monsoon. Rivers are in spate, villagers living near overflowing rivers and lakes need a Plan B to move residence to higher ground,' Vijay said.

'Village elders are working overtime with civil defense workers in each village,' Dhoomal added.

'In the summer, gramikas organized wooden planks or bamboo tied together like a catamaran, plus coracles and boats, so each household could save livestock, precious household objects, and family, and move to safer ground, but only with partial success,' Vijay continued.

'Monsoon being the provenance of divine mediation, floods destroying everything in their path,' the king said thoughtfully. 'Set up rice kitchens, *annadanam,* for the refugees,' he instructed officials.

Morvati Palace's Monsoon Woes

A middle-aged man, in a state of distress, was agitatedly talking to King Chandragupta and Guruji in a hunting tent a slight distance from Morvati, the finally renamed Nandawati. Dhoomal, in a metal helmet, was weaving something stylish in chain mail for the king's battle kit. Next to him was an old man bare to the waist with sacred thread and ash markings, the royal purohita.

'O King, Morvati royal quarters are having a rat influx followed by another of poisonous snakes. Morvati palace roof looks like it will blow away in the wind or catch fire in a lightning storm. It is already leaking with continuous rains,' the housekeeper complained.

'There is only one way out,' Guruji grunted. 'Non-stop homas, also havans or fire rituals, in the center of the royal residence. Every room will have a homa, done daily till the monsoon ends, to keep evil at bay,' he added.

'Holy smoke deters scorpion, centipede and ant infestations,' the Purohita interjected, fire homas being his specialty.

'Besides, monkeys, bats and wild bees cannot thrive with smoke or fire. Snakes too keep away. The rooms remain dry, a bonus,' the king added.

'The fire threat, Guruji?' Dhoomal cut in, the royal housekeeper and Purohita unable to imagine anything going wrong with a homa.

'As destructive fire can become a tool of divine intervention, each homa will be supervised carefully by acolyte priests, from start to finish,' the old man instructed. 'Roof repair will be taken up after monsoon,' he added.

The housekeeper and the Purohita left together to set up the homas.

The Seleucid Palace

General Seleucus was disturbed. The usual ministrations of the male love expert had failed to please. Not that the excellent finger skills of the expert were in any way lacking, but the general was in such deep mental distress, his reproductive system had to take a back seat.

The reason, a double whammy.

First, the love expert, instead of leaving his messages till after the massage, had become chatty with the general halfway through.

'Have you heard, Taxiles citadel after Sandrakottus' conquest, has become a regular garrison town, with more than 300,000 soldiers,' he said.

Before the general had time to digest this bit of unpleasantness, his trustworthy Indian double agent, a weaver of exceptional skill, had marched into the bedroom where he was lying prone and oily, and informed him, 'King Sandracottus has amassed an army of 400,000 plus soldiers on the east of your Indian territories, close to Gandhara and Kambhoja.'

'Four hundred thousand plus soldiers? Near the Paropamisadae?' Seleucus asked, alarmed.

'Next to it, Sire!' the agent replied.

'Ask my secretary to summon all my commandants and double agents to the war room. Instruct the cartographer,' the general roared.

The urgency of the matter was soon apparent. Without waiting for the collection of aphrodisiacs from the love expert, otherwise an important monthly activity, Seleucus rushed to the war room nearly naked. The love expert guessed that Apama, the general's Sogdian consort, could give up all hope of a pleasant time with her husband that night.

In the war room, the cartographer, instructed by the Indian weaver and the just-arrived balladeer, was making a map with colored sand, pebbles and children's wooden toys. Commandants of the infantry, cavalry, navy, were spread all around the room, their eyes rivetted grimly on the map coming to life before them. Behind them, several double agents were also waiting attentively.

On the long wooden table lay sandy versions of Arachosia, Gedrosia, Sapta Sindhu, Kambhoja and Gandhara, with toy armies spread all over these territories.

'Lord Alexander's Indian territories, now all yours, general,' the cartographer said with a flourish, quite clearly clueless about recent events.

General Seleucus frowned. The '...all yours' rankled.

Intelligence Gathering, end July 303

Across the porous border of the late Alexander's Indian territories, a similar situation was taking place, an *idée fixe*. In the Varana war room, King Chandragupta, his Amatya, Guruji, General Ramagupta, double agents, the Purohita, and a troupe of soothsayers, astrologers, omen readers and black magic priests, were patiently waiting for the royal cartographer to finish his map on the battle strategy table.

When he was done, the king growled, 'Ramagupta, briefly.'

Ramagupta plunged in, waving his sword erratically to make his point.

'Five hundred thousand soldiers are now in Taxila garrison town, southeast of Varana. Not just soldiers, your vassals are sending war elephants as we speak,' the general was saying.

'As many as?' the king interjected.

'Several thousand,' the officer replied.

'We have stretched Seleucus thin,' the king said thoughtfully.

'But he has yet to commandeer his soldiers on Parthia border to return,' Ramagupta mentioned.

'So, speed is of the essence. Send pigeon posts to Sapta Sindhu post boxes. From Patala harbor, to all places on the rivers, I want our Yavana and Persian mercenaries, disguised as pirates, to scuttle anything Seleucid, anything naval,' Chandragupta barked orders.

Guruji now asked, 'How many more soldiers expected, Ramagupta?'

'Another 100,000,' the general replied.

'Ok, let's play it like this. Mercenary pirates for the Sapta Sindhu and Patala, camel troops for Gedrosia, Arachosia and the Thal Desert, and let's decide where to conduct direct battle with Seleucus,' King Chandragupta had taken charge.

'Dhara and her young beautiful courtesans can enmesh the Seleucid commandants, and feed them slow-acting poison that takes effect on the third day after ingestion,' General Ramagupta said.

The group hunkered down, Ramagupta and the king taking the lead, double agents supplementing them with important info.

More Intelligence Gathering, August 303 BC

Many miles away, in the Seleucid war room, double agents were giving information to their boss, unwelcome though it was.

'General Seleucus, bad news! Not only has King Sandracottus now amassed 500,000 plus soldiers, he has managed a terrifying 9,000 elephants,' the Indian weaver said, in his open palm a curl of parchment with details.

'Nine thousand elephants!' Seleucus growled, slashing the strategy table with each word.

'General, soldiers remember the Porus-Alexander battlefield, this battle will be lost before it starts,' Seleucus' infantry head lamented.

'Keep this news secret or our soldiers' morale will plunge badly,' Seleucus snapped.

'Too late, General! Brothel owners, wine mongers, cooked-meat sellers from highway inns are telling all and sundry about the elephants, which passed them on the highway,' the madaari said.

'Any other news?' Seleucus asked grimly.

'Up and down the Indus, pirates have attacked your naval brigade and cargo boats. The area around Patala harbor has been captured, and Sauvira, east of the Indus, is totally enemy-powered,' the traveling balladeer spoke, adding to the general gloom.

'Gedrosia is out too. Your soldiers, ill with water-borne illnesses, can neither travel nor fight,' the toy trader added.

'Arachosia is bordered by Sandracottus' camel troops. Any movement will invite a fight to the death,' the kapata sanyasi said.

'Commandants, call in your regiments, no more guarding wells, Parthia's border, etc. All regiments to march back,' Seleucus barked. 'And I need more intel,' he demanded.

Commandants set off to send pigeon posts and pony posts ment to recall their able-bodied soldiers. Double agents scattered to gather military intelligence.

The Worries of Seleucus, September end 303

Weeks later…

In the Seleucid war room, all pretense of peacetime was long gone. The war table took centerstage, and commandants and double agents crowded the room.

'What is the composition of Sandracottus' army?' General Seleucus asked the double agents.

The kapata sanyasi bowed as he answered. 'King Sandracottus' army is heterogenous, Mallas, Matsyas, Vitihotras, Surasenas, Kurus, Panchalas, Asmakas, Kashmiris, and other conquered peoples, number nearly 600,000 troops and 9,000 elephants,' he informed Seleucus.

'Sandracottus will eat us alive,' Seleucus said bitterly, venting his temper by slashing the table with his Mauryan wootz steel sword.

A painful silence followed.

'Foreigners?' Seleucus snapped, his voice deliberately low to control any tremor.

'Include Yavana, Kambhoja, Scythian, Kirata, Persian and Bactrian mercenaries,' the balladeer answered.

'Can we retreat?' the Yavana head of Seleucus' infantry asked in a cowed voice, the thought of battle with 9,000 war elephants having destroyed any vestige of martial spirit he had formerly.

'If we give up without a fight, then all of Alexander's Indian territories will be lost to King Sandracottus,' Seleucus snarled testily.

This outburst was followed by silence, due more to craven fear than respect for the boss.

'How do we march? Where do we battle?' General Seleucus asked, slashing irritably at the war table.

'The closest flat ground is the area southeast of Aornos Varana, and northwest of Taxila. The River Indus can secure our backs, the Indians won't attack from behind. And the good news, our men from Parthia have arrived,' the Yavana head of infantry said. 'We have now at our disposal at least a 100,000 troops and mercenaries from Parthia and other areas,' he added, sanguine about their prospects.

General Seleucus looked doubtful. 'Let's send our troops now, with an infantry-cavalry-infantry battle line. I will lead from the west and all commandants will lead from the front,' Seleucus ordered.

General and commandants, with the help of the cartographer, began to detail the coming battle.

'The troops will leave as soon as the battle formation is final,' the general said.

'The enemy's 600,000 troops are an unwieldy number, and can lose contact in battle, which we can utilize to our benefit,' the infantry head sounded slightly more confident.

'The best tactic of all, General Seleucus, is to send assassins to kill King Sandracottus,' came a suggestion.

'Undoubtedly, the best,' General Seleucus said, sounding somewhat positive.

March to Gandhara

Within an hour, the pigeon postman came hurrying in to meet Guruji, Rakshash, King Chandragupta and General Ramagupta at Varana. A few double agents were also present.

'All details of the Seleucid meeting are contained here, thanks to our planted double agent,' the king pointed out, passing the parchment to Guruji to peruse. 'We march to the battlefield of their choice, Gandhara, tomorrow. Let's take back our ancestral lands. Where do we set up base camp?' This question was addressed to General Ramagupta.

'Base camp should be a brisk two-hour march, and from base camp to the battlefield, a one-hour brisk march,' the general said.

'Base camp should mimic the Varana township as far as possible,' the king said, 'so our soldiers know their way around.'

All present, including the double agents, nodded in agreement.

'*Yana,* movement of troops, will be coordinated from base camp, our battle HQ. Important is the appropriate selection of forces,' King Chandragupta dictated.

'The elephants can start right away for base camp,' General Ramagupta said. 'Early morning for foot soldiers, he added.'

'Keep 24x7 surveillance on the elephant corps chief. He is our key to success,' the king emphasized.

'Sire, several trained mercenaries have been sent to assassinate you,' the woman mendicant interjected.

'The solution, distrust all foreigners.' Rakshash said.

'Not always possible,' Chandragupta sounded doubtful.

'Not always possible. Let's copy Alexander. Send three lookalikes of me on black horses, to fool the enemy west, southwest and south of the battlefield,' Chandragupta said calmly, as if assassination attempts were an hourly occurrence in his life. 'I myself will go to battle HQ, nearest the eastern block of foot and cavalry soldiers,' he added.

'You will go, Chandra, in disguise, on a brown horse with white ankles and golden ponytail,' Guruji was quietly insistent.

His protégé grinned in agreement. Then he, General Ramagupta and the rest played with several battle formations before they came up with the appropriate strategy, and back up plans.

The Battleground

On the plains, the next day, mid-afternoon...

The battlefield stretched seemingly endless on both sides. Corpses of soldiers and horses littered the ground as far as the eye could see. A lone, dusty horseman rode up to a burly Mauryan commandant on the eastern front.

'Sire, two of the king's doubles are dead, ambushed and speared dead by the death squads. Guruji and Rakshash are both worried sick for your safety,' the inconspicuous horseman spoke in a low voice to the burly elderly commandant, who had a second-in-command in tow.

'How did they know?' he asked.

'Sire, there's an informer in our midst,' another scout had caught up. 'Seleucus' head of infantry has been killed, and the general has sent a couple more death squads to the east to base camp as we speak,' the king was informed.

'Vijay!' General Ramagupta's voice had a definite tetchy tone. 'We need a distraction. Buy us some time,' he yelled.

The horseman immediately made hurried changes to his attire, mounted a black, riderless horse nearby and rode towards the massed Seleucid forces.

An hour later…

'Sire, Vijay was viciously attacked by the death squads, thinking he was you because his black horse had a diamond mark,' a scout wearing a non-combatant's water carrier uniform, reported.

'Dead?' the second-in-command asked, anxious.

'No! Injured and sent to Seleucus' tent for leverage,' he replied.

'Our Amatya will be upset. Enemy infantry, cavalry, archers?' the nondescript second-in-command, his head covered against the vile winds, asked in a low voice.

'All a mess, our pachyderms took good care of that,' the scout said.

The second in command now spoke in the king's commanding tone the non-combatant was familiar with. The order was clear, 'Enough delay. We now have Seleucus where we want him, in the battlefield he himself chose. Let's finish this. Ramagupta?'

'A pincer move will pin the Seleucid army against a rain-swollen Indus behind, and 9,000 elephants in front. Retreating backwards, the Seleucids will drown, forwards, the elephants will gore them dead,' the burly commandant spoke in Ramagupta's voice.

'No more hiding from assassins, General Ramagupta, let the elephants take over, west, south, east. Dhoomal,' this was addressed to the non-combatant water carrier, 'go to the elephant corps chief.'

'About?' he waited for the order.

'Ask him to release his secret weapon, three wild elephants kept calm with *Sarpagandha,* Rauwolfia roots. Tell the elephant handlers to feed them with rage-inducing herbs so that their wild nature is again uncontrolled, and let tame elephants and drummers drive them towards the Seleucids. When their soldiers scatter, tell our commandants to finish them,' came the precise instructions.

Dhoomal, temporary water carrier, departed.

In the War Room, Varana

Two hours later…

Back in Varana, Guruji was especially stressed. He spent half his time with the troupe of soothsayers, astrologers, omen readers, intuitionists, fire priests, and the royal Purohita, performing a continuous homa for Chandragupta and Ramagupta's safety and success. The other half he spent with Rakshash in the war room surrounded by double agents and messengers, who gave them an hour-by-hour account of the ongoing battle, making updated changes to the 'battleground' on the table. Even though there was no news of Chandragupta being attacked, he was tense, repeatedly telling Rakshash that, 'Power is not constant, victory is not constant. Darius, though having a much larger force than Alexander, still had several crushing defeats. Take nothing for granted.'

A Defeated Seleucus, October 303

But by end of the next day, it was clear who had won. The 'battleground' showed a definite overpowering from the Mauryan side.

'The wild elephant handlers drove their charges towards the unfortunate soldiers of Seleucus, every man, every battle formation is in utter chaos,' Dhoomal reported.

'Now what?' he asked.

'Time for ill omens to spook the enemy further. A Naga, one of our own, has emerged from a secret chamber in the north side of the river, covered in white, "holy" ash in full view of the Seleucid war tent,' the old man said.

'And?' the agent asked.

'General Seleucus and his surviving commandants are closeted in the tent for hours, consulting the Naga and the fake "king,"' he replied.

'Doing what?' the agent was puzzled.

'Being convinced to ask for peace,' the old man chuckled.

Very early next morning, the Seleucids finally sent off a messenger to the Chandragupta base camp.

Seleucus Asks for a Truce

A day later. Morning in the war room.

Guruji was pacing up and down, waiting for news from the battlefield; Rakshash leaning against the wall with a strained look. No fresh news had come their way, except that there was a cessation of hostilities.

From far away, Rakshash, who had very keen eyesight, spotted a pigeon postman, and Tan Mei, the Kushan, rushing towards the building.

Tan Mei reached first.

'Our 9,000 elephants, having done psychological mayhem on the war-weary Seleucids for several days, yesterday did physical mayhem,' Tan Mei gasped, simultaneously happy and breathless.

'Thank the gods for elephants,' Guruji raised his hands to a generous almighty and his minions for the good news. 'But Chandra and Rama?' Guruji asked anxiously.

'Both await General Seleucus' official acceptance of defeat at base camp,' he informed them.

'Guruji, a special message from the king,' the pigeon postman had reached, and now handed over a small chit wrestled from a reluctant pigeon.

'The Seleucid hold on Lord Alexander's Indian territories has crumpled. General Seleucus has asked for a truce,' Guruji read out loud.

'Our two years of warfare without war has paid rich dividends, sooo…' Amatya Rakshash's voice trailed off, astounded. Their normally austere Guru had buried 'General Seleucus' under a bunch of toy elephants on the 'battleground'.

The Mauryan Empire

Mauryan Takeover of Alexander's Conquests

THIS WAS THE final meeting, end October.

The two powers, Seleucid and Mauryan, sitting on opposite sides of the war-cum-map table in Morvati palace, had come to an understanding that reflected on the map.

'Arachosia, Gedrosia, Paropamisadae, areas of the Sapta Sindhu including Patala harbor and Sauvira are all King Chandragupta's territories,' General Seleucus remarked, with a tinge of regret in his voice.

'All Alexander's Indian conquests are now mine,' Chandragupta stated calmly.

Guruji, General Ramagupta and Rakshash, all three excited, kept total silence, as the king led all the negotiations with the Seleucid party.

'Alexander's posthumous hold on Indian conquests is now extinct,' General Seleucus stated, standing up and bowing to Chandragupta who bowed in return.

'With these acquisitions, Chandra, you unite the Sapta Sindhu and Gangetic plains, making it the most powerful mahajanapada in our history,' Guruji commented.

A Political Alliance – Queen Helen

The meeting had ended, and both leaders faced each other as equals.

Now that the dreaded battle with elephants was over, and Alexander's Indian territories handed over to King Chandragupta, General Seleucus looked relaxed.

'King Sandracottus, please accept a marriage alliance between my beautiful daughter Helen and yourself,' Seleucus offered.

The royal wedding was celebrated with Indian pomp and show. Helen's background, daughter of Seleucus Nikator and a Persian noblewoman, made for a good political liaison.

After the wedding, King Chandragupta turned generous.

'Father-in-law, I gift you 500 war elephants as bride price, so that if ever you need to, you can replicate the mayhem that Porus' war elephants wreaked on Alexander's troops in the battle on the Jhelum river,' the king said.

General Seleucus looked pleased.

'I cannot match you, but I too send a unique gift, Ambassador Megasthenes to your court,' General Seleucus said to his son-in-law.

The Mauryan king accepted gracefully.

Megasthenes

'Tell me about this brilliant man, Megasthenes,' King Chandragupta said to Xerxes.

Both veterans were sitting relaxed under a tarpaulin roof outside the restored Varana palace. A bonfire with roasting goat and sweet potato sent sparks into the evening sky, wafting a mouth-watering aroma into the night.

'Megasthenes was born 47 years ago in Ionia, Turkish territory. He is a scholar, ethnographer, geographer, and historian,' Xerxes began in his inimitable style.

'And he came here?' the king wanted more details.

'Through the Pentapotamia of rivers, probably the Sapta Sindhu,' the old expressman said.

Banana leaves shaped like bowls were placed in front of both men. The cook placed piping hot goat and sweet potato on them, smothered with burnt butter and a sprinkling of pink mountain salt.

'What exactly does Megasthenes want?' Chandragupta was curious.

'A good observer, he has sent letters about the worship of Hercules and Dionysus by the natives of India,' Xerxes told him.

'Any connection to our late King Alexander?' came another question.

'Alexander had erected twelve stone altars to twelve Macedonian gods, a few who the Indians also worship. Hercules and Dionysus, may have been part of the original 12 altars, according to Megasthenes,' Xerxes explained.

'We'll send him to our second, brand new Patala capital,' the king said.

'The Pataliputra of yore?' the drinking companion asked.

'We'll gift him a horse of good stock for his travels through our kingdom,' the king added and gave a small yelp as the hot meat singed his fingers.

Both men settled down to do justice to their meal, carefully tearing off chunks of meat and sweet potato, dipping them in the drippings of the goat and burnt butter, and stuffing their mouths with heavenly, greasy deliciousness. A contented silence reigned.

Mauryan Administration, 302 BC

Chandraguta's coronation had thrown up various administrative issues.

'Coronation is over but unification is not,' King Chandragupta Maurya was deep in discussion with Guruji and Rakshash about the future of their kingdom as their caravan traveled back and forth from Patala to Varana.

'I think it is best to emulate the Achaemenid administrative model, now that our kingdom has grown,' Guruji said.

'With satrapies,' Rakshash added.

'I agree, nothing else comes close,' King Chandragupta said.

'All the territory acquired by conquest should be assimilated properly. The first thing we should do is to avoid your father's mistakes,' Guruji said.

'Our rural poor should be protected from greedy administrators,' Rakshash added ruminatively, still in shock with the way corrupt Nanda administrators had looted the poor.

'For internal peace, I must dress like the high-born of acquired territories to convince subjects that I am not a foreigner,' King Chandragupta said. 'Guruji, instruct me on how to be a better king than my wretched father,' the king sought counsel.

'The duties of a wise king are *yogakshema*, people's prosperity, *raksha,* the kingdom's protection from external aggression, and *palana,* internal peace,' Guruji advised.

'Covered in *Arthashastra*?' King Chandragupta asked.

'In detail,' Guruji answered.

'Let us occupy vacant land, so our subjects live comfortably,' Rakshash added.

Seleucus on the Move

In his camp quarters somewhere close to Parthia, Seleucus Nikator, who was homeward bound, was being entertained by the Indian madaari who had come with a couple of snakes, who did nothing but sleep the whole time, and some bears and monkeys, who earned their keep by performing amusing tricks. After an hour, feeling a slight fatigue with so many animals, he asked for a halt in the proceedings.

'What's new in my son-in-law Sandracottus' kingdom?' General Seleucus asked.

'Basic administrative work. Maurya coinage has completely replaced Arrhidaeus coins in the empire. Compulsory standardized weights and measures for the whole kingdom. Separate departments for foreigners, importers and exporters, mines, and metals. Chancellors are responsible for internal security and espionage. Special department for foreigners like Yavanas, Persians, Scythians, Pahlavas, Bactrians, who work in far-flung reaches of Sandracottus' northwest territories,' Seleucus was informed.

'They seem to copy the Achaemenid admin structure,' the general said, not surprised.

'But tailor-made for Indika,' the madaari, a double agent reputed to be an expert in governance, said with conviction.

General Seleucus was thoughtful, wondering how much of his son-in-law's work ethic would apply to his own empire. A few weeks later, General Seleucus was having another audience with the Indian madaari. His menagerie of wild animals was outside this time, as the general did not wish to see them.

'Update me on my son-in-law,' Seleucus said.

'The Indians dabble in a lot of black magic in politics. And vice versa,' he began.

'As in?' the general asked.

'Protective white magic to cancel black magic and keep evil spirits under control. The royal court commissions Brahmin priests of the highest order, to offer continuous prayers with offerings, day and night, to placate and appease the gods. Regular feasts and gifts for scholarly and holy Brahmins are supposed to give the kingdom a protective aura,' the madaari explained.

'Who is the authority on these issues?' Seleucus was curious.

'To get rituals right, the benchmark *Atharva Veda* is the go-to text for all rites that the holy ones must perform, to protect the kingdom from baleful influences. Free accommodation is accorded to the holy ones so that they stay within the kingdom and bless the location they reside in with a protective aura,' he replied.

'Well, Lord Alexander performed a sacrifice to the gods daily, but he still died young. Luck must accompany the work of the holy ones, and that we have no control over,' the General said thoughtfully.

War Elephants Win the Battle of Ipsus, 301 BC

A grey-haired Xerxes was visiting again.

'I have great news for you, King Sandracottus and Queen Helen,' he said bowing to the king and queen, sitting at the head of a full court.

'Which is?' the king said.

'Queen Helen, the 500 war elephants given as bride price by Emperor Chandragupta came in very useful in your father King Seleucus' victory in the battle of Ipsus,' Xerxes said.

'The enemy?' Chandragupta asked.

'Western Hellenistic kings, especially Antigonos Monophthalmos, who was defeated and killed,' the visitor replied.

'The 'one-eyed'? Good! Reward him with a special horse from the royal stable,' King Chandragupta said, smiling at his wife.

For the rest of the court session, Xerxes stayed in court, grinning through all the proceedings.

The End of Chandragupta's Reign, 297 BC

The palace of General Seleucus somewhere in Asia Minor…

For a change, the traveling balladeer was not planning to shatter anyone's eardrums. In fact, he was silent. After waiting for a while, Seleucus waved him in towards the throne.

'What ill news do you have for me?' the General asked, noticing his unusual silence.

'King Seleucus, your daughter is now a widow,' he said solemnly.

'How did this happen?' Seleucus asked.

'King Sandracottus was a good man, who ruled for 24 years. In the past year-and-a-half, the end of his reign, there was terrible famine and drought in the kingdom. When his coterie of astrologers, omen readers and intuitionists were consulted, all warned of the disappearance of his empire if he continued as king. Converting to Jainism, an Indian religion of much austerity, he abdicated in favor of his son Bindusara, who is now king,' the balladeer said.

'Bindusara?' the General asked.

'A motherless boy barely in his twenties called Amritochates by the Greeks, Amritaghata by the Indians,' he replied.

'And Sandracottus?' Seleucus wanted to know.

'He traveled south to Sravanabelagola in the entourage of Acharya Bhadrabahu, a famed Jain monk. Your daughter, Queen Helen, did not accompany him. The king starved to death, a practice common among Jains,' he told the General.

'Helen, my beloved child, a widow? If she wishes, she can return to her natal home again,' the General gave a deep sigh. 'Anything else?' This question was addressed to a trader of children's toys from the west, who was standing quietly next to the balladeer.

The Curses of the Alexanders

'Sire, Indian kings are not the only ones to die of personal travails. Prince Cassander has died too,' the trader said.

'Of?' Seleucus asked.

'Ostensibly of dropsy and worms,' he replied.

'Ostensibly?' Seleucus asked, curious.

'According to common gossip, from the bad karma of getting rid of Alexander's family one by one. Everyone believes Alexander's family's curses finally did him in,' he replied.

'He deserved every bit of the suffering,' Seleucus said unemotionally.

Seleucus is Assassinated in Thrace, 281 BC

Rakshash was in court when the travelling balladeer asked for an audience. Since King Bindusara had next to no patience with the balladeer's old-fashioned songs, it was left to Rakshash to extract info.

'What is new in the West, balladeer?' Rakshash asked.

'King Seleucus, Queen Helen's father, is dead,' he informed.

'Dead? Killed? From natural causes?' Rakshash asked.

'After having enjoyed a fruitful tenure, where he consolidated his kingdom, Seleucus was assassinated by Ptolemy Keraunus, King of Macedonia. Seleucus' son, Antiochus Soter, is now coronated king,' he said.

'The old guard goes, replaced by the new guard,' Rakshash sighed.

The Five Empires, 276 BC

Within five years of Seleucus' death, Alexander's conquests had permanently split five ways – Macedonia and the Greek states, Egypt, Thrace, northwest India, and the rest of Asia.

Antigonos II Gonatas, grandson of Antigonos Monophthalmos, controlled Macedonia and the Greek city states. Ptolemy ruled Egypt. Lysimachus ruled Thrace. Bindusara, Chandragupta's son, ruled the Mauryan Empire combining Indus and Gangetic areas. Antiochus Soter, son of Seleucus, ruled the Seleucid kingdom comprising the rest of Asia, that is Asia Minor.

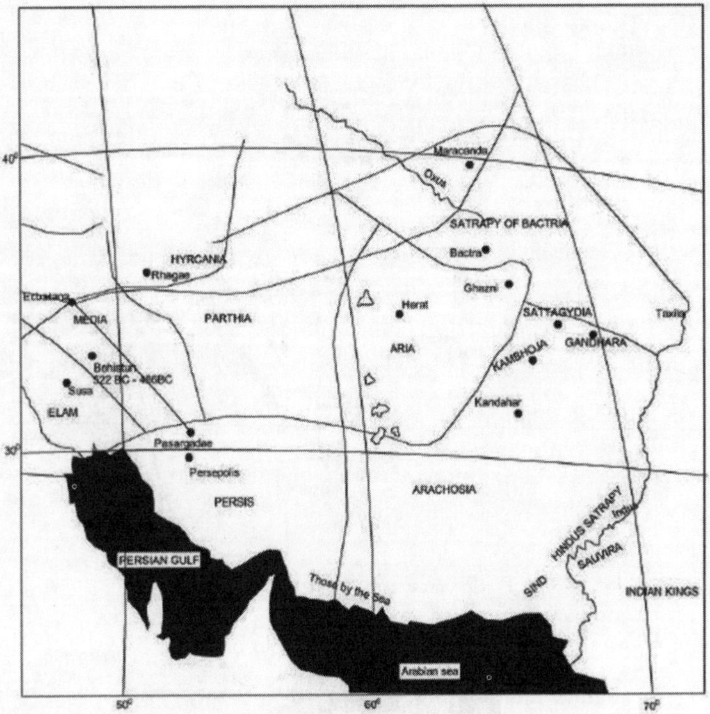

A. Map Info

1. Behistun Inscription of Darius I (522-486 BC) mentions a. Sattagydia, b. Gandhara, c. Arachosia, d. Aria, e. Persis., f. those by the sea (Gedrosia ?)
2. Herodotus (425 BC) mentions a. Gandhara and b. Hindush satrapies.
3. Dhanananda (326 BC) paid 360 talents of gold for a. Hindush, b. Gandhara (?) paid 170 talents of gold .

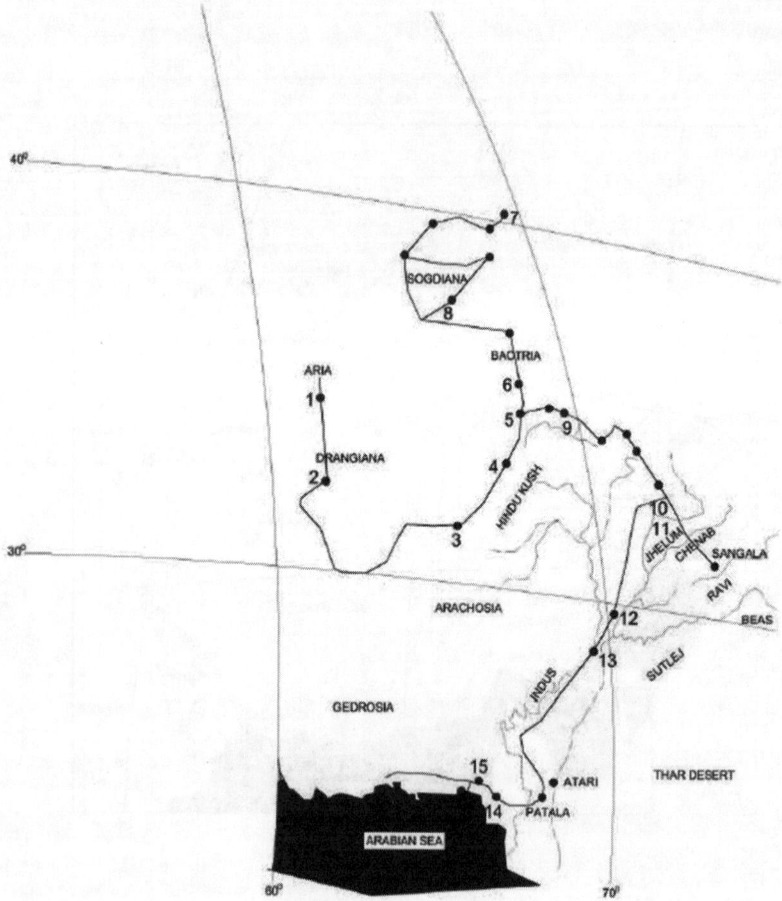

B. Map Info

Alexander's route

Rivers crossed

Alexandrias (1- 15)

1.HERAT
2.PROPHTHASIA
3.KANDAHAR
4.GHAZNI
5.NICAEA
6.AD CAUCASUM
7.ESCHATE
8.AI KHANOUM
9.NYSA
10.BUCEPHALA
11.NICAEA
12.UCCH
13.OPIANA
14.PERTUS
15.KHAMBAKA

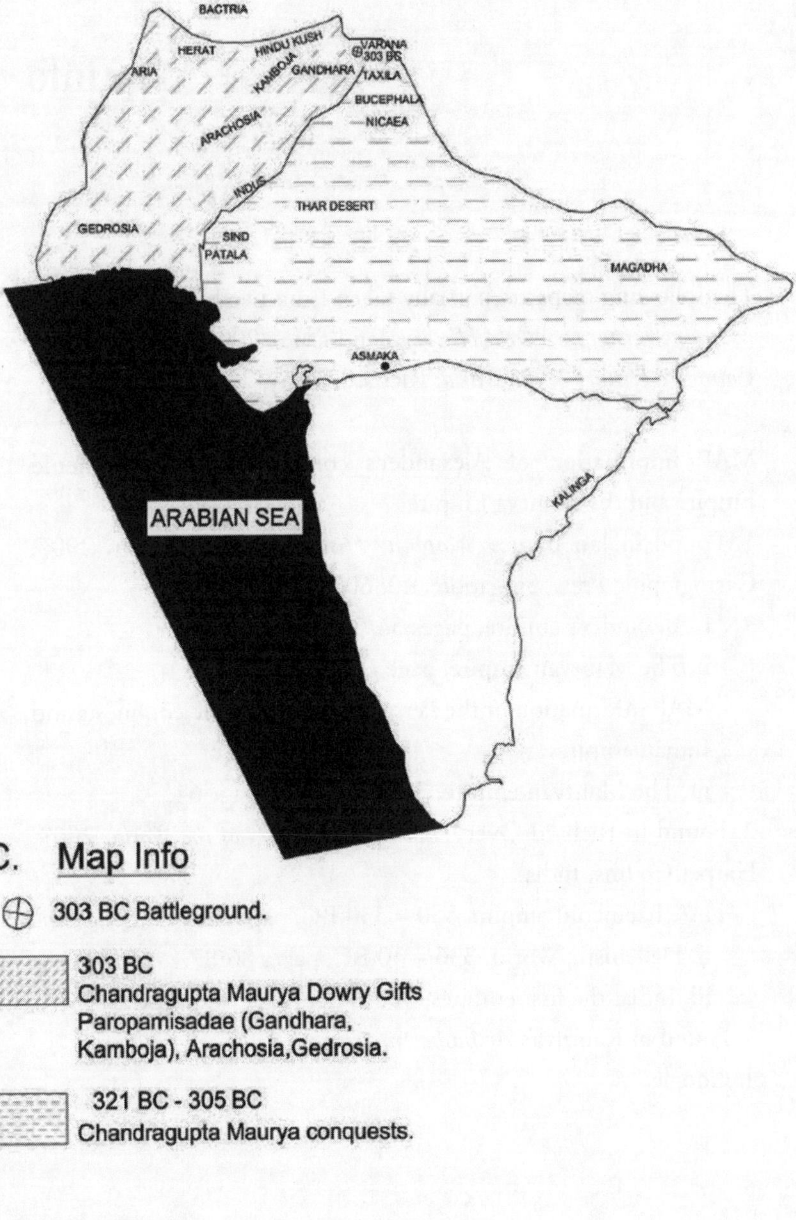

C. Map Info

⊕ 303 BC Battleground.

303 BC
Chandragupta Maurya Dowry Gifts
Paropamisadae (Gandhara, Kamboja), Arachosia, Gedrosia.

321 BC - 305 BC
Chandragupta Maurya conquests.

Map info

The following maps are partially taken from two books:
Mapping History – World History: Ian Barnes, 2007.
Complete History of the World: Richard Overy, 2009.

MAP information of Alexander's conquests, the Achaemenid Empire and the Maurya Empire

1. Found in Ian Barnes' *Mapping History - World History*, 2007, Cartographic Press, Singapore, 408600.
   i. Alexander's empire, pages 54/55.
   ii. The Mauryan empire, page 64.
   MAP information of the Persian and Hellenistic conquests and Indian empires
   iii. The Mauryan empire, 322 – 297 BC, page 64.
2. Found in Richard Overy's *Complete History of the World*, 2009, Harper Collins, India.
   i. Achaemenid empire, 550 – 330 BC, page 82.
   ii. Hellenistic World, 336 – 30 BC, pages 86/87.
   iii. India: the first empires, 500 BC – AD 550, pages 92/93.
3. Found in Kautilya's *Arthashastra*.
4. Google.

Map 1
Indian territories in
Darius's *Behistun* Inscription (521 BC) mentions (i) Sattagydia, (ii) Gandhara, the 7th satrapy, which paid the second highest tribute – 170 talents of gold to the Achaemenid Empire, (iii) Arachosia, (iv) Aria, (v) Persis and (vi) those by the sea (Gedrosia?).

Herodotus (425 BC) - the world's first historian - mentions the Hindush satrapy covering middle and lower Indus, as the 20th, eastern-most satrapy paying 360 talents of gold. Herodotus also mentions (ii) Gandhara that paid 170 talents.

Dhananda's tribute (prior to 330 BC) - Sind (a.k.a. Hindush) - the 20th satrapy, included middle and lower Indus; Dhanananda paid 360 talents of gold annually in **336 BC**.
Gandhara (and Kambhoja) covered upper Indus areas, included Kashmir, east Afghanistan, west Punjab and Taxila covering Sattagydia, and was the 7th satrapy paying 170 talents. Kambhoja - famed for its horses, may have covered Nysa, Ora and Massaga, all animal husbandry candidates for ancient Sattagydia (a.k.a. *Thatagus*, Old Persian for country of a 'hundred cows').

Map 2

Alexander's conquests in and around India

Rivers crossed in India include **Indus, Jhelum, Chenab, Ravi, Beas** and **Sutlej**

Territories captured or acquired include Gedrosia, Arachosia, Paropamisadae, Varana, Sangala, Porus the Elder's area, Porus the Younger's area. Abhisares of Kashmir, and Ambhi Raja of Taxila freely became his satraps without battle.

Alexandrias set up by Alexander near or within **India**

1. In Aria, **Herat.**

2. In Drangiana, **Prophthasia .**

3. In Arachosia, **Arachoton (Kandahar).**

4. In Arachosia, **Ghazni.**

5. In India, **Nicaea 1.**

6. In India, **ad Caucasum.**

7. In Sogdiana, 329 BC, – **Eschate** – 'the Farthest'.

8. In Sogdiana, **Oxiana, Ai Khanoum.**

9. In India, **Nysa.**

10 & 11. In India, 326 BC, **Nicaea 2** & **Bucephala** on banks of the Jhelum.

12. In 326 BC, in India, **Uchch.**

13. In India, **Opiana.**

14. In India, **Pertus (Karachi).**

15. In Gedrosia, **Alexandria Khambakia.**

Harbors constructed included **Patala.**

Map 3 – The empire of Chandragupta Maurya (321 – 303 BC).

Patala – **336 BC.**

Varana - the second innings of the Mauryan empire begins – **326 BC.**

Indian territories added from **321 – 303 BC**

Possible route for Chandragupta's conquests in Gangetic and nearby areas: Kuru, Surasena, Panchala, Haihaya, Vitihotra, Maithila, Kashi, Magadha, Asmaka.

Possible battlefield where Chandragupta defeated Seleucus in **303 BC:** west of Kashmir, north of Taxila, between Varana and Massaga (which is northwest of Varana), below a bend in the Indus River, and in the greater Gandhara satrapy.

Dowry given to Chandragupta Maurya by Seleucus in **303 BC:**

Arachosia (around Kandahar and the Arghandab Valley, south Afghanistan)

Gedrosia (around coastal Baluchistan, the Makran), covered from the west of River Indus to the southern edge of the Straits of Hormuz, south of Bactria, Arachosia and Drangiana

Paropamisadae - beyond the Hindu Kush - included **Gandhara** and **Kambhoja**

Chandragupta also recaptured **Patala** harbor in **303 BC,** rebuilt by Alexander, defeated five of Alexander's satraps, and later on annexed their territories either from Seleucus or on his own.

Epilogue

By 500 BC, North India had 16 polities or 'mahajanapadas' – some republics, some monarchies. 'Janapada' means 'tribal foothold'. Agriculture advanced and this led to cities, political systems, and 'mahajanapadas'. Among the sixteen mahajanapadas, Gandhara and Kambhoja consistently paid tribute to the Achaemenid Empire. **During the fifth century**, there were four mahajanapadas in the Indian subcontinent – Vajji, Kosala, Kasi and Magadha.

The *Behistun Inscription* of the sixth century speaks of 23 different satrapies. Gandhara and Sattagydia were the two important sub-continental Indian satrapies mentioned in the inscription.

Thanks to political fragmentation in India, the Achaemenids entered and established a foothold. The upper Indus areas including Gandhara and Kambhoja formed the seventh Gandhara satrapy. Gandhara was in the Peshawar basin, in Afghanistan and Pakistan, and partly at the confluence of the Kabul and Swat rivers. The Gandharan king was probably a vassal of Dhanananda, who paid the maximum tribute among the satrapies to the Persians around the time Alexander invaded India.

Sattagydia, a.k.a. Thataguš (Old Persian for country of a 'hundred cows') was among the eastern-most satrapies of the Achaemenids. A very unruly satrapy, Sattagydia revolted against Darius I, who stamped out the insurgency in **515 BC**. Possibly with time, Sattagydia, the country of a 'hundred cows', morphed into the animal-husbandry territories of the Ashvakas of Ora, Nysa and

Massaga. In 1982, the cultural historian David Fleming proposed that Sattagydia was located in the region of Bannu in the southern part of the Pakistani province of Khyber Pakhtunkhwa.

The middle and lower Indus (including Sindh and Sauvira) was the twentieth, Hindush satrapy, and paid 360 talents (11,880 kg) of gold as annual tribute; the Gandhara satrapy came second with an annual payment of 170 talents of gold.

Important north west Indian communities of the time included Kambojas (a.k.a. Ashvakas), Taksas of Gandhara, Sindhis, Madras, Kathaioi on the River Chenab, Mallas of the Ravi river, and Tugras on the River Sutlej.

In the 300s BC, the Nanda satrapy and territory in the Sapta Sindhu (renamed Punjab centuries later) was known for its gold and paid the Achaemenid empire 360 talents of gold dust as yearly tribute – they were the richest tribute givers among the 23 satrapies. Just prior to Alexander's invasion of India, Raja Sarvarthasiddhi paid this wealthiest of tributes to the Achaemenids, earning the moniker, Dhanananda.

The **battle of Guagamela,** in October **331 BC,** is one of the decisive battles of the civilized world, because, after this, the dominant Achaemenid Persian culture waned in Asia (including northwest India), and Alexander tried to replace it with Macedonian culture.

After King Emperor Darius III was assassinated by his cousin, satrap Bessus in **330 BC**, Alexander became king of Asia. In the hierarchy of satraps, the satrap of Bactria, *Mathista,* was next in succession to the Persian throne. When traitor Bessus – the *Mathista* – crowned himself king, Alexander was infuriated. Bessus was captured and executed in **329 BC.** Bactria (and Sogdiana) had many rulers after the execution.

All Asia had taken a violent beating at the hands of Alexander. But it was India which crumbled his army's morale, particularly the nightmarish pachyderm terror encountered in the battle with Porus in **326 BC**. Alexander's troops revolted against engaging the 'dirty' Indian battle zone, and mutinied, forcing Alexander to abandon further invasions into India.

When the Achaemenid Empire collapsed, its satrapies came under Alexander's rule, but after his death, his conquests fragmented. To mark victory or commemorate an important event, Alexander set up Alexandrias near Issus, Siwa, the second citadel of the Agalossoi, Susa, on the Nile, in Media, Parthia, Aria, Drangiana, Arachosia, Bactria, Scythia, Sogdia, Nicaea, at the Jaxartes river, the confluence of Jhelum and Beas, the Sindhu river and a stream, and for Bucephalus. Some Alexandrias still survive. Alexandria Arachoton survives as Kandahar, and Ghazni and Ucch are the other Alexandrias.

In **June 323 BC,** Alexander died in Babylon poisoned by his close aides, his death preceded by several human-intervened omens. His body was placed in a gold coffin, hijacked, and put in a beautiful tomb; currently rumored to lie beneath the Prophet Daniel's tomb in Alexandria, Egypt.

After his death, Alexander's mother Olympias, and his widow Roxanne were determined that Alexander's posthumous, legal son – Alexander-IV Aegus – inherits his empire. World history would have been different, if the only legitimate son of Alexander the Great had become the ruler of the empire of his father. But this was not to be.... Olympias was assassinated in **315 BC**. Alexander's widow Roxanne and Aegus were assassinated in **310 BC**, his illegitimate son Heracles and his mother Barsine, in **309 BC**.

Post-Alexander, India's first historically documented dynastic empire – the Maurya – lasted from **321 BC** till **185 BC**. Chandragupta Maurya was the first king to unite the Indus valley and Gangetic valley into one empire. He had two capitals: Patala on the Indus, which was destroyed repeatedly (and finally abandoned like many flood-prone sites), and Pataliputra (which translates loosely as 'son of Patala'), the regional capital in east India that has a much older pedigree than just being the Mauryan capital. Chandragupta ruled from **321** to **297 BC**.

The former Sashigupta's rule brought much-needed peace to the territory; the common man and rural India thrived. During wartime, even if a battle broke out in land adjoining agricultural fields, farmers were left undisturbed, to farm their land. Chandragupta's multiethnic army had Yavana, Kambhoja, Shaka (Scythian), Kirata, Persian and Bactrian soldiers – a reflection of a cosmopolitan time.

The original *Arthashastra,* a classic on economics and administrative strategy and the wealth of a nation, was discovered in Mysore, in the Oriental Library archives. Mysore is an overnight journey from Sravanabelagola, which has two hills – Chandragiri (Chikkabetta) and Vidyagiri. One can infer that King Chandragupta Maurya and much later, his Guru, settled in this area near the end of the king's lifetime. There is a Chandragupta *basadi* built by his grandson Ashoka the Great on Chandragiri hill. Basadi is a Jaina structure.

Megasthenes, the ambassador to India, sent in **303 BC** by Seleucus Nikator, recorded the way of life in the Mauryan empire.

Chandragupta's son **Bindusara** a.k.a. Amritochates (*Amritaghata)* by the Greeks, was coronated king after Chandragupta left in **298 BC** – and ruled till **273 BC**, a period of 25 years. Chanakya or Rakshash helped Bindusara destroy 19 towns, and settle and rule most of India from East to West. Amatya Rakshash may have stayed back to help Bindusara consolidate the empire. The wealth of the Nandas and later on the Mauryas, was based on the extraction of minerals and metallurgy.... Rakshash, chief minister of both the Nanda and Maurya kings, may have helped forge that aspect of empire.

Bindusara was succeeded by Ashokavardhan Maurya, a.k.a.

Ashoka THE GREAT. Ashoka was appointed the Governor of Avanti and became emperor in **273 BC**. Ashoka conquered Kalinga in a vicious, life altering battle. This conquest and his subsequent conversion to Buddhism, was a prelude to Ashoka being called 'Great'.

List of Events 563 BC Onwards

India

Republics and kingdoms increasingly replaced north Indian tribal structure.

549 BC **Persia**

Cyrus the Great (Cyrus II) overthrew the Medes, named his kingdom the Achaemenid Empire.

546 BC **Persia**

Cyrus seizes Lydia. [Lydia was an Iron Age kingdom situated in the west of Asia Minor, in modern-day Turkey. Later, it became an important province of the Achaemenid Empire.]

539 BC **Persia**

Babylon (Iraq) surrenders to Cyrus.

525 BC **Persia**

Egypt surrenders to Cyrus.

521 BC **Persia**

Darius I organizes empire in the satrapy system.

Behistun Inscription records details of 23 satrapies of Darius I.

518 BC **Persia-India**

Achaemenids conquered the Sapta Sindhu (the area of the Indus river basin and around its tributaries, modern day Punjab).

515 BC **Persia-India**

Darius I puts down a revolt by Sattagydia in the Sapta Sindhu.

490 BC **Persia-Macedonia-Greece**

Darius sends an army to Greece.

480 BC **Persia-Macedonia-Greece-India**

Xerxes invades Greece with Indian infantry and cavalry; proof Indian territories were Achaemenid satrapies, and is defeated.

413 - 363 **BC India**

Amatya (minister) Shishunaga deposed the Haryanka dynasty.

357 BC **Macedonia-Epirus**

Princess Myrtale of Epirus marries King Philip of Macedonia.

356 BC **Macedonia-Greece-India**

Alexander is born to Olympias (Myrtale) and Philip.
Sashigupta Maurya may have been born the same year.

346 BC **Macedonia-Greece**

Alexander tames wild stallion Bucephalus at age 10.

342 BC **Macedonia**

Alexander becomes Aristotle's student at age 14.

336 BC **Macedonia-Epirus**

Alexander's sister, Cleopatra, weds her mother's brother, King of

Epirus. At the wedding, Pausanius of Orestis kills King Philip. Alexander becomes king at twenty.

334 BC **Greece-Persia**

Alexander defeats Darius III on the banks of the River Granicus.

333 BC **Greece-Persia**

Alexander defeats Darius III in Issus, captures his family.

331 BC **Greece-Persia**

Alexander defeats Darius III at Guagamela (in modern Iraqi Kurdistan). Indian soldiers fought for Darius III as chariot and cavalry troops in this battle.

September 331 BC

Statira dies during childbirth. The father of the dead baby was Alexander.

330 BC **Media-Bactria**

Darius III flees to Bactria, where satrap Bessus treacherously executes him. [Country lying between the mountains of the Hindu Kush and the Amu Darya (ancient Oxus River) in what is now part of Afghanistan, Uzbekistan, and Tajikistan.]

329 BC **Ecbatana-Bactria**

Bessus is taken prisoner by Alexander, sent to Ecbatana and beheaded.

328 BC **Marakanda**

Alexander kills his savior Cleitus the Black in a drunken brawl [Ancient Samarkand was Marakanda.]

327 BC **India**

Ambhi of Taxila connives with Alexander, offering his troops as backup against the Nanda rulers of India.

326 BC **India**

Varana (Aornos) defeated and given to Prince Sashigupta as satrapy. Alexander defeats Porus [a king whose territory spanned the region between the Jhelum river (Hydaspes) and Chenab river (Acesines), in the Punjab], in the most fierce battle his army fought.

325 BC **India**

Abhisares of Kashmir dies and is replaced by Pushkaraksha.

324 BC **Persia-Susa-Opis**

Macedonians marry local noblewomen, following Alexander's example. Alexander's Oath at Opis (modern Iraq) combines Greek and Indian philosophy. Hephaestion dies in October.

323 BC **Babylon**

Alexander dies. Five people chronicle symptoms leading to his death. Sisygambis – mother of Darius III – dies five days after Alexander.

321 BC **India**

The Mauryan dynasty takes center stage.

310 BC **Amphipolis**

Alexander's wife Roxanne and son Alexander Aegus are assassinated by Cassander.

309 BC **Pergamon**

Darus III's daughter and Alexander's consort Barsine and her son,

Heracles, are assassinated by Cassander.

308 BC **Epirus-Sardis**

Cleopatra, Alexander's sister, assassinated by Antigonos Monophthalmos.

305-303 **BC India**

Chandragupta Maurya defeats Seleucus in one decisive battle, winning Arachosia, Gedrosia, Sapta Sindhu and Paropamisadae. Seleucus' daughter, Helen, marries Chandragupta, who gives Seleucus 500 war elephants as bride price.

304 BC **Egypt**

Alexander's general, Ptolemy, is crowned pharaoh in Egypt.

301 BC **Ipsus**

Seleucus' 500 war elephants win battle and are instrumental in the death of Antigonos.

300 BC **India**

Chandragupta Maurya unites the Indus Valley and Gangetic plains to bring about the greatest *mahajanapada* in India's history.

297 BC **India**

Chandragupta abdicates in favor of his son Bindusara, departs for Sravanabelagola.

276 BC **Alexander's Empire**

Alexander's conquests are divided into Antigonid Macedon, Seleucid Asia, Ptolemic Egypt, Thrace and Mauryan India.

Cast of Characters

The Indians

Abhisares (d. 325 BC): The king of Kashmir was friend and ally of Paurava the Elder. By the time Prince Malayaketu and Rakshash forged alliances with five princely states, Abhisares had been replaced by Pushkaraksha.

Ambhi Raja (d. 318 BC?): of Taxila was called Oomphis of Taxiles by the Yavana. An opportunist and groveler, he befriended Alexander in order to use him against his long-time enemy, Paurava.

Calanos (d. 323 BC): Sage cum teacher Calanos became Alexander's second mentor after Aristotle. His gentle influence is evident in the speech at Opis. He immolated himself on an Indian-style funeral pyre in Persia.

Chanakya, a.k.a. Kautilya or Vishnugupta (d. 283 BC): Chanakya helped Sashigupta Maurya set up the Maurya dynasty. Sashigupta met Chanakya at his forest gurukul, school. The connection between Sashigupta and Chanakya was so strong, that not many attempts were made on the old scholar's life out of fear of deadly revenge on Sashigupta's part. The guru's strong intuition helped save Sashigupta, known later as Chandragupta, from burning to death in the former Nanda palace. Later, after Chandragupta's abdication in favor of his son Bindusara, the guru followed his protégé south to Sravanabelagola, Karnataka.

Guruji Chanakya incorporated many Achaemenid administrative features into Maurya infrastructure. For instance, there was a special department that only took care of Yavana and Persian foreigners. Chanakya, a scholar in politics and economics, was the author of *The Arthashastra,* a world classic on wealth generation and political stability for nations. A copy of *The Arthashastra* was found in Mysore in the twentieth century, after going missing for centuries. This copy of the *Arthashastra* in Sanskrit, written on palm leaves, was presented by a Tamil Brahmin from Thanjavur to the newly opened Mysore Oriental Library, founded by the Wodeyar kings in 1891 and headed by Benjamin Lewis Rice. Rudrapatna Shamashastri, a Sanskrit scholar and librarian, discovered the manuscript in 1905 among the mounds of palm leaf documents lying in the institute, which has been part of the University of Mysore from 1916, and is home to about 70,000 rare palm-leaf manuscripts. Shamashastri transcribed the *Arthashastra* on to fresh palm leaves and published it in 1909. He translated it into English in 1915.

Chanakya also authored the *Niti Darpan* (The Mirror of Justice).

Chandragupta Maurya (356 - 297 BC): Chandragupta Maurya was the founder king of the Maurya dynasty, who rose phoenix-style in 321 BC from the ashes of Alexander the Great's crumbling empire after his death. He is believed to be the same person as Prince Sashigupta.

From 305-303 BC, Chandragupta waged 'warfare without war' – a war of attrition – against the Seleucid forces. In 303 BC, after the Seleucids were defeated in a life-altering battle, the Mauryan and Seleucid forces came to a truce. Arachosia, Gedrosia, Paropamisadae (Kambhoja and Gandhara) and many areas around the Sapta Sindhu were transferred to the Mauryan Empire. Today's Herat (Aria) was also part of the transfer.

Helen, daughter of Seleucus Nikator, married Chandragupta,

cementing political ties between the two kings. India only developed her greatest *mahajanapada* under Chandragupta's reign, when the Gangetic plains and Indus river valley territories were cemented as one. Ashvakas, Sakas (Scythians), Bahlikas (Bactrians), Pahlavas, and Kiratas of the northwest, helped Chandragupta set up his empire. Singlehandedly, Chandragupta Maurya replaced Alexander's rule (and satraps) with his own via a very astute war policy. Alexander's Indian territories had been Mauryan holdings for decades when Chandragupta Maurya died.

At the end of Chandragupta's reign, the king converted to Jainism, traveled to Sravanabelagola as a Jaina monk. Very close to Sravanabelagola, is a small hill called Chandragiri named after Chandragupta. Chandragupta starved himself to death through the Jaina practice called *Sallekhana* – a vow observed by Jaina ascetics to reduce the intake of food and fluids on each following day, daily. Chandragupta's two known wives were Durdhara and Helen, and his successor was Bindusara, born through Durdhara. The Mauryan dynasty ended in 184 BC.

Dhananandа (d. 322 BC): Dhanananda, the rich Nanda a.k.a. **Raja Sarvarthasiddhi**, was a showoff, debauch and a man of low origins. Dhanananda earned his nickname, the 'rich' Nanda – Dhanananda – as he was the richest satrap of King Emperor Darius Codomannus. Kings in the surrounding areas looked down with contempt on this man and his siblings. Protected by chief minister Rakshash, Dhanananda made the fatal error of insulting a scholar of Chanakya's caliber in his court. He also erred in trying to wipe out his bastard sons through the courtesan Mura, which earned him a life-threatening enmity with his only known surviving illegitimate son, Sashigupta. Dhanananda's brothers were Pandugati, Bhutapala, Rastrapala, Govishanaka, Dashasiddhaka, and Kaivarta. His legitimate son was Panduka. None survived.

Durdhara (d. 320 BC) was Chandragupta's Indian queen. Chandragupta was fed small doses of poison by his guru Chanakya to immunize him. By mistake, Chandragupta fed Durdhara the poisoned food when she was just seven days from delivery. She died, and Guru Chanakya cut open the queen and extracted the baby boy in her womb. This son of Chandragupta was his only known offspring.

Malayaketu (d. 299 BC): Malayaketu, son of Raja Parvataka, was coronated as king after his father's assassination. His allies were Chiravarma of Kaulutu, Megaksha of Parasika, Narasimha of the Malaya Mountains, Pushkaraksha of Kashmir, and Sindhusena of Saindara on the Sindhu.

Maurya (321 – 185 BC): The Maurya and Kambhoja clans were called Warrior clans as well as Asuras – which might point to an Iranian connection, as Asuras peopled Persia, where they worshipped their God Ahura Mazda.

Mura (d. 331 BC): Mura, the mother who gave her name to the Maurya dynasty, was accused of being of a low caste – a manipulation Dhanananda used when he wanted to rid himself off his concubine after he tired of her and her 'low-born' sons. In reality, if Mura had Asura (Persian) ancestry, she was actually on par, if not superior to, the low-born Nandas.

Porus, a.k.a. **Paurava the Elder (d. 316 BC):** Paurava was defeated by Alexander in battle by the banks of the Jhelum. Alexander won the battle, but it demoralized his troops so much that Alexander had to give up all ambitions to go eastward into India. Porus is famously known for his answer to Alexander after defeat, when asked by Alexander how he wanted to be treated: 'Treat me like a king.'

Porus's kingdom lay between the Jhelum and the Chenab. His nephew Porus the Younger, fled when Alexander crossed into his kingdom, which was then gifted to Porus the Elder. Porus was killed by Alexander's general Eudemus in 316 BC, after which Eudemus used Porus' elephants against the Diadoch Antigonos, who then executed Eudemes, leading to the Third War of the Diadochi. Many small principalities were captured by Alexander, but only the fight with Paurava the Elder was recorded in detail by Alexander's chroniclers.

Raja Parvataka (d. 322 BC): Raja Parvataka appointed Rakshash as chief minister after Dhanananda's death. His son Malayaketu was a foolish boy who did not quite understand politics, and the art of ruling.

Rakshash: Amatya Rakshash was the intelligent, loyal chief minister successively of Raja Dhanananda, Raja Parvataka, Prince Malayaketu and Prince Sashigupta. It was his idea to turn Sashigupta's newly renovated palace into a firetrap to kill Sashigupta. Later, thanks to Guru Chanakya's psychological manipulation, Rakshash became a loyal chief minister to King Chandragupta Maurya.

Sashigupta (d. 297 BC): Sashigupta, the ruler of Varana fort (today's Pir-sar) was a loyal satrap of Alexander, but broke free after Alexander died. His war games were all strategies to destroy the Nandas and Alexander's conquests. Sashigupta a.k.a. Chandragupta after his coronation, converted to Jainism. Both 'Chandragupta' and 'Sashigupta' mean 'moon-protected'. Greek writer Phylarchus (3rd century BC) called Chandragupta 'Sandrakoptus'. Other writers called him Sandrakottus, or Andrakottus.

The Greeks and Macedonians

Alexander (356 - 323 BC): Alexander, of the Argead dynasty, world-altering monarch of Macedonia, also called the Great, the Accursed, and *Iskander Gujaste*. Alexander was known as Eskandar-e-Maqduni in Persian, Al-Iskandar Al Makadoni in Arabic, Alexander Mokdon in Hebrew, and Tre-Qarnayia (the two-horned one) in Aramaic. Alexander slept with a copy of Homer's *Iliad* and thought he was a reincarnation of Achilles. Alexander was very influenced by Greek culture and architecture, and all his Alexandrias were built as rectangles, with high walls, and public buildings (acropolis) like temples, and an agora (marketplace) in the classical style. The period that followed Alexander's death is called the Hellenistic age. Early in his career, Alexander humbled his enemies in Greece. The main Greek cities were Sparta, Athens, Corinth and Thebes, and when Thebes refused to join the league of cities of which Alexander was the leader (*hegemon*), he burnt it and sold the citizens as slaves. After more than twelve years as conqueror, king and master of genocide, Alexander had made enough enemies to die a treacherous death. Alexander was mostly poisoned through alcohol and died in 323 BC. Just before his death, when asked who he was leaving his kingdom to, he replied: 'To the strongest, for I foresee that a great combat between my friends will be my funeral games.' Sure enough, by 276 BC, Alexander's Empire split into five parts ... Antigonid Macedon, Thrace, Seleucid Asia, Ptolemic Egypt and Mauryan India.

Antigonos Monophthalmos (382 – 301 BC): Antigonos Monophthalmous, the 'one-eyed', was the founder of the Antigonid dynasty of Macedonia, becoming king in 306 BC. He, along with Peithon and Seleucus, killed Perdiccas. Next, Peithon, satrap of Media, was killed by Antigonos. Antigonos himself died in battle against Seleucus Nikator's troops and 500 war elephants in the battle of Ipsus, Phrygia. Nikanor was the Macedonian satrap of Parthia under Antigonos.

Antipater (d. 319 BC): Elderly Antipater was viceroy of Macedonia. His two sons were Cassander and Iollas – Alexander's wine pourer; his daughter Nicaea was married to Perdiccas. Antipater divided the conquests of Alexander the Great – for Ptolemy, Egypt; for Antigonos, Asia; and for himself, Macedonia.

Aristotle (384 – 322 BC): Aristotle – philosopher and teacher of Alexander in his teen years, was the third in the trio of Greek philosophers and thinkers following Socrates and Plato. Aristotle joined Plato's school – the Academy – at the age of 18, and for the next twenty years Plato called Aristotle, '*the intelligence of the school*'. When Plato died, Aristotle married Pithias, the adopted daughter of King Hermias of Atarneus. Aristotle's father Nichomacus was personal physician of Amyntas II – father of Philip and grandfather of Alexander. In 343 BC, Philip II invited Aristotle to oversee Alexander's education. Aristotle helped Alexander become king. Later, he became an enemy who might have masterminded Alexander's death by remote control after Alexander killed his grandnephew, the historian Callisthenes. Some of Aristotle's main lessons were that reason was a good alternative to violence (that the Greeks-Macedonians had a propensity for) and his definition of happiness was that it was composed of good health, friendship, enough money, a job, and a family.

Arrhidaeus (d. 317 BC): Arrhidaeus a.k.a. Philip Arrhidaeus, and son of King Philip through the Thessalian dancer Philinna of Larissa, was poisoned by Queen Olympias, which affected the child's brains. That should have taken Arrhidaeus out of the race for the throne. However, Arrhidaeus was made king in 323 BC, with Perdiccas as regent. Coins minted in his name were used in the Mauryan kingdom. Arrhidaeus's wife Eurydice, was made to hang herself by Olympias after he died.

Callisthenes (d. 327 BC): Historian Callisthenes was the grandnephew of Aristotle through his sister Arimneste. In the beginning, Callisthenes – who was Alexander's childhood friend – had fawned upon Alexander, ignoring Alexander calling himself son of the god Zeus. He set up Alexander's publicity and propaganda department, that made the king look good in the Greek city states. But he was a harsh critic of the Persian practice of *Proskynesis,* imprisoned, and died of torture or disease.

Cassander (d. 297 BC): Prince Cassander, a Macedonian prince and son of Antipater, rebuilt Thebes, out of hatred for Alexander. He singlehandedly eliminated Alexander's family. First, Cassander paid Polyperchon 100 talents to get rid of Alexander's son Heracles and his mother Barsine. Cassander also had Roxanne and her son – Alexander's heir – killed. He captured Olympias, the mother of Alexander. In the end, Cassander fell ill with dropsy and worms. He was king from 305 to 297 BC, when he died of dropsy (edema).

Charidemus (d. 333 BC): Charidemus was a Greek mercenary, with Athenian citizenship. After Alexander threw him out in 335 BC, he left for Persia and joined the army of Darius III. Darius had him foolishly executed because he criticized the composition of the Persian army.

Cleopatra (d. 308 BC): Cleopatra, Alexander's sibling, was a pawn used by both her mother and father for political intrigue. The girl was made to marry her uncle – her mother Olympias's brother. . Cleopatra had two children – Neoptolemus II and Cadmeia. The former was king of the Molossian kingdom. After her husband, who was King of Epirus died, Cleopatra who became the regent, was assassinated by Antigonos who held her prisoner in Sardis.

Cleitus the Black (d. 328 BC): Cleitus the Black saved Alexander during the battle of the Granicus river in 334 BC. Years later – 328 BC – when Alexander hosted a party to send Cleitus to some god-forsaken barren areas with a host of defeated Greek mercenaries, there was a bitter, drunken fight between him and Alexander. While drunk, Alexander had a very short memory, and no gratitude towards Cleitus, whom he speared dead during the drunken brawl. But when Alexander sobered, he wanted to commit suicide from remorse.

Coenus (d. 326 BC): Coenus was a commander of a few infantry divisions, who opposed Alexander's foray eastwards into Indika. Alexander was forced to accept that his army did not want any more battles within India. When informed by Coenus, the army cheered loudly at the prospect of leaving snake-ridden, rain-soaked Indika for more predictable and easier conquests. Veteran Coenus died mysteriously. It was rumored he was killed for being the voice of the malcontents in Alexander's army. Coenus may have been married to Parmenion's daughter.

Eudemus (d. 316 BC): Eudemus was Alexander's general, and was appointed satrap of few of his Indian territories. In 317, a powerful Eudemus supported Eumenes in his war against Antigonos by sending 500 cavalry, 300 infantry and 120 war elephants. Then in a political move, Eudemus betrayed Eumenes to Antigonos. After he killed Eumenes, Antigonos killed Eudemus for whom he had a deep antipathy.

Eumenes (d. 316 BC): Eumenes was private secretary first to Philip II of Macedon, and after his death, to Alexander the Great. He married a daughter of Artabazus in the internation marriages that Alexander organized. When Eumenes's baggage train lost 30 years of war loot, belonging to the Macedonian Silver Shields, he was betrayed by them for the loot loss and for being Greek. Antigonos then had Eumenes as well as the commander of the Silver Shields put to death.

Helen (m. Chandragupta Maurya 303 BC): Daughter of Seleucus Nikator and a Persian noblewoman, Apama, she married King Chandragupta. In return, Chandragupta gifted his father-in-law 500 war elephants as bride price in exchange for Gedrosia, Arachosia, Paropamisadae and parts of Aria, Drangiana, and the Sapta Sindhu. Helen had no known children through Chandragupta.

Heracles (327 – 309 BC): Heracles – Alexander's first but illegitimate son through Barsine, and named after the Greek hero of the same name – lived in obscurity at Pergamon, with his mother. Polyperchon received a sum of 100 talents from Prince Cassander to kill Heracles. Polyperchon invited Heracles for dinner, and when Heracles intuitively refused, made up a story that his father King Alexander always obliged a friend, and 'so should you, unless you fear me as a plotter.' Fooled, Heracles attended the dinner, where he was strangled. Next, his mother Barsine was also killed, and both bodies secretly buried, since a grand funeral would invite unwelcome attention.

Iollas (d. 318 BC): Iollas was Alexander's alcohol server and wine pourer, and, son of Antipater. Antipater sent Iollas through Cassander poison in the hoof of a mule, packed in an iron box. After Alexander's death, Iollas was honored. But after Iollas died,

Olympias had his ashes scattered in the wind as punishment for his part in poisoning Alexander.

Kleopatra Eurydice (d. 336 BC): Kleopatra Eurydice, wife of Philip of Macedonia, was killed by Philip's ex-wife Olympias after Philip's death, as her son Caranus – could have posed a challenge for the throne to Alexander, his half-brother. Olympias got Caranus and his elder sister killed, and then forced Kleopatra Eurydice to hang herself.

Megasthenes (350 – 290 BC): Megasthenes – ambassador, ethnographer, travel writer – had taken back with him several manuscripts on India, which was the basis for later European and other writers to expand on their understanding of India. Megasthenes visited Madurai, the capital of the Pandyan kingdom, where women were preferred to men for administrative jobs –- a gender difference that he mentioned in his encyclopedic series of travel books, called *Indika,* which later historians and writers extensively referred to. Megasthenes gave a bird's eye view of Indian society – where all the people were divided into two groups – *Arya* and *non-Arya.* The first three *Arya* groups were Brahmin, Kshatriya and Vaishya, and the fourth, Sudra. Only the last three were preferred for settling virgin lands as they made good contributions to the economy, according to his observations.

Memnon (d. 333 BC) and **Mentor (d. 340 BC):** Memnon and Mentor of Rhodes were Greek mercenaries who commanded King Emperor Darius's mercenary troops. Both brothers were married to Barsine, first one than the other.

Neoptolemus II (d. 297 BC): Neoptolemus II was king of Epirus for a brief period from 302 to 297 BC. His grandmother Olympias was daughter of King Neoptolemus I. His mother Cleopatra was first niece and then wife of Alexander, the king of Epirus, who happened to be the brother of Olympias.

Nikanor (d. 304 BC): Nikanor was appointed satrap of Parthia, under Antigonos Monophthalmous, after the assassination of General Eudemus. He was assassinated by Chandragupta's mercenaries to indirectly weaken General Seleucus' hold on northwest India.

Olympias (375 – 315 BC): Princess Myrtale – sister of the king of Epirus - was christened Olympias after her husband King Philip's race horse won in the Olympics in 356 BC, the same year she gave birth to her first born, Alexander. The Albanian daughter of King Neoptolemus I of Epirus, she was the fourth wife of Philip, and a member of the snake worshipping cult of Dionysus. Olympias – a master of intrigue and a schemer – was probably stoned to death in Pydna, Greece, by the families of victims she had destroyed. Her other names were Stratonice and Polyxena.

Parmenion (d. 330 BC): Parmenion was a general in Philip's army and was responsible for defeating Memnon, the mercenary general of Emperor Darius. He defeated the Illyrian and Paeonian armies, the year Alexander was born. A dependable man, Parmenion occupied the coast around Issus, while Alexander attacked Miletus. During the battle of Issus, Parmenion faced the first charge by the Persian cavalry with the Thessalian cavalry, and did a brilliant job… he held the battlefield much after Alexander's Companion Cavalry attacked the forces of Memnon. He fell out of favor when his son **Philotas** openly opposed Alexander's adoption of *Proskynesis.* Alexander first executed Philotas, and then his father Parmenion, shortly after.

Parysatis (d. 323 BC): Daughter of Artaxerxes III, she married Alexander in 324 in Susa. She was murdered by Roxanne after Alexander died as she was rumored to be pregnant.

Peithon (d. 305 BC): Peithon was made satrap by Alexander, of territories south of the Jhelum, around Sindimana. He and Seleucus were good friends and allies. He was killed by King Chandragupta's mercenaries.

Peithon (d. 316 BC): Peithon, son of Agenor, was made satrap of Media. He made his brother Eudemus satrap of Parthia. Peithon had Philip, satrap of Sogdiana killed. He allied with Seleucus and Antigonos to kill Perdiccas. Was probably killed by Antigonos.

Perdiccas (d. 321 BC): Perdiccas helped save Alexander in a battle with the Malloi. When Alexander was struck in the left lung by an arrow, Perdiccas surgically removed it. Perdiccas was married to Antipater's daughter, Nicaea. He backed Roxanne's son, Alexander IV Aegus to take over Alexander's throne, and was regent for Alexander's mentally deficient brother Philip Arrhidaeus. Alexander trusted Perdiccas with his signet ring. After Alexander's death, Perdiccas and Roxanne plotted to kill Alexander's wife, Parysatis, suspecting that she was pregnant too. But Perdiccas was killed by Peithon, Seleucus and Antigonos, leaving Roxanne on her own.

Philip II (d. 336 BC): King Philip II of Macedonia was Alexander's father, and held hostage from 368 to 365 BC in Thebes. Born in Pella, he was the youngest son of King Amyntas II and wife Eurydice, and a pronounced pedophile. His death can be attributed in part to his pedophiliac abuse of two young boys. One of them – Pausanius of Orestes assassinated him on his daughter's wedding day. Philip – of the Argead dynasty – was a mere 46 years old when he died, and left Alexander one of the most powerful armies in Europe.

Philip (d. 318 BC): Philip, satrap of Sogdiana, was killed by Peithon before 316 BC.

Philip (d. 305 BC): Philip – son of Machatas – was made satrap of the areas next to Paurava's satrapy by Alexander the Great, when the Yavana left. He took over Paurava's territories after he was killed by Eudemus. Philip himself was killed by Chandragupta's Yavana mercenaries.

Polyperchon (d. 304 BC): Polyperchon worked under Philip II, and then under Alexander. After the battle of Issus in 333 BC, he headed the Tymphaean battalions till 324 BC. After Antipater died in 319 BC, Polyperchon was appointed regent and supreme commander. Polyperchon killed Heracles, Alexander's son, on payment from Prince Cassander.

Ptolemy (d. 283 BC): Ptolemy was made governor of Egypt and became pharoah in 305 BC. The Ptolemaic empire came to an end when Cleopatra, the last of the Ptolemies, committed suicide in 30 BC through cobra bite.

Seleucus Nikator (d. 281 BC): Seleucus Nikator rose from humble soldier to general in Alexander's army. His promotion as commander of the Shield Bearers, the elite infantry that protected Alexander was the starting point for his later successes. Seleucus learnt a tough lesson when Porus's enraged elephants caused chaos and mayhem in the battle with Porus. Later, when Seleucus helped Alexander defeat the Malloi, Alexander put him in charge of an entire regiment.

In the internation marriages between Alexander's men and the local noble women, Seleucus married Apama, daughter of Spitamenes, leader of the Sogdians. This was one of the exceptionally happy marriages that lasted beyond Alexander's death. The couple had a son – Antiochus Soter – who became the leader of the Seleucid kingdom. Seleucus was one of the Diadochi, the generals who came up after Alexander's death. He was appointed satrap of Babylon at the partition of Tripara-Disus by Antipater in 321 BC, but immediately lost this territory due to the Wars of the Diadochi. He only regained Babylon with Ptolemy's support. The Seleucid empire began in 312 BC, and lasted till 64 BC, and extended from the Indus till Phrygia. Seleucus minted coins in India from 306 to 303 BC.

From 305 to 303 BC, Chandragupta Maurya chipped away at the Seleucid forces, and finally routed them in battle with an estimated 9,000 elephants, and 600,000 men in 303 BC, after which both Mauryan and Seleucid forces came to a truce. Arachosia, Gedrosia, Paropamisadae and areas around the Sapta Sindhu were allotted to the Mauryan Empire. Seleucus was assassinated in Thrace by Ptolemy Keraunos, who was king of Macedonia for a brief period.

The Persians

Bagaos (d. 336 BC): The downfall of the Persian Empire would not have happened so swiftly if not for Bagaos, a politically manipulative eunuch, who assassinated Artaxerxes III Ochus, and his sons. Bagaos then crowned Ochus's cousin Darius Codomannus (Darius III) as the next king emperor. When Bagaos became greedy for the crown, he offered Darius a glass of poisoned wine, which a suspicious Darius forced the eunuch to drink, thereby killing him.

Bagaos (death unknown): Bagaos, the younger eunuch, was a dazzling beauty, cherished by king emperor Darius III. When the king emperor was on the run, his general Nabarzenes met Alexander with many gifts, one of them being the stunning Bagaos, whom he presented at Hyrcanus in 330 BC. Alexander was so enamored by the young eunuch, he was often spotted kissing him on the lips in public, in front of his soldiers. Bagaos was given the post of one of the 33 Trierarchs, commanders of the triremes (the boats with three rows of oars), but this was a mere title, as Bagaos had no battlefield experience.

Barsine (d. 309 BC): Barsine was the daughter of King Emperor Darius Codomannus. After Darius' family was captured in 333 BC, at the battle of Issus, Barsine became mother of Alexander's son, Heracles, in 327 BC. After Alexander's death, she and her son relocated to Pergamon, and were murdered by Polyperchon on order from Prince Cassander.

Bessus (d. 329 BC): Bessus, satrap of Sogdiana and Bactria, betrayed his cousin king emperor Darius. After Darius' death, Bessus – who was a *Mathista*, next in line of succession to the throne – crowned himself Artaxerxes V. Alexander deeply detested Bessus's treachery. When Bessus was captured, his nose and ears were chopped off in the Indo-Iranian style of punishment. To add insult to injury, Bessus was tied naked to a stake next to the highway so that soldiers could heckle him as they marched past. Adding more injury to insult, he was then sent to Ecbatana to be executed by Darius's brother in the summer of 329 BC.

Darius Codomannus (d. 330 BC): Darius was a mere courtier picked by the eunuch Bagaos to replace King Ochus and his son Arses, whom he assassinated by poison to get rid of them. Darius was chosen for his personal bravery in a war with the Cadusans, whose representative set up a challenge. Darius took up the challenge and killed the challenger, for which he was rewarded with gifts and honors and the satrapy of Armenia. This brave man became a weak and vacillating king emperor of the Persian Empire (a.k.a. *Darayavaunsh* meaning 'he who is holding the good'), and was killed treacherously by satrap and cousin Bessus in July 330 BC. Darius was taken hostage by Bessus, his general Nabarzenes, and Barsaentes, but assassinated by Bessus. A day before he was assassinated, he was warned of the plot to kill him, but Darius vainly refused to escape on horseback, saying it was too demeaning for him. The next day, a Macedonian soldier – Polystratus, noticed a driverless bullock cart meandering off the battlefield between the Ahuran Pass and the city of Quse, and riding up to investigate, found the king emperor dying, attended by one faithful dog. Darius took a sip of water, and died. Alexander took Darius's signet ring and sent his body back to Persepolis to be buried in the royal tombs. Alexander now became king of Asia. Darius was also called Artašata.

Mazaeus (d. 328 BC): Mazaeus was the cowardly saptrap of Babylon who was first a satrap of the Achaemenid, and then later Alexander's empires. He fought against Alexander in the battle of Guagamela commanding Scythian, Sacesimian, Syrian, Median, Mesopotamian, Parthian, Tapurian, Hyrcanian, Cappodochian, and Armenian cavalry. Alexander, however, made him satrap of Babylon later for reasons no one could fathom.

Nabarzenes (d. 330 BC): Nabarzenes was a general in Bessus' army. When Darius was on the run, Nabarzenes met Alexander and handed him many gifts, including the stunning eunuch Bagaos. Nabarzenes was one of the trio who took Darius prisoner, and may have had a hand in his assassination, but was not punished.

Ochus (d. 338 BC): Ochus, also called Artaxerxes III Ochus, was the eleventh emperor of the Achaemenid dynasty. A son of Artaxerxes II, Artaxerxes III became king after his father died, when one brother was executed, one more murdered, and one died. Ochus then murdered the rest of the royal family, and reigned till the age of 87. Ochus and his sons were assassinated by Bagaos, the older eunuch. Alexander married Parysatis, the youngest daughter of Ochus so that he could claim to be a legitimate successor to the whole of Asia.

Roxanne (d. 310 BC): Roxanne was the daughter of Oxyartes, a former nobleman of Balkh, the principal city in Bactria. The sixteen-year-old Roxanne, whose Persian name *Roshanak* meant 'Little Star', met Alexander in 327 BC during a wedding dance he attended, and offered to become his wife. Alexander fell in love with Roxanne who the Macedonians pronounced as the loveliest woman in Asia. Roxanne was enchanted by exotic India – its plants, its rare animals, its religious practices, its Arya temples.

Roxanne lost her first child, but gave birth to a posthumous baby boy, the only legal child that Alexander the Great ever had, recognized by the Greeks and Macedonians. This child – Alexander IV Aegus – was the heir to the empire of Alexander, which included today's Greece, Macedonia, Egypt, Turkey, Iran, Afghanistan, Pakistan, parts of India, Uzbekistan and much more.

Roxanne was as vicious as her mother-in-law Olympias when it came to protecting her son's inheritance. She tricked Alexander's other two wives Barsine and Parysatis to travel away from their homes. Roxanne killed Parysatis who she thought was pregnant, and a future threat to her son Alexander IV Aegus's takeover of the throne. After her husband's death, Roxanne knew that she was in danger. She ran. Her journeys with her baby boy took her thousands of miles, all the time being pursued by the jealous generals who wanted to kill the boy so that they could divide the empire of

Alexander among themselves. Roxanne and her son's brutal deaths were remote controlled by Prince Cassander through Glaucias.

Sisygambis (d. 323 BC): Queen Mother Sisygambis was the mother of King Emperor Darius Codomannus. Sisygambis and her family were captured by Alexander after the battle of Issus in 333 BC. After her capture, she visited the tent of Alexander where he was in discussion with his friend Hephaestion, who was taller than Alexander. She mistakenly addressed Hephaestion as Alexander, who nobly forgave her mistake, saying 'Your confusion over the name is unimportant, for this man is also Alexander.'

When Sisygambis was informed about Alexander's death, she stopped eating and drinking, and died five days later. Her reaction to Alexander's demise was stronger than her reaction to her own son Darius's death. Sisygambis and Ada were mother figures who revered, and were in turn, adored by Alexander.

Spitamenes (d. 328 BC): Spitamenes, leader of the Sogdians and former commander in Bessus's army, had a daughter Apama who married Seleucus Nikator. Their son, Antiochus Soter, later became the ruler of the Seleucid kingdom. Apama's exceptionally happy marriage was one of very few internation marriages that survived Alexander's death.

Statira (d. 331 BC): Statira, mother of Barsine and Drypetis, was captured in 333 BC and became Alexander's mistress. She died of childbirth after living with Alexander; this illegitimate child (sired by Alexander) did not survive.

Relevant info

Achaemenid Empire (559- 330 BC) was known as the Hakhamanishiya in ancient Persia.

Alexandria

An Alexandria was a city laid out in rectangles, defended by walls, with an acropolis (temple and public buildings), and an agora (a marketplace) in the classical mould, built by Alexander. The first township Alexander founded, was called Alexandripolis Maedica, in Thrace in 340 BC.

Asiatic lion a.k.a. Persian Lion

The Asiatic lion ranged all over Gujarat, Delhi and the long-grasslands of the tributaries of the Indus rive during the time of Chandragupta Maurya. There are two legends (legends are stories with a basis in truth) about Chandragupta's interaction with lions, both of which are covered in this book. Plutarch, centuries later, mentions one of the lion stories of Chandragupta, in a patronizing fashion. The mention of the lions not only pins Chandragupta to the northwest of India, especially today's Punjab, it is also a pointer to the rich ecosystems in existence in Chandragupta's time. There is early proof that the lion existed in northwest Indian jungles, as there are seals found in the Indus Valley civilization cityscapes with lion images. Historically, the lion occurred in Saudi Arabia, Iran, Iraq, Turkey, and ranged from the Indus to Bengal, in Sind, Rajasthan, Rewa, Haryana, Bihar, and included the Narmada River.

Asskenoi

The Asskenoi a.k.a Ashvakas and Aspasoi, were known for their horse rearing and cattlebreeding skills. So impressed was Alexander with the cattle that he captured in what is today's east Afghanistan and west Pakistan, 230,000 superior cattleheads, and thousands of good breed horses, and sent them to Macedonia. The Ashvakas have been also called Kambhojas. The Macedonians picked up the stirrup – a metal loop supporting the horse rider's foot – from India.

Behistun Inscription – 521 BC,
Indian territories of Darius the Great

The *Behistun Inscription* of Darius the Great (522-486 BC, Darius I) has the first written proof outside India of Sattagydia and Gandhara. In the *Inscription,* Darius I says: *These are the lands that came to me. I became their king by the will of Ahura Mazda: Persia, Elam, Babylonia, Assyria, Egypt, those by the sea, Sardis, Ionia, Media, Armenia, Cappodocia, Parthia, Drangiana, Aria, Khwarazm, Bactria, Sogdiana, Gandhara, Shakaland, Sattagydia, Arachosia, Maka, a total of twenty-three lands.*

Behistun (**Mount Behistun** in Kermanshah Province of Iran), was also called **Bagastana** (Old Persian for 'place of God'.) In Devnagari, it can be loosely translated as 'Bhagvan ka stan', or 'place of God'.

Paropamisadae was a satrapy of Alexander's empire, located today in Afghanistan and Pakistan. Alexander had given a part of Paropamisadae to his father-in-law Oxyartes as satrapy. Paropamisadae comes close to the Achaemenid province of 'Parupraesanna', which means beyond the Hindu Kush. Paropamisadae (around Kambhoja and Gandhara) also became part of the Mauryan Empire.

Sattagydia is described as a troublesome satrapy that revolted against Darius I when he was visiting Babylon. The rebellion was put down in 515 BC, and the satrapy is not mentioned post 480 BC. After Alexander colonized it, the satrapy became part of the future Seleucid kingdom. Sattagydia, a.k.a. *Thataguš* (Old Persian for country of a 'hundred cows') was an eastern satrapy, on the River

Indus, possibly named for its animal husbandry expertise. During Alexander's invasion, he encountered the Ashvakas who were expert in breeding cattle and horses.

Diadoch means 'successor'; and refers to the first generation of military and political chiefs who came to power after Alexander's death.

Dionysus was the god of wine in Greek mythology. According to legend, he founded Nysa, which was conquered by Alexander in his push towards India.

Ecbatana was in Hagmatana Hill, in Hamadan province of Iran.

Gandhara was an ancient kingdom in the valleys of Swat and Kabul rivers, around Purushapura and Taxila. It was the birthplace of *Mahabharat's* Gandhari. It may have covered modern Peshawar and Rawalpindi in today's Pakistan and areas of east Afghanistan. A Susa palace inscription of Darius III mentions that teak was brought from Gandhara for the construction of the emperor's palace. It was one of the sixteen mahajanapadas, and its capitals were Charsadda (ancient Pushkalavati), Kapisa-Begram, Taxila, and Peshawar/ Purushapura.

Gangaridae, the Gangetic delta lay east of the Beas river, covering the five mouths of the river, and included Kalinga. It had a massive, intimidating elephant army, which reputedly defeated any enemy that threatened the kingdom. The Nandas could have allied with the Gangaridae in a power sharing equation.

Granicus river is today known as the Kocabas river.

Indus-Hndush satrapy was, according to historian Herodotus (484 – 425 BC), the twentieth and richest tax province of the

Achaemenids.

Lampaka is situated in present day Afghanistan, where the Indian emperor Ashoka inscribed a rock in Aramaic around 260 BCE. The inscription is called the Pul-i-Darunteh Aramaic inscription and was discovered in 1932 at Pul-i-Darunteh in the Laghman valley.

Kurus were an ancient Indian tribe settled in Delhi, Haryana, Punjab and western UP, of the mid-Vedic period (1200 – 900 BC), who developed into India's first state-level proven polity. By the mahajanapada time (500 BC) of the late Vedic period, stories of the Kurus contributed to the *Mahabharat.*

Mahajanapada means polity, or kingdom. India had, prior to 500 BC, 16 mahajanapadas. The mahajanapadas were, from west to east, Kambhoja and Gandhara in the northwest. East of the Indus River, they included Maccha, Kuru, Surasena, Panchala, Avanti, Vamsa, Cetiya, Malla and Anga. Down south, Asmaka. The four mahajanapadas that survived were Vajji, Kosala, Kasi and Magadha.

Oxus River is also called the Amu Darya.

Panini, was a linguist and grammarian, 5th century BC. The Panini clan is supposed to have lived in **Śalatura** in ancient Gandhāra during the Mahajanapada era. His full name was Daksiputra Panini, with Dakṣi suggesting his mother's name. He was the person who first codified the Sanskrit language, spoken at that time in north India. His work *Aṣṭādhyāyī* mentions that the people of the northwest frontier provinces (NWFP) of greater Punjab lived by the profession of arms. The clans mentioned are republics or oligarchies that thrived by the force of arms, as mercenaries or kshatriyas perhaps.

Poison of every sort was tried to kill the kings and their top officials in the subcontinent. To protect against food poisoning, a food taster, and a mother-and-son pair of monkeys were the first and second line of defense against poison in food for the king. Since the monkeys had smaller bodies, they displayed symptoms of poisoning by food faster than the food taster.

Aconite poisoning

Aconitum luridum (Linn.), a.k.a. Ativisha in Sanskrit, and Himalayan Monkshood in English; also has the botanical name Aconitum ferox. Its poison was also called Beesh.
Part used: Root
Habitat: Himalayas
Commonly used to trap animals today.

Clinical Features:

Victims have a combination of neurological, cardiovascular, and gastrointestinal symptoms. Neurological symptoms can be sensory (numbness of face, and the four limbs) and/or motor (muscle weakness in the four limbs). Cardiovascular features include hypotension, chest pain, palpitations, bradycardia, sinus tachycardia, ventricular ectopics, ventricular tachycardia, and ventricular fibrillation. The gastrointestinal symptoms include nausea, vomiting, abdominal pain, and diarrhea.

Strychnine poisoning

Srychnos nux-vomica (Linn.), a.k.a. Kupila in Sanskrit.
Part used: dried ripe seeds
Habitat: throughout India
Has no odor but has a bitter taste. Seeds have the shape of flattened disks. In large doses, strychnine poisoning causes symptoms that lead to death.

Clinical Features

As described in the Grant Dictionary of Toxicology:

'*Strychnine interferes with inhibitory transmitters, which produce a state of muscle rigidity and stimulation. Soon after ingestion, the first clinical signs are uneasiness, anxiety, muscle twitching, and stiffness of the neck. After about an hour the solar plexus tightens causing extreme pain. Periods of delirium, hallucinations, and tonic convulsions occur shortly afterward, characterized by sudden contractions of the muscles followed by complete relaxation. The patient may be particularly sensitive to light and noise, and can experience a painful reaction to pressure on the skin. Other symptoms include a temperature rise of 2 to 4 degrees above normal, sweating, elevated blood pressure, episodic rapid heart rate, and intense thirst. The final stage of poisoning resembles tetanus with the jaw muscles being locked.*

Punjab is an exonym or word given to a place by outsiders. 'Punj' meaning 'five' and 'ab' meaning 'water' make up the name given by Turkic conquerors of India. The *Rig Veda* called the Punjab, the Sapta Sindhu, for the six rivers which merged into the seventh, Sindhu. The Sapta Sindhu had ancient mahajanapadas (polities) of Gandhara and Kambhoja.

Proskynesis – Proskynesis was the ancient Persian ritual of prostrating to some one of higher rank. *Proskynesis* in Greek means, 'kissing forward.' The payer of *proskynesis* brought his right hand to his lips and kissed the tips of his fingers, and then blew the kiss in the direction of the king or god. If he was of a very low rank, he did this prostrate on the ground. Many of Alexander's commanders detested the practice of *Proskynesis*, especially Philotas, son of Parmenion, Alexander's second in command, for which Parmenion and his son were both executed. Historian Callisthenes too may have been killed for his opposition of *Proskynesis.*

River names of northwest India and Alexander's travels

Greek	Sanskrit	Modern
Hydaspes	Vitasta	Jhelum
Hyphasis	Vipasa	Beas
Hydroatis	Airawati	Ravi
Ascesines	Asikini	Chenab
Hesidros	Sutudri	Sutlej
	Sindhu	Indus

The rivers of the northwest of India were referred to as the Sapta Sindhu in the *Rig Veda.* Alexander's travels took him through the Indus first, then Jhelum, where he battled Porus, next, the Chenab, after that the Ravi, and the Beas. Alexander's conquests were only up to the Beas as his army mutinied from further eastward incursions into India. Going southward, he crossed the Sutlej.

Salt Range is a hill system in the Punjab province of today's Pakistan, north of, and next to, the Jhelum river, south of Potahar Plateau, and north of Thal Desert. The Plateau borders western parts of Kashmir and southern parts of Khyber Pakhtunwa. 32.40.30 degrees N. and 72.47.35. E. Rock salt from the range was supplied to various kingdoms.

Sogdian Rock a.k.a. Rock of Ariomazes was a rock fortress north of Bactria in Sogdiana (in current day Uzbekistan). Alexander attacked it in 328 BC. It was considered impregnable, and Oxyartes sent his wife and daughters, one of whom was Roxanne, to the Sogdian Rock.

Strabo (63 BC – 24 AD) was a Greek geographer and historian who lived in Asia Minor during the time when the Roman republic evolved into the Roman Empire. He described the people living in the territories handed over to Chandragupta by Seleucus.

Territories handed over to Chandragupta Maurya by Seleucus
Arachosia, Gedrosia, Paropamisadae, and Sapta Sindhu

Arachosia is the Hellenized version of a satrapy in the eastern Achaemenid, Seleucid, Parthian, Greco-Bactrian, and Indo-Scythian empires. Arachosia is situated around the Arghandab valley of south Afghanistan.

Gedrosia is the Hellenized name for a part of coastal Baluchistan that could be part of today's Makran. Gedrosia – in the accounts of Alexander's and Seleucus' record keepers – starts from the Indus river, and spans an area up to the southern edge of the Strait of Hormuz.

Paropamisadae includes both Gandhara and Kambhoja. Gandhara today is part of Afghanistan and Pakistan. Its center was the confluence of the Kabul and Swat rivers, with the Sulaiman Mountains on the west and the Indus river in the east. During the Achaemenid and Hellenistic periods, Gandhara's capital was Pushkalavati, modern Charsadda.
Strabo describes the tribes of these three areas as follows: Along the Indus are the Paropamisadae, besides which lie the Paropamisus mountains (the Hindu Kush); south, the Arachoti; further south, the Gedroseni, who occupy the sea board.

Sapta Sindhu, the ancient Indian name for areas covered by Patala, and many battlefields like the one with Porus, enclosed the territory of at least six rivers (the Saraswati having gone extinct) – Sindhu, Jhelum, Beas, Chenab, Ravi, Sutlej.

Talents – Talent is a measure. The value of a talent depends on the context, whether it's a unit of weight or a unit of coinage. The talent was a unit of weight used in ancient times to weigh gold, silver, and other metals. The weight of a talent varied by region and time period; One talent weighed about 8.5 grams of gold in Homer's Greece. In Alexander's time, a gold talent was on average 33 kilos of gold. Dhanananda, easily paid 360 talents of gold as tribute or tax to the Achaemenid empire, in modern terms, 11,880 kilos of gold, or 505 million USD, per year (value as in 2024). Gandhara paid 170 talents of gold, 238 million USD per year.

Torsion Catapults

Alexander made excellent use of Torsion Catapults, which his father Philip II of Macedonia had invented, against the Malloi. The Torsion Catapults used torsion springs, which worked by torsion or twisting through a flexible elastic object that stored mechanical energy. When it was twisted, it exerted a force in the opposite direction in proportion to the angle it was twisted.

Vitihotras – vanquished by the Maurya war machine, were the dominant clan of the Haihayas.

Water harvesting

In ancient India, water was used as a weapon of war. Since open and public water bodies could be poisoned and made unfit for human and animal consumption, water harvesting was of very great importance. Some of the richer villagers had, apart from ponds and wells, water storage tanks under their ground floors, which collected water from outer walls that were porous and had water seeping into the tanks underneath. So, while public waters could be poisoned, silver calx purified public waters, and underwater tanks kept the rural population supplied with drinking water. Wetlands also were preserved, and these swamps led to water collection. Trees of a certain kind and termite mounds indicated the presence of water below ground surface.

Wootz steel

In ancient times, swords made from Wootz steel were preferred by warriors of repute within India. Wootz steel originated in the mid-1st millennium BCE in India. These swords had special banding and mottling patterns which resembled the flow of water. Testing by weapons specialists has revealed that Wootz steel contained nano wires and carbon nanotubes. Wootz steel, famous from the 300s BC, was sent to Persia and Damascus to make their famed sword blades. Most Wootz steel was manufactured in south India. (Tamil Nadu has had an iron mining culture for 4,172 years according to archaeological discoveries.) It was made in Golconda in Telangana and Karnataka. The word Wootz is an anglicized version of the Kannada word for steel, ukku.

Yavana

Yavana in Sanskrit denoted Greek speakers. Yavana is a transliteration of the Greek word 'Ionian'. Yavanas were first mentioned in the *Mahabharata*, where they fought in the war against the Pandavas under king Sudakshina. Greece is called Hellas, and the Greeks called themselves Hellenes. Alexander considered himself a Hellene.

Wootz Steel

Bibliography

Alexander the Great – Journey to the End of the Earth: Norman F Cantor.

Complete History of the World: Richard Overy.

Google.

Grant Dictionary of Toxicology.

Historynet.com/battle-of-guagamela-alexander-versus-darius.htm/5

Mapping History – World History: Ian Barnes.

Monuments of Civilization – India: Maurizio Taddei.

Mudrarakshasha: Vishaka Dutta

Paurava and Alexander: Amar Chitra Katha

World Book Encyclopedia.

A History of India: Vaman Soranarayan Dalai, et al.

Cities of Alexander the Great: P M Frazer

There are several translation of the play *Mudrarakshasa*, since the 18th Century.

Mudrarakshasa: Kashinath Trimbak Telang (1884). With the Commentary of Dhundiraja (written in 1713 CE) edited with Sanskrit text, critical and explanatory notes, introduction and various readings, Tukârâm Javajī. Second edition 1893, Fifth edition 1915.

Teatro scelto indiano tr. dal sanscrito (Italian translation), D. Salvi e c. Antonio Marazzi (1871).

Mudrarakschasa: oder, Des kanzlers siegelring (German translation), P. Reclam jun. Ludwig Fritze (1886).

Le sceau de Râkchasa: (Moudrârâkchasa) drame sanscrit en sept actes et un prologue (French translation), Maisonneuve & C. Leclerc. Victor Henry (1888).

Mudrārākshasa or the Signet Ring: a Sanskrit drama in seven acts by Viśākhadatta (with complete English translation) (2 ed.), Poona Oriental Series (Volume 25). K H Dhruva (1923).

There is a Tamil version based on the Sanskrit play and Keshavlal Dhruv translated the original into Gujarati as Mel ni Mudrika (1889).

There is a Kannada version of the play, *Mudramanjusha written by* Kempunarayana.

Bengali playwright Dwijendralal Ray's 1911 historical play, *Chandragupta* has a scene where Alexander of Macedon is standing on the bank of the Indus, staring at the expanse before him that he plans to conquer. He tells his trusted general Seleucus Nicator, "Satya he Seleucus, ki bichitro ei desh… How strange is this land.'

Acknowledgement

Let's start with family…

I thank my Dad, who had faith that I was very intelligent, in spite of all experiences to the contrary, my mom who thought I was perfect except for my paunch, and my sister who kicks my ass, every time I lapse into 'laidbackness'.

I also thank this beautiful planet for the daily blessings she showers on me.

I started this book in Purdue, and repeatedly lost it. My final edit was in Mysore, a calm place to 'just be'. Writing this book was like piecing together a large jigsaw puzzle.

My beacons in this quest for the past were the *Arthashastra,* of Kautilya, the *Behistun Inscription,* of ancient Persia, Herodotus, the founding father of history, his Book III, of the *Histories* and Cantor's *Alexander the Great, Journey to the end of the Earth.*

The Internet, Google, Wikipedia, Creative Commons much gratitude… they confirmed and reinforced nebulous truths in my head. Libraries of my maternal grandad, mom, Purdue, Deccan College, Manasagangotri also shaped my thoughts.

I am not a trained cartographer, and quite the most difficult work was making of the 3 maps; difficult because there was a plethora of info, and I had to decide what to include, or exclude. Overy's *Complete History of the World,* Barnes' *Mapping History – World History,* Taddei's *Monuments of Civilization - India, World Book*

Encyclopedia, and a couple of pre-Independence maps aided me, though the final maps are entirely my doing, as precise info about incidents like the 303 BC battlefield was lacking.

Thanks, Ranjit Monga for putting me in touch with Sagar Azad, who connected me to editors Papri Sen Sri Raman, Ashwin Raj and designer Somesh Kumar Mishra.

Glossary

Amatya: a political position in ancient India. An official or minister.

Agalossoi: The Agalassoi were a tribe that lived in modern Pakistan in the lower Indus Valley. During Alexander's invasion of India, the Agalassoi fought against the Macedonian army. Women here committed self-immolation rather than be captured by the enemy.

Alexandria Nicaea & Alexandria Bucephala: Boukephala and Nikaia were two cities founded by Alexander the Great on either side of the Hydaspes (modern-day Jhelum River, Pakistan). They are mentioned by Pliny.

Antapura: Anthapura, also known as Antaḥpura, is a Sanskrit word that refers to the women's quarters or royal harem of an Indian palace. It is a suite of apartments that are usually located in a secluded area of the palace and are reserved for the women of the royal household.

Aghora: a sanyasi of the Aghora Saivite Sect; mostly with ash-covered body.

Arya: The Aryan race is a historical race concept that emerged in the late-19th century to describe people who descend from the Proto-Indo-Europeans as a racial grouping. The terminology derives from the historical usage of Aryan, used by modern Indo-Iranians as an epithet of 'noble'. Aryan, Arian is a term originating from the ethno-cultural self-designation of the Indo-Iranians. In ancient India, the term was used by the Indo-Aryan peoples of the Vedic period, both as an endonym and in reference to a region called 'Aryavarta', where their culture emerged. Also mentioned in the Avesta.

Ashram: an Hermitage; an exclusive residential school.

Ashvakas: Sanskrit: Aśvaka were an ancient people from Gandhara in the present-day Pakistan and Afghanistan. The region in which they lived was also called *Aśvaka.* The Sanskrit term aśva, Prakrit assa and Avestan aspa means horse. The Asvakas were especially engaged in the occupation of breeding, raising and training war horses, as also in providing expert cavalry services. The name of the Aśvakan or Assakan is believed by some scholars to have been preserved in that of the modern Pashtun, with the name Afghan being derived from Asvakan.

Historical texts mention the Aspasioi of Kunar valley, the Guraeans of the Guraeus (Panjkora) valley, and the Assakenoi of the Swat and Buner valleys; also the Ossadai and Abastoi tribes, all Himalayan kingdoms.

Bahirika: Outsider, foreigner.

Bali: Sacrifice, killing before a deity; can be fruit, vegetable, animal or human sacrifice.

Dahae: The Dahae were an ancient eastern Iranian nomadic tribal confederation, who inhabited the steppes of Central Asia.

Denari: The denarius was the standard Roman silver coin, struck as early as 211 BC. It continued to be minted in very small quantities, likely for ceremonial purposes, until 293–313 CE.

Deva: Hindu Gods

Gurukula: Gurukula is a type of education system in ancient India with shishya ('students' or 'disciples') living near or with the Guru (teacher) in the same premise.

Hetaera: Hetaera was a type of courtesan or prostitute in ancient Greece, who served as an artist, entertainer and conversationalist in addition to providing sexual service.

Himavatkuta: A Himalaya kingdom, a mountainous country in the Himalayas, mentioned in the Puranas. Himavat was its ruler and his daughter Parvati was a princess from this kingdom.

idée fixe: an idea that dominates one's mind especially for a prolonged period. Obsession.

Kanaganahalli village near Sannathi is where Emperor Ashoka of the Mauryan dynasty left his mark. Located on the banks of the Bhima river in Chitapur taluka of Gulbarga District of northern Karnataka, about 400 kms south of Sravanabelagola, the remains of a Buddhist stupa were excavated here almost 27 years ago by the Archaeological Survey of India(ASI).

Kambhojan: Kambhoj was a kingdom in ancient India that was part of the 16 Mahajanapadas. It was located near Gandhara.

Kathoians, Xathroi: The Xathroi were an ancient Indian tribe who lived in the Punjab region, between the Hydaspes and Acesines rivers, or east of the Hydraotes. The Xathroi were also known as the Kathaioi. Supposed to be forefathers of the modern Khatris.

Khuskhus: Chrysopogon zizanioides, commonly known as Vetiver and Khus, is a fragrant grass.

Kshudrakas: The Kshudrakas were an ancient tribe in India that are mentioned in the Mahabharata, by the grammarian Panini (born in Kandahar region), and in coins.

Magi: a priest

Madaari: Is a Indian word which means 'street performer'or 'street magician'. It refers to a person who performs tricks and illusions, performs with animals like bears and monkeys.

Maidans: Open space, a parade ground, playing field.

Malloi: The Malloi, also known as the Mallian people or Malavas, were an ancient Indian tribe that lived in the Punjab region during the 4th century BCE.

Mufti: civilian clothing.

Nagariks: Citizens, people of Nagaras, towns.

Padmasan: Padmasana, also known as the Lotus Pose, is a seated meditation pose in yoga where you cross your legs and place each foot on the opposite thigh. It is an ancient practice that originated in India and is considered one of the most important asanas in yoga.

Panas: The pana was a silver coin that was a standard currency during the Mauryan period. The name pana comes from the Greek word pani, which means 'hand'. The coin was based on the weight of 80 rati seeds, or almost 9.5 grams.

Panchayats: Panchayats are local self-government institutions in India that provide basic services to rural communities. The word 'panchayat' means 'assembly of five'. Panchayats were and are the first level of government interaction for more than 60 per cent of India's population, even today.

Parvataka desh: King of the mountains, of Parvataka Desh. Parvata kingdom refers to the territory of a tribe known as Parvatas (mountaineers), mentioned in the epic Mahabharata. Tribes belonging to other mountainous regions in the north west, west and the east of the Indo-Gangetic Plain were also known as Parvatas.

Persepolis: Also called Takht-e Jamshīd, was the ceremonial capital of the Achaemenid Empire (c. 550–330 BC). It is situated in the plains of Marvdasht, encircled by the southern Zagros mountains, Fars province of modern Iran.

Prasanna: Prasanna was a spiced barley or wheat beer consumed in ancient India: Kautilya mentions Prasanna as an intoxicating beverage made from rice during the Mauryan era.

Sauvira: The territory of Sindhu-Sauvīra covered the lower Indus Valley with its southern border being the Arabian Sea. Sindhu was the name of the inland area between the Indus and the Sulaiman Mountains, while Sauvīra was the name for the coastal part of the kingdom extending to modern-day Multan.

Shoulder cloth: Angavastram. Or Vastram, Vastra.

Siboi: The Siboi were an ancient tribe that lived in the region between the Indus and the Chenab river (Akesines).

Sivi cloth: The second book of the Pali Vinaya Pitaka, one of the three major 'baskets' of Therevada canonical literature, explains it as a special cloth woven by the women of the Sihivi tribe, who were supposed to inhabit the Kabul river valley in 800 BC. There is reference to it being fit only for a king like Bimbisara (Bindusara).

It could also mean a fine funerary cloth used to wrap the dead. The Mahabharata too mentions a king called Sivi and fine muslin-like cloth from his kingdom, also called Sivi.

Susa: was an ancient city in the lower Zagros Mountains about 250 km (160 mi) east of the Tigris, between the Karkheh and Dez rivers in modern Iran. It was the winter capital of the Achaemenid Empire, and remained a strategic centre during the Parthian and Sasanian periods.

Thal Desert: In Pakistani Punjab

Tumulus: In Greek, 'tumulus' directly refers to a burial mound or tomb; essentially the same meaning as in English.

Yojana: The word yojana is a Hindu unit of distance that means 'distance traversed in one yoking'. About 5 miles, can vary from 3.5 to 15 km depending on the county.

Vrshala: a common nun